I0692699

A GIFT OF FIRE

Also by Stephanie Stamm

A GIFT OF WINGS

A GIFT OF SHADOWS

A GIFT OF FIRE

THE LIGHT-BRINGER SERIES: BOOK THREE

STEPHANIE STAMM

ZEKE & ME BOOKS
ATLANTA, GEORGIA

This book is a work of fiction. Any references to historical events, real people, or real places are used fictitiously. All other names, characters, places, and incidents are the product of the author's imagination, and any resemblance to actual events, places, or persons, living or dead, is purely coincidental.

Tree of Life image at chapter heads modified from original by Unknown Author licensed under CC BY-SA (https://creativecommons.org/licenses/by-sa/3.0/).

Published by Zeke & Me Books, March 2024

Copyright © 2024 by Stephanie Stamm
Cover by Ravven, www.ravven.com

All rights reserved. No part of this book may be reproduced, scanned, or distributed in any form or by any means without the prior written permission of the author.

ISBN 978-0-9883042-4-6

For Dad
&
For Terri

TERMS & CHARACTERS

Adrigon	First of the Metatron
Alicia	A member of the Bound, friend of Bryn and Lucky
Archangels	The four angelic beings who hold order in all creation
Ba'al	Lucifer's Second in Command, former ruler of the Dark realms
Bonding	A ceremony in which a Naphil is bonded to a specific weapon they can then summon when needed
Book of Life	The energetic source and record of all that is
Bound	Humans who attached their lives to Lilith in exchange for learning magic
Cherub (pl. Cherubim)	An angel who can take the form of man, bull, lion, or eagle, or all at once, usually with multiple pairs of wings
Danel	A member of the Forces of the Dark
Dominion	A warrior angel
Elsewhere	A neutral zone for Light, Dark, and Fallen

Fallen	An angel who chooses to live in the earthly realm among humans
Gabriel	An Archangel
Galiel	Third of the Metatron
Gareth	A member of the Forces of the Fallen
Gates of Heaven	Portals used to connect the earthly realm to the Heavens after direct pathways between the realms were closed, also used to connect to Else-where
Grevyadach	The Still Ones' Home World
Halls of Hell	The home/seat of the Light-Bringer, visible from all the Dark realms
Ha-Satan	An official who facilitates communication between the Light-Bringer and the Metatron
Helel	An angel, installed as Light-Bringer
Jahoel	Deceased, former First of the Metatron
Jaime	A resident of Nadach and friend of Bryn and Alicia
Katrin	A half-Seraph Naphil healer, daughter of Semyaza, mother of Kev, former General in the Forces of the Fallen
Luil	Son of Lilith, father of Lucky
Making	A ceremony in which angelic or Naphil beings grant power to a Sensitive human, who then becomes Naphil

Margash	Fourth of the Metatron
Metatron	The Heaven's ruling council, made up of four members, the First, Second, Third, and Fourth
Michael	An Archangel
Miguel	A member of the Forces of the Fallen
Nadach	The Dark world to which Lilith was Banished
Naphil (pl. Nephilim)	An angel-human hybrid
Power	A warrior/ruler angel
Raphael	An Archangel
Sambethe	A visionary and healer
Semyaza	One of the original Watcher angels, father of Katrin and grandfather of Kev
Seraph (pl. Seraphim)	An angel with flaming wings, usually Gifted with Fire
Still One	A furry, gargoyle-like creature who feeds on suffering
Striking	A ceremony in which the commitment to be Made Naphil (i.e., to undergo a Making) is written into the Book of Life
Tatriel	Second of the Metatron
Uriel	An Archangel

CHAPTER 1

Where had he gone this time?

When Kev had said he was going to work out, Lucky had assumed he'd headed for the extensive gym in the basement of Zeke's brownstone. The unoccupied exercise equipment proved her assumption incorrect.

Maybe he'd gone to the training center. Maybe he'd decided to go for a run despite the cold of Chicago late winter. Maybe he'd zapped himself back to Colorado.

Lucky sighed. Wherever he'd gone he clearly had no interest in her joining him.

She sensed a pattern.

Over two weeks had passed since Kev had finally awakened after her attempt to integrate him with his dragon had left him unconscious for more than three days. Other than the brief, joyful hours after he'd first awakened and a few scattered encounters during the week that followed, they'd had little time alone together.

Lucky knew Kev was busy working with Zeke and Malachi and the rest of the Forces of the Fallen to figure out how to rescue Lucifer and the Dark Forces, after Adrigon, the first of the Metatron, the Heavens' ruling council, had gone rogue, invaded the Halls, and imprisoned them there. Still, she couldn't help but feel that he was avoiding her. The passionate Kev who had declared his love in the Colorado snow seemed to have disappeared.

Maybe the integration had changed how he felt about her.

Well, her feelings hadn't changed. She felt her connection to him with every beat of her heart.

She traced the outline of the dragon on the Light-Bringer's medallion before she tucked the amulet inside her shirt.

With another sigh, she stepped onto one of the treadmills to begin her solitary workout.

Several sprints around the training center's track had finally quieted the sound of the dragon's heartbeats and muted the interference of the beast's heat-sensitive sight with Kev's human vision.

Kev kept running.

A few more laps and he should be able to function like a normal three-quarter Seraph Naphil with a dragon alter ego.

At least, he should be able to function more like he did before Lucky had used her Gift to integrate him and his dragon. He had asked for her help when his unruly emotions had caused him to lose control of the dragon. But now he was beginning to question the wisdom of his request.

The changes had seemed subtle at first. Just as he had hoped, the dragon had stopped taking control when his emotions ran high. And he found he could call the shift to and from dragon form even more easily than he could before.

But then his senses had gone haywire, his dragon perceptions merging with his human ones.

He'd tried shifting, but it didn't seem to matter. In either form, he shared the perceptions of both. And, in either form, he felt overwhelmed to the point of short-circuiting.

Only exhaustion dulled the flood of sensory information to a level that allowed him to function. And each day, he had to drive himself harder than the one before to reach that sweet spot.

He had to find another solution. Or he was going to lose his newly integrated mind.

He knew he should talk to Lucky about what was going on with him, but he couldn't bring himself to do it. She had been so worried about her Gift, so afraid of what she might do to him. He didn't want to add to her worry. He had asked for this. He would find a way to deal with it.

He'd learned to control his dragon before. He could figure out how to manage this—whatever this was—as well.

If only he could talk to his father. Lucifer's dragon had always seemed an integrated part of him. Of course, Lucifer was fully Seraph. He didn't have that problematic human element added to the mix like Kev did. Still, Kev felt sure Lucifer could help—if Kev could only find a way to contact him.

Kev pushed himself beyond the point where the dragon's perceptions finally faded away. Several minutes later, he allowed his steps to slow to a walk and caught his breath.

His mind clear again, he knew what he needed to do. Zeke had suggested another look at Semyaza's record might provide more information about the robed figure who'd copied Lucifer's sigil from Semyaza's arm when he was imprisoned.

That additional information might enable Kev to free his father—or at least provide a reason for Kev to see him.

Aidan was waiting when Bryn and Lucky materialized outside the training center. Her heart fluttering with anticipation, Bryn watched him peel himself from the wall on which he'd been leaning. This was her first trip to the training center, the first of what she hoped would be many, as she began her new life among the Fallen.

Zeke had invited her to join them, to become one of them, even though she was a Raven. She knew he had had some initial misgivings, but he had put them aside after witnessing her behavior fighting the Wraiths and in training. He'd even praised her for her discipline and called her wise.

Bryn didn't know if she deserved his praise. She certainly hadn't relinquished all her own misgivings about her Raven tendencies. But she was going to do her best to live up to Zeke's good opinion. She didn't want to give him any reason to regret taking a chance on her.

Aidan pressed his hand to the sigil-activated security panel and opened the door for them.

"When will I get approved to open that with my sigil?" Lucky asked.

"When you graduate from training to become an official member of the Forces," Aidan said. He didn't smile.

Bryn could tell he still smarted from Lucky's choice of his brother over him. At least, he found it possible to be civil to Lucky now. And he seemed to be on slightly better terms with Kev—if only because they were united in their desire to release their father from his wrongful imprisonment. Bryn hoped Lucky and Aidan could heal their friendship soon. She liked spending time with both her cousin and her cousin's handsome ex-boyfriend. But when she was with both of them together, the tension became somewhat difficult to bear.

"What about those of us who don't have a sigil?" Bryn asked.

This time Aidan did smile. "Maybe we'll give you one as a graduation present."

Bryn looked at her palm. "How would that work, I wonder?"

"If it's anything like how I got mine," Lucky said, "I warn you, it hurts."

Before Bryn could respond, Aidan answered for her. "From what I've seen, Bryn's no stranger to pain."

"True." Lucky cast Bryn a rueful smile. "I didn't mean to imply..."

Bryn stopped her cousin's words. "It's okay. I know what you meant."

And so did Aidan—if he could only get beyond his own defensiveness.

Inside the center, Aidan led them through a large gym to a hallway lined with simulation rooms, classrooms, and smaller gyms designed for specialized training. He ushered them into one of those smaller, specialized rooms.

Bryn suppressed a grin when she saw the trainees donning fencing gear and choosing their weapons.

At the front of the room, Malachi stood talking to a tall, dark-skinned woman with close-cropped hair. Aidan led Bryn and Lucky toward them.

"Dominique, meet your two new trainees," Aidan said.

"Welcome to official training." Dominique smiled and shook their hands as Aidan introduced them.

"I'm going to steal Lucky for a while," Malachi said once the introductions were over. "But I will have her back to you by the beginning of your next session."

Bryn had only a moment to wonder where Malachi might be taking Lucky before her new trainer led her toward the equipment so she could get ready for her first class.

Malachi held the door to the weapons room open so Lucky could enter, then followed her inside.

Cases and cases of gleaming weapons surrounded them.

So many ways to die.

Lucky remembered thinking that same thing when Kev had shown her this room on her first visit to the training center. Before she had gone to Nadach with Lilith. Before her Gift had manifested. Before she knew the depths of darkness she possessed.

She still found herself drawn to the swords, with their elaborate hilts and gleaming blades. More so now that she knew the heft of a sword in her hand and the impact of blade on blade in the muscles of her sword arm.

But her dismay at the capacity for destruction contained inside a single room overshadowed the attraction of the blades.

"Take your time," Malachi said. "Don't worry if you do not know how to use a particular weapon—or even what it is. Don't simply see with your eyes. Listen with your heart for what calls to you. There may be more than one that speaks, but one will call more strongly."

Lucky shifted her gaze from the weapon-filled cases to Malachi's face. "What called to you?"

Malachi raised his right hand, his fingers curving around the long grip of the thin curved blade that took shape before him. His left hand joined his right on the grip, and he executed a series of graceful moves. To Lucky, his movements seemed like a dance, his whole body aligned with the sword, the sword an extension of his body.

"It's beautiful," Lucky said, when he again held the blade still before him. "What kind of sword is it?"

"It is a Japanese sword, called a katana."

"What's its name?"

"Masamune."

"What does it mean?"

"It comes from a legend about a great Japanese swordsmith. The legend says Masamune's apprentice Muramasa challenged him to see who could create the better sword. According to the legend, Masamune won the contest, and his sword was deemed to be holy, because it would not cut the innocent or undeserving."

"I like that." Lucky smiled. "You knew about the legend when you named the sword?"

Malachi shook his head. "I did not name it. The name is revealed in the Bonding. I did some research afterwards."

"That's right. Kev told me about that. He said his sword, Pacifer, would have a different name if it belonged to someone else."

Malachi nodded. "Yes. As would Masamune."

Lucky took a deep breath. "I'm not sure I want to be Bonded to a weapon."

Malachi gave her a reassuring smile. "The weapon doesn't own you, nor do you own it. But when you are Bonded, your weapon will always appear at your call."

"That's handy, I guess."

Malachi smiled again. He gestured toward the weapon lined walls. "Walk around. Look. Listen."

Lucky sighed but did as he asked. She felt Malachi's eyes following her as she moved slowly about the room.

"Are you going to keep watching me?" she asked. "It makes me nervous, like you're pressuring me."

"I do not intend to pressure you—only to observe. To notice any response you might have."

"Don't suppose I could convince you to go away?"

Malachi chuckled. "No."

After two slow trips around the room, her vision full of swords, daggers, sabers, lances, spears, staffs, maces, throwing stars, bows and arrows, and many more weapons she couldn't name, Lucky stopped in front of a case of swords with long narrow double-edged blades and delicate looking basket hilts.

She looked at Malachi and raised her shoulders. "I think these are lovely, but I'm pretty sure I'm just looking with my eyes. I don't hear or feel anything calling to my heart."

She studied the swords for a moment more, then asked, "Did you notice any response?"

"No." A slight frown knit Malachi's brow. "I did not."

"Should I keep going?"

Malachi shook his head. "No. If one of them were going to speak to you, it would have."

Lucky sighed. "It took a long time for my Gift to show up. Could this be the same way?"

"Perhaps." Malachi's frown deepened as his gaze dropped to the medallion and locket resting on Lucky's chest.

"What?" Lucky reached up to touch the amulet.

Malachi raised his eyes to hers, his frown disappearing as a smile curved his lips. "Nothing really. I was just thinking that sometimes a weapon doesn't always look like a weapon." He gestured toward the door. "Let's get you back to class, before Dominique comes looking for us both."

Kev showered and dressed in record time. A workout as hard as the one he'd just put himself through should buy him a few hours of normalcy, but the stretches of mental calm got a little shorter each day. He wanted to make sure he had enough time to see what he needed to see in Semyaza's record before the dragon's perceptions disrupted his focus again.

He fastened the cord bearing the obsidian pendant of *Ha-Satan* around his neck. With Helel, the new Light-Bringer, reporting directly to the Metatron, the need for *Ha-Satan* had disappeared. But no one had yet demanded the amulet's return. Kev hoped the pendant still retained its powers. If not, he'd have to go through Zeke to contact Uriel, the Book's keeper.

Closing his hand around the pendant, he sent a mental message to the Archangel, requesting access to the Book. Then, anticipating success, he headed down the stairs to the basement. By the time he reached the Gates, the Archangel's response had already scorched a trail through Kev's thoughts.

Placing his hand on the warm, vibrating wood of the Gates of Heaven, Kev activated his palm sigil. He focused his thoughts on Uriel and the Book. The great carved wings lifted, revealing a blazing light.

Kev stepped into that light.

And, for the second time, he found himself in a completely empty white room. This time, though, he stood on his own feet rather than dangling from the hand an angry Uriel had wrapped around his throat. Instead, the Archangel stood across from him, his flame-filled eyes looking at and beyond Kev.

No more problems with your dragon then?

As always, Uriel's voice burned in Kev's brain more than it fell on his ears. He wondered if the comment was the Archangel's attempt at a joke.

"I wouldn't say that exactly," Kev replied, "but I'm not shifting against my will these days."

Good. Otherwise, I might be forced to send you back to your own realm. You wished to see Semyaza's record again?

"Zeke said I should try changing the angle I viewed it from. I hadn't realized I could do that."

Uriel nodded and waved his hand. The room shifted, and a screen containing Semyaza's record flickered on the wall in front of Kev.

I will return when you have finished.

The Archangel vanished in a flash of light, even as his words sparked in Kev's mind.

Kev sped through the record until he reached the place where the cloaked visitor appeared. He slowed the images and watched the visitor soften his hand like wax to copy the sigil Lucifer had burned into Semyaza's forearm.

Slowing the images even more, Kev experimented with the angle of vision. Maybe if he looked out from where Semyaza sat, seemingly unaware of his cloaked visitor.

The figure turned to go, and Kev followed his passage to the cell door. The door opened, and the cloaked figure showed his marked hand to whoever had opened the door. Then the two shook hands. All Kev could see of the second person was the hand the cloaked man shook. No matter how he shifted the angle, the body of the mysterious visitor blocked his view.

Then the man in the cloak stepped aside.

Kev sucked in a breath, even as his thoughts stilled the image in place.

The person on the other side of the door was Ba'al, his father's second in command.

CHAPTER 2

"That has got to be one of the stupidest plans I've ever heard." Aidan could keep his thoughts to himself no longer. "You can't really think Adrigon and Helel are just going to let you waltz into the Halls, have a nice chat with Dad, and then waltz right back out again."

His brother rubbed a hand over his eyes and shook his head as if to clear his vision. "I don't expect it to be that easy, but I need to see Lucifer. If I have new evidence that suggests his innocence, if Ba'al betrayed him..."

"Adrigon trusts Ba'al enough to keep him on as Helel's Second. Why would he believe you? It's not as if you can show him Semyaza's record as proof." Aidan slid to the edge of his chair, the tension in his body punctuating his words. "What if Adrigon already knows, what if he and Ba'al worked together to frame our father and put Helel in his place?"

Kev closed his eyes and let his head fall back against the leather chair in which he sat. "Don't think I haven't thought of both of those options."

"Then you have to know this won't work." Aidan left his chair to pace back and forth between the grouping of leather chairs and Zeke's desk.

"I have to try." Kev sounded both weary and desperate.

"Why is this so important to you, Kevin?" Zeke leaned forward to rest his elbows on his knees, his penetrating gray gaze locked on Kev's face. "I sense it is about more than proving your father innocent of Jahoel's murder."

Kev opened his eyes, blinked several times, and shook his head again. "Yeah, it is."

Aidan frowned. "Are you all right?"

"I'm fine, just tired. It's been a long day."

Zeke's glance told Aidan the Cherub didn't believe Kev any more than he did. But neither of them commented on the obvious lie.

"We know your feelings on the subject, Aidan," Zeke said. "Give me a few minutes to talk to Kevin alone, please."

Aidan nodded. "Fine."

He opened the door, but couldn't resist giving his brother one last bit of advice before he left. "Don't be an idiot, Kev."

Staring at the cell walls around him, Kev wished he'd listened to his brother. And to Zeke for that matter. The angel had also cautioned Kev to rethink his plan, even though Kev had told him his more personal reason for wanting to see Lucifer. And Zeke's advice hadn't changed after he had contacted Adrigon and received his promise that Kev would have safe passage into and out of the Halls.

Zeke hadn't trusted that promise.

Zeke had been right.

They hadn't even allowed Kev to speak to his father. The guards who had put him in this cell had stopped outside

Lucifer's only long enough for Lucifer to witness them injecting his oldest son with something that had rendered Kev immediately unconscious.

Kev had come to with a splitting headache and cursed himself for being every bit the idiot Aidan had warned him not to be.

He failed to see why Adrigon hadn't simply granted him the promised safe passage. They had to know that if they kept him imprisoned, Zeke and the rest of the Fallen wouldn't simply ignore it. They had no cause to imprison him. The fact that he'd served as *Ha-Satan* for the last several months wasn't enough to incriminate him in any way.

Unless they planned to implicate him in Jahoel's murder too.

Kev pushed himself up to sit on the edge of the narrow bed and rested his throbbing head in his hands. He had no idea how long he'd been out.

His hand rose to touch the place on his chest where the obsidian pendant normally rested. They must have stripped that from him while he'd been unconscious. Guess they hadn't completely forgotten about it after all.

His gaze fell on his hand as he lowered it back to his lap. The dragon's heat-sensitive vision was beginning to overlap his human vision again.

Seven hells. That was the last thing he needed.

Doing his best to ignore the pain in his head, he dropped to the floor and began a series of one-handed push-ups. He didn't bother to count them. He'd just keep going until his vision cleared.

"He went *where?*" Lucky almost shouted the question. "And no one told me? *Kev* didn't tell me?"

It had been over twenty-four hours since she'd seen or heard from Kev, and she'd finally gone to Zeke. She hadn't let Aidan's presence in Zeke's study deter her from asking about Kev's absence. She was happy to ask them both at the same time.

The answer she'd received hadn't made her so happy.

"Now you know how we felt when *you* disappeared," Aidan muttered.

Lucky glared at him. The person she really wanted to light into was Kev, but since he wasn't there...

Zeke sighed. "He didn't want to worry you. And he assumed he would be back in a couple of hours."

Lucky glanced from Zeke to Aidan and back. "But neither of you assumed that. You said you both warned him not to go."

Aidan propped his backside against the back of one of Zeke's leather chairs and crossed his arms over his chest. "I knew nothing good could come of it."

Zeke leaned back in his desk chair. "I doubted Adrigon's promise, but Kevin would not be dissuaded."

Lucky paced in front of Zeke's desk. After a couple of trips across the rug and back, she stopped and looked from Aidan to Zeke and back to Aidan, her hands on her hips. "We're going after him, right?"

Zeke stood up and leaned forward, his hands on his desk. Lucky could see the shadows of bull, lion, and eagle, as well as several pairs of blue wings, flickering around him. "I do not think that is wise," he said. "If they are holding Kevin, what is to keep them from capturing you as well?"

"For one thing," Lucky said, "I don't plan on letting them know we're coming."

"And how exactly do you plan on getting into the Halls?"

Lucky shrugged. "We'll figure something out."

Zeke sighed. "Lucky, let Malachi and me do the figuring. We do not yet know for sure that Adrigon is keeping Kevin against his will. But if he is holding Kevin prisoner, he must know we will take some action against him."

"All the more reason to do something now, before Adrigon expects it." Lucky was about to jump out of her skin. Why did Zeke have to be so sensible all the time?

"Lucky, we will take care of it." Zeke's voice brooked no further argument. "Aidan, convince her I am right."

Lucky threw up her hands in protest, but headed toward the door, Aidan following behind her.

He started up the stairs without so much as a word. Lucky raced after him.

"I can't believe you would agree to wait and do nothing. Now they have both your father and your brother."

Aidan waited until they reached the top of the stairs before he turned toward her. "You might have noticed I didn't exactly promise to abide by Zeke's request. But I keep remembering what happened to my mother when I didn't listen to Zeke. We can't rush into this."

His mother. Lucky had forgotten.

She sighed. "You're right. And I kind of get what Zeke's saying. But I can't help thinking the element of surprise is our best weapon right now. We need to act before Adrigon expects we will."

Aidan was quiet for a moment, then he sighed. "Much as I hate to admit it, I agree with you. But we need a plan—a good one. I don't even know how we can get into the Halls. They've blocked access through the Gates. None of us can transport there. It seems to me like we're pretty much stuck."

Lucky thought for a moment. "What about Lilith?"

Aidan raised an eyebrow. "You might be on to something there. It's at least worth a shot."

"I'm going to go find Bryn," Lucky said. "I think the two of us need to pay a visit to our grandmother."

Kev slowed his circuit around the perimeter of his cell. His vision had finally cleared—or, if not cleared exactly, had stabilized to a degree he no longer found disorienting. Good thing too, because the heat rushing through his veins was distraction enough. He almost believed he could feel every single drop of super-heated blood circulating throughout his body.

He leaned against the cell wall, closing his eyes and pressing as much of his skin as he could against the cool stone.

The slide of metal against stone had him off the wall, fists clenched and legs bent, ready to spring. When the door slid open to reveal Ba'al on the other side, Kev almost growled. "What in seven hells did your people shoot into me?"

"Something to keep you from shifting, from calling your Gift." Ba'al's eyes slid away from Kev's. "And they are not my people."

"Right. I saw you, Ba'al. When I looked at Semyaza's record, I saw you let the thing that stole Lucifer's sigil out of Semyaza's cell. He showed it to you like maybe you were the one who wanted it." When Ba'al made no reply, Kev asked, "Just how long had you been planning to kill Jahoel and frame my father?"

Ba'al shook his head. "I had no plans. I took advantage of having one marked with Lucifer's sigil and a Morpho demon in our cells at the same time, no more. I paid the Morpho and drugged Semyaza. Having the copied sigil, knowing I could use it if I ever needed to, was enough."

"Why would I believe you? Now that I know every word you said about trading your resentment of my father for respect for him was a lie. When he and I are both imprisoned for a murder he did not commit—while you, a prime suspect, are free."

"It was not my idea to imprison you. I would have granted you safe passage." At Kev's indication of disbelief, Ba'al shrugged. "Believe me or not."

Kev let his hands unclench, hoping to lessen the heat building in his palms. "Why are you here, Ba'al?"

"I wanted to assure you your father is unharmed. And to assure myself you are as well, so I can pass that information on to him." He held up a wineskin he'd had pressed against his side. "I also brought you this. Water. I thought you might be thirsty—and a bit too warm."

Kev raised his eyebrows.

"Your father had a similar reaction to the injection. The worst of the effects should be over soon."

Ba'al extended the wineskin to Kev, his arm passing safely through the warded door. After a brief hesitation, Kev accepted the gift, careful not to allow his fingers into the warded area. Ba'al and the guards—and probably Adrigon and Helel—could cross the cell door wards without harm, but for Kev or anyone else to do so would mean death.

"Use as much as you need," Ba'al said. "The water will replenish itself." He flourished his hand in front of his chest. "A gift from a former storm god."

"Thanks." Kev's eyes narrowed. "But I still don't understand why you would feel the need to offer any support to my father or me."

"You may find that many things are more complicated than they seem."

Ba'al stepped back and triggered the door to slide closed.

Aidan scanned the tapestry-covered walls and lofty ceiling of the castle's entryway. Magicked torches floated above him and Lucky and Bryn, providing light enough to see some of the stonework on the walls and the sweep of an uneven looking stone stairway curving upward to their left. Outside the reach of the torchlight, the details faded into obscurity.

So, this medieval-looking place was where Lucky had lived when she ran away with Lilith.

Aidan gave himself a mental slap. Why did his first thought on reaching Nadach have to be about Lucky? Instead of remembering this was the place where everything between them had changed, he needed to focus on why he was here now, why Lilith had temporarily altered the wards that kept him out—so he could be part of the rescue committee that infiltrated the Halls to free his father and brother.

Still, he couldn't help but wonder if things would have turned out differently if he had been able to enter Nadach before, if the Light-Bringer's medallion had reached out to him and not to Kev when Lucky's Gift had first manifested. Aidan had been the one to give her the medallion in the first place, and before Nadach—no, before Lucky's Making—he had been the one the medallion alerted. But, afterwards, any connection he had had to the amulet had disappeared.

He sighed. He could wonder all he liked, but that wouldn't change anything. He saw the way Lucky and Kev looked at each other. And, though it pained him to admit it, Aidan knew Lucky had never looked at him in quite that way. Yes, she had cared about him—he even believed her when she said she still did—but what she felt for his brother was on a whole other level. And Kev felt the same way about her.

Aidan knew he had to let her go, but his chest still tightened when he watched the two of them together.

"This way." Bryn's voice drew his attention back to the matter at hand. "Lilith's apartments are up the stairs."

She led them up the curving stairway. More torches lit before them as they climbed, and those behind them faded away. Aidan was grateful for the light. Even his heightened Naphil senses didn't allow him to see in the dark.

When they had climbed several flights, the stairs ended at a small landing with a single closed door. Almost as soon as Bryn knocked, Lilith opened the door to usher the three of them inside.

They passed through a foyer furnished with an understated elegance into a sitting room that somehow managed to convey both elegance and comfort.

A young man Aidan had never met rose from one of the settees, brushing a fall of chestnut hair back from his face.

"Jaime!" Bryn and Lucky spoke at the same time.

Bryn rushed forward to embrace the young man, and something tightened in Aidan's middle. The tightness didn't lessen when Lucky stepped into Jaime's welcoming arms.

"What are you doing here?" Lucky asked when Jaime released her.

"I will explain all," Lilith said. "But first things first."

She made the introductions, and Aidan somewhat reluctantly offered Jaime his hand. He told himself he distrusted the young man because he was a stranger seemingly intruding on a mission which didn't concern him. It had nothing to do with the affectionate smiles on Bryn's and Lucky's faces.

And it wasn't because, when Lilith encouraged them to sit, Jaime sat in the middle of the settee with Bryn and Lucky on either side of him.

Aidan dropped onto an ottoman across from them.

Lilith settled into a high-backed armchair, looking like a queen ready to hold court. "Now, back to Lucky's question. Why is Jaime here?" She glanced at Aidan, and her lips curled in a slow smile. "I can tell by your scowl, Aidan, that you are even more curious about the answer than Lucky is. Jaime, do you want to tell them about your special talent?"

Jaime looked first at Bryn and then Lucky before he spoke, as if, Aidan thought, he feared their response to what he was about to say. "Well, let's just say I've never met a ward I couldn't penetrate—or a spell that could bind me."

Bryn gasped. "And you never told me this?"

Aidan's distrust ratcheted up another few notches. That was a dangerous talent to have. "How is that possible?" he asked.

"My father was part Morpho demon, and my mother apparently had some angelic blood—though we didn't discover that until we started investigating why I could do what I do."

Aidan raised an eyebrow. "Someone with that kind of talent could become a master thief—or a master spy."

This time it was Lucky who gasped. She had been watching Jaime as Aidan spoke. "That's why you thought I came here as a spy. Because that's what you were doing while you were away from Nadach. Wasn't it?"

Jaime's expression leaned toward sheepish. "Not the whole time I was away, no. I really did just travel a lot. But I did do a little investigative work for Lilith while I was away."

"Jaime has a strong moral sense—a good thing for someone with his gift," said Lilith. "I never asked him to do anything that would compromise those values."

Aidan wasn't as ready as Lilith to trust Jaime's morality. "And how exactly is your ability supposed to help us?" he asked Jaime.

"When I pass through a ward, it's disrupted for a while," Jaime said. "I can help you free your father and brother. If you can get through the physical barriers, I can get through the wards."

"Yes!" Lucky grinned and looked at Aidan. "He's exactly what we need."

"All right." Aidan nodded at Jaime, trying to set aside the distrust that neither Lucky nor Bryn seemed to share. "Welcome to the team."

"Now that that's settled, let's talk about the portal," Lilith said. "It has not been used for many, many, many years. I created it shortly after Lucifer came into power, hoping I would somehow be able to sneak through the Halls into the Heavens and stage some rebellion, or perhaps use the power of the Halls to get around the strictures of my Banishment. Neither proved to be possible, so I stopped using the portal. Until Lucky asked if I might know of any way of sneaking into the Halls, I had almost forgotten about it."

For a moment, Lilith appeared to lose herself in thought, then she waved a hand in the air. "Anyway, the point is that portals, like all created things, require a certain amount of upkeep, and this one has not exactly been, shall we say, upkept. I have spruced it up as much as the limited time allowed, but the ride might be a little bumpy."

She looked at Aidan. "Someone who knows the layout of the Halls should serve as the portal guide. Given your parentage, I assume you've been there."

Aidan heard the question beneath Lilith's statement. He shook his head. "No. As Fallen, I have never been permitted entry into any of the Dark realms—until now. But I have this."

He withdrew a small holographic device from the pocket of his leather jacket. Crouching, he placed the device on the floor and activated it. A three-dimensional model of the Halls appeared in the air above the device. "I made a copy of the plans Zeke and Malachi have been poring over. I've committed them to memory."

Lilith pursed her lips. "Not ideal, but it will have to do. Can you direct the portal to a hidden place, somewhere the new Light-Bringer and his troops would never think of placing a guard or an alarm?"

Aidan pointed to the spot he'd chosen. "Best I can tell, this room is an unused wine cellar. Adrigon and Helel would have no reason to take notice of it. Even better, it's only one level above the cells."

"Good," Lilith said. "Make your way to the cells from there then."

Aidan deactivated the device and pulled two others like it from his pocket. "I have two more of these." He glanced at Jaime. "I didn't realize there would be four of us." He tossed one of the devices to Bryn and another to Lucky. "When activated, they'll show our locations inside the Halls—in case we get separated. We can also use them to talk to each other." He reached into his pocket again and handed each of them an even tinier device. "Put that in your ear. Then press the green button on the holocom and speak into it."

He spoke the last few words into his holocom, and Bryn and Lucky both indicated they heard him clearly through their earpieces.

"Excellent," Lilith said, as Aidan returned to his seat. "The portal will close once you are all through it. It can only be opened from that same location. The key is my blood."

She stood, pulled four tiny vials from the pocket of her robe, and gave one to each of them. "Bryn and Lucky, as my granddaughters, you might be able to open the portal with your own blood, but I prefer not to take any chances."

Raising her hand, index finger extended, she continued. "Place a drop of the blood on your finger and draw a spiral"—she traced an ever-enlarging circle in the air with her finger—"in the place where the portal releases you. The portal will open again to return you here."

Lucky held up her vial. "And we each have one—"

"In case you get separated," said Lilith.

"Or in case any of us are captured," Aidan added.

Lilith nodded. "That too."

She glanced at each of them in turn. "Are you ready?"

"Yes." Aidan rose to his feet. He could almost feel the adrenaline surging through his veins.

"Ready," said Bryn and Jaime.

"I was ready hours ago," Lucky said.

Lilith drew them all into the center of the room. "Once the portal opens, you have only thirty seconds to make it through. Remember that for the return journey."

She took a small, curved blade from another pocket in her robe and pricked her finger with the blade's point. Then she traced a spiral in the air with her blood-stained finger.

A swirling portal opened in front of them. It looked nothing like the portals opened by the Gates of Heaven. Instead of bright almost blinding light, Lilith's portal swirled gray on gray, like moonlit water shot with mercury.

"Aidan, you go first. It will take its direction from you."

Aidan glanced at Lucky and Bryn and Jaime. Then he stepped through the portal, leaving them to follow behind.

CHAPTER 3

The former storm god's gift was a blessing.

Kev drank his fill and then emptied the wineskin over his head. The relief was short-lived. The water heated as it ran over his skin, causing steam to rise from Kev's body. But he didn't have to wait long to repeat the process. The wineskin refilled within seconds.

Apart from the agonizing burning when Lucky had integrated him and his dragon, Kev had never felt such heat. Fire, not blood, filled his veins and pumped through his searing heart. If he cut himself, Kev thought, flames would leak from the wound.

He wondered again what exactly they had injected into him. Something to keep him from shifting, Ba'al had said, something to keep him from calling his Gift.

He had had to try it, of course. The cell they had put him in was spacious enough to hold the dragon if he had shifted. But it needn't have been. Whatever else it might be doing to him, the mystery injection had indeed blocked his ability to shift, which meant he couldn't call his Gift. His father's Gift was not bound to his dragon the way Kev's was. Lucifer could call the Fire in human form as well as dragon. But, for

Kev, the two had always come in one combined package. No dragon, no Fire.

He wondered if whoever had created the substance they'd shot into him had known how it would affect him. Because Kev was beginning to think the Fire might come whether or not he could call his dragon. He felt as if he might burst into flames at any moment.

Maybe that was the point. Maybe the drug was designed to make him burn out, to make his Gift eat away at him, so he couldn't use it as a weapon.

Ba'al had said the worst of the injection's effects should wear off soon. Kev wondered how long it would take before the drug left his system altogether.

He lost count of how many times he'd dowsed himself with the contents of the wineskin. He was pouring the water over his shoulders yet again when the cell door slid open a second time.

Ba'al's eyes narrowed as he took in the steam rising from Kev's shoulders, chest, and arms. "Your reaction to the drug is much stronger than your father's. He had stabilized by this time." A frown knitted the skin between his dark brows. "I can feel the heat radiating off you from here." He wiped sweat from his brow and stepped back from the open doorway. "Lucifer was somewhat uncomfortable, but he was not so hot no one could get near him. Maybe instead of a wineskin of water, you need a tub of ice."

"Maybe," Kev agreed.

His own eyes narrowed as he realized he could see the temperature changes in the air currents as the heated air within his cell mixed with the cooler air entering through the open door. He could also see the heat of Ba'al's body, many degrees cooler than the furnace of his own.

And his human vision was still intact.

Somehow the dragon's heat-sensitive vision and his human vision seemed to have fused—in a way that didn't leave him dizzy and disoriented.

He wondered if that was an effect of the injection as well. But he wasn't about to ask. He didn't want to reveal to Ba'al that anything of his dragon was still present.

"I brought you food." Ba'al set a tray on the floor inside the cell door and stepped quickly back away from the heat. "Though it may char before you can get it into your mouth."

Kev gave a half laugh at the statement. "Thanks anyway."

Ba'al frowned again. "I will tell them to wait another few hours before questioning you."

"Questioning me? About what?"

Ba'al sighed. "Jahoel." He slid the cell door closed.

Kev's temperature rose another few degrees.

Lilith had told nothing less than the truth when she said the ride might be bumpy. By the time the portal spit them out, Bryn felt like she might lose the contents of her stomach.

"Ooh," she moaned, bending forward with her arms around her waist.

"Yeah," Lucky muttered. "She wasn't kidding, was she?"

"Bumpy was an understatement," Jaime said.

Aidan said nothing, but he looked as if he felt as uncomfortable as the rest of them.

As her nausea dissipated, Bryn scanned their surroundings, her Nadachi vision piercing the darkness. Broken crates and dust-covered casks and barrels littered the room.

"Good call on the abandoned wine cellar," she said to Aidan.

He grunted.

A light flared, and Bryn saw that Aidan held a small flashlight. He scanned the room as she had a moment before, locating the door and a pathway to it.

"Has everybody recovered?" he asked.

When they all answered in the affirmative, he led them through the remains of wooden crates and empty casks to the door. There he signaled for silence and then doused the flashlight. He inched the door open and peeked out, then eased the door closed again.

"From the lack of light, it looks like this level is as abandoned as I hoped it would be. But I'd feel a little more confident about that if one of you took a look—since I'm the only one of us who can't see at all in the dark."

"I'll do it." Bryn moved forward to stand beside him.

Aidan opened the door, so she could peek through. She could feel the heat of his body close behind her as she scanned the darkness outside the room.

She was vaguely disappointed when he stepped back and closed the door.

"It's definitely abandoned," she said. "The dust out there is as thick and undisturbed as it was in here before we arrived."

"The plans indicated the stairs to the cells are about fifty paces ahead and off to the right," Aidan said. "Bryn, you want to lead us down a level?"

She nodded, then realized he couldn't see her. "Sure."

Aidan held out his hand to her. "You'll have to be my eyes."

For some reason, Aidan's comment penetrated Bryn's alert battle-ready calm, causing her heart to skip a beat. She took a breath to steady herself and then took his hand.

"Let's go," she said.

She slipped through the door, Aidan at her side. Lucky and Jaime followed close behind.

They had almost reached the stairs when Lucky's gasp drew Bryn to a halt.

"I know where Kev is. I have to go to him." Lucky's hand had closed around the medallion she always wore.

"You can't rescue him on your own," Aidan said. "Without Jaime, how are you going to get him past the wards?"

But it was too late. Lucky had already dematerialized.

When she materialized inside Kev's cell, Lucky felt as if she had entered the world's hottest sauna. Heat and steam filled the room, radiating from Kev's body.

"Lucky!" Kev shouted, backing as far away from her as the cell walls would allow. "Get out of here! I don't know how you managed to materialize inside this cell, but get out."

"But—"

"My body feels like it's about to go supernova. And I will not be responsible for killing you. Get out! Now!"

"I love you," Lucky whispered. Tears filling her eyes, she dematerialized and reformed outside the cell door.

Fortunately, the stone-walled hallway was empty. Lucky offered a silent thanks to the powers that be that no one was standing guard.

She didn't know how to help Kev. The medallion and everything in her told her she should, but he was right. If his temperature kept rising, she couldn't withstand the heat pouring from his body. And she didn't think getting into his head would help. Whatever was going on wasn't about his mind. She would just have to stand by, watch while everything played out, and do what she could.

She pressed her hand against the cell door. Even that was warm. She couldn't imagine what Kev must be feeling. She scanned the area around the doorway until she found what looked like the control to operate the door. She moved the control into various positions and finally felt it click into place.

The door slid back and the heat from the cell washed over her. She moved as far away as she could, stopping when her back pressed against the stone wall. Her eyes widened as her gaze pierced the cloud of steam inside the cell.

Kev was glowing, his whole body like a bronze statue heated to the point of going molten but solid still, retaining its shape. If lava could take on human form, it would look like Kev did now.

As Lucky watched, the glow grew brighter and brighter. She could feel the increasing temperature even as far away as she was. When the light radiating from Kev's body began to pulse, Lucky dove down the hall away from the open cell door. Seconds later, a huge ball of fire exploded from the cell, blasting the area where she'd been standing.

"Kev!" Lucky screamed.

Finding no fuel in the stone walls and ceilings, the flames quickly died away. Lucky raced back toward the cell, whispering Kev's name like a mantra. She stopped in front of the blackened stone wall and looked toward the cell door, afraid of what she might find.

She sobbed with relief when she saw Kev standing just inside the door, staring at the hand he had extended through the opening. He stepped out of the cell and turned a shell-shocked expression toward Lucky.

"I burned away the wards," he said.

"That's not all you burned away." Lucky's gaze swept his naked, smoke-stained body.

"Huh," Kev said. He seemed too stunned by what had happened to be bothered by his nakedness. "I've always been able to keep my clothes when I shift from dragon back to human. It's just part of the magic. But even battle gear isn't designed to withstand that kind of heat."

"Well, we'll have to find you something to wear. If not here, then back in Nadach." Lucky took a few tentative steps toward him. "Is it safe to touch you?"

"I think so. I'm still a little warm, but my temperature isn't too much above normal."

"Good." Lucky flung her arms around his neck and pulled him close, another sob catching in her throat. "Hold on while I get us out of here."

Kev's arms closed around her, and she transported them back to the abandoned wine cellar where the portal had dropped them.

Lucky's arms refused to release Kev even when they had fully rematerialized. "For a minute there, I thought I'd lost you," she whispered.

Kev hugged her closer and buried his face in her hair. "Nope. You're stuck with me."

Lucky smiled against his chest. "I'm good with that."

"Me too." Kev's fingers slid under her chin, and she tilted her face to receive his kiss.

His lips tasted smoky, and she told him as much when the kiss ended.

His embrace loosened, then he caught hold of her again, leaning against her for support. "Not surprising, I guess. I'm feeling kind of burned out."

"We need to get you home. Hang on for a few minutes, while I check in with Aidan. Then we can get out of here." Lucky pulled the holocom Aidan had given her from her pocket as she spoke.

Kev looked around, his eyes searching the darkness. "Where is here anyway? I can't see a thing."

"Sorry," Lucky said. "I didn't bring a light."

"With your extra senses you don't need one. Not to worry."

Kev lifted his free arm and Pacifer, his broadsword, appeared in his hand, luminous enough to light the room as well as a flashlight. Lucky could see him struggling to hold the sword steady.

She placed the holocom on top of the nearest cask and activated it. Two glowing dots indicated Bryn's and Aidan's positions. They were together, at least, but Lucky had no idea if they had found Lucifer's cell yet.

Lucky pointed at the two dots. "Aidan and Bryn. Our friend Jaime is with them too, but he doesn't have a holocom. Are they anywhere near where Lucifer is being held?"

"It looks like they're right there. They might need help. Guards are posted outside Lucifer's cell. At least they were when the ones who locked me up took me by his cell on the way to mine."

"Where is your cell in relation to his?"

Kev shook his head, leaning a little more of his weight against her. "I don't know. They injected me with something while we were at his cell. It knocked me out, and when I came to, I was already inside my own."

Lucky glanced at him. "Is the injection what caused the supernova thing?"

"Some of it at least." Kev pointed to a spot not too far from where Aidan and Bryn's locators glowed. "That's a supply room. I might be able to transport us there."

You're not going anywhere but through the portal, Lucky thought. "I'll see if I can contact Aidan."

She pressed the green button on the holocom. "Aidan?"

"Yeah, I'm here." Aidan's voice was as quiet as hers.

"I have Kev, but I need to get him back home." Lucky ignored Kev's muttered protest. "Are you all okay?"

"How did you...? Never mind, you can tell me later. Jaime just sprung the wards. You two go on home. We got this."

"Okay. See you all back home."

"See you soon."

Lucky deactivated the holocom and put the device back in her pocket. "They've gotten through the cell wards. Aidan said we're good to go."

"That seems way too easy," Kev said.

Lucky offered no reply, though she secretly agreed with him.

She guided Kev to the place where the portal had dumped her and the others earlier and opened the tiny vial Lilith had given her. She wet her finger with the blood.

"This portal will take us back to Nadach," she said as she drew the spiral that would bring the portal to life.

When the portal opened, just as it had in Lilith's sitting room, Lucky sighed with relief. Holding tightly to Kev, she stepped through.

Springing Lucifer from his cell was surprisingly easy. The glamour Aidan had thrown over Bryn, Jaime, and himself fooled the on-duty guards long enough for the trio to put them out of commission. When the last guard had fallen, Aidan opened the cell door. Then, with Jaime standing in the doorway disrupting the wards, Lucifer strolled past him to freedom.

He had barely voiced his thanks, when Aidan heard shouts and the sound of booted feet running toward them.

"Company's coming," he said as he summoned his sword.

By the time he felt the heft of the blade in his hand, Jaime had unsheathed the sword he had strapped to his back, and

Bryn had shifted to her half-Raven form. A weapon very like Aidan's appeared in Lucifer's hand. When the four guards reached them, they were ready.

Four on four was hardly a fair fight. Within minutes, Aidan, Lucifer, Bryn, and Jaime had defeated the guards. None of their wounds were mortal—no one had been beheaded—but healing would not be quick.

"Let's get out of here," Aidan said. He held out his hand. "Hold on to me, and I'll transport us to the portal room."

Three hands landed on his arm, and Aidan locked onto his companions. But when he tried to dematerialize them, nothing happened.

Aidan cursed. "They must have wards that prevent transporting. Any chance you can disrupt this one, Jaime?"

"No." Jaime shook his head. "If I could find the source, yes. But a ward like this could originate from anywhere, and we don't have that kind of time."

"Then I guess we leave the way we came—on foot." Aidan motioned for the others to precede him. "Go!"

With Bryn and Jaime in the lead, they raced toward the intersecting hallway where they'd find the stairs that would take them up a level to the abandoned wine cellar. They were a few yards from the intersection when Aidan heard more guards coming after them. He ran faster.

Seconds later, he crashed into a wall he couldn't see. Then he hit the floor.

CHAPTER 4

Bryn and Jaime had reached the hallway to the stairs when Bryn realized she no longer heard Aidan's and Lucifer's footfalls behind her. Glancing at Jaime, she stopped and turned around.

A few yards back, Aidan was getting to his feet, and Lucifer's hands were in front of him, palm forward, as if pressed to an invisible wall.

"What the—?" said Bryn.

Jaime frowned. "Those wards must have gone up just now. Otherwise, I would have disrupted them when I ran through."

They began to run back toward their friends but stopped when two figures Bryn could only assume were Adrigon and Helel materialized between them and the wall that had trapped Aidan and Lucifer.

"Well, that complicates things," Jaime said. "But we can still do this. If we act like we're surrendering, we might get close enough I can disrupt the wards."

Bryn nodded. "Sounds like a plan."

They strolled back the way they'd come, hands held up in surrender.

The taller of the two figures, an angel with long white hair, turned toward them as they approached. His cold, handsome mouth turned up in a smirk.

"Such loyalty you show. We would have let you escape, yet here you are still. How laudable." His laugh was as cold as his expression. "And how stupid."

They were close now. Just a little bit more.

Bryn drew the dagger from the sheath on her thigh and closed the distance between her and the white-haired angel. The smaller dark-haired angel lifted a hand, and the impact of the dagger against some solid invisible barrier jarred up Bryn's arm.

The white-haired angel laughed his cold laugh. "Oh, you'll have to do better than that."

But Bryn had provided the distraction Jaime needed. He'd gotten close enough to step through the wards. Aidan and Lucifer were free.

They moved toward the two angels, swords raised.

His expression hardening to ice, the white-haired angel raised his hand toward Lucifer. Then, apparently reconsidering, he lowered it again. "You will regret this," he said.

He called to the guards, "Stop them!"

Then he and the dark-haired angel dematerialized.

"Bryn, go! Now! We're right behind you." Aidan yelled, even as she caught the sound of booted feet coming toward them from the other end of the hall.

She turned and sprinted down the hall toward the on-coming guards. She reached the hallway that led to the stairs before the guards reached her. Skidding around the corner, she beat a path to the stairway door. The sounds of footfalls on stone told her two of the guards had peeled off to follow her. That meant two less facing Aidan and the others.

She had almost reached the door when pain sliced through her thigh. She stumbled but kept moving, gritting her teeth as the blade embedded in her flesh cut deeper with each step. Grabbing the door with one hand, she grasped the dagger's hilt with the other and yanked it from her leg. She tossed it into the air and caught the bloody tip between her fingers as it came back down. Lifting her arm over her head, she brought it forward and straight down, releasing the dagger and sending it spinning end over end toward the guards. She slipped through the stairway door before she saw the blade make contact, but her lips curled when she heard a pained grunt that assured her she'd hit her mark.

She pounded up the dark stairs, her wounded thigh burning. She reached the top just as the door opened and found herself hoping full-blooded angels had as much trouble seeing in the dark as her Nephilim friends did. Slowing her steps, she moved as quickly and quietly as she could toward the door to the abandoned wine cellar. She sped up when a light flickered to life behind her.

She slipped through the cellar door and closed it as quietly as she could. She pulled some dusty pallets in front of the door to block it, before heading toward the back corner where the portal had dropped them. She could hear the angel guards pushing at the door as her hand slipped into her pocket to withdraw the vial of her grandmother's blood. She hated to leave without Aidan, Jaime, and Lucifer, but with

Adrigon's angel guards so close on her heels, it seemed better not to wait. She had to trust that Aidan could use the vial of blood Lilith had given him.

She pulled the stopper from the vial just as the door gave way with a crash. She wet the tip of her finger with the blood and traced a spiral in the air. The portal spun, gray on gray, in front of her.

Before she could step through, a hand closed on her wounded thigh and yanked her backward. She fell forward, the vial of blood dropping from her hand. Gritting her teeth against the pain in her leg, she called her Raven form. Like always, pain ripped through her with the shift, and she couldn't suppress the rough caw that escaped her Raven beak. Twisting, she drove that beak toward the guard's face as she reached for his throat with her taloned hands.

She knew enough about angel physiology to know she couldn't kill the guard without beheading him, so she had no qualms about wounding him as badly as she could. She just needed to put him and his companion out of commission long enough to make it through the portal. She held his neck with one hand, as she sliced her beak across it. The wound was not quite deep enough to behead him. He fell back, breath gurgling, his own hands reaching for his wounded throat.

Bryn launched herself at his companion just as he launched himself at her. She drove her beak into one of his eyes, then drew back and opened his throat as well. He too crumpled to the floor.

Turning, Bryn dived toward the portal.

It collapsed before she reached it, and her body slammed into the cellar floor.

The tension permeating the air of Zeke's study didn't prevent Kev from relaxing into the embrace of one of the big leather chairs. It was good to be home.

Lilith had been waiting when he and Lucky had stepped through the portal into her sitting room. Her brows had risen at the sight of his naked body. In addition to a robe, she had offered him the use of her bath, but he'd accepted only the clothing, wanting to return to Zeke's as quickly as possible.

Back at the brownstone, he'd showered while Lucky had alerted Zeke and Katrin of their return. He was still weak, but the shower and clean clothes—as well as the food on the table in front of him—went a long way toward making him feel more human.

Though perhaps human wasn't the best way to put it.

It seemed his human vision and the dragon's vision were now permanently entwined. He not only saw shapes and colors, but temperatures, heat signatures. Even in the dark of the abandoned wine cellar in the Halls he'd been able to "see" Lucky's body and his own because of the heat they generated.

His hearing was more sensitive too. He could pick up a much larger range of pitches and tones.

These changes made him wonder just how much the super-heating of his body and the subsequent explosion of power had been due to the injection and how much was a result of his integration with his dragon.

"You disobeyed me." The rumble of Zeke's voice brought Kev back to the room.

"Yes." Lucky's voice held a hint of defiance. "And I'd do it again. I couldn't just leave him there."

Zeke ignored the comment. "Where are Aidan and the others?"

"They should be here soon."

Zeke raised his eyebrows in question.

"They had freed Lucifer when I last spoke to Aidan. They should have been close behind us." A frown gathered Lucky's brow. "I expected them to be back by now."

"Unless they ran into trouble." Zeke's voice was very quiet, a signal to all who knew him that the angel was furious. "Which is more than likely. Which is why I asked you both to leave this matter to Malachi and me."

Kev watched the movement of Lucky's throat as she swallowed. He wanted to pull her into his arms and comfort her, but he knew now wasn't the time.

He wanted to hold her and never let her go.

He had never been as afraid as when she'd appeared in his cell as the Fire in him was building to explosion force. If anything had happened to her because of him, he would never have been able to forgive himself.

He understood that she felt something similar now. She had convinced Aidan and the others to break into the Halls. She would feel responsible if they didn't make it back safely.

Aidan had said they'd freed Lucifer. Kev didn't know any more capable fighters than his brother and father. But he also didn't know how badly Lucifer had been affected by Adrigon's injection. Nor did he know what other tricks Adrigon and Helel might have up their collective sleeves.

"They'll be back soon," he said. He hoped he was right.

Bryn's searching gaze landed on the fragments of the vial that had held Lilith's blood. The remaining drops of red blood mingled with tiny glass shards and the golden ichor that had spilled from the necks of the angelic guards, the same ichor that stained Bryn's fingers.

The guards began to stir even as she wiped her hands on her leathers and the fabric of the black tank she wore beneath her jacket. *Seven hells.* Where were Aidan and the others? When she had cleaned her hands as best she could, she carefully touched a finger to the wound in her thigh.

Bryn's hand shook as she drew a spiral in the air. *Please let this work.*

A portal took shape before her, spinning gray on gray, but the outline wavered, and flashes of silver shot like lightning in patterns across the swirling gray.

Behind her, the movements of the guards grew louder. She didn't have much choice really. Stay here and be imprisoned or jump into the mystery portal.

Filling her mind with the image of Lilith's sitting room, Bryn took a deep breath and leapt.

Pain assailed her. Her body stretched, burned. She felt as if she were being ripped limb from limb, flattened thin as a pancake, and exploded from the inside out, her body replaced by an amorphous field of screaming, burning, crushing pain.

Then she lost all consciousness.

"Aidan, behind you!"

Aidan spun and ducked in response to Jaime's warning; blade raised to block the thrust of his attacker's sword. The clash of steel on steel punctuated his movements as he backed toward the intersecting hallway.

The guard drove his sword at Aidan's midsection. Aidan brought his own blade down and around, leaping and twisting as he did so, using the impact of sword on sword to propel himself away from his opponent even as it drove the guard's sword toward the floor. In the seconds before the guard could renew his attack, Aidan summoned his spear and thrust it into the guard's side. Then he sliced the edge of his blade across the guard's throat. Golden ichor gushed from the wound. The guard would survive, but he no longer posed a threat to Aidan and his friends.

Aidan swung his blade up to block another guard's sword thrust. He and Lucifer and Jaime were outnumbered. He didn't understand why his father fought with his sword. If Lucifer called the Fire, they could easily best these guards.

Lucifer disabled the guard he was fighting and, as if sensing his son's thoughts, swung his gaze to meet Aidan's. His eyes began to glow. He opened his mouth and issued a roar that could have come from Kev's dragon. That roar quickly morphed into a high-pitched sound that sent the guards to their knees, their hands over their ears.

Aidan suffered no such reaction. His Gift of Song gave him the ability both to create and tolerate pitches outside the range of normal hearing.

The same could not be said for Jaime. Like the guards, the young Nadachi was on his knees.

Dismissing his spear, Aidan rushed to Jaime. He lifted the young man with one arm, tossed his over his shoulder, and raced down the hall toward the stairs. Lucifer followed behind, still emitting that high-pitched whine.

He stopped when they reached the door to the stairs. "They'll recover quickly now. You go on. I'll wait here and give them another sound blast when they get close."

Jaime had recovered enough to protest when Aidan tossed him over his shoulder like so much baggage. Aidan released him, dismissed his sword, and pulled his small flashlight from his pocket.

Lucifer let loose the next blast as they started up the stairs. Jaime stumbled but kept climbing.

"You okay?" Aidan asked.

"It's painful, but the door blocks the worst of it."

Aidan opened the door to the unused wine cellar in time to see Bryn disappear into the portal. Flashes of silver lightning split the swirling gray on gray. Then the portal winked out.

Aidan shone his flashlight around the room, cursing when it revealed a mess of blood and ichor and two angelic guards beginning to show early signs of revival. Bryn's departure through the portal had apparently been hard won.

Aidan's booted foot connected with the head of the nearest guard before he could stand. That should keep him still for a little longer. It didn't take long for Aidan and Jaime to deliver the other guard back to unconsciousness as well.

Aidan stepped into position to call the portal. Something crunched beneath his boot. He lifted his foot to see the remains of one of Lilith's tiny vials.

Hearing the door open, he pulled his own vial of blood from his pocket.

"Now, Aidan!" Lucifer yelled.

Aidan wet his finger with the blood and shaped the spiral. All three of them leapt into the portal as soon as it formed.

Bryn groaned and pushed herself up to sitting. Her thigh throbbed and burned, and her head spun. She opened her eyes, and then quickly closed them again as a wave of nausea hit her. She took deep breaths, hoping to quell her rocking stomach and slow the pounding of her heart.

She needed to pull herself together. Because, if the brief glimpse she had gotten before she slammed her eyes closed was any indication, she had bigger problems than a wounded thigh and a headache. She didn't know where she had landed, but it wasn't Lilith's sitting room.

Feeling a little steadier, she slowly opened her eyes. Something like fog surrounded her, though the shifting mist was more silver than white. The surface she had landed on felt solid, but it looked no more substantial than the silvery fog.

She waved a hand in front of her face. The fog shifted, and the skin on her hand tingled as if the atmosphere carried a slight charge.

Slowly she pulled herself to her feet, favoring her wounded leg. Turning in a circle, she scanned her surroundings. Silver fog in every direction.

"Wish I had a clue where I am or which way to go," she said aloud.

As if responding to her words, the fog in front of her thinned, parted.

"And that's not at all creepy." This time she spoke under her breath.

Even though she knew it was probably futile, she took the holocom from her pocket and pressed the button as Aidan had shown her. "Aidan? Can you hear me?"

Nothing. Just as she'd expected.

She tried twice more, with the same result.

Shoving the device back in her pocket, she stared at the clear spot in the fog.

After a few moments, she took a step forward. As she stepped, her surroundings began to change, the fog dissipating, solidifying into shapes. With each step she took, the shapes became clearer and the surface under her feet changed texture. She was walking on a path in a forest, skeletal trees rising on either side.

Bryn was reminded of the night she and Lucky had wandered into the forest beyond Lilith's garden in Nadach. As that thought took shape, a full moon, blood-tinged, rose above the trees, lighting the path before her.

Okay, Bryn thought, *probably best not to recall the other things that happened that night.* She didn't know if this strange place could conjure people as well as landscapes, but she didn't want to take any chances that a phantom William would appear to drag her into a clearing and hold her captive in magical bonds.

She had a moment to wonder if following the path was a good idea, but her intuition didn't send up any red flags. And if wasn't as if she had a ready supply of alternatives. She had asked for direction, and a path had been laid before her. For now, she would limp down it and see where it led.

The portal dropped Aidan, Lucifer, and Jaime onto the floor of Lilith's sitting room in a pile, with Aidan sandwiched between his father and the Nadachi. After Jaime's weight lifted from him, Aidan rolled off Lucifer to lie on his back and catch his breath.

"Where's Bryn?"

At Lilith's question, Aidan leapt to his feet. "What do you mean? She should have made it here before us."

"Lucky and Kev came back through the portal," Lilith said. "It didn't open again until you arrived."

"But I saw her go through it," Aidan said.

Lilith paled. "Aidan, what did the portal look like? The one Bryn went through? Did it look exactly like the one you opened to return here?"

"No. It was similar. But it looked kind of like it contained flashes of lightning." Aidan frowned. "I stepped on a broken vial before we came through the portal. What might have happened if Bryn used her own blood to open it?"

"Oh gods." Lilith closed her eyes as her skin went even paler. After a few breaths, she whispered, "I have to talk to Zeke."

CHAPTER 5

"What?!"

Zeke's question penetrated the closed study door like a bullet. Lucky, Kev, Aidan, and Jaime exchanged looks.

Lucky and Kev had been in the study with Zeke when Lilith, Aidan, and Jaime had arrived. Lucky's relief at seeing them had faltered when she realized Bryn wasn't part of the group. Before anyone could ask any questions, Lilith had shooed them all into the hallway, insisting that she needed to talk to Zeke—alone.

The four of them had waited outside the door and had heard nothing of the conversation inside the study until now. But this they definitely heard.

While they waited, Aidan had told them everything he knew, which was very little. He had seen Bryn go through the portal, but it had looked somewhat different. When he had told Lilith, she had rushed them all here to see Zeke.

They wouldn't know any more until Lilith and Zeke decided to fill them in.

"And you never told me?!"

This time the question shook the door and the walls. Lucky sat on the floor, leaning against the wall, and she could feel the vibration at her back. She sent a wide-eyed glance to Kev, who sat beside her. He raised his eyebrows.

They both looked at Aidan.

He shrugged and shook his head. "Not a clue."

Several more minutes passed, and then the door opened.

Nobody moved.

"Well, come in," Zeke said, his voice still rumbling like thunder.

No one spoke as they moved into the study.

Zeke was leaning back in his desk chair, eyes closed, while Lilith perched on one side of the desk.

Shortly after Zeke opened his eyes, Malachi and Lucifer appeared.

"Sit," Zeke ordered.

They sat. Malachi took his usual cross-legged position on the floor.

Zeke closed his eyes again, but this time he didn't seem to be summoning anyone, only gathering his thoughts. With his eyes still closed, he said, "'In front of the garden of Eden he posted the cherubs, and the flame of a flashing sword, to guard the way to the tree of life.'"

Zeke opened his eyes, and his gaze settled on Lucky where she sat on the arm of Kev's chair. "Sound familiar?"

Lucky nodded. "It's from Genesis. After Adam and Eve got kicked out of Eden."

"Yes." Zeke's smile looked weary. "And as with all sacred stories, this one contains seeds of truth. One of those truths is the part about the Cherubim guarding the Tree. At least, that is what we were supposed to do."

"The Tree of Life," Lilith interrupted, "is not a tree that grows in an earthly garden though. It has branches and leaves, but its branches are pathways, and its leaves are worlds. The Tree of Life, or the World Tree, connects all the worlds. All worlds can be accessed through the Tree."

"The energy of all those worlds pulses through the Tree. Inside the Tree, those worlds intermingle." Zeke took up the story again. "We tap into the Tree's pathways when we dematerialize from one world to another. That's how we can move freely among the worlds within our branch of the Tree." He glanced at Lilith. "No one but trained Cherubim Guardians were ever meant to enter the Tree directly."

"But I did," Lilith said softly. "And what I did wounded the World Tree."

"What did you do?" Lucky asked.

"I was young and foolish," Lilith said. Her gaze turned to Zeke. "And greatly enamored of a handsome Cherub I wanted desperately to impress."

The corners of Zeke's mouth turned upward in a sad smile. "You had already impressed me, Lilith."

Lilith's lips tightened. "How quickly things changed."

She sighed and resumed her story. "I was studying magic, sorcery, and I excelled at it. My teachers had filled my head with dreams of being the greatest adept the worlds had ever known."

"And I was training to be a warrior, a protector, a Guardian," said Zeke.

"The sorcerers told me of the Tree's power."

"The Guardians warned me of the Tree's fragility."

"They said the Tree could grant power over all the worlds."

"They said the Tree must be protected for the sake of all the worlds."

"I needed to touch that power."

"I needed to safeguard it at all cost."

Zeke and Lilith stared at one another, as if they had forgotten they were telling a story for the benefit of others. Lucky held her breath, her fingers locked with Kev's.

Zeke tore his gaze from Lilith's. "The only direct entrance into the Tree in our branch was in my home world."

"Our home world," Lilith interrupted.

"Our home world," Zeke conceded. "And I was assigned to guard that entrance. Lilith knew. I had told her about my assignment." He looked at Lilith again. "You were not the only one who was young and foolish. I trusted you."

"And I betrayed your trust," she said. "I tricked you."

Zeke sighed. "She showed up at the entrance during my shift, tried to convince me that the Cherubim leaders were wrong, that she could enter the Tree without endangering anyone, that she just wanted a glimpse of the power of the worlds."

"He would have none of it. He has always been stubborn—and completely committed to his role as Guardian. When I couldn't convince him to take me into the Tree, I tricked him. I let him think he'd brought me round to his way of thinking, that I'd left. Then I used my magic to slip past him. I had already used it to steal some of his blood without his knowledge. And that blood gave me access to the Tree."

Lilith's gaze sought Zeke's. "I thought when you realized I'd caused no harm, when you saw I was right, you'd forgive me."

"But you did cause harm," Zeke said. "You were wrong. You ripped holes between the worlds." Zeke looked at Aidan and Kev and Lucky. "You may have wondered why I am so insistent on returning the Wraiths to their world instead of killing them. It is because our worlds were never meant to connect. They are in completely different branches of the Tree. But what Lilith did that day fractured the Tree, opening passages where none should ever have been opened, connecting incompatible worlds."

Lilith sighed. "Getting in was easy. But when the entrance closed behind me, I was lost. I wasn't a Cherub. I couldn't find my way out. The energy of all the different worlds swirled through the Tree, obscuring my senses. I panicked. I cut myself and used my own blood to open a portal back to my home world. But I used too much blood, drew too much of the Tree's power, and the backlash ripped through the Tree, creating fissures in the boundaries between worlds."

Lilith paused, her eyes downcast, long enough for Lucky to sense the regret that remained unspoken. "Zeke started to work repairing the obvious damage as soon as the portal dropped me back home. But he didn't know—neither of us knew—just how bad it was. Only later, when the Wraiths and other creatures started entering the worlds in our branch of the Tree did we begin to understand."

She raised her eyes to Zeke, and he took up the tale. "Far too many lives were lost. But, eventually, the Cherubim

Guardians, together with the Archangels, found all the fissures and repaired them as best we could. But our seals are imperfect, and sometimes, as you are all aware, the creatures from those worlds break through."

Aidan shifted in his chair. "This is all really fascinating. But what does it have to do with Bryn?"

Zeke looked at Lilith.

"That's where she is," Lilith said. "She's in the Tree."

"But how could she—?" Lucifer glanced from Zeke to Lilith and back again, then let out a low whistle. "Holy hell. She's—"

"Start with the portal," Zeke said to Lilith, cutting off Lucifer's comment.

"As some of you know"—Lilith looked pointedly at Lucifer—"the Halls exists at a nexus in the Tree. That's how it can be in all the Dark realms simultaneously. Well, when I created the portal, I drew on that energy, I tapped into the nexus."

"And you activated the portal with blood magic," Zeke said. He shook his head. "You never really grasped the enormity of what you did, did you? Even though you were Banished because of it."

"I knew." Lilith's voice trembled. "What I did then cost me everything. The portal seemed a small enough magic. I never intended to use it to enter the Tree. The blood that activated it was my own. When I told Lucky and Bryn their blood might work, because they are my granddaughters, I didn't think—"

"Only a Cherub's blood can open the Tree," said Lucifer.

"Then how did Bryn end up there?" Aidan asked. "Even if she used her own blood..." His voice trailed off, as all eyes swung to Zeke.

The Cherub sighed. "It seems Bryn is not just Lilith's granddaughter. She is also mine."

Bryn had no idea how long she'd followed the path through the trees. Sometimes she thought it had been only a matter of minutes, but other times she believed she'd been walking the path for hours.

She had no measure by which to judge how far or how long she'd walked when she rounded a bend to find a clearing open before her. The path by which she'd entered the clearing was one of four. She had a choice to make.

Bryn moved to the center of the clearing, and every inch of her exposed skin began to tingle as if the charge in the atmosphere had increased. Her heart sped up. She didn't know how she knew it, but she knew this decision was about more than whatever destination she might reach in this strange realm in which she found herself.

Her choice of path would determine her future.

Turning slowly, she faced each of the three new paths. Something in her swung like a compass needle.

Again, she turned, pausing to look at where each path opened between the trees. Again, the compass needle swung. To her eyes, the three paths were virtually identical.

She turned a third time with her eyes closed. This time she sank into the sense of that internal compass needle. When it settled, like true north, she opened her eyes.

Without hesitation, she set off down the path before her.

Bryn was Zeke's granddaughter. Zeke's and Lilith's. Lilith and Zeke. Aidan would wrap his mind around all that later. What mattered now was Bryn.

"So, we know she ended up in the Tree because she has Cherub blood," he said. "But how do we get her out?"

"I am going into the Tree after her." Zeke captured Aidan's gaze with his own. "And you are coming with me."

Aidan raised an eyebrow. "Me? You know I'm happy to help, but I'm no Cherub Guardian."

"Nor am I anymore, at least not officially," Zeke replied. "But I know how to navigate the Tree, and Bryn is my granddaughter. That should convince the Guardians to let me in. I want you with me because of your Gift."

"You think Bryn might be hurt?" Aidan's worry for her kicked up another notch.

Zeke frowned. "It is possible. But that is not what I meant."

"How long can Bryn survive there?" Lucky asked. "Lilith, you said you panicked. How long were you there?"

Lilith slid off the desk. "To me, it seemed like maybe an hour at most. But when I returned to my world, two days had passed. Time moves differently in the Tree."

"So, what do we do?" Aidan asked. The sooner they got going, the sooner they could rescue Bryn. "How do we get into the Tree? Do we have to go to your home world?"

"I cannot go back to my home world," Zeke said. "The entrance is no longer there anyway. After what happened, access to the Tree, for all but Guardians, was bound to the Book. With the Guardians' permission, I will contact Uriel."

Kev stared at the phone in his hand and the name on the screen. Katrin. He'd pulled up the contact, but he hadn't made the call.

Kev was alone in Zeke's study.

Zeke and Aidan had left to prepare for their trip into the Tree. Lucifer and Malachi had headed to the training center to strategize about next steps. Lilith had returned to Nadach, so as not to use up her limited time in the earthly realm. And, when Kev had insisted, Lucky had reluctantly gone without him to catch up with Jaime and get more details about what had happened inside the Halls.

Kev had intended to call the Fallen's healer—his mother—and have her run some tests. He hesitated because he wasn't sure she'd be safe in his presence.

Because, with his finger poised to make the call, he'd felt again as he had when the Fire had begun to burn in his veins when he was imprisoned in the Halls.

With a muttered curse, he shoved the phone into his pocket. He dematerialized and reformed inside the mudroom of his cabin. As the fire in his blood ran hotter, he stripped off his clothes and stuffed them into the backpack that hung from one of the hooks on the mudroom wall. He grabbed his barn coat from another hook and shoved it into the backpack as well.

Then he slung the pack over his shoulder and zapped himself to the clearing where he had trained with Lucky, hoping the coming blast of Fire would be quenched by the Colorado snow.

The harsh caw took Bryn by surprise.

She had again lost track of time as she followed the forest path, her boots creating shifting patterns in the tendrils of silvery mist. She had no idea where she was going, no idea what she would find when she reached that destination, no idea what she might encounter along the way.

But something in her told her to follow this path, so she kept moving. Her wounded thigh ached with each step, but the pain had faded to a dull throb. The repetitive movements of her steps, the constant presence of the skeletal trees on either side, the silver mist shifting in the moonlight, all combined to lull her into a dream-like state. She moved along the path without thought or conscious volition.

The cry startled her from her waking dream. She recognized the sound as soon as she heard it. It was one she'd heard coming from her own throat often enough. The strident rasp of a Raven's caw.

For a moment, the moon was obscured by dark wings, then the human-sized bird landed on the path in front of her. Folding its wings against its sides, it stared at her. Its beak glistened red-black with blood, as did the taloned feet that brought the creature a few steps closer to Bryn.

Her heartbeat accelerating, Bryn called her own shift. She chose the half-Raven form she favored, her own harsh cry spilling forth as her hands morphed into talons, her human face elongated into a Raven beak, and wings sprang from her back. She had never encountered another Raven before, never been forced to defend herself against another of her kind. She hoped the combined human-Raven form would give her an advantage.

The fully formed Raven cawed and took to the air. Bryn's gaze followed the Raven's flight as it circled above her. Then it dived toward her. Bryn issued her own harsh caw and, thrusting herself upward with her wings, she crashed into the Raven, her taloned hands closing around the huge bird's throat.

Then the feathers beneath her hands shifted to human skin. The face above the neck Bryn's half-shifted hands encircled was her own.

Bryn sucked in a breath and released her hold. The other Bryn fell toward the ground, dissolving into silver mist.

As soon as Bryn's feet touched down on the forest path, she shifted back to her fully human form, the cry that escaped her morphing into a wail. She sank to her knees and sat back on her heels, her body folding forward over her thighs, her arms encircling her middle. She made no effort to silence the sobs that escaped her. She couldn't have even if she'd wanted to. She had no defense against the pain that shuddered through her.

When her wails subsided into sniffles and a trickle of tears, she crawled to the base of one of the trees framing the path and curled up in the hollow of its roots. Spent, she closed her tear-stained eyes and slept.

When he followed Zeke through the Gates, Aidan had no idea what to expect on the other side. Now, he found himself standing on a rocky plain with Zeke and the Archangels Uriel and Gabriel. A twilight glow lit the sky.

Before him, Uriel held the leather-and-gold-bound Book Aidan had last seen at Lucky's Striking. Gabriel's hands were outstretched, palm up. The Archangels' hair, as always, appeared to be stirred by a gentle breeze. The wind that flattened Aidan's curls and whipped Zeke's long hair about his face and shoulders seemed to pass over the Archangels and the Book with no effect.

Supporting the Book with one hand, Uriel placed his other hand on its cover. His flame-filled eyes gazed beyond Aidan and Zeke.

The Book is bound to the Tree as the Tree is bound to the Book. As usual, Uriel's words danced through Aidan's head like flames. *In opening this Seal, we open the way to the Tree.*

As Uriel spoke, the Book began to glow. When the Archangel removed his palm from the cover, the Book sprang open, pages turning, light radiating out in all directions. When the pages stopped moving, a scroll hovered above them, as if released from inside the Book. The scroll glided to Gabriel and dropped into his waiting hands.

Aidan saw Gabriel's lips move, and the Archangel's words flashed like lightning in his mind. Aidan had no sense of what the words meant, but he could sense their power.

As Gabriel finished speaking, the large golden seal on the scroll released, and the scroll unfurled. Clouds raced across the twilight sky, lightning flashed, and thunder rumbled. A huge tree appeared before them, its branches tossing in the wind.

The way is open. This time Aidan caught the meaning as well as the lightning sensation of Gabriel's words. *Go with care. Retrieve the lost. Repair the breach.*

"Come." Zeke motioned for Aidan to follow him.

They fought the wind for every step. The closer they drew to the tree, the harder the wind pushed back.

When only a few feet separated them from the tree's trunk, a large sword appeared before them, turning in every direction. Aidan went to step around it, and the sword moved as well, blocking his way. He started to shift to the opposite side, but Zeke's hand on his arm stopped him.

Bowing to the sword, Zeke said something Aidan couldn't understand. He'd studied several different angelic languages as part of his training, but the one Zeke spoke hadn't been among them. Its use was probably limited to the Guardians.

The sword stopped turning and hovered hilt down. Zeke spoke more words and held his hands out palm up. In one swift motion, the sword sliced across his upraised palms. As blood welled from the wounds, the sword disappeared, and the wind died away.

The sudden silence charged with anticipation.

Zeke pressed one bleeding palm to the center of Aidan's forehead. Then he marked Aidan's palms with his blood.

Aidan followed Zeke to the tree. Zeke pressed his palms against the trunk, indicating that Aidan should do the same. When Zeke removed his hands, Aidan did likewise. The tree absorbed Zeke's blood, and an opening the size of a doorway glowed silver in the thick trunk.

"The energy of the Tree can be overwhelming for one without Cherub blood," Zeke said. "My blood on your forehead and hands should help to steady you as well as allow you entry, but I cannot predict what you will experience. The Tree interacts with each of our energetic signatures to create something unique. You may find yourself facing your deepest fear, living out your greatest dream, reliving a scene from your past, or something else. Do not get caught up in it. Remember our purpose here, focus on our connection to one another and to Bryn, and the initial experience will pass. Ready?"

Aidan nodded. He pictured Bryn as he had last seen her, disappearing into the lightning-shot portal.

Then he followed Zeke through the silvery opening into the Tree.

CHAPTER 6

She ran down the forest path, her heartbeat loud in her ears. Something pursued her, but she didn't know what. She only knew she had to run. She couldn't let it catch her.

Shapes rose from the silvery mist. Angelic guards, their slit throats dripping golden ichor.

She stumbled over something and looked down to see the body of a Wraith, its throat slit, and its eyes pecked out. The bodies of countless more lined the path in front of her.

A sob caught in her throat. She tried not to look at the bodies as she passed them. But the empty eye sockets and opened throats drew her gaze. She had done this to them.

"Bryn!" A voice called from behind her.

"No," she sobbed and kept running. She couldn't stop, couldn't turn around.

"Bryn!" The voice called again, closer this time.

And there was no more path. A wall of silvery fog pressed against her, forcing her to turn.

She squeezed her eyes shut.

"No." Her sobs grew louder. "No, no, no."

"Open your eyes."

"No," she said again, even as her eyelids lifted.

She knew what she would see. She had seen it when she'd first turned, before she'd closed her eyes.

Her mother, her body red with blood from the waist down, her eyes empty and lifeless, her mouth shaping the name "Bryn" over and over again.

It was like walking through a bank of silvery fog. And when Aidan emerged on the other side, there was Bryn, clothed in her fighting leathers just as he had last seen her. She was lying under a tree, sleeping. A bandage decorated her left thigh, and blood marked the leg of her leather pants.

Aidan remembered the red blood mixed with golden ichor on the floor of the wine cellar where they'd accessed the portal. It had been hers.

She moved restlessly, making noises of distress, dreaming.

"Bryn," he called.

"No," she sobbed. Aidan could see tears glistening on her cheeks.

"Bryn, wake up," he said. "We're here. We've come to take you home."

"Aidan?" Bryn sat up and looked around her, rubbing the tears from her cheeks. "Aidan, is that you? Where are you?"

The silvery fog swirled up around Aidan again, blurring his view of Bryn. He pushed through the fog.

"I'm right here," he said. "I'm right in front of you."

Bryn got to her feet, favoring her wounded leg. "Aidan!" she cried.

Then she half-ran, half-limped to him and threw her arms around his neck. She clung to him, saying nothing.

Aidan held her, all his questions stunned into silence.

Then, just as suddenly as she had embraced him, Bryn pushed back out of his arms and squared her shoulders. "Sorry about that," she muttered.

"You've got nothing to be sorry for." Aidan rested his hands on her shoulders.

She stiffened but didn't pull away. Her gray eyes were red-rimmed.

"You okay?" he asked.

Bryn nodded, then shook her head. "I don't know." Then her gaze locked on his forehead, and her brow knotted in concern. "You're bleeding."

"What?" Aidan had forgotten that Zeke's blood marked his head and hands. "Oh, that's not my blood. It's Zeke's."

"Zeke's? Is he—?"

"He's fine too," Aidan interrupted. "We just needed his blood to get here."

"Where are we anyway? I had to use my own blood to open the portal, and then I ended up here. But I have no idea where here is."

"We're inside the Tree of Life, the nexus of energy that connects all the worlds." Aidan looked all around them. "And I seem to have lost the entrance."

He had the fleeting thought that maybe Bryn was a Tree-induced illusion, based on his desire to find her. But he tossed the thought aside as quickly as it came. The Bryn standing before him was as real as he was. Not only did she carry a wound from their adventure in the Halls, but she'd talked about the portal. And, while the way she had clung to him was more than unusual, she had felt warm and alive in his arms.

And if she was real, then he had to assume the Tree had somehow transported him to her. He didn't imagine for a moment that they had been fortunate enough to find her right inside the entrance they had opened. If that had been the case, Zeke would be with him.

"Entrance?"

"Yeah. We—Zeke and I—we came through a physical entrance in what looked like an actual tree."

Bryn frowned. "If you came through the same entrance, how did you end up here when Zeke didn't?"

"I don't know. I just stepped through the door and wound up here." Aidan sighed as he did another 360. "But where here is in relation to the entrance is a mystery to me."

"Is there a map to this place?"

Aidan shook his head. "Maybe on a grand scale. I mean, it does connect all the worlds, and Lilith apparently knows the Tree's pathways well enough to have tapped into one to create that portal. Which, I gather, is how it dumped you here." He skipped over the bit about her Cherub blood. He figured it was Zeke's place, not his, to share that detail. "That may mean we are in some branch close to the Halls. The entrance Zeke and I used was in the Place of the Book. Uriel and Gabriel may know how those realms are aligned in spacetime, but I don't have a clue. Odds are good that multiple dimensions are involved."

"So, what you're saying is that we're both lost now?" Bryn asked.

Aidan raked a hand through his hair. "Yeah," he said. "I guess that about sums it up."

The explosion, when it came, was less of an uncontrolled blast this time. As the heat and pressure built inside him, Kev could feel the energy pulsing in his arms. His palms burned but not the way they did when he activated his sigils. He aimed his palms toward the biggest snowdrift he could find and channeled the blast down his arms. He couldn't control when the Fire started or when it ended, but he could control what he flamed.

While the Fire streamed through him, it completely claimed his awareness. When it stopped, he saw he'd not only melted the drift but had also vaporized the resulting water. The heat from his body had melted the snow around him. He stood inside a snow-free circle six to eight feet in diameter.

His body hadn't burned as hot as it had in his cell, and he didn't feel as burned out.

Kev looked down at his upturned palms. Could he...?

He turned his right palm toward another bank of snow and called the Fire.

It came. Shooting from his palm, it vaporized the snow in an instant.

"Sweet," Kev breathed.

The left hand worked just as well.

Kev laughed as he alternated hands to fire several shots into the snow.

He tried shifting, but he couldn't call the dragon. The blasted drug still polluted his system.

The dragon didn't come, but the Fire did. The heat inside Kev started building again, this time much more rapidly than before. And this time, he couldn't control it. He roared as his whole body flamed, the heat and Fire blasting outwards as it had in the Halls.

When the Fire subsided, he felt as burned out as the blackened, smoking pines at the clearing's edges.

When his legs felt steady enough to carry him, he made his way back to where he'd stashed the backpack. He dressed, then slipped the pack onto his back and checked the perimeter of the clearing to make sure there was no fire left to spread. The snow had melted from the first rows of trees beyond those blackened by the blast, but further out the snow blanketing the trees remained intact.

Looked like he shouldn't try shifting for now, but at least he could call the Fire in human form. He fired another blast from his palm to reassure himself.

He waited long enough to make sure there were no unexpected side effects—no sudden rise in temperature, no feeling that an explosion was imminent—then he zapped himself back to the cabin.

"Should we stay put or keep moving?" Bryn asked. "Does it even matter?"

"I don't know. I don't want to make it harder for Zeke to find us, but I hate the idea of just standing around here doing nothing."

No sooner had Aidan finished speaking than the silvery mist beyond the trees parted to reveal a strip of sand, the water beyond stretching away to what passed as a horizon. The moonlight sparkled on the water and soft waves lapped the shore.

"It's like Lake Michigan," Aidan said, moving toward the beach. "Is this place for real?"

Bryn followed him onto the sand. "It's freaky. Most of what I've seen seem like illusions created from my thoughts and memories. They fade in and out. But sometimes they seem way too real."

"What do you mean?"

Bryn didn't reply.

A few feet from the water's edge, Aidan dropped down onto the sand, stretching his legs out in front of him. He patted the sand next to him, inviting Bryn to join him.

She winced as she bent her legs.

Aidan gestured to her bandaged thigh. "Let me take a look at that leg."

"It's all right. It should heal soon."

"I can heal it faster. Let me help you."

Bryn sighed but shifted onto her side, so Aidan could remove the bandage.

"This cut is deep. What happened?" he asked.

"One of the angelic guards threw a dagger at me." Bryn sucked in a breath as Aidan's fingers probed her wound. "I got him back though."

"Yeah, we saw what you did to them." Aidan pressed his hand against the gash. "Hold still."

Then he began to sing. He never chose the song when he healed someone. He simply concentrated on the wound and what needed to be healed, and the necessary notes just came. He was getting better at sensing the right way to heal and when to stop. His hand grew warm as the notes passed his lips. When the warmth began to fade, he stopped singing.

He lifted his hand from Bryn's thigh. The gash had closed. "There," he said. "That should feel better."

Bryn touched the place where the wound had been. "It's completely healed." She sat up and turned to face him. "That's the second time you've healed me. I don't know how to thank you."

Aidan grinned. "Gotta say this time was a lot easier." After a moment's pause, he added, "You can do something for me too if you would. Will you tell me why you were so upset when I first found you?"

Bryn picked up a handful of sand and watched it sift through her fingers.

"This place," she finally said. "It's like it knows everything about me."

Aidan nodded. "Zeke said our experience here is shaped by what we bring with us."

Bryn chuckled bitterly. "Yeah, I kind of guessed that."

"What happened to you?"

Bryn let a second handful of sand fall through her fingers before she replied. "Another Raven attacked me. Only she wasn't another Raven at all. When I tried to kill her, she shifted to her human form. She was me."

The bleakness on Bryn's face made Aidan want to hold her, but he just waited for her to continue.

"I've always hated being a Raven. I'm a killer. I even killed my own mother."

"That wasn't your fault. It was beyond your control."

Bryn sniffed, and Aidan knew she was fighting back tears.

"I've killed others, because of the Raven bloodlust."

"And you've done everything in your power to control that. You've trained, gained discipline. You didn't kill those angelic guards. You could have, but you didn't."

"I tried to kill the Raven—before she turned into me. It's like this place was mocking everything I've tried to do to overcome my Raven. I'll never be anything but a killer." Bryn's hand clenched in the sand.

"That's not how I see it." Aidan covered her clenched hand with his own. "I think it was showing you how much you've fought against your Raven side. And that maybe you don't have to fight it anymore."

Bryn let out a sob, and the tears she'd been holding back rolled down her cheeks. She half-turned toward him, and Aidan pulled her into his arms.

Kev awoke with a start. He'd decided to rest at the cabin a bit before returning to Zeke's, but he hadn't intended to fall asleep. He checked the time on his phone and found that several hours had passed.

Lucky was probably wondering what had happened to him—and he should have been at the training center a while ago.

Without bothering to change his sleep-rumpled clothes, he zapped himself to the training center.

He found only Malachi and Lucifer in the war room, which meant Zeke and Aidan must still be in the Tree. Somehow Kev didn't think their absence was enough to account for Malachi's and Lucifer's grim expressions.

"What's happened?" he asked.

"The Metatron has demanded I return to the cell in the Halls," Lucifer said, "or else they will destroy Nadach."

Kev's jaw dropped. "How could they do that? Destroy an entire world and everyone in it?"

"They said it was a suitable punishment, considering that Lilith provided the means for Lucifer's escape," Malachi said. "And they know he would never sacrifice all those lives for his own."

Kev shook his head, his lips compressing into a thin line. "Still, such a threat amounts to terrorism."

"It does," Lucifer agreed. "But with the Halls in their hands, they have the ability to carry out that threat. And since Nadach was created specifically for Lilith's Banishment, the world does not have the same rights within the Alliance as any other Dark Realm."

"And, in Zeke's absence, there is no one to speak for it but you," Malachi added.

"Which is to say, no one." Lucifer lips curled sardonically. "The only means of speaking for it I have is to return to my cell."

Kev's hands clenched into fists. "While the one who stole your sigil continues to serve as the Light-Bringer's second."

"They insist Semyaza's record does not prove Lucifer's innocence." Malachi crossed his arms over his chest. "And it doesn't. It just shows someone else had access to his sigil. It casts doubt on his guilt but does not disprove it."

Lucifer frowned. "I cannot see Ba'al harming Jahoel. No matter how much resentment he may have harbored for me."

Kev leaned forward, propping his elbows on the conference table. "He told me he only had the sigil copied because he could, that he took advantage of having a Morpho demon imprisoned at the same time as Semyaza. That he had no plan to kill Jahoel."

Lucifer's frown deepened. "But he did not deny that the copied sigil was used to mark Jahoel's body?"

Kev shook his head. "No, he didn't."

"Perhaps you can use your return to prison to find out more from Ba'al," Malachi said.

"Yes." Lucifer nodded. "Perhaps I can."

CHAPTER 7

When her anguish had receded enough that she became aware of how tightly she clung to Aidan, Bryn pulled away from him and lunged to her feet.

"Thanks," she muttered, making a show of brushing the sand off her pants, so she didn't have to look at him.

"Any time."

Bryn pretended not to hear the concern in Aidan's voice. Despite having spent she didn't know how long crying in his arms, she didn't want him feeling sorry for her.

Perhaps the Tree interpreted that thought as a dismissal, because the lake and sand faded away, leaving them surrounded once again with dark trees and silvery fog.

Fog that parted to reveal a familiar figure.

"Zeke!" Bryn exclaimed.

Aidan grinned. "You found us."

"Blood calls to blood," said Zeke.

Bryn glanced at the blood marking Aidan's forehead. "That explains how you found Aidan. But how did he find me?"

"I think that may be due to a combination of things." Zeke pointed at the white streak in Bryn's black hair. "The side-effect of Aidan's healing created an energetic link between the two of you."

"And?" Bryn asked. "You said a combination of things."

Zeke swallowed. "There's also the blood on his face and hands."

Bryn frowned. "He said that's your blood. How would that draw Aidan to me?"

Aidan cleared his throat. "I'm going to go over there"—he gestured toward a tree a few feet away—"and give you two some privacy."

"What?" Bryn looked after Aidan's retreating figure.

Zeke took a step closer to her. "What I am going to say may come as a shock to you. I know it did to me." The softness of his voice wrapped around her like an embrace. "My blood drew Aidan to you, and drew me to you, because you share that blood."

"I what?" Bryn whispered.

"You are my granddaughter, Bryn," Zeke said. "Mine as well as Lilith's."

"You're my grandfather?" Shock was an understatement. Bryn thought she might lose her balance.

Zeke extended his arm, and she latched onto it as to a lifeline.

"Your mother was my daughter, though I never knew. I do not think Lilith would ever have told me had you not found your way through the portal into the Tree."

She would never have told me either, Bryn thought. "She's kept a lot of secrets, hasn't she?"

"Indeed, she has. I wish I had known your mother."

The mixture of affection and sadness in Zeke's eyes near-ly undid Bryn.

She nodded, blinking back tears. "Can we go home now?"

"Soon," Zeke said. "There is something we have to do first."

The ferret looked up from the bowl of kibble Lucky had set in front of him and chittered.

"I know, Harley," she said. "I want him to come back too."

She wanted all three of them to come back. All four of them really. At least she knew, theoretically, where Aidan, Zeke, and Bryn were. Even if she didn't know exactly where it was in relation to Zeke's brownstone, she could intellectual-ly grasp that they were inside the Tree somewhere. Kev, on the other hand...

Once again, he'd disappeared without so much as a word. She'd left him in Zeke's study, expecting to catch up with him later. But he hadn't come to find her.

Now, nearly twenty-four hours had passed since she'd seen him. And since Zeke and Aidan had gone to find Bryn.

Maybe they were on their way home right now.

Maybe Kev was too.

Lucky sighed. "I'll check on you later, if Aidan's not back," she told the ferret.

She descended the stairs to the gym to change into train-ing clothes, the emptiness of the brownstone pressing on her like a weight. She was glad she had training to attend.

Dominique's class kept Lucky too focused on swordplay to worry. Lucky left the class covered in sweat and with an aching sword arm.

Instead of heading to the exit, she turned toward what Zeke and Malachi referred to as the war room, hoping she might find Zeke had returned while she was in class. At least she could find out if Malachi had any updates. She might even run into Kev.

Speak of the devil. Kev stepped out of the war room just as she approached.

She started to ask him where he'd been, but the expression on his face stopped her.

"I don't suppose you've heard from Zeke or Aidan?" he asked.

Lucky shook her head.

Kev cursed under his breath.

"What's going on?" Lucky asked.

"The Metatron threatened to destroy Nadach if Lucifer didn't return to the Halls. So, he went back."

"Destroy Nadach?" Lucky gasped. "They can do that?"

"Apparently so."

Lucky repeated Kev's muttered curse.

He gave her shoulder a squeeze, his hand lingering to caress her upper arm.

Lucky was torn between the desire to pull her arm away—he'd left her hanging for hours—and the need to move closer and touch him back. The latter won.

"Where have you been?" she asked, trailing her fingers down the back of his free hand.

"The cabin."

A needle of pain pierced Lucky's heart. "You went without me?"

Kev continued to caress her arm. "It wasn't a pleasure trip. I felt like I was going to supernova again."

Concern crowded out Lucky's sense of hurt. She stepped closer, her hand rising to cup his cheek. "And did you? Are you okay?"

He nodded. "I'm okay. I even learned some new tricks. I can't shift though. I think trying is what brings on the explosion."

"You need to have Katrin run some tests."

"Yeah, I might as well do that while we wait for Zeke and Aidan—and try to figure out how to prove Lucifer's innocence once and for all."

With Zeke as a guide, they moved swiftly through the Tree. The silver fog parted, and they seemed to travel on paths of light, or energy, or thought. Or perhaps the paths moved through them.

Bryn couldn't be sure. She lost all sense of time and place and distance.

But even though she had no idea where they were going, she knew beyond her trust in Zeke that they went exactly where they needed to go. The internal compass she had felt when she had had to choose from the available paths in the clearing asserted itself again, pointing unerringly along the path they followed.

When their motion—or the motion of the energy around them—slowed, Bryn had already anticipated it would. Something in her knew they were about to reach their destination.

The silvery fog Bryn had become accustomed to was nowhere to be seen. They appeared to be surrounded by shifting streaks of colored light. Bryn gasped in wonder. It was like the pictures she had seen of the aurora borealis, like they were inside it.

"There," Zeke said.

He pointed to where a jagged gray opening slashed through the streaks of color. The colored light at the edges of the opening seemed to be leaking through in silver drops.

Bryn touched the colored streaks with delicate fingertips. The light offered a slight resistance and emitted a bit of a tingle, as if it were a kind of cloth that carried an electrical charge. Bryn slid her fingertips to the silver drops on the edge of the tear. A zing of energy shot up her arm. She lifted her fingers and extended them into the opening itself. The opening tugged on her fingers, and she quickly withdrew them.

"You see it, feel it?" Zeke asked.

She nodded. "Something is drawing the Tree's energy."

"Yes." Zeke took her hands and placed one on each side of one end of the gash. "Help me seal it."

He placed his own hands in similar positions at the opening's opposite end. "Press it together, so the silvered edges meet."

Bryn couldn't quite understand how she could press something that felt so insubstantial together, but the harder she pressed against the light the more resistance it gave, until she could draw the edges together just as Zeke asked. She zippered the wound closed from her end to the center, and Zeke did the same, until they met in the middle.

Zeke turned to Aidan, who had watched the whole proceeding in silence. "What do you see?"

"Well, it sort of looked like you two just mended a tear in a curtain of light. I can see the seam there." He pointed to the thin silver line that marred the aurora-like streaks.

"Yes," Zeke said. "We sealed the breach. But I believe you might be able to heal it."

Aidan looked stunned. "You want me to try to—heal—the Tree?"

"Yes," Zeke said again. "Want to give it a shot?"

Katrin slipped the needle from Kev's vein and pressed a bandage over the mark in his arm. "That's it. You are free to go now."

"Are you sure you got everything you need?" Kev muttered, rolling down his sleeve.

He glanced at the lab table where several small vials of his blood sat next to closed containers of different shapes and sizes in which flames of varying colors and temperatures danced. He had breathed the Fire into some of the vessels. Others Katrin had used to capture flames he shot from his palms.

She had also tested the sensitivity of his heat vision, as well as performed scans to measure his body temperature and to track his brain waves, both when he was and was not calling the Fire. Kev had lost patience with the poking and prodding a while ago.

Katrin raised her eyebrows. "You were the one who came to me, remember?"

Kev sighed. "I know. I just didn't realize what I was signing up for." He shrugged into his battered bomber jacket. "Do you think you can find out what's blocking my ability to shift?"

"I don't know. I hope so." She gestured toward the containers of blood and Fire. "It will take time to run all the possible tests on these. I will let you know what I discover."

"Thank you." Kev held out his hand, feeling awkward.

After a slight hesitation, his mother put her hand in his. Her fingers tightened momentarily, and Kev had the fleeting thought that she might pull him into an embrace.

But the moment passed.

Katrin released his hand. "Enjoy your dinner," she said.

Kev nodded his thanks and exited the lab.

Lucky, Josh, Ben, and Mo already had plates of burgers and fries in front of them, when Kev arrived at the Medici. Once he'd realized Katrin's tests would take longer than he'd thought, he'd texted Lucky to tell them to start without him.

He slid into the empty seat next to Lucky and dropped a kiss on her cheek.

"How'd it go?" she asked.

Kev shrugged. "We won't know until the tests are done. But she's got enough samples to keep her busy for a while." He looked across the table at Ben. "I guess you were able to get out of tonight's gig?"

"Yeah. No one wants to see Icarus without a lead singer. I told them Aidan's got the flu, so they let us reschedule." Ben eyed the fully loaded cheeseburger he held with anticipation. "The only bright side to no Icarus show is that we get to have burgers at the Med for dinner." He bit into the burger, his eyes closing in pleasure.

"I hope they get back soon." The worry that threaded Lucky's voice found an echo in Kev's thoughts.

Aidan and Zeke had been in the Tree for over two days now. Lilith had said time moved differently there, so maybe it had been only a few hours for them. Still, Kev couldn't quiet the troubled murmurings in his head. What if they couldn't find Bryn? What if something had happened to all three of them? He knew Lucky had similar fears.

He closed his hand on her knee. "They will be." He meant the words to reassure himself as much as her.

"Yeah," Mo said around a mouthful of burger. "This is Zeke we're talking about. He can do anything. He'll find Bryn and get them all back here in no time."

Lucky grinned, and Kev shot Mo a grateful look.

The girl with the unruly blonde curls was the only fully human being at the table since Lucky had been Made Naphil, and Josh had become, through a combination of Sambethe's meddling and Lucky's mixed-up demon-Naphil blood, some kind of human-Wraith-angel hybrid. Kev remembered sitting in a different restaurant with Lucky, Mo, and Aidan when Mo had first learned the truth about her best friend. It had been the day of the Striking, the day Kev had first met Lucky, and already something had drawn him to her. He'd been the one to describe the Striking to Mo when he'd seen that Lucky couldn't. His brother, who had been Lucky's boyfriend then, had taken her hand, offering physical comfort. All Kev could do was give voice to the story Lucky couldn't seem to speak.

And Mo had taken it all in stride—bearing up even when, shortly after, a Power had slid a poisoned sword through Lucky's middle. Kev had been impressed with the girl then, and his opinion hadn't changed.

Mo flagged down the server. "This guy," she said, pointing a ketchup-laden fry at Kev, "needs a burger and fries, stat."

Kev laughed and gave the server his order. He understood why Mo's friendship meant so much to Lucky.

Aidan had never contemplated healing something like the Tree. It was, well, primordial. But if it could be wounded, he supposed it could be healed.

And Zeke believed he could do it.

Aidan ran his fingers along the silver seam, feeling the light give like cloth. He flattened his palm over the sealed wound, and the suddenly more solid energy field suctioned his hand flat, even as his mouth opened without his conscious will. Song spilled like light from his lips, and his hand moved slowly from one end of the seam to the other.

Aidan had never felt so much a vehicle for his Gift as he did now. He did not so much heal the Tree as the Tree's energy worked through him to heal itself. His body, his voice, his breath were not his own.

When the Tree released him, he stumbled and bent over to catch his breath.

"I knew you could do it."

Even through the blood pounding in his ears, Aidan could hear the satisfaction in Zeke's voice.

He drew himself upright and looked to where the silver seam had been. The unbroken streaks of light undulated and pulsed as if the wound had never existed.

"Wow," he breathed.

Zeke smiled. "Indeed. Lilith may not be pleased though. Her portal will not work now that it can no longer pull energy from the Tree."

Bryn shuddered. "She might not be happy about it, but I am. I never want to go through that portal again."

"Because it brought you here?" Zeke asked.

Bryn slowly shook her head, her brows drawing together in a frown. "If you'd asked me that when Aidan first found me, I'd have said yes. But now... I don't necessarily want to spend a lot of time in the Tree, but something about it—fits—somehow. I didn't know we were coming here, to this spot, to heal this wound, but somehow I knew we'd arrived where we needed to be."

"I thought as much," Zeke said. "Do you want to help guide us back to the entrance?"

Bryn's eyes widened. "I wouldn't know how to begin."

"I will teach you." Zeke smiled at her reassuringly.

Still Bryn hesitated.

"Give it a shot, Bryn," Aidan said. "I saw the way you sealed your end of that tear. You're a natural."

"Okay." Bryn took a deep breath and grinned at Zeke. "Show me what to do."

Zeke alternately navigated the Tree's pathways and guided Bryn as she navigated. She learned how to recognize the distinctive vibration of their branch of the Tree, so as not to stray down pathways that led to other branches. And she learned how to feel the shift in energy that signaled an entrance. When they reached the entrance that opened to the Place of the Book, she was exhilarated, her head full of information and vibrational frequencies.

"Way to go!" Aidan held his hand up high, palm facing Bryn, and looked at her expectantly.

"What?" she asked.

He chuckled. "Slap my palm with yours. It's called a high five. It's something we do to celebrate or say 'Good job.'"

Bryn slapped his palm as requested. "Good job to you too. You healed the Tree like you healed the cut on my leg."

Aidan frowned. "Not quite like that. But thanks."

Bryn would have questioned him about his response, but Zeke was ushering them through the silvery gateway he'd opened in the Tree.

When she stepped through to the other side, the windy, rocky plain and the literal tree behind her took Bryn by surprise. As did the two larger than human figures standing some distance from the tree. One had hair like spun gold and eyes like flame. The other had eyes like the sky and white hair that shimmered like lightning.

"Who are they?" she whispered to Aidan.

"The Archangels Uriel"—he indicated the one with flame-filled eyes—"and Gabriel."

When they had pushed through the wind to stand beside the Archangels, Gabriel said something in a language Bryn didn't understand and sensed more than heard. The open scroll in his hands rolled up, sealed itself, and disappeared into the light spilling from the open Book Uriel held before him.

The tree disappeared, the wind dropped, and the Book closed.

Well done. Gabriel's words sizzled in Bryn's mind, though her attention strayed to the Gates that had appeared nearby.

She barely heard what Zeke said as he thanked the Archangels for their help. But she was close behind him when he strode to the Gates to open the way home.

CHAPTER 8

Josh raised his beer. "To a night out with friends—who are all back where they belong."

He gave Lucky a meaningful glance as she clinked her glass against the bottle he held, and she knew he meant more than Bryn and Aidan's safe return from the Tree. This was the first Icarus show she'd been to since she'd started dating Kev. And Kev was there with her. Aidan had made a point of asking them both to come.

Bryn had told them how Aidan had healed the Tree after she and Zeke had sealed the gap. It looked as if that breach wasn't the only one he wanted to see mended.

Kev's fingers closed around hers, and she smiled at him before directing her attention to the stage, where Aidan was stepping up to the microphone.

He started to sing, and that beautiful voice that had first drawn her to him began to wrap around her. She wanted to open her senses as she had before, to see and touch that voice, but it seemed too intimate, a violation of both Aidan's privacy and her commitment to Kev. So she kept her extra senses locked down and just listened, as she had before her Sensitive abilities had asserted themselves.

And she was just as enraptured with the music as she had been when she'd first heard Icarus. Only now her enjoyment was tinged with a hint of sadness—for all she'd gained and lost since she'd first seen Aidan on a stage, flaming wings extending from his back.

Kev squeezed her hand. "You okay?" His eyes met hers, a concerned frown creasing his brow.

She nodded. "I was just thinking about how much has changed since the first time I saw them play."

Kev's frown deepened. "You looked sad. Do you wish you could go back?"

"Of course not." Lucky threaded her fingers through his. "I wouldn't have you. It's just..."

"You miss what you had with Aidan."

Lucky searched his eyes and found no judgment there. "Yes," she said.

"You love him." Kev's words held no accusation, merely a statement of fact.

Lucky's eyes filled with tears. "I do," she whispered. "I think I always will." She tightened her hold on his hand. "But my love for you is—more."

Kev lifted his free hand and pushed the curls back from her face. "I know. Though sometimes I still find it surprising." His lips curved in a gentle smile. "I also know that what you feel for me doesn't cancel out what you feel for Aidan. I never expected it to."

Lucky cupped his cheek. "How did you get so wise?"

Kev chuckled. He captured her hand with his and pressed his lips to her palm. "I don't know that I am."

"You are," Lucky said.

She turned her attention back to the stage and the music, her fingers folding against her palm to enclose the warmth of Kev's kiss.

A slender blade twisted in Aidan's gut as he watched his brother thread his fingers through Lucky's hair and press a kiss into her palm. He channeled the pain into the song he sang, even as he wondered how long it would be before seeing them together ceased to hurt. The pain wasn't as acute as it had been—otherwise he'd never have asked them to come tonight—but it still hurt more than he'd like to admit.

Then Lucky looked right at him, his eyes caught and held hers, and, for a moment, the mixture of joy and sadness Aidan saw reflected there nearly undid him. Then his gaze travelled past her into the crowd, and he sang on, never missing a note.

When he next glanced at the table where his friends sat, it was Bryn who caught his eye. She was smiling, her eyes sparkling, her face aglow. His mouth curled into a grin in response, and he closed one eye in a wink. She laughed and raised her glass in salute.

He scanned all the faces at the table—Bryn, Lucky, Kev, Josh, and Mo—and again felt a slither of pain in his belly. This time though it wasn't about what he'd lost, but about how very much he had.

The show was over, and the band had nearly finished packing up their equipment, when Zeke's summons settled into Kev's brain. He glanced at Lucky, Bryn, and Josh, and they all nodded to show they too had gotten the message. On the stage, he saw Aidan and Ben exchange looks and say hurried goodbyes to their band mates.

"What?" Mo asked, noting all the shared glances. Then, "Oh, don't tell me. Zeke's doing his mind-meld thing again, isn't he?"

"Yup." Josh blinked and shook his head as if trying to dislodge the message. "This is the first time I've been the lucky recipient of one of these. I gotta say it's creepier than I expected. Can we go now? If we don't, I think my head might explode."

Ben and Aidan arrived in time to catch Josh's last words. "We just need to get to an alley where we can dematerialize," Ben said.

"And where are you off to?" Mo asked as they headed for the door.

"Elsewhere," Lucky answered, breaking into a run.

"Don't worry about me. I'll find my own way home," Mo called after them.

Kev spared a moment to wonder what it must be like for Mo, always getting left behind by her non-human friends. Then Zeke's summons intensified, eclipsing all other thoughts. He raced after the others.

They ducked down the closest alley. After a quick check to make sure no humans were around, they clasped hands and zapped themselves to Elsewhere, neutral ground for Light, Dark, and Fallen. Kev and Aidan led the way into the

Alliance Council Hall and up the stairs to the meeting room that matched Zeke's coordinates.

"What's up?" Kev asked, as he pushed through the door, the others close behind. "Whoa. What's going on?"

Zeke, Malachi, Lucifer, Ba'al, Lilith, and Margash, the Metatron's fourth, stood around the table, staring at a holographic map, their expressions marked with urgency. Zeke's form flashed from man to bull to eagle to lion and back in such rapid succession Kev could barely look at him.

Before Kev could ask any one of the many questions clamoring to escape his lips, Zeke spoke, his voice as multi-layered as his shifting form. "Adrigon and Helel have moved ahead with their plans to destroy Nadach. The process is already in motion."

"What?!" Aidan exclaimed. He glanced at Lucifer. "But you met their demands. You returned to your cell."

"Yes," said Margash. "But once the idea took hold of Adrigon, he could not let it go."

"Couldn't you or the other members of the Metatron stop him?" Kev asked.

"The question was not posed to the Metatron council. I know only because I overheard Helel telling Adrigon that the destruction process had been started as requested. From what I heard, once the process has begun, it cannot be reversed."

"That is true," said Ba'al. "We cannot stop it now."

Kev's heart began to race. "How long?"

Ba'al shook his head. "A few of your earthly hours. Four or five at most."

"So, the question is," said Lilith, "how do we evacuate?"

Lucky watched as people poured through the portals opened all around the sanctuary area of St. Stephen's, the seemingly abandoned church at Blackstone and 57th Street that served as a safe house for the Fallen.

And now for the people of Nadach. The Bound.

Or those who were formerly Bound. When Lilith had learned of the imminent destruction of her world, she had broken the Binding spell she had laid on her people as the price of coming to her world and learning her magic. Released from the Binding, they could now freely remain in the earthly realm.

But their homes were in Nadach. In the earthly realm, the only home they had for the moment was the Fallen's safe house.

Lucky helped hand out water and blankets and directed people to areas where they could claim a small space for themselves. As she grabbed more blankets and water from the supply table, she saw Mo pointing out an open area to a young couple with a small boy. Mo was the only human Lucky knew who could so calmly aid refugees who had stepped through portals from another world.

"Lucky!"

She turned to see a girl with long blonde hair pushing through the crowd toward her.

"Alicia!"

Lucky dropped the supplies back onto the table and pulled the blonde girl into a hug. "Are you okay? It's so good to see you—though I wish, well, the reason was different."

"I wish it was too," Alicia said, "but it is good to see you. Is it bad that I'm excited about being in the earthly realm, even if I'm sad about the reason?"

Lucky remembered when Alicia had first told her about the Bound, how she had explained that her own mother had bound her as well as herself to Lilith and Nadach in exchange for learning Lilith's magic. Lucky shook her head. "No, it's not bad. I'd be excited too if I were you."

She scanned the crowd around them. "Where's Jaime?"

"He stayed behind to help get everyone out of Nadach. He'll be one of the last ones through." Both admiration and concern colored Alicia's words. "So will Bryn."

Lucky nodded. She hadn't been surprised when Bryn had asked to return to Nadach to assist with the evacuation. Bryn had lived most of her life there, and despite her love for the earthly realm and her new life among the Fallen, she still considered Nadach home.

Kev and Aidan had gone too, along with Lucifer and a few other members of the Fallen's Forces. Zeke had assured Lucky and Josh they would be of more help on the earthly side. Her cousin was somewhere on one of the safe house's other levels, helping get the newly arrived Nadachis settled.

"They'll be okay," she said, reassuring herself as much as Alicia. "Lucifer and Lilith won't leave anyone behind."

Lucky didn't feel as sure as she sounded though, and she was especially unsure about Lilith's safety. While Lilith had released the Bound from her spell, she could not release herself from the Banishment that bound her to Nadach and limited the amount of time she could spend away from the

Dark world. Lucky didn't know if her recently discovered grandmother would be able to escape Nadach or, if she did, how long she would survive in the earthly realm.

"Can I help you with those?" Alicia gestured to the tables of supplies.

"Absolutely," Lucky said, grateful for the distraction of the work. "Make sure everyone has at least one blanket and two bottles of water."

They had distributed only a few more blankets and water bottles when the din of conversation that filled the safe house turned to sounds of alarm.

"They're all hurt," someone shouted.

The group gathered around the closest portal parted long enough for Lucky to see for herself. All the people coming through the portals now were injured, limping, bleeding.

"It's starting," one of the injured women said through her tears. "The ground is shaking. The buildings are falling."

Lucky thrust the blankets and water she held into the hands of the person closest to her and cast a desperate glance toward the far side of the sanctuary where Zeke had set up his command post. She longed to run to him and beg him to compel Kev and Aidan and Bryn to come back now.

Instead, she followed his orders and grabbed a stash of bandages and a container of medical supplies.

"Let me do that," said Alicia, taking the supplies from her hands. "This is something I'm good at."

Lucky nodded. "Thank you."

As Alicia moved into the crowd toward the nearest group of wounded, Lucky turned and caught Mo's eye. She was afraid her own smile of reassurance was as weak as her friend's.

She continued to hand out blankets, water, and medical supplies and direct people to available space in the various levels of the safe house, but as time passed and more and more wounded came through the portals, she couldn't help wondering if her friends would make it out of Nadach alive.

The city was falling fast. Kev circled over the rubble, looking for the best place to blast a route out for the last of those trapped when the buildings began to crumble.

There. That would do for a starting point.

He shot a flare from his palm to catch his father's attention. Lucifer, in dragon form, turned in Kev's direction. Kev wished he could call his own dragon, but the fear of going supernova in what was already a disaster zone kept him from making the attempt. At least, he could call the Fire without the dragon. Using both hands, he directed dual streams of flame at the location he'd spotted.

He and Lucifer, who alternated bursts of flame with carefully directed sound waves powerful enough to break rock, soon cleared a trail through the debris. Then Lucifer shifted back to human form, and they hurried to help Aidan, Malachi, Ben, and the other members of the Forces usher the wounded through the rubble.

The ground shuddered beneath their feet, and more stones and beams fell from the buildings. Kev grunted as a rock hit his shoulder, but he kept his footing, using his body to shield the wounded Nadachi children in his arms.

Once free of the rubble, he summoned his wings and flew to the clearing where the nearest portals waited. Leaving the children in the care of the portal attendants, he returned to the ruins.

His father met him as he touched down and dismissed his wings. "Aidan is coming with the last of the survivors," Lucifer said. "She is badly wounded. I will let the rest of the team know we have them all. You and Aidan get the girl and yourselves to the portals. We need to get out of this world before it blows."

Lucifer winged skyward without waiting for a reply, just as Aidan came into view. The little girl in his arms was covered with blood.

"Lucifer says she's the last," Kev said. "Let's get her to the portals and get out of here."

Aidan shook his head. "She's not going to make it to the portals. I need to heal her now. Hold her for me."

No sooner had Kev gathered the unconscious girl into his arms than the ground beneath them shuddered and split. Kev lost his footing, but kept tight hold of the girl, absorbing the force of his fall with his shoulder. As he hit the ground, he saw Aidan slide into the newly formed crevice.

"Aidan!"

By the time Kev had scrambled to his feet, the girl still cradled in his arms, Aidan had winged up out of the break in the ground.

He dropped to his feet beside Kev and ran his hands over the little girl's body, searching for wounds. "Got them," he said as the ground rumbled once more. "Hold her tight."

Kev watched as his brother pressed his hands to the deep gashes in the little girl's side and arm. Then Aidan opened his mouth, loosing multiple notes in multiple octaves, singing as only one with his Gift could sing.

The little girl twitched and moaned in Kev's arms. Her wounds were beginning to knit when another tremor hit.

Kev summoned his wings and lifted into the air as the ground gave way beneath them. Aidan was right beside him.

"Just a little more," Aidan said, hovering inches away. "A few more seconds and she'll make it to the portals."

Kev nodded. "Do it."

Aidan pressed his hands to the girl's wounds once more and sang those impossible notes. When he removed his hands, the wounds had closed.

But, beneath them, the world was folding in upon itself.

Lucky could barely focus on the bandage she and Mo were applying to a wounded woman's leg. She kept glancing at the one remaining portal. Lucifer, along with Malachi, Ben, and the other members of the Forces who had been part of the evacuation team, had come through several minutes ago, after all the other portals had closed. But she had seen no sign of Kev, Aidan, Bryn, or Jaime yet.

She was staring at the empty portal when Kev and Aidan stumbled through, Kev with a little girl in his arms, and all three of them covered in blood.

Lucky gasped and leapt to her feet.

"Go on," Mo said. "I got this."

Lucky was already moving. "Thanks, Mo."

Heart pounding, she pushed her way through the crowd.

By the time Lucky reached them, the little girl lay on a pallet of blankets. Aidan knelt beside her, conferring with Katrin, who leaned on her cane at his side. Kev stood close by.

He looked up as Lucky approached, and his face lit up at the sight of her. He opened his arms. She flew into them, undeterred by the blood on his clothes. He kissed her, and she clung to him, her return kisses conveying all the worry of the past hours and the intensity of her relief at having him back.

When he raised his head, she pressed her hands to his bloody shirt. "You're not hurt?"

Kev shook his head. "Not my blood. That little girl was in bad shape though, before Aidan did his thing."

"What about Bryn? Is she—?"

Before Lucky could finish the question, Bryn, Jaime, Luil, and Lilith fell through the portal. It closed behind them with a boom that shook the sanctuary.

Nadach was no more.

CHAPTER 9

When Kev and Aidan returned to the Council Hall meeting room, they found Margash and Ba'al waiting for them, as promised. Not that Ba'al had much choice in the matter, Kev thought. Before Kev, Aidan, Lucifer, Lilith, and Zeke had left to see to the evacuation of Nadach, Zeke had warded one end of the room to create a kind of holding cell for Lucifer's former second-in-command. Ba'al was confined behind silvery lines that stretched like bars from floor to ceiling.

He had been sitting on the floor but rose to his feet when Kev and Aidan entered the room. He scanned their bloody clothes. "I trust that blood does not belong to either of you."

"Nope. You're not that lucky," said Aidan.

Ba'al sighed. "I do not wish you harm. Nor did I wish Nadach to be destroyed."

"Were there many casualties?" Margash asked.

"A few," Kev said. "More wounded than dead. Some people were crushed when the buildings began to fall. We were able to get the rest out in time."

"That is mostly good news at least," said Margash.

"Yes, about the best we could have hoped for," Ba'al agreed, some of the tension visibly leaving his frame.

Kev noticed Ba'al tense once more when Lucifer entered the room, looking as if he'd come fresh from a shower rather than a dirty, bloody rescue mission. Despite appearances, Kev knew his father had not taken the time to clean up. No matter the battle or mess, Lucifer always managed to look unsullied by it. That particular trait must have aggravated Adrigon to no end when he'd kept Lucifer imprisoned in the Halls.

"Zeke said we should carry on without him. He has something else he needs to take care of." Lucifer pulled out a chair and sat, his long legs stretched out and crossed at the ankles, arms crossed over his chest. "As you know, Ba'al, my son viewed Semyaza's record. He saw you letting the Morpho demon out of Semyaza's cell after said demon had copied my sigil. Why don't you tell us the rest of the story? How were you planning to use the stolen sigil? Did you have plans for killing Jahoel even then?"

"As I told your son when he was imprisoned in the Halls, I had no specific plans. Having Semyaza and the Morpho in the cells at the same time simply seemed too good an opportunity to waste."

Lucifer leaned forward, elbows dropping to his knees. "You really resented me that much? I made you my Second. I thought I treated you fairly."

"From your perspective, I suppose you did. But I had ruled the Dark realms—I was a god—and suddenly I had to take orders from you, the 'Light-Bringer' sent to civilize the worlds that had been under my command. *I* did not see that arrangement as fair."

For an instant, Lucifer seemed to deflate.

Then he nodded, squared his shoulders, and leaned back in his chair again. "Please tell us the rest of the story. What did you end up doing with the sigil?"

His voice seemed gentler than before. Kev wondered if Lucifer's own ouster by Helel made his father more sympathetic to Ba'al than he might once have been.

"For a very long time, I did nothing with it." Ba'al paced behind the silvery bars. "Then, some earthly months ago, Adrigon contacted me, convinced me to meet him in Elsewhere. He told me he thought the Light had gotten it wrong when they sent you to the Dark as the Light-Bringer all those years ago, that he was convinced we would all be better off if the Dark were given our independence from the Light, and I was reinstated as the Dark's ruler." His lips pursed, and he shook his head. "He told me what I wanted to hear and, fool that I was, I believed him. When he said he had a plan to make it happen, that all he needed was a copy of your sigil if I could get one for him, I told him I already had one."

"So, Adrigon killed Jahoel?" Aidan asked.

"We have no absolute proof," Margash said, "but all the evidence says so."

Kev frowned. "But Adrigon isn't a Seraph. Whoever killed Jahoel had to have the Gift of Fire. His burns were too precise to have been inflicted by someone without the Gift."

"One does not have to be a Seraph to possess the Gift of Fire," said Margash. "It is rare for another type of angel to bear that Gift, but not unheard of. It is also rare, but not impossible, for an angel to have more than one Gift. Adrigon is known for having the Gift of Order. But I have found records—records someone tried very hard to hide—that he also has a second Gift—of Fire."

"What made you look for those records?" asked Aidan. "Why suspect Adrigon?"

"Yes," said Lucifer. "Why did you not just assume I killed Jahoel, like the rest of the Metatron?"

Margash looked at Lucifer. "That explanation never made sense to me. Why would you have done it? What would you have gained by killing him—and by marking the kill as your own? I had had suspicions about Adrigon for many years. As did Jahoel. I believe those suspicions are why he was killed."

"Suspicions of what?" asked Kev.

"That Adrigon meant to change the Metatron from ruling council to dictator. When Jahoel lived, Adrigon, as the Metatron's Second, was tasked with improving the harmony of the Heavens' cities. And he has succeeded beyond anything we could have imagined. Our people are happy and well-provisioned, and our cities have few disturbances. Those we do have are usually prompted by the presence of an outsider." Margash looked at Kev. "Like the one you experienced during your recent visit."

Kev nodded. He recalled a comment Margash had made then, something about the price of the Heavens' order, which had struck him as curious at the time. He guessed he was about to find out what the angel had meant.

Margash abandoned his seat to move about the conference room as he spoke. "During Adrigon's time as Second, the number of angels requesting to join the Fallen decreased sharply, and those who did make the request always changed their minds after their interviews with Adrigon. In addition, anti-Dark and anti-Fallen sentiments have risen just as sharply. Whatever harmony we might have gained within our own worlds seems to have cost the ability to see the good in worlds outside of our own. That is a price many of us are unwilling to pay."

Margash stopped his pacing and turned to where Kev and Aidan leaned against the table near where Lucifer sat. "Several weeks before his death, Jahoel had formed a secret coalition to investigate Adrigon's history and his activity since he joined the Metatron. Jahoel wanted to determine if Adrigon had unlawfully used his position on the Metatron Council to promote the rise of extremist views the Council ostensibly opposed, or if he had somehow abused his Gift of Order to persuade those who disagreed with him to adopt his positions. I was part of that coalition." He glanced at Aidan. "That is what first made me look for the records on Adrigon's Gift. When it seemed some records were missing, it only made me search more. When I finally found them, I discovered not only that the persuasive abilities associated with Adrigon's Gift of Order have grown stronger and stronger over the years, but that he has taken pains to hide his secondary Gift of Fire."

Kev frowned. "You said Jahoel formed this coalition several weeks before his death. Do you think Adrigon found out about it? Could that be why he killed Jahoel?"

Margash nodded. "I believe so."

"Did you know Adrigon planned to kill Jahoel when you gave him the sigil?" Lucifer asked Ba'al.

Ba'al shook his head. "No. I knew he meant to use the sigil to incriminate you in something, but he did not reveal his plans to me. By the time I heard of Jahoel's death and realized what Adrigon had done, I regretted my part in the scheme. But I still hoped to have my former leadership of the Dark restored, so I kept silent. The destruction of Nadach was too much though. I was on my way to release you myself when I ran into Margash."

"Once I realized Ba'al and I had the same mission," Margash said, "I decided to get you both out of the Halls, so we could do what we could to save the people of Nadach."

"What about the other two members of the Metatron?" Kev asked. "Are they aligned with Adrigon? Do they know what he's done?"

"I do not know if they are aware of his role in Jahoel's murder. But they are aligned with him in his positions on the Dark and the Fallen. I suspect, though I do not know for sure, that he may have used his Gift to influence them."

"If I may ask," said Aidan, "how did you manage to become a member of the Metatron when you clearly don't agree with the rest of them?"

"I have spent years carefully cultivating an image of complete compliance with Adrigon's more extreme separatist views. Otherwise, I would not even have been considered. He may have discovered Jahoel's secret council, but he did not guess I was a part of it. He never saw me as a threat."

"Well, I guess he does now, doesn't he?" Aidan said.

"By now he will have discovered our absence," said Lucifer. "You will not be allowed to reenter the Halls, Margash."

The angel nodded. "I knew that when I left."

"What about the Heavens?" Kev asked. "Won't they have had time to block you from returning there as well?"

Margash's mouth turned upward in a smile equal parts smugness and steel. "While you were saving Nadach, I ensured my means of entry into the Heavens. I will not be returning to the Metatron's chamber, but to an outpost in another Heavenly realm where others of like mind are preparing a revolt."

"Your people will fight with us, then, to depose the current Metatron and their puppet Light-Bringer?" Lucifer asked.

"We will," said Margash. "Though our numbers are small in comparison to Adrigon's supporters."

Lucifer nodded. "Even so, we must prepare for war."

War.

The word chilled the blood in Kev's veins.

"She is breathing easier now," Luil said softly near Lucky's ear.

Lucky nodded. She had caught the change in Lilith's breathing seconds before Luil spoke, his voice pitched low to keep from waking the Nadachis sleeping nearby.

The two of them sat on the floor near Lilith's pallet, leaning back against the wall. Lilith had collapsed soon after the portal closed, remaining conscious only long enough to refuse Zeke's offer of more comfortable accommodations at his brownstone. She insisted on remaining with her people in the safe house for as long as she had left.

Bryn fidgeted on Lucky's other side. She was practically vibrating with energy. Lucky had tried to convince her to go for a run or take a walk, promising to call or text her if Lilith's condition worsened. But Bryn wouldn't leave her grandmother. Lucky understood.

Knowing she had limited time in the earthly realm, Lilith had remained in Nadach until the last possible moment. Bryn and Luil had refused to go through the portal without her, and Jaime had refused to go without Bryn. They had all dived through the portal as the ground collapsed under them, Bryn and Luil holding on to Lilith.

Once they had settled Lilith onto a pallet in the safe house, Bryn and Jaime had helped Lucky, Alicia, and the others get the remaining Nadachis situated and treat their wounds. Luil had not left his mother's side.

"I assume that's a good sign?" Lucky asked.

Luil shrugged. "I hope so, but I do not know for sure. She stretched herself to the limit holding all those portals open for so long. And she said she had only a few hours left of her allotted time away from Nadach."

The door to the sanctuary opened, and two figures entered. Even with the lights turned down low for sleeping, Lucky couldn't mistake Zeke's tall, long-haired form weaving a path through the sleeping Nadachi refugees. Only when they drew close to Lilith's pallet did she recognize the small, white-haired woman trailing behind Zeke.

Lucky leapt to her feet. "What's she doing here?"

She had forgotten to lower her voice, and a few nearby Nadachis awoke with mumbled protests.

Zeke held up one hand. "I know you do not want to see her, Lucky, but Sambethe can help Lilith."

"Help? She almost killed my cousin. Josh could have died—or, even worse, become a Wraith—because of her."

Sambethe stepped forward. "I regret the pain I caused you and your cousin, Lucky. I did what I felt necessary to ensure you would undergo the Making. Soon you will understand your own importance." She gestured toward the sleeping forms around them. "That which I foresaw has already begun."

"And what do you feel is necessary now?" Lucky asked.

"Keeping Lilith alive."

"Let her do what she came to do," Zeke said to Lucky, as he motioned Sambethe toward Lilith's pallet. "She can save your grandmother."

Bryn moved to stand with Luil, her foot tapping with nervous energy, and Sambethe knelt beside Lilith. She murmured words Lucky couldn't understand as her hands traced patterns, hovering over but not quite touching Lilith's body.

Lucky moved closer to Zeke.

"Do you really trust her?" she whispered.

"Would I have brought her here if I did not?" he asked.

A flush of embarrassment flooded Lucky's face. Once again, she had let her anger with Sambethe eclipse her trust in Zeke. "I'm sorry," she murmured. "Of course, you wouldn't. I know you care about Lilith too."

Zeke nodded, his eyes on Lilith's still form. "I do. No matter what she has done, no matter that she betrayed me, lied to me, I do care. She has paid for what she so foolishly did so long ago. And her actions this day proved that she has learned to think of more than her own power."

"She was very brave," said Luil, who had come closer to them as Zeke spoke. "She only cared about getting all of the people of Nadach to safety."

Sambethe's hands had settled into place over Lilith's mid-section. Her head was thrown back, her long white hair brushing her feet, as her body swayed in rhythm with the words she spoke.

"What's she doing?" Lucky asked.

"Breaking the bond that connects Lilith to Nadach," Zeke replied. "It was weakened when the world collapsed, but not destroyed. If it is not broken, Lilith will die when her allowed time away from Nadach has passed."

Lucky's eyes widened as one of Sambethe's hands sank into Lilith's abdomen. There was no blood, but Lilith moaned and shifted as if in pain. Sambethe's arm moved, her hand apparently searching for something inside Lilith's body.

After a few moments, Sambethe withdrew her hand, her fingers closed around something. When her hand was several inches above Lilith's body, Sambethe twisted her hand and gave a yank. Lilith screamed, her body arching up off the pallet. Then she sank back down with a sigh. Her breathing deepened as if she'd finally fallen into a restful sleep.

Lucky could hear worried murmurs from the Nadachis who had been awakened by Lilith's scream.

Sambethe rose to her feet, the thing she had removed from Lilith's body still hidden in her closed hand, and walked over to Zeke. He held out his hand, and she dropped what she held onto his palm. His fingers closed around it before Lucky could see what it looked like.

"She will live now," Sambethe said, her voice loud enough to carry to all the Nadachis in the sanctuary. "Her Banishment is broken."

"Thank you, Sambethe," Zeke said softly. "I could not retrieve it, though it fell to my hand to apply it. That was part of *my* punishment. To be forced to be the instrument of her Banishment and to be powerless to remove it."

Sambethe looked at his closed hand. "Now you can destroy it."

"Yes," Zeke said. "That I can."

He closed his eyes and tightened his fingers. For several seconds, his form shifted rapidly from man to bull to lion to eagle and back to man to start the cycle again. For a moment, all four forms coalesced as if superimposed upon one another. Then Zeke was a man again. He spilled the crushed remains of whatever he had held onto the sanctuary floor, and then he dusted off his hands.

He looked at Lucky and Bryn. "You two should go home and get some sleep, because this"—he indicated the roomful of Nadachi refugees—"is only the beginning."

CHAPTER 10

Zeke might have thought she needed sleep, but sleep was the furthest thing from Bryn's mind. Her grief for the destruction of Nadach and her anger at Adrigon and Helel combined with the adrenaline still rushing through her from the evacuation had left her so keyed up she couldn't imagine even lying still, let alone falling asleep. Even knowing her grandmother was now safe hadn't calmed her. If anything, her nervous energy only seemed to have increased since Sambethe removed Lilith's binding spell.

She walked Lucky to her apartment instead of heading straight to Zeke's brownstone, hoping the additional exercise would help rid her of excess energy. When Lucky, apparently sensing Bryn's wakefulness, invited her to come up, Bryn turned down the invitation. Lucky looked ready to fall off her feet, and the apartment's darkened windows indicated Josh had already gone to bed.

Instead of heading toward Zeke's, Bryn just walked. She didn't know how many blocks she'd covered or how long she'd been walking when she finally climbed the stairs to the brownstone's door. Sleep still seemed far away, but she felt a little calmer than she had.

She was heading for the stairs to her bedroom when she heard noises coming from the kitchen. Peeking into the dining room, she saw light spilling through the kitchen door. She stepped into the kitchen to find Aidan leaning against the counter, a steaming cup in his hand.

He wore only a pair of sweatpants.

The sight of his bare chest and abs made Bryn's breath catch in her throat. And that made Bryn want to kick herself.

"Hey," he said. "Do you want some?"

Bryn tore her gaze away from his chest. "What?" she asked.

"Tea." His lips curled in a half smile. "I needed something to take the edge off, and it was either this or alcohol. I've been trying to cut back, so..." He saluted Bryn with the cup.

She smiled. "I'd love a cup, if you don't mind the company."

"Not at all."

He pulled a wooden box from one of the cupboards, lifted the lid, and held it toward her. "Pick your poison."

Bryn wasn't familiar with the phrase, but given that the box held a selection of teas, she could guess what it meant. She plucked a packet from the box and handed it to him.

"How long have you been back?" she asked, her eyes drawn to both the sigil between his shoulder blades and the play of lean muscle as he replaced the tea box on the shelf and found a cup for her. She wanted to trace the lines of his sigil with her fingers and glide her palms over the planes of his back and chest.

She swallowed and forced herself to look at anything except him. It wasn't as if she had never seen him shirtless before. They had worked out together plenty of times. And, yes, she had noticed his body. But she had always been able to push her attraction to him to the back of her mind. Now, the energy buzzing through her heightened her awareness, making it impossible to ignore his near nakedness.

"Just long enough to ditch the bloody clothes and take a shower." He handed her the cup of tea, and a flash of heat rushed through her at the brush of his fingers against hers.

Aidan leaned back against the counter across from her. "I needed a little help to get to sleep though." He took a sip from his cup and grimaced. "In all honesty, I'd prefer the scotch."

"Yeah. I'm not much of a drinker, but tonight it doesn't sound like a bad idea." Bryn's shoulders sagged as she let herself relax against the counter behind her.

"You do seem to be wound pretty tight." Aidan studied her for a moment. "I can only imagine what this must be like for you. It's not every day your home world is destroyed. For what it's worth, I'm sorry."

She nodded, squeezing her eyes shut against the tears. A shaky sip of tea gave her voice time to steady. "Thanks."

"How's Lilith?"

The gentleness of Aidan's voice made her want to rush into his arms like she had when he'd found her in the Tree. It took all her strength not to do so.

She sipped her tea again before she answered. "She's sleeping, but I think she's going to be okay. Sambethe removed the spell that bound her to Nadach, and then Zeke destroyed it."

"So that's where Zeke went. I'd wondered what could be more important than getting back to Margash and Ba'al."

"Did you know Zeke was the one who placed the spell on her?" Bryn asked. When Aidan replied in the negative, she continued, "He said that was his punishment, to have to apply the spell, but to be unable to remove it."

Aidan whistled. "That sheds a little more light on their relationship."

One corner of Bryn's mouth curled. "It couldn't get much more complicated, could it?"

They sipped their tea in silence for a while. Then Bryn asked, "What more did you learn from Margash and Ba'al?"

Aidan sighed. "We're pretty sure Adrigon killed Jahoel. He apparently has the Gift of Fire as well as that of Order."

Bryn gasped. "But they destroyed Nadach because Lilith helped Lucifer escape. If Adrigon knew Lucifer wasn't guilty..."

"Yeah. I can't imagine colder blood," Aidan said. "Anyway, Margash and a small group of rebels are on our side. They'll publicize what he's learned about Adrigon. And they'll fight with us against Adrigon and his supporters."

"How can anyone still support him after they learn the truth?" Bryn's fingers clenched around her cup. Her Raven side clamored for Adrigon's blood. He'd destroyed her world, nearly killed her grandmother. For all he knew, the entire population of Nadach had been wiped out.

To uphold a lie.

"According to Margash, Adrigon's Gift of Order makes him very persuasive. It sounds like he can make his followers believe what he wants them to believe." Aidan drank the last of his tea and set the empty cup on the counter.

An incoherent sound of anger and despair escaped Bryn.

Aidan wrapped a hand around the back of her neck. "He won't get away with it, Bryn." His thumb caressed her jaw. "We'll defeat him. He'll be punished for what he did—to Jahoel and to Nadach."

Aidan's touch pushed Bryn over the edge. She was sick of death and destruction and lies. Aidan was alive and beautiful, and he promised her justice. He made the blood sing in her veins.

She wrapped her hand around Aidan's neck and pulled his head down to hers. "You bet he will," she said and kissed him hard.

For just a second, shock paralyzed Aidan's body. But then the warmth of Bryn in his arms and the hard pressure of her lips against his had him pulling her against him.

Her teacup, caught between them, bit into his abdomen, and he reached down to remove it from her hand and place it on the counter, even as he pressed his body closer to Bryn's.

She moaned and sank her teeth into his lower lip as her other hand slid up over his chest to tangle in his hair.

Aidan had kissed her once before, but then he hadn't really been aware of the girl in his arms. That kiss had been about getting even with Lucky and Kev. Far from returning his kiss then, Bryn had slapped him.

Well, she wasn't slapping him now, and he was more than aware of her this time.

She still wore her fighting leathers, and the feel of her leather jacket against his bare chest sent his pulse racing even faster. Without removing his mouth from hers, Aidan lifted her onto the counter. She wrapped her legs around his waist.

"Gods, Bryn," he groaned.

Her hands slid down over his shoulders, her fingers feathering over his sigil. Aidan shuddered and deepened the kiss.

Lifting his mouth from hers, he unzipped her leather jacket and dragged the jacket and the strap of her tank off one shoulder. His mouth found her collar bone, and he traced the tantalizing pattern of her Raven Mark with his tongue.

Bryn stilled. She leaned back and pushed her hands against his chest. Though he felt the emptiness in his arms like a wound, he allowed her to push him away.

"I can't do this," she said, as she slid off the counter. "I'm sorry."

Then she ran out the door.

Flattening his hands on the counter, Aidan released the breath he hadn't realized he'd been holding.

He waited until he was sure Bryn had reached her room before he headed upstairs.

Josh had already left the apartment by the time Lucky was up and dressed. Feeling lonely for family, she decided to visit G-Ma before heading to the safe house.

She found G-Ma asleep in her rocking chair near the window. A tiny Still One perched on her shoulder, its hand gently stroking her hair.

Lucky sat on the wide windowsill, smiling at the Still One as she did so. The small furry gargoyle inclined its head.

"Hi, G-Ma," Lucky said quietly. She didn't want to wake her grandmother, but she wanted to talk to her. And, since G-Ma was sleeping, she could speak more honestly than she could have otherwise.

"I miss you. You already know that. And things are going crazy in my world." Lucky's eyes shifted to the Still One. "Maybe you already know that too. I haven't been able to tell you that I met my other grandmother—and my—father— too." She couldn't help it. She still felt reluctant to acknowledge Luil as her father. "Her name is Lilith. His is Luil. They... well, neither of them is exactly human. They lived in another world, a place called Nadach. But now that world is gone. Some people destroyed it, just because they could. They said they did it to punish Lilith, but..." Lucky stopped, tears blocking her words. "I went there. I made friends there. And now it's gone."

Lucky closed her eyes, her fingers wiping at the tears that leaked out.

She opened her eyes when a hand touched her hair. A full size Still One stood beside her. She gave the creature a watery smile. It pressed its clawed hand to her cheek, and a wave of comfort washed through her. She smoothed her cheek against its palm.

Then the Still One's fingers tightened, its claws digging into Lucky's hair and scraping her cheek hard enough to break the skin, as the creature let out a low wail. And, instead of comfort, Lucky was filled with fear and grief.

Her eyes flashed to the Still One's and found them wide with pain. The tiny creature that had perched on G-Ma's shoulder now stood, at full size, beside its fellow. Their hands were clasped.

Hoping to learn something about the source of the Still One's feelings, Lucky opened her senses. Though she could now see the colors and textures of the emotions rushing through them and hear the hum of their vibrations, she came no closer to understanding their cause.

"What is it?" she asked them. "What's happening?"

In response, the second Still One pressed its free hand against the other side of Lucky's head.

Lucky gasped and switched off her extra senses as her mind flooded with too many sensations to process.

With the rush of sensory input dammed, she realized the Still Ones and the other creatures from their world were connected telepathically, and that these two now shared that connection with her. She could sense that something terrible was happening to the Still Ones in their home world. Many were injured, dying. She could sense the lessening of life force as each connected individual fell.

Lucky would have fallen off the windowsill when the Still Ones broke the connection if the one who had first stroked her hair had not held her steady. With shaking hands, she pulled her cell phone from her pocket and dialed Zeke. He answered after the first ring, and she explained what she had learned as quickly as she could.

"Return to the safe house, and prepare for more guests," Zeke said. "I fear the Tree may have fractured again."

Lucky wouldn't have believed the safe house had room for any more inhabitants, but it seemed to expand as need demanded. Still Ones entered through portals into more underground levels than Lucky remembered the safe house possessing.

Some of the creatures had only minor injuries, while others suffered possibly fatal wounds. Katrin, Aidan, Sambethe, Alicia, and the few Nadachi healers worked to heal or treat all those they could. Lucky, Josh, Bryn, Jaime, and the remaining Nadachis did their best to make the creatures comfortable in the safe house.

Even William and Mather seemed to be doing their part. Lucky had caught a glimpse of the father and son from a distance when they had arrived from Nadach, but neither had seemed to notice her. Now, William looked up and briefly caught her eye before looking away. Lucky wondered if he felt at all guilty for what he and his father had done to her, or if he still blamed her for burning his arm with her palm sigil.

As Lucky watched the Nadachi refugees and the Still Ones huddle together, she hoped the arrangements would benefit both groups. The Nadachis could provide comfort to the Still Ones, even as the Still Ones could relieve the Nadachis by feeding on the suffering they felt over the loss of their world.

At least, the Still Ones' world, Grevyadach, had not been destroyed. The Guardians had discovered the places where an alien world, with an incompatible atmosphere, chemistry, and physics, had overlapped and distorted Grevyadach. They worked to seal the holes and repair the Tree, even as Lilith, Zeke, and members of the Forces ushered Grevyadach's affected inhabitants to safety. Those who had not survived would receive death rites later.

"Hey, you."

Lucky turned to find Josh beside her. "Hey, yourself."

"The portals have closed, and everyone seems to be settled," Josh said. "Zeke wants us all to head back to his place. He promised there'd be pizza involved."

They made their way toward the stairs through the groups of Nadachi and Still Ones. On the main level, Bryn, Jaime, Alicia, and Mo waited for them near the door.

"Katrin said for us to go ahead," Alicia informed them. "There are a few Still Ones she wants to check on before she leaves."

Lucky tensed. "Katrin can't leave until Sambethe's escort arrives. We may need Sambethe's help with the injured, but she's still officially under house arrest."

Josh's hand settled on Lucky's arm. "Katrin won't leave Sambethe unsupervised," he said. "Though I'm not convinced she really needs supervision."

"How can you say that?" Lucky fell into step beside her cousin as the group moved outside. "After what she did to you."

Josh sighed. "She had her reasons. I'm not saying I condone her methods or anything, but she felt like she had no choice. She saw all this—what's happening now—and she knew you had to be Made Naphil to help us get through it. I don't know what exactly you're supposed to do, but I know she believes you're important."

"How do you know all this?"

"I talked to her earlier today. She pulled me aside and apologized. Well, sort of apologized. She said she couldn't have done things any differently, but she regretted the pain her actions caused me."

"Pain? She could have killed you."

"I know. But she also made me what I am." Josh paused a beat before he continued. "Don't get me wrong. This isn't something I would have asked for. But..." He hesitated again. "With you being what you are, and Ben what he is, and with everything that's happening, well, I guess I'm glad I'm not human anymore. This way I can help."

"I'm helping, and I'm still human." Mo said over her shoulder. "Sorry to eavesdrop, but I couldn't help overhearing. As the only human left here, I feel a need to speak up in our defense."

"I'm human," Alicia, who walked beside Mo, joined the conversation.

"You are?" Mo looked surprised.

"Yes. Many of the people who were in Nadach are."

"Really? Do tell."

As Mo and Alicia fell into their own conversation, Lucky looked at Josh. "You're really glad this happened?"

He nodded. "Yeah. I am. I haven't told Mom and Dad. I don't know if I should." He chuckled. "They handled me being gay pretty well. I guess they'd be okay with this too. But how do I even begin...?"

"I know." Lucky sighed. "If they find out about either one of us, they'll have to find out about both. When I first got pulled into this world, I thought I had to hide it from everyone—you, Mo, Uncle Matthew, and Aunt Beth. But then you were attacked. And I couldn't go through the Making without telling Mo. Maybe we should tell your parents."

"And maybe we shouldn't. It's not like they don't worry about us already. And do they really need to know how much trouble the entire world may be facing right now?"

"Yeah," Lucky said. "It's hard to say if they're better—or safer—knowing or not knowing."

When he opened the door to Zeke's brownstone, Aidan was assailed by the din of conversation and the smell of pizza. The normally empty formal living room was crowded with people, pizza and drinks in hand.

"Hey, nobody told me we were having a party," he said.

Josh paused with his pizza halfway to his mouth to answer. "We were starving. We talked Zeke into ordering pizza."

"He didn't take much convincing," Ben added. He gestured to where the tall, long-haired angel stood talking with Lucky, Lilith, and a dark-haired man Aidan didn't recognize.

Zeke's plate held several slices of pizza. "I think he was hungry too."

Aidan grinned. "And I'd bet his pizza is loaded with bacon."

"Now that you mention it," Josh said, "I think more than a few of them had bacon as a topping."

Chuckling, Aidan made his way into the kitchen to wash his hands. His gaze fell on the counter onto which he'd lifted Bryn the night before, and his heartbeat accelerated at the memory of her mouth on his, her hand on his neck, her legs wrapped around his waist. He didn't know what had stunned him more, her initial embrace or her subsequent rejection.

No, he did know. Her sudden departure had been a surprise only as a sequel to her passionate advance. Otherwise, the exit had been pure Bryn. That she had chosen to kiss him so passionately in the first place—that was the real shocker.

He filled a plate with a selection of pizza slices and headed toward Zeke's group. Bryn had joined them. A flush tinted her cheeks when she saw him moving in their direction. She had managed to avoid him the whole time they were at the safe house. For a second, he thought she might leave now, but she stood her ground as he approached.

Aidan positioned himself across from Bryn and offered his hand to the man he didn't know, who stood between Bryn and Lilith. "I don't believe we've met," he said. "I'm Aidan."

A smile curved the man's lips, and one dark eyebrow lifted as he shook Aidan's hand. "Oh, we have met," he said. "We had a little bit of a fight once. But I had a rather different form at the time. My name is Luil. I am Lilith's son, Bryn's uncle, and Lucky's father."

"It was you? At the country club? But..."

"As I said, I had a different form. Since then, I have gone back to the one I had when I knew Lucky's mother." The curve of his lips took a wry turn. "Having met my daughter, I find I want to look like the man who fathered her."

Glancing from Luil to Lucky, Aidan found he could see something of the man in the shape of her face, her cheekbones, her lips.

He also found it didn't hurt so much to look at Lucky anymore. A smile lit her face, and he followed her gaze to see his brother approaching from the kitchen. He noticed with some surprise that his gut didn't clench with the wish that her smile was directed at him. And when Kev took his place beside her and slipped an arm around her, giving her a quick squeeze, Aidan felt only a slight constriction in the region of his heart, nothing compared to the biting steel band he'd felt before.

"I can see the resemblance," he said, turning back toward Luil. His gaze collided with Bryn's, but she quickly looked away, her lips tightening.

A moment later she left the group.

Aidan asked Luil a question, even though he didn't really care about the answer, just to keep from following her.

They gathered in the living room after they'd cleaned up the remains of the pizza. The group was too big to fit in Zeke's study.

Kev settled next to Josh and Ben on the sofa. Lucky and Mo sat on the floor in front of them, Lucky leaning back into the space between Kev's knees. He resisted the urge to stroke her hair.

Bryn and Katrin had joined the group from Nadach—Lilith, Luil, Jaime, and Alicia—on the opposite side of the room.

Aidan stood at the back of the room with Miguel and Gareth, two members of the Forces that Malachi had brought with him.

Malachi and Lucifer flanked Zeke at the front.

The murmur of conversation stopped when Zeke stood.

"First, I want to offer thanks to all of you for your response to the situation with the Still Ones today—to Lucky for sounding the alarm and to everyone who helped get those affected to safety. Though too many lives were lost, many more were saved. The Guardians have sealed the fracture in the Tree that allowed the two worlds to collide. The damage to Grevyadach cannot be fixed as easily, but enough of the world remains undamaged to provide habitation until the damaged parts can mend. The Still Ones we brought here have a world to return to when they have healed."

"Do you know what caused the Tree to fracture?" Bryn asked. "Was it because of us? Because we went inside it?"

Zeke shook his head. "It was not because of us. We think the fracture was caused by the destruction of Nadach. The Halls exists at a nexus in the Tree, which enables it to be in all the Dark realms at once. When Adrigon and Helel used the power of the Halls to destroy Nadach, they damaged that nexus."

"Can the damage be repaired?" asked Kev.

"The Guardians have repaired what they have found, but there may yet be ruptures of which they are unaware."

"What Zeke is trying to say," inserted Lilith, "is that we may only find out as other worlds are affected. Last time, the ripples of the Tree's damage spread out over many worlds and many months."

Malachi stepped forward. "That means we must be prepared for an invasion, an attack, or some other unnatural disaster. Pockets of Fallen around the globe are on alert, and the members of the Forces are ready to deploy as needed. We are also prepared to move against Adrigon and his supporters once we have a solid plan of attack."

"And those plans are taking shape," Lucifer said, moving forward to stand with Zeke and Malachi. "I have met with Margash and his team to discuss possible ways of retaking the Halls. Their spies inside the Metatron's court are keeping us apprised of the activities of the Metatron's supporters and alerting us to any information they receive from Adrigon and Helel. Together, we will defeat the fraud of a Metatron and their usurper Light-Bringer—and we will bring Jahoel's killer to justice."

Lucifer's voice softened as he spoke Jahoel's name, and Kev understood his father wanted to see Adrigon punished not only to clear his own name, but to do right by Jahoel. Lucifer had respected the angel and had mourned his death.

"We must all be prepared as well," Zeke said. "Josh, could you join Lucky and Bryn at the training center tomorrow?"

"I—yeah—of course," Josh answered. "I want to do anything I can to help."

"Is there anything I can do?" Mo asked.

Not for the first time, Kev felt a rush of admiration for Lucky's best friend. She had no angelic or demonic powers, but her bravery belied the fragility of her fully human form.

Zeke smiled down at the girl where she sat cross-legged on the floor. "Just keep doing what you are doing," he said. "All those at the safe house appreciate your assistance, as do I, Mo. Thank you for your help and your bravery."

Mo's smile lit her face.

Lucky reached over and squeezed her best friend's hand.

"I want to help too," Jaime said. "Bryn and I have been training together for years. She can vouch for me."

"I have no doubt of your skill," said Zeke. "We would be grateful for your help, Jaime. Please accompany the others to the training center tomorrow."

"And come to see me after your training is done," Lucifer added. "I want to discuss that special talent of yours."

Kev could guess the direction of his father's thoughts. With Jaime's ability to pass through and disrupt wards, he might be the key to their attack on the Halls.

CHAPTER 11

The next day, Jaime and Josh joined Bryn and Lucky at the training center. All four of them spent the morning working with swords under Dominique's direction. The weapons master seemed to Bryn to have an extraordinary capacity to track the movements of all four of her students simultaneously.

She paired them based on skill levels, teaching Bryn and Jaime more advanced techniques, while starting with the basics for Lucky and Josh. Lucky had a few lessons on her older cousin, but from what Bryn could see Josh learned quickly.

Bryn needed the physical exertion as well as the mental concentration necessary to master the intricate moves. The excess energy that had filled her with the destruction of Nadach had not abated, and the emotional turmoil generated by her late-night encounter with Aidan had given her even more energy to burn.

How could she have let herself grab him and kiss him the way she had when she knew how he felt about Lucky? Before that night, she'd convinced herself she saw him only as a friend. She hadn't allowed herself to acknowledge the attraction she felt for him, because she had no interest in being a substitute or stand-in. But her emotions had been so raw that night. If the surprising touch of his tongue on her Raven Mark hadn't jarred her to consciousness, she didn't know how far she might have let things go.

She had stayed away from Aidan since. As best she could. She didn't want to explain herself. And she had even less desire to hear any excuses or apologies he might offer. Watching him studying Lucky at last night's gathering, hearing him comment on her resemblance to Luil, had only strengthened Bryn's resolve to keep her distance. She didn't want to be a temporary bandage for the wound her cousin had left behind.

Whether due to the energy buzzing through her, her preoccupation with Aidan, or something else, she'd also had trouble sleeping. The past two nights, what little sleep she'd gotten had been riddled with dreams. If she wasn't traveling down forest paths that ended in jagged cliffs or wandering through corridors blocked with piles of rubble, she faced roomfuls of intertwined branches that she was somehow supposed to untangle. She could feel Aidan's presence in the dreams too, though she never saw him.

Both days she'd awakened feeling as if there was something she was supposed to do, but which she had forgotten.

Bryn realized she had allowed her thoughts to distract her too late. Jaime hooked an ankle around one of hers, and she fell backward, his sword-point at her throat.

"Where are you today?" Jaime pushed his chestnut hair off his face with his free hand. "I've never bested you so quickly before."

Bryn shoved his sword away and jumped to her feet. "I just got distracted for a minute."

Jaime narrowed his eyes but kept his silence.

"Again," Dominique ordered. "Bryn, get your head back in the game."

Bryn nodded. Clenching her jaw, she forced Aidan and her disturbing dreams to the back of her mind. She narrowed her focus to her movements and Jaime's and settled into battle stance. Jaime would fall to her this round.

Bryn was about to make good on that promise when all hell broke loose.

At first Aidan thought it was part of the simulation. But then the lights flickered and died, killing the program. And the building still shook, the far wall continued to fall, and the Zahhaks continued to spill into the simulation room through the hole in the wall. Forked tongues flicked from their mouths, while the serpents that grew from their shoulders lashed the air, looking for a victim to strike.

In the time it took Aidan to grasp that nearly a dozen very real Zahhak demons had somehow entered the training center, the confusion on the creatures' vaguely humanoid reptilian faces had shifted to anger, and the demons were advancing on the troop Aidan had been training.

"Miguel!" he yelled, looking around for the troop's leader, even as he summoned his wings, sword, and spear. The soldier had been working on some exploding arrows that could come in handy about now.

A Zahhak bent from its nearly two-story height to grab one of Aidan's trainees in a huge, clawed hand and lift him toward one of the serpents that grew from its shoulders. Aidan zoomed toward the creature. Dodging the serpent that struck at his face, Aidan launched his spear toward the Zahhak's arm. The spear hit its target, but too late. The other serpent had already sunk its fangs into the soldier's head. The man's screams died as the serpent sucked out his brain.

Aidan shuddered and sliced his sword through the shoulder-serpent he'd been dodging. Even as the serpent fell, writhing, to the ground, two more sprouted from the demon's shoulder to take the place of the one Aidan had lopped off.

Aidan swore and shot backward as both serpents lunged at his face.

"Miguel!" he yelled again.

Then he saw the arrow sink into the Zahhak's chest. Aidan didn't have time to brace himself. The impact from the explosion sent him into the side wall, where he fell to the floor amid pieces of Zahhak.

Lucky lost her footing as the floor buckled beneath her. Josh had managed to shift the position of his sword before she stumbled into him. Even so, the blade's edge sliced the outside of her arm. She tossed her own sword aside to avoid impaling either herself or her cousin as they fell to the floor.

When she'd pushed herself off Josh and sat back, she wished she still held the weapon in her hand.

Masses of scorpion-tailed snakes slithered from the hole that had erupted in the middle of the training room floor, separating her and Josh from Bryn, Jaime, and Dominique.

The creatures tested the air with their forked tongues. Then, fangs exposed and scorpion tails arched to sting, they headed straight toward the warm-blooded.

Lucky scrambled to her feet. Too late to dive for her abandoned sword. The stinging serpents already covered it.

At her side, her scholarly, brown-eyed cousin went red-eyed Wraith-hybrid, his muscles filling out so that his training gear fit like a second skin. Lucky's eyes widened. She'd seen Josh in fighting mode, but she hadn't witnessed the transformation. Unlike Bryn's, it seemed painless.

"Can you do anything to control these things?" Josh asked. "I'm not going to be able to slice and dice them all."

"You don't have to slice and dice any of them yet," Lucky said, as she summoned her wings. "Hold onto me."

"Are you kidding me? I'm huge."

"I'm not human anymore either, remember? I'm stronger than I look." She hooked an arm around Josh's waist as the serpents reached the toes of her boots. "Now hold on."

Lucky shot upward as fast as she could bearing Josh's extra weight. Looking down, she could see a serpent clinging to one of her boots with two tiny arm-like appendages. It drew back its head, preparing to strike, as its scorpion tail curled upward.

Josh's boot slammed into the creature's head, preventing the strike but not breaking the creature's hold. Lucky kicked at the scorpion tail with her other foot.

"Don't move your leg," Josh said. He still held his sword in his free arm.

This time when the serpent drew back its head, Josh sliced it off. Even as the head fell away, the scorpion stinger stabbed through the leather of Lucky's boot.

"Ow!" She kicked at the thing's headless body, but the stinger stuck fast, and the little arms clung to her boot like Velcro.

The pain spread from her ankle up to her calf, and Lucky felt herself weakening. She muttered a curse as she battled to keep herself and Josh aloft.

"Hand him over to me," said Dominique. She and Bryn hovered nearby. Bryn, in her half-Raven form, held Jaime in her arms.

Josh grabbed onto Dominique, his arm wrapping around her back below her glistening gray wings.

Lucky forced the pain creeping up her leg and her growing weakness to the back of her mind and sent her power toward the mass of stinging serpents that now swarmed over the training room. Maybe she could make them attack each other.

Their minds were surprisingly easy to access. She touched their fear, their desire to destroy whatever threatened them. And she recognized the same fear and desire in herself.

She could destroy them, turn them against one another, but she didn't want to. Could she neutralize the threat another way? She searched through their primitive emotions, looking for something she could use. She could feel herself growing weaker and her thoughts getting fuzzy as the poison spread through her system.

She could feel their fear. Their fear. She latched onto the strands of emotion and twisted them a tiny bit. The fear she felt ratcheted upward. Altering her hold on the emotional ribbons, she twisted again. And the fear decreased. She twisted a little more, and the fear decreased a little more. Finally, she had calmed the serpents enough that they seemed almost docile. Then she nudged them back toward the hole in the floor.

She struggled to hold onto her focus and her strength as the creatures began to move. Their thoughts were easier to manipulate than before. But her own grew fuzzier by the minute, and every beat of her wings took more out of her than the one before.

Maybe a third of the serpents had slithered back into the ground when her hold on them broke. She felt a flare of heat at her chest before she lost consciousness.

Aidan picked himself up off the floor, relieved to see the other troop members the explosion had sent flying do the same.

Between the exploded Zahhak and the fallen troop members, the simulation room was a mess of blood and gore. His troop did their best to battle the remaining demons, but their efforts seemed ineffectual. And too many of the soldiers had fallen—or worse.

A Zahhak lifted a fallen soldier in each massive fist, holding the men so his shoulder-serpents could feast on their brains. One of the soldiers was still alive. He screamed as the serpent sank its fangs into his skull.

Stomach churning, Aidan located Miguel amid the chaos. He beckoned the other soldiers to follow him and made a beeline for the source of the exploding arrows.

"How many of those things do you have?" he shouted, as Miguel notched another into his bow.

"Not enough. *Sólo prototipos.* No time to make more."

"We'll have to make do," Aidan said. "Do your arrows have enough explosive power to take the rest of those blasted things out if we can get them all together?

Miguel's expression lightened. "That could work. If we hit them with all the arrows at once."

"Okay. Miguel, you're in charge of rounding up some more archers and getting them in position. The rest of us will corral the Zahhaks. As soon as they're in a bunch, fire those arrows."

"Yes, sir."

Arrows in hand, Miguel took off running.

"Time to herd some demons," Aidan said to the others as he summoned his wings.

He winged toward the hole in the wall where a group of soldiers fought a trio of Zahhaks. Positioning himself between the demons and the broken wall, he flamed his wings. Then he buzzed the demons' heads, hoping they would find his flaming wings a threat.

It worked. Even the serpents drew, hissing, back from the flames.

"Where's Kev when we need him?" Aidan muttered under his breath.

The vision invaded Kev's mind, obscuring the schematics and attack plans that floated in the middle of Margash's war room. Piles of scorpion snakes. Lucky falling toward them.

"Gotta go. Training center. Now!" Kev summoned his wings as he spoke.

Malachi yelled something in response, but Kev was already dematerializing and only half-caught the words.

He reformed inches above the mass of scorpion snakes. Lucky landed in his outstretched arms, and he gathered her close. Winging upward, he opened his mouth and loosed a geyser of flames onto the swarming creatures below.

Only after he'd fried the last of them did his awareness shift to the room's other occupants. Bryn and Dominique hovered a few yards away, Bryn holding Jaime and Dominique holding Josh. All four stared at Kev. Even Bryn, in her half-Raven form, looked shocked.

"What?" he asked.

"Weren't you in the Heavens with Margash?" asked Dominique. "How were you able to transport here? And how did you get through our wards?"

Don't forget the wards. That's what Malachi had yelled.

"I don't know." Kev looked down at Lucky's unconscious form in his arms. "And, right now, I don't really care. We need to get Lucky to someone who can heal her."

Kev lowered to the floor, and the others followed suit. Fried scorpion snakes crunched under their feet as they made their way to the exit.

As soon as they opened the door, Kev heard screams and sounds of combat coming from the other end of the training center. Smoke drifted from the gaping hole in the outer wall of one of the simulation rooms.

He cursed and dropped into a crouch to place Lucky on the ground.

"Stay with her," he said to Josh. Then he summoned his wings and took off after Dominique and Bryn, who were already in flight. Jaime raced after them on foot.

Kev, Dominique, and Bryn had nearly reached the hole when another section of the wall exploded outward. The blast knocked the breath out of Kev and sent him sailing.

He hit the ground. Debris rained around him. And some of that debris looked like bloody, charred flesh.

Dominique also climbed to her feet. But Bryn, now in fully human form, stayed down.

"Make sure she's okay," Kev yelled to Dominique, gesturing at Bryn's still body.

Then he raced toward the smoke-filled hole.

He stepped over the remains of the wall. Through the haze he saw a far too small band of Forces soldiers, battered and bloody, fending off two equally battered looking Zahhaks. Burns and bleeding wounds marred the demons' reptilian hides, but the wounds seemed only to spur the creatures to fight more fiercely.

Dodging building debris and Naphil and Zahhak body parts, Kev raced toward the small group of soldiers. He recognized his brother's golden blond hair among them.

Kev heard Aidan call his name as he tried to call his dragon. The dragon didn't come, but the heat began to build in his body. His body just kept getting hotter, his veins running fire. The dragon's heat-sensitive vision overlay his normal human vision, so he could even watch his temperature rising.

"Everyone out now!" he yelled. And his voice reverberated with the roar of the dragon. The soldiers cleared the space between him and the Zahhaks and headed for the door.

When he felt himself go supernova, Kev did his best to direct the brunt of the blast at the demons, hitting them with everything he had. At first, their hides resisted the flames, and the demons moved a step or two toward him, the serpents on their shoulders crisping. Kev continued to flame them, ratcheting up the heat.

And the fire did its work. The demons roared as the flames consumed them.

It took a few minutes for Kev to turn off the flames. He scanned the blackened room, hoping everyone had made it out before he'd blown. He looked down at his body. Still clothed. The fireproof gear he'd had specially made had held up.

He climbed through the opening in the wall and looked around for his brother.

Aidan limped to his side. After making sure his body temperature had dropped enough to be safe, Kev pulled Aidan into a fierce embrace.

"How many did we lose?" Kev asked.

"Too many," Aidan replied, sounding far older than his years. "Way too many."

CHAPTER 12

The haunting notes Aidan sang faded away, and the warm weight of his hand lifted from Lucky's ankle. Katrin had extracted the stinger and what venom she could, but they had needed Aidan's Gift to heal the tissue damage the scorpion snake venom had caused.

"That should do it," he said. "You won't feel quite your-self until your body's natural healing ability gets rid of any residual venom in your system. But I've healed all the dam-age."

"Thank you, Aidan," Lucky said. She hesitated, her eyes searching his face, then held out her hand.

After a split-second pause, Aidan clasped her fingers with his own. "You're welcome."

Lucky gripped his fingers more tightly. "Are you okay? Kev told me about the Zahhaks—and about our losses."

Aidan glanced at Kev, who sat on the bed next to Lucky, an arm around her shoulders, and then his gaze dropped before lifting to meet Lucky's once more. He shook his head. "No. I'm not. I can't bring them back." He squeezed her hand. "I'm glad I could heal you though. That helps. To know I could do something."

Lucky blinked back tears. She didn't trust herself to speak. What more could she say anyway?

Aidan released her hand. "I'm gonna get cleaned up. See you two later."

After the door closed behind him, Lucky curled into Kev's arms and let the tears fall.

Bryn stepped out of her room and almost collided with Aidan.

His hands caught her shoulders, and her gaze skimmed up his bare chest to his face. He looked shattered.

Without a word, she slipped her arms around him and pulled him close. His arms wrapped her so tightly she could feel the muscles of his forearms denting her back. His breath shuddered through him.

Bryn choked back a sob. She had regained consciousness before they left the training center. She had seen the devastation in what remained of the simulation room.

She increased the pressure of her embrace, sensing that Aidan needed to be held as tightly as he held her.

They remained like that, holding on to each other as if their lives depended on it, for several minutes. Then Aidan took a deep breath and loosened his arms. Bryn stepped back, one hand lifting to push the shower-damp curls from Aidan's forehead.

"I was going downstairs to get something to eat. Do you want to join me?" she offered.

"Yeah," Aidan said. "Let me grab a shirt."

He ducked into his room and came back out wearing a faded blue t-shirt that made his eyes look even bluer. Harley was curled upside down in his arms.

When Harley saw Bryn, he climbed up Aidan's chest to stand on his shoulders, wrapped around the back of his neck. He chittered at her as if asking a question. Bryn chuckled and scratched the top of the ferret's head.

"Do you mind if he comes with?" Aidan asked.

"No. Maybe we can find him a snack too."

"I'm sure he'd love an egg. Wouldn't you, Harley?"

They started down the stairs, and Harley scrambled off Aidan's shoulder to curl up in his arms again.

"What made you decide to get a ferret for a pet?" Bryn asked.

"I didn't. Kev gave him to me. After my mom—died—and I renounced my wings. He thought I needed the company—and something to care for. He was right. That condo would have been even lonelier without Harley."

"You lived there alone?"

"Yeah. I had lived there with my mom. After—I stayed there both because I missed her and to punish myself. The place was a constant reminder that she wasn't there anymore—and why."

"Does the fact that you're spending most of your free time here these days mean you've finally decided to forgive yourself?"

Aidan stopped to let Bryn precede him into the kitchen. Then he set Harley on the floor and washed his hands.

Bryn had almost decided he wasn't going to answer her question when he finally responded.

"Maybe." Aidan opened the fridge and pulled out eggs, butter, and cheese. "How about a cheese omelet?"

"Sounds good. I'll make toast."

Aidan broke the eggs into a bowl, added some salt and pepper, and whisked everything together.

"I hadn't really thought about it," he said. "What it means that I'm spending so much time here. Kev and Lucky and I were all coming here for work and training. Zeke had the space, and we were putting in long days. So, we started staying the night sometimes too. Even Lucky, though the apartment she shares with Josh isn't too far away. We seemed to just end up here more often than not."

"Often enough that you moved Harley here."

"Yeah. Poor little guy was missing me." While the omelet cooked, Aidan broke another egg into a small bowl and put it on the floor for the chittering ferret. "Weren't you, buddy?"

Harley stopped his chatter so he could give the egg his undivided attention.

Aidan chuckled. "Then again, maybe he just felt like he wasn't getting fed often enough."

Bryn smiled. Kev's gift had been a wise one. Harley was good medicine for Aidan—now as then.

She slathered butter on the toast while Aidan divided the omelet between two plates.

"This smells great," Bryn said as they settled on to barstools at the end of the counter to eat.

"It's one of the few things I know how to cook."

They ate without speaking for several minutes, then Aidan broke the silence. "There's going to be a ceremony—to honor the people we lost today."

"And for the deceased Nadachis and Still Ones." Zeke's body followed his voice into the room. "We decided we should honor them all at once."

Bryn thought the ancient angel looked almost as shattered as Aidan had when she had run into him in the upstairs hallway.

"Would either of you like some tea?" Zeke asked. "I feel the need for a cup."

"Sounds good," said Aidan.

"I'd love one," said Bryn, trying not to think about the last time she'd had tea with Aidan in this room.

Zeke began the tea preparations.

"Want me to make you an omelet?" Aidan asked. "Nothing fancy. Just eggs and cheese."

"I would like that very much, thanks."

Zeke leaned back against the counter and closed his eyes. Grief etched his features. Bryn sliced bread for toast to add to Zeke's plate and wondered how many times in his long, long life he had had to suffer such loss. Now that she knew he was her grandfather, she was even more curious about him than she had been before.

"The Guardians have repaired the ruptures between the Zahhak world and the training center, and Malachi and I have restored the training center's wards," Zeke said after he had eaten a few bites of his omelet.

"I guess it was a good thing the collision with the Zahhak realm broke the wards," Aidan said. "Otherwise, Kev wouldn't have caught Lucky in time."

"The collision did not break the wards. Kevin burned them away when he flamed the Zahhaks."

"But the wards should keep anyone outside from transporting into the training center," Aidan said.

"Not to mention that Kev was with Margash, in the Heavens." Bryn waited for her words to sink in.

Aidan's eyes widened. "He wouldn't have had time to use the Gates. Zeke, how did he...?"

Zeke shrugged and took another sip of his tea.

Lucky awoke to find herself alone in Kev's bed. After she had cried herself out, he had held her until she fell asleep. A glance at her phone told her only a couple of hours had passed.

The room was brighter than usual. Must be a full moon, Lucky thought. She slid from the bed and walked to the window to look out. The moon rode high in the sky, silvering everything with its light and reflecting off the late-winter snow.

Kev was sitting on top of the picnic table on Zeke's patio. He wasn't wearing a coat.

Lucky slipped on boots and added a sweater and jacket to her long-sleeved t-shirt and leggings. After grabbing a sweater for Kev, she crept down the stairs and out the back door.

Kev didn't turn around, though he must have heard the door. Respecting his stillness, Lucky climbed onto the picnic table and sat down beside him. He slid his arm around her waist and drew her close to his side. The warmth from his body sank through her coat.

"I brought you a sweater in case you were cold," Lucky said, "but I can tell you don't need it."

"No." Kev pressed his lips to Lucky's hair. "I came out here because I was hot."

"Afraid you were going to supernova?"

Kev chuckled. "If it had been that bad, I would have zapped myself to the cabin. I think it's just the after effect of blasting the Zahhaks. I tried to call my dragon, but still no shift. Instead, my temperature just shot higher and higher." He ran a hand through his hair. "I'm beginning to wonder if I'll ever be able to shift again."

Lucky rested a hand on his thigh. "When I helped to integrate you and your dragon, I never intended to make the dragon go away."

"I know. I still think this is some combination of the integration and the drug Adrigon's men injected me with."

"Any word from Katrin about the test results?"

Kev shook his head. "The Nadachis and Still Ones have kept her pretty busy. You know what else I was thinking?"

"What?" Lucky looked up at him. His hair glistened in the moonlight. She brushed some silky strands back from his face and tucked them behind his ear.

"When I appeared in the training room and caught you, Dominique asked me how I was able to transport there. I was at Margash's outpost in the Heavens, and when the vision came, I didn't even think about the Gates or the wards. I just knew I had to catch you. If either the Heavens' wards or those on the training center had blocked me, I wouldn't have reached you in time." Kev's arm tightened around Lucky's waist.

"But they didn't block you," she said.

"No, they didn't. But they should have," Kev said. "Just like the wards on my cell in the Halls should have kept you from materializing inside it before I supernovaed the first time."

He slid his hand inside the neck of her sweater and hooked a finger around the chain she wore, lifting her locket and the Light-Bringer's medallion free of her clothing.

Lucky caught the medallion between her thumb and forefinger. "You think this had something to do with it?"

"Yeah, I do. Don't you?"

Lucky remembered the way Malachi had frowned at the amulet at the end of their unsuccessful trip to the weapons room. "I think it might."

"You called me as your Maker with this. Do you think somehow you called *it* too?"

"I don't know. Maybe."

Kev studied the medallion in silence, then Lucky felt a shiver go through him.

"Do you want this sweater now?" she asked.

"No." Kev nuzzled the side of her neck. "I want to go back to bed."

"Mmm." Lucky put her arms around his neck. "Me too."

CHAPTER 13

They held the memorial ceremony in Elsewhere.

Because Elsewhere was neutral territory, many of the attendees, including the displaced Still Ones, could simply materialize there. Others, like the mostly human Nadachis streamed through the Gates in Zeke's basement. He had temporarily altered the wards on his home and on the Gates themselves to allow more open access.

Lucky, Josh, Bryn, and Jaime waited in line with Alicia and Mo. Since the two human girls could not dematerialize, the others had agreed to accompany them through the Gates. Their group brought up the end of the line. Once they were through, Zeke would reset the wards and then zap himself to Elsewhere for the ceremony.

"Is it wrong that I'm completely excited that I get to go to Elsewhere this time instead of being left behind like usual?" Mo said into Lucky's ear. "I mean I hate why we're going—that worlds have been destroyed or mangled and people have died—but to get to go someplace that isn't, well, *here*... I mean, *Who gets to say that?* I can't help it. There's a lot of excitement mixed in with the sad and angry."

"Believe me, I get it, Mo. Emotions are complicated."

"Almost there," Josh said behind them. "Is there anything we should know about going through these Gates?"

"You feel like you're getting squished, but it doesn't last very long." Lucky spoke over her shoulder so all her friends could hear.

She watched the next group step into the glowing opening revealed beneath the lifted wings of the Gates. The first time she had gone through them had been before her Striking, and Zeke had been beside her, holding her hand.

Lucky reached for Mo's hand as they approached the Gates and gave her friend's fingers a reassuring squeeze. "Ready?"

"Oh, yeah. Let the squishing begin."

Lucky chuckled. Then she and Mo stepped through the Gates.

After the familiar sensation of compression and stretching, she stood on the hill outside the Alliance Council Hall, sunny skies above, green grass beneath her feet, and her hand still in Mo's.

"You okay?" she asked.

Mo looked around, wide-eyed. "I feel a little queasy, but that's a pretty small price to pay for this."

They moved forward, following the line of people snaking over the hill.

"Is that where it happened?" Mo gestured toward the Council Hall. "Your Making?"

Lucky nodded. "Both the Striking and the Making were there—in different rooms."

"I take it that's not where we're going today though."

The crowd followed a path around the Council Hall and down the hill behind the tall building.

"Looks that way," Lucky said. "I've only ever been to the Council Hall, so I don't really know where the ceremony is being held. I guess we'll find out when we get there."

"Oh, wow!" Mo breathed when they reached the top of the hill.

Below and to their left stood a massive structure that reminded Lucky of an ancient temple. Statues of angels, wings outspread, alternated with gargoyle-topped columns to frame the rectangular structure. Multiple pairs of angel statues, facing one another, marked an entryway on each of the rectangle's shorter sides. Apart from the statues and columns, the structure was open. Looking down from the top of the hill, Lucky could see the stone floor and the stone benches that filled as guests entered through the nearest angel-framed entrance.

Beyond the opposite entrance, outside the temple walls, a bier, ringed with flaming torches, held several wooden coffins. Some, too small for the Naphil soldiers, must belong to the deceased Still Ones.

Of course, Lucky thought, looking again at the columns that framed the temple. Not gargoyles, but Still Ones. She wondered if the furry creatures had been the original models for the gargoyles that decorated Gothic cathedrals.

At the base of the hill, to the right, a road wound toward what looked like a small city.

"Do people actually live here?" asked Mo.

"I was wondering the same thing myself," Lucky said.

"They do." Jaime moved forward to better talk with the two girls. "Since Elsewhere is neutral territory for Light, Dark, and Fallen, many beings have come here to escape unpleasant situations in their home worlds. Others came to make a living, running inns, bars, or less savory businesses."

"Did you spend time here while you were away from Nadach?" Lucky asked.

"Yes. You can learn a lot about the world hanging out in the bars in Elsewhere. In fact, we should all go to one after the memorial."

"You've been holding out on us," Bryn accused. "Why didn't you ever tell us about your trips to Elsewhere and all the interesting things you learned in the bars?"

Jaime grinned. "I didn't want to make you jealous."

"Jealous is right," said Bryn. "You got to travel around while I was stuck in Nadach." She sighed. "I so wanted to get away from there, but now I can't believe it's gone."

"Me either." Alicia sniffled. "I hated being Bound, but Nadach was the only home I ever had."

Jaime put his arm around her shoulders to draw her to his side. "You'll make a new home, sweet one. We all will."

Their conversation faded as they drew closer to the temple. They processed in solemn silence past the angels framing the entrance. Inside the temple, they moved toward the benches nearer the far end. Scanning the crowd, Lucky noticed many beings she didn't recognize as Nadachi or Still One. She guessed some to be inhabitants of the other Dark realms, or, given what Jaime had said, perhaps they were residents of Elsewhere.

Lucky spotted Lilith's scarlet hair and made her way toward her grandmother. The others followed close behind.

From her seat beside Lilith, Lucky could see the bier with its flaming ring of torches beyond the temple's second entrance. Kev and Malachi stood, feet apart, arms behind their backs, on one side of the raised dais in front of the doorway, Aidan and Lucifer on the other side. All wore the formal Forces uniform of black trousers and high-collared jackets.

The quiet murmurs of the crowd gradually ceased, and Lucky turned her head to see Zeke making his way down the aisle. He wore a black robe, topped by the breastplate he had worn at her Striking. His long wheat-blond hair, tied back at the temples, fell over his shoulders.

Zeke moved to the center of the dais and turned to face the crowd. When he spoke, his resonant voice filled the temple. "We gather here today to mourn our recent losses: the destruction of Nadach and those who died there, the loss of land and lives in the Still Ones' Grevyadach, and the deaths of the Fallen's Forces at the hands of the Zahhaks. We are many peoples, but our grief makes us one. And, as one, we honor those who have gone from us too soon."

After the echo of Zeke's voice had faded away, he stood unmoving for a few moments, allowing those there to grieve in silence. Then, looking at Lilith, he gave a slight nod.

Lilith rose and moved toward the dais. Like Zeke and the others, she wore black. But for her, mourning wear took the form of a slim, elegant black dress and stylish, heeled boots. She carried something wrapped in black velvet.

Standing beside Zeke, she folded back the velvet to reveal a silver bowl. She then placed the bowl, resting on its velvet wrapping, in Zeke's hands and reached inside it to retrieve something. Standing to the side, Zeke held the bowl in front of her. Lilith lifted her hands over the bowl, and Lucky saw that she held the small, curved blade she often carried in the pocket of her robes.

Lilith opened her empty hand and sliced her palm with the knife, allowing her blood to drip into the bowl. "For those who died with Nadach, I offer my blood. I grieve that I could not save you. I honor you with this sacrifice."

She lowered her hands and whispered words Lucky couldn't hear. When she stopped speaking, golden flames flared up from the silver bowl.

When Zeke had returned the flame-filled bowl to Lilith's hands, she spoke again. "I honor your lives. I honor your deaths. I honor you."

Zeke then moved to one side of the dais and Lilith to the other. The flame in the bowl she held continued to burn.

A group of Still Ones moved up the aisle and on to the dais. Holding hands, they formed a circle. Then they tilted back their heads and, as one, raised a ululating cry to the sky. Lucky's eyes filled with tears and a sob caught in her throat. Listening to them, she felt the same pain and grief she had when the two Still Ones in G-Ma's room had touched her. The wails of the Still Ones on the dais were the wails of all Still Ones everywhere, their grief a shared grief, their loss a shared loss. Every one of them had felt the presence, the life-force, of each individual who had been lost, and every one had experienced the lessening when each life ended. They wailed for each lost life, for their own pain at each loss, and for the pain they all shared through their connection.

Lucky wanted to wail along with them.

When the Still Ones ceased their mournful cry, silence fell over the temple. After several minutes, the creatures broke their circle and moved to stand beside Lilith.

Aidan stepped to the front of the dais.

When he began to sing, Lucky pressed her hands to her mouth to keep from sobbing outright. The melody he sang was the most hauntingly beautiful thing she had ever heard. It held the sound of ocean waves and heartbeats and blood pumping through veins, of bravery and heartbreak and the soul-deep grief she had seen on his face when he'd healed her. By the time the last note died away, she feared her heart might burst.

Through her tears, she watched Aidan turn and walk through the doorway and past the paired angels toward the bier. The others on the dais fell in behind him.

Then she was rising along with everyone else. No one spoke as they all made their way to the bier, but she heard lots of sniffling and a few muffled sobs.

Once everyone was in place around the bier, Lilith handed her burning bowl to Malachi. His great black wings sprang from his back, and he flew upward to place the bowl on top of the casket at the center of the bier.

Then the Still Ones who had stood on the dais raised their cry once again. And all the Still Ones in the crowd joined in. Aidan's voice rose above their wails, his melody weaving the notes of their cries into a song of deep mourning and much honor.

Kev and Lucifer summoned their wings and flew to opposite sides of the bier, hovering just outside the circle of torches. A signal passed between them, and each held up a hand, sigil activated. A ball of blue flame appeared above each of their upturned palms.

They tossed the balls of flame into the air above the bier, where the flames spread and fell like particles of soil onto the coffins of the Fallen's soldiers and the Still Ones. The tiny flames licked into the wood and rose higher, as the fire in Lilith's silver bowl flared skyward and then rained down to join its golden tongues with their blue ones. The crackle of the flames mingled with the song of mourning.

The magical fire burned quickly. When the song ended, the bier, the coffins, and their contents had burned to the ground. The silver bowl, charred but whole, rested on a pile of ashes that circled outward from the bowl in patterns, like a mandala.

Zeke hovered several feet above the ashes upheld by multiple pairs of blue wings. Lucky could see the shadows of bull, eagle, and lion flickering around his human form.

"The ashes will blow away with the wind." Zeke's words rang over the crowd. "But we will not forget those we have mourned here, those we have honored here. They live in us."

Around her, Lucky heard the words repeated: "They live in us." She added her voice to the chorus.

Bryn scanned the occupants of the Elsewhere City bar where Jaime had led them after the memorial was over. She had never seen so many different beings in the same place before. Even the attendees at the temple service had been less diverse.

"You have to try this one," Jaime said, pushing a pink drink into her hand.

"I can't believe *you've* tried this one," she responded, studying the bright concoction. "It's so very...pink. Are you sure this is safe?"

"Just try it."

Reluctantly, Bryn raised the glass to her lips and took a sip. Despite its shocking color, the drink was surprisingly tasty, even refreshing. "It's good."

"You sound so surprised," Jaime said. "Don't you trust me?"

"I trust anything you might tell me about swordplay. Pink drinks are something else altogether." Bryn passed the glass to Alicia. "Want to try it?"

Alicia sipped the drink. "Ooh, I like this one best of all."

Bryn, Jaime, Alicia, Lucky, Mo, Josh, and Ben had been hanging out in the bar for the better part of an hour, people-watching and trying the different drinks that Jaime and the green-skinned server recommended. Aidan and Kev had been unable to join them, as they had to report to Margash's war room to help plan their next moves.

Bryn wanted to enjoy the light-hearted interlude, but she felt detached from it all. Scenes from the memorial service kept playing in her head, along with memories of the destruction of Nadach, interspersed with the images of blocked pathways and tangled branches from her dreams. Aidan's haunting song provided a soundtrack for it all. How could they drink and make jokes and laugh when so many lives had been lost, when more were going to be lost?

She pushed back her chair. "I'm going to get some fresh air."

"Do you want some company?" Lucky asked.

Bryn shook her head. "I just need a few minutes of quiet."

Lucky smiled sympathetically, and then laughed at something Josh said as he thrust a smoking acid-green drink into her hand.

Bryn weaved her way through the crowded bar, side-stepping to avoid stumbling patrons. When a man with too-bright eyes and too-sharp teeth propositioned her, she drove her elbow into his stomach, without breaking her stride.

"A simple 'no' would have sufficed," he called after her.

The bar door closed behind her, shutting in the sounds of laughter and revelry, and Bryn breathed a sigh of relief. Few people were out in the street, and the quiet provided a welcome respite.

She walked slowly down the stone-paved street, with no particular destination in mind. An odd glow caught her attention as she passed an alley, and she ducked down the alley to explore.

Refuse and bundles of rags littered the alley, but at its end, Bryn found a kind of shrine. Candles flickered in votive holders placed among bouquets and strewn flowers. Bryn studied the offerings, wondering who they honored.

"That's where it happened." The voice from behind her was so quiet and shaky Bryn had to struggle to catch the words.

"Where what happened?" she asked, turning slowly.

"Where he was killed." Searching the shadows, Bryn found that what she'd thought was a bundle of discarded rags was a woman dressed in a long, ragged cloak, crouched against a wall, her eyes locked on the candles. "Jahoel."

"That happened here?"

The woman nodded, but she didn't lift her gaze from the candle glow. "I saw it," she whispered.

Bryn gasped. "You saw it?"

She moved toward the woman but stopped when the woman scuttled farther into the shadows. "I'm sorry. I don't mean you any harm." Bryn dropped into a crouch, so she was on a level with the woman. "Could you tell me what exactly you saw?"

"Dark." The woman continued to stare at the candles as she spoke. "Talking, arguing. Two men. One shiny bright. Jahoel." The woman frowned. "The other, almost shiny bright, but dimmed, smoked glass, tarnished silver. Pushed Jahoel against the wall, held something against his chest. Fire came out of his hand. Fire went into Jahoel. And then—no more shiny bright. Empty container fell to the ground. Tarnished one laughed. Then he was gone. I saw. I saw."

Bryn waited, not moving or speaking. Finally, the woman turned her head and looked directly at Bryn. "I never told no one. Before now. But I bring candles. I light them. For Jahoel."

"Did you recognize him—the, uh, tarnished one?"

The woman shook her head. "Should have been shiny bright like Jahoel, but dirty, polluted."

"You said you never told anyone else about this. What made you decide to tell me?"

"You saw my shrine. You didn't just look. You saw. And I saw you. You have blood on your feathers, bird girl, but you shine bright too."

Bryn blinked back the tears that filled her eyes. "I do?"

The woman nodded. "I see you."

Bryn started to speak, but the woman faded back into the shadows at the sound of footsteps at the entrance to the alley.

"Bryn? Are you ready to go?"

"Yeah." Bryn rose from her crouch as Lucky approached.

"Who were you talking to?" Lucky gestured toward the shrine. "And what's all this?"

"It's for Jahoel." Bryn moved toward the mouth of the alley, drawing Lucky away from the shrine and the woman hiding in the shadows. "I'll tell you all about it on the way home."

Back at the bar, they found their friends waiting outside for them. Lucky led the way back to the Council Hall and the Gates that would take them back home, while Bryn filled them all in on everything the strange woman had told her about Jahoel's murder. She kept the things the woman had said about seeing her and her brightness, despite her bloody feathers, to herself.

Bryn hardly noticed the squishing of the return trip through the Gates, so focused was she on telling Zeke about the woman she'd met. When the others headed upstairs, she knocked on the door to Zeke's study, hoping he'd returned from the latest strategy meeting.

She was relieved when she heard a muted "Come in."

Zeke sat in one of the leather chairs, a glass of scotch in his hand.

"Have a seat, my dear." The smile he offered Bryn was tempered by the deep sadness in his gray eyes.

Bryn sank into the chair across from him. "I thought you might still be in Margash's secret lair."

Zeke chuckled and shook his head. "No." He swirled the scotch in his glass. "I cannot visit Margash's outpost, as it happens to be in my home world, to which I am forbidden entry. The others will report back to me upon their return."

"Why are you forbidden entry to your home world?" Bryn asked. "Does it have something to do with my grandmother?"

Zeke raised one index finger and deliberately placed it on the tip of his nose. "She was Banished to Nadach. I was barred from the Dark realms and the world we called home. I carry a similar spell to the one I was forced to apply to her. If I ever return to my home world, it will cost me my life."

"I'm sorry," Bryn whispered.

Zeke shrugged. "It has been a long time. This world is my home now." He downed the rest of his scotch. "So, what is it you wanted to see me about?"

Bryn told him about the strange woman and her shrine, including something that had puzzled her. "She told me she saw Jahoel's murder. But she didn't mention beheading, only fire. Isn't beheading the only way to kill an angel?"

"Beheading is the most efficient method, but there are other ways. Burning one's internal organs away, as Jahoel's killer did, is no less effective." Zeke sat up straighter in his chair, as if the weariness that had weighed him down had lifted. "You say this woman saw Jahoel's murder?" he asked. "She saw who killed him?"

Bryn nodded. "She didn't recognize the murderer, but she saw him."

Zeke stood and held out his hand. "My dear granddaughter, will you take me to see this woman?"

CHAPTER 14

Bryn led Zeke down Elsewhere City's cobblestone street to the alley that held the shrine. She motioned for him to wait at the alley entrance before proceeding slowly toward the shrine, her eyes searching the shadows for the woman. Like earlier, she initially missed the woman, mistaking her for a pile of discarded rags. Then she looked again and caught the flash of the woman's eyes as she glanced at Bryn before quickly looking away.

"Hello," Bryn said. "It's me again." She dropped to a crouch, so her eyes were on a level with the woman's. "I'm sorry to disturb you again, but I was wondering if you would be willing to speak to someone—about what you told me earlier."

The woman shook her head and moved farther back against the alley wall.

Bryn resisted the urge to creep closer. "It's okay. He won't hurt you. He was a friend to Jahoel, and he—he shines very bright."

"Shiny bright?" The woman crept slightly forward.

"Very bright," Bryn repeated.

The woman moved closer to Bryn, and Bryn beckoned for Zeke. He approached slowly and settled into a crouch beside Bryn.

"Hello," he said, his resonant voice cloud soft.

The woman looked at him in wonder, her lips slightly parted. "Shiny, shiny bright," she breathed. She placed her hand over her heart. "With such an ache here."

She glanced from Zeke to Bryn and back to Zeke. "You shine different but the same."

Bryn found it difficult to speak. "He's—well—he's my grandfather."

The woman nodded. "Shiny bright," she said, as if that explained everything.

"I understand you saw Jahoel's murder," Zeke said gently. When the woman nodded again, he added, "Would you be willing to let me see that memory? I will not hurt you, I promise."

The woman did not answer at first. She simply stared at Zeke, her eyes searching. At least she didn't shrink back into the shadows, Bryn thought.

Finally, the woman nodded a third time. "I see you. You see me," she said.

"I will need to touch you—like this." Zeke put his fingers against the side of his head. "Is that okay?"

The woman nodded again.

Very slowly, Zeke reached his hand toward her. Even though she had consented to his touch, the woman initially jerked her head back. When Zeke stayed still, his hand outstretched, she gradually moved forward again. Zeke raised his hand and rested his fingers against the woman's temple.

"Just relax. It will not hurt. You have my word."

The woman did not move. Zeke pressed his fingers more closely against her temple and closed his eyes. For a second, the woman's eyes widened, then they too closed.

Bryn's heart sped in anticipation while she waited, her ears trained for any noise that might indicate another's approach. More than once, she caught the sounds of people who had had perhaps too much to drink stumbling past the alley entrance. But no one turned down the alley.

After what seemed like a long time to Bryn, Zeke opened his eyes and lowered his hand. The woman's eyes fluttered open.

"Thank you," Zeke said. "Your help has been invaluable."

The woman's smile lit her face. "I see you. You see me."

"Yes." Zeke returned her smile. "Yes, I do."

When he stood up, Bryn rose to her feet as well. "Thank you," she told the woman.

"You are welcome, bird girl," the woman said. Then she faded back into the shadows.

Halfway down the alley, Zeke took Bryn's hands and transported them back to his study.

"Did you get it?" Bryn asked.

Zeke's lips curved in a slow smile. "The woman may not have recognized Jahoel's killer, but I did. We now have proof it was Adrigon."

Aidan grinned as Jaime disrupted the last of the ever-more-complicated wards Zeke and Margash had created to test him. None of them had given him the slightest resistance. It appeared that Jaime really could penetrate any ward he wanted. His passing rendered the ward ineffective for a few minutes but left no other trace.

"Excellent!" said Margash. "Jaime should be able to enter the Halls without Adrigon, Helel, or their Forces suspecting a thing."

"Miguel, did you get the readings you require?" Zeke asked.

"*Sí.*" Miguel held up a small device. "It should take me no more than a few hours to make the alterations you requested." He moved toward the door as he spoke, obviously anxious to start work in the training center's lab.

They had been near to readying their attack plan, and the discovery of proof that Adrigon was Jahoel's killer had intensified their efforts. After Bryn and Zeke had visited with the woman in Elsewhere, Zeke had contacted Uriel, who had extracted the woman's memory from Zeke's mind. Soon after that Aidan, Kev, Margash, and Malachi had received a summons to meet Zeke at the training center. There they had viewed the memory that provided the proof they needed. They hadn't yet shared the information with anyone outside the Forces and Margash's team, so as not to risk alerting Adrigon they were on to him.

Things had been happening so fast, Aidan hadn't had a chance to talk to Bryn. He hoped her part in collecting the evidence that proved Adrigon's guilt gave her satisfaction.

The lie the angel had used to support the destruction of her world would soon be exposed to everyone in both the Light and Dark realms.

Now that Jaime had passed all his tests, they were that much closer.

"You mentioned you had a way to get Jaime into the Halls without a portal or the use of the Gates," Kev said to Zeke.

Zeke nodded. "Provided Jaime is willing."

"Why not?" said Jaime. "I've come this far. What would I be signing up for in addition?"

Zeke smiled at the young man's enthusiasm. "A temporary transfer to you of my ability to dematerialize."

"Transfer?" Aidan frowned. "Does that mean you wouldn't have that ability as long as Jaime does?"

Again, Zeke nodded. "That is exactly what it means. But *I* am unable to transport into any of the Dark realms anyway, including the Halls. Jaime can put my power to good use. And he should not need it for long. If Miguel can do what we think he can, all Jaime will need to do is get inside the Halls long enough to use Miguel's device to dismantle the wards. Then he transports back here, and our Forces invade."

"Okay, I'm in," Jaime said. "When would we do this?"

It was Malachi who answered. "As soon as possible. While Miguel finalizes the device and we gather the Forces, Margash and I will return to the Heavens to mobilize his soldiers there. As soon as we are all in place, Zeke will transfer his power to Jaime—and our attack will begin."

Lucky strapped daggers to her thighs and then slid her arms into the straps of the back sheath for the sword she had chosen from the collection in the weapons room. She adjusted the straps and then turned to Kev. "Will this do?"

A slow smile spread across his face as his green gaze travelled from her head to her booted feet and back again. "You look even more powerful and beautiful than you did the night your Gift manifested. I like you in leather and weapons."

Lucky smacked his leather-clad arm. "That's not what I meant, and you know it. Do I need more weapons, or are these enough?"

"Forgive me for trying to distract myself from the fact that you're going into the Halls with us." Kev sighed. "They should be enough. And you always have your Gift."

"Right," Lucky said.

Kev's hand cupped her cheek before sliding under her braid to wrap the back of her neck. His thumb caressed the soft skin under her ear as his mouth settled on hers.

Lucky kissed him back, her fingers threading through his silky hair. His other arm snaked around her, lifting her and pulling her body tight against his.

"You do remember you're not alone, right?"

At the sound of Aidan's voice, Kev broke the kiss, and Lucky lowered her arms. Kev loosened his hold but didn't release her. "You were way on the other side of this very large room," he said with a grin.

"Yeah, well, we're not anymore." Aidan gestured at Bryn. "We found what she needed."

Lucky saw that Bryn too had daggers strapped to her thighs. A belt holding throwing stars circled her waist.

Bryn held up her hands, her fingers bent to mimic talons. "My built-in weapons are only good up close," she said. "I wanted something I could use from a distance."

"Do you have experience with those things?" Lucky asked.

Bryn nodded. "I used to train with them in Nadach."

They left the weapons room and made their way to the main training field where the members of the Forces had gathered and separated into groups. Lucifer and Ba'al moved among them, providing them with coordinates for various locations within the Halls. Each team would transfer to their specified coordinates once Jaime had returned with confirmation that the wards were down.

Lucky, Kev, Bryn, and Aidan had already been assigned their coordinates. They would work with Lucifer to locate and apprehend Adrigon and Helel, while the Forces of the Fallen freed their Dark counterparts from their cells.

Lucky searched for Ben, but she couldn't find him among the sea of soldiers. She knew he was there somewhere though. Just as she knew Josh was at the safe house with Katrin and Mo, probably still chafing at being left behind when she and Bryn were going after Adrigon and Helel, no less.

Lucky understood his irritation.

But she also knew her Gift and Bryn's Raven abilities and training gave them advantages Josh didn't yet have. He had grudgingly admitted as much himself.

Lucky stopped looking for Ben and turned her attention to the raised platform in the middle of the gathered Forces, where Zeke and Jaime were clearly visible to all. Everyone would be able to see when Zeke gave the signal for them to transport. Zeke had already transferred his power of dematerialization to Jaime and given him lessons on its use. Over and over, Jaime disappeared and reappeared on the platform, while Lucifer and Ba'al made their rounds.

When all the Forces had been given their transport coordinates, Lucifer and Ba'al approached the platform, where Zeke stood alone after another of Jaime's disappearances. After a minute or two, Jaime reappeared. The four conferred. Zeke nodded to Jaime, Jaime nodded back, and then he disappeared, presumably to rematerialize within the Halls.

It seemed to Lucky as if they all held their breath awaiting Jaime's return. He was gone too long for that, she knew. She had to breathe. And everyone else did too. But the company stood so still, remained so quiet, every eye fixed on the spot Jaime had vacated, it was as if time had stopped, suspending their breath.

She wasn't sure how long they waited, not moving, hardly breathing. And then Jaime was back, gasping for breath as if his too had been suspended.

"The wards are down," he cried. "But they're setting the Halls to self-destruct—and to take all the Dark realms with them."

All the movement that had been suppressed during Jaime's absence unfurled in seconds, amid expressions of shock. Jaime communicated Adrigon and Helel's location to

Zeke, and soon Lucky felt new coordinates slide into her mind. Then Zeke gave the signal and, along with everyone else, Lucky transported to the Halls.

She had little experience dematerializing and rematerializing based solely on mental coordinates. Usually she could picture her destination, aim at something more concrete. Now she relied on the dimensional equivalent of latitude and longitude, which seemed a little too abstract. But other than the increased anxiety, the experience was much the same. Nowhere and everywhere and then reforming in a large room at the center of which pulsed a glowing ball of energy.

Even from inside a spherical enclosure made of something dark and crystalline, the brightness of the energy ball made Lucky wish for double-strength sunglasses. Columns attached to the top and bottom of the crystalline sphere channeled the energy somewhere. Lucky had heard that the Halls brought light to all the Dark realms. She guessed that she and her friends now stood near that light's source.

And they weren't alone.

Roughly halfway between Lucky's position and the pulsating energy sphere, two beings she could only assume were Adrigon and Helel turned as they realized they had company. Both had skin so pale it looked almost silver. The taller of the two had silvery white hair that spilled over his shoulders. The other's hair was dark, stark against the pallor of his skin.

"Well, if it isn't the deposed Light-Bringer and his mutt children," said the taller of the two. His silver-white hair spilled over his cape-covered shoulder as he turned his head toward Lucky and Bryn. "Who are your little friends?" Eyes narrowing, he settled his gaze on Bryn. "This one looks familiar. Oh, yes, you were part of Lucifer's ill-fated rescue, weren't you? Lilith's granddaughter, am I right?" He chuckled. "Too bad that little mission cost you your home world."

Lightning fast, Bryn whipped one of her throwing stars toward his head. The star dropped to the floor a yard or so from its target.

"Temper, temper," the tall one said. "Thank you, Helel. Please hold them off while I start the process."

"Of course, Most High," said Helel.

Adrigon's gaze shifted from Bryn to Lucifer, Kev, and Aidan. "An ally with the Gift of Protection can be ever so handy."

With a smirk and a swirl of his cape, Adrigon turned and strode toward the crystal-enclosed energy ball.

Kev and Lucifer each released simultaneous blasts of fire from both palms. Helel's protective shield held, but Lucky could see his face contort with the effort to hold the shield as the fiery blast continued.

Adrigon had almost reached the crystal sphere when Aidan began to sing. Strictly speaking, Lucky wouldn't have called it singing. The notes weren't particularly melodious. She opened her senses, wondering what he hoped to accomplish with his song.

With her senses turned on, Lucky could see a current stretching from Aidan toward Adrigon, passing through Helel's protective shield. When the current touched the silver-haired angel, he faltered. But only for a moment.

"That trick will not work on me, little Naphil," Adrigon said, directing a superior look toward Aidan.

Well, let's see if this does, Lucky thought. If Aidan's Gift could make it past Helel's protection, maybe hers could too.

She reached out for Adrigon's mind with everything she had. She couldn't let him reach the sphere.

Helel's shield offered no resistance. The same could not be said for Adrigon's mind. She had an impression of tangled darkness, then her own power rebounded back at her, dropping her to her knees. She staggered to her feet to see Adrigon turning toward her, his features contorted with hate. Then lightning shot from his fingertips toward her.

"NO!"

Lucky heard Kev yell as if from a distance. Then his body launched in front of her. The impact of Adrigon's lightning propelled Kev's body into her. She flew backward, then hit the floor, Kev heavy and unmoving on top of her.

"Kev!"

Lucky struggled to pull herself from beneath him. His body and limbs were dead weight, lifeless as a rag doll.

Sobbing his name, she scrambled to her knees. Her eyes locked on the hole burned through Kev's supernova-proof jacket and the charred flesh beneath just as the atmosphere in the room charged enough to lift the hairs on her skin.

"It is done."

She looked up at the sound of Adrigon's satisfied voice. She saw him and Helel fade away. Then the pulsing ball of energy grew too bright for her to see anything at all.

She wrapped herself around Kev's body and willed them both back to the training center as the energy ball exploded.

CHAPTER 15

It took several seconds for the materialization to complete. Aidan flickered back and forth between the solidity of his human form and the everywhere and nowhere sense that came with dematerializing before he finally took shape on the training field, Bryn in his arms. They struggled for balance, knocking into some members of the Forces, Fallen and Dark, who had materialized in almost the same place.

Aidan grasped Bryn's shoulders. "Are you okay?"

She nodded. "Yeah. You?"

"I'm good."

His gaze was already sweeping the crowd. "Lucky!" he yelled. "Lucifer!"

There hadn't been enough time. Aidan had grabbed Bryn, but he hadn't been able to make sure the others were all safe. He had to trust that they too had gotten themselves out of the Halls before it exploded. But he'd like more to go on than trust.

"Lucifer!" he yelled again, pushing through the crush of bodies. "Lucky!"

Bryn caught his arm. "Over there."

He looked to where she pointed.

A break in the crowd. Lucky and Lucifer kneeling beside Kev's prone body.

Relief crashed through Aidan. He grabbed Bryn's hand and shouldered his way toward the others.

Lucky jumped to her feet at their approach. "You're all right!" She flung her arms around Bryn.

She almost did the same to Aidan, but then stopped, hesitating. Without a second thought, he opened his arms. She barreled into him. He felt her sob as he pulled her close.

"How's he doing?" he asked. "I saw him go down. I couldn't get to either of you..."

She shook her head. "I don't know. He's breathing, but it's shallow."

"Let me take a look."

Aidan knelt next to Kev and pulled the charred jacket away from his chest.

"The wound has healed," Lucifer said, confirming what Aidan's eyes had already told him. "But something still holds him."

Aidan pressed his fingers to his brother's wrist. A pulse throbbed, thin and thready. Aidan reached into the shallowness of the beat and opened his mouth.

Usually, the right notes presented themselves. This time, though, nothing came. The breath intended for song left his lips in silence.

No visible wound. No available song. Aidan sighed.

He looked up at Lucky and shook his head. "Get him to Katrin. Maybe she'll know what to do."

Lucky nodded, then, frowning, looked from Aidan to Bryn to Lucifer. "Did any of you have trouble materializing?"

"Yeah." Aidan raised his hand to wave at Jaime, who was pushing through the crowd toward them. "We flickered in and out a few times."

"As did I." Lucifer rose to his feet. "It might be a result of the explosion. The Halls was at a nexus in the Tree, and we tap into the Tree's pathways when we dematerialize and rematerialize somewhere else."

"Do you think there will be a problem getting Kev to Zeke's?" Lucky asked.

Lucifer shrugged. "We won't know until we try."

"You and Aidan can't go," said Jaime, who had reached them in time to hear Lucky's question.

Aidan raised his eyebrows. "Why not?"

"Because no one can find Malachi or Zeke," Jaime said. "Someone has to take charge."

The light flickered on and off, like when a bulb was about to die. But Kev could find no source for the unsteady light. Like sunlight or moonlight belonged to the earthly realm, this flickering light seemed to be a part of his current location.

And he had no idea where that was.

He remembered diving between Lucky and Adrigon's lightning blast. He remembered pain. Then nothing. Then this flickering light, this unrecognizable place.

His hand moved to his chest, where the lightning had hit. No wound. His body seemed whole under the smooth cloth of his shirt.

Cloth?

Kev scanned his body. He wasn't wearing fighting gear, but his favorite, faded green button-down, open and untucked, over a t-shirt and jeans. Odd.

No sooner did he have the thought, than his clothes shifted to the fighting gear he'd assumed he would be wearing.

Frowning, Kev passed a hand over his unmarred jacket. What was this place?

He looked around trying to see beyond the flickering light. In flashes, he caught glimpses of dark trees and wisps of silvery mist.

Then the light caught and held, narrowed like a flashlight beam illuminating a path through the trees. Far off in the distance, he could see a ruddy sunset glow. The light seemed to usher him toward it.

With no better options, he started to walk.

Everywhere and nowhere. Kev's bedroom at Zeke's. Everywhere and nowhere. Kev's bedroom. Lucky flickered between the two, a radio signal disrupted by static. By the time her body and Kev's had finally solidified in his bedroom at the brownstone, her heart was pounding with the fear they might be permanently lost in translation.

She settled Kev on the bed and called Katrin's name.

While she waited for the healer—Kev's mother, she reminded herself—to appear, she did what she could to make Kev comfortable. She tugged off his boots and carefully removed his ruined jacket. Her fingers explored the charred edges of the hole in the jacket and then dropped to his perfectly healed chest to trace the place the wound had been. She slid her hand up to his neck to feel for a pulse. It was there, stronger and steadier than before.

She sat down on the bed beside him and clasped one of his hands in both of hers. She activated her extra senses and carefully, carefully, reached out for his mind.

She found only a pair of intertwined threads trailing away into a mist that blocked her like a wall. Wherever they went, she couldn't follow.

"Where are you, Kev?" she whispered. "Come back to me."

After tucking the covers around Kev's body, she stepped out into the hallway, calling Katrin's name again. No one answered.

The emptiness of the house pressed in on her. No one was here. But a faint hum came from somewhere below.

She had started down the stairs when she heard a key turn in the front door.

Mo's voice was close behind. "Anybody home?"

"Just me." Lucky raced down the rest of the stairs. "And Kev, sort of."

Mo raised an eyebrow. "Sort of?"

"He's unconscious." Lucky frowned and shook her head. "More than that. His body's here, but he's somewhere else."

"What happened?"

Lucky didn't answer right away. She couldn't. She hadn't let herself think of the enormity of what had happened. Of what should never have happened, but had.

"Adrigon hit him with something that looked like a lightning bolt. Adrigon meant it for me, but Kev blocked it." She swallowed. "Then the Halls exploded, taking the Dark realms with them."

"Holy hell," Mo breathed. "Does that mean Adrigon got away?"

Lucky couldn't summon the will to tease her friend about the expression she'd picked up from Aidan. "Yeah. Adrigon and Helel both."

In the silence following Lucky's statement, she once again became aware of the humming sound. "Do you hear that?"

"I think it's coming from the basement," Mo said.

The humming got louder as they descended the stairs. It came from the Gates.

They were half open, their impossible wooden wings partially spread, the bright light beyond them flickering erratically. A body lay prone on the floor, half in and half out of the Gates.

Lucky gasped. "Malachi!"

Bryn followed orders. She was too numb to do anything else. She moved robotically, hardly even aware of her body except for an occasional odd tingling in her palms. The only emotion she allowed herself was gratitude—gratitude that Aidan had transported her out of the Halls, gratitude that Lucky and Kev and Lucifer had escaped as well, gratitude that Lucifer and Aidan had taken charge as Jaime had asked. If they hadn't told her what to do, she might have just collapsed.

All the Dark worlds....

No. She couldn't think about it. Not yet.

So, she helped the rescued Dark Forces find rooms in the barracks, made sure they each had the necessary bedding and towels and a clean change of clothes. She did what she could to make them feel welcome while holding her feelings at bay.

Most of them seemed to move as automatically as she did, calling on the stoicism enforced by their training to get through what could not be borne but somehow had to be.

She was about to leave another soldier in his tiny room when he stopped her.

"Would you—sit with me a moment?" he asked.

She turned slowly. Since first greeting him, she had done her best to avoid his sad lavender eyes. She couldn't deny a direct request though.

He was sitting on the narrow bed, and he patted the mattress beside him. "Please," he said. "Only for a moment."

He looked mostly human, apart from his odd eye color and the points on his ears which pushed through his curly blue-black hair. His skin was the color of creamed coffee.

Bryn sat down beside him. "What's your name?"

"Danel. And yours?"

"Branwen."

"You are from the earthly realm?"

Bryn shook her head. "I live there now, but I am from Nadach."

"Your world is gone as well?" Those sad eyes caught hers.

Bryn nodded. She could not speak over the grief clustered in her throat.

When Danel's arms went around her, she embraced him too. They wept together.

Kev had walked for hours, but the sunset glow didn't seem any closer than when he'd first started his trek. Though he hadn't felt thirsty before, he did now that he thought about how long he had gone without water. He wondered if the forest he walked through might be hiding a stream somewhere.

He stepped off the path and the light opened up, no longer a flashlight beam, but sunlight filtering through the trees to the forest floor. To his left, he could hear the gurgle and splash of water spilling over rocks.

He followed the sound to the stream. With less surprise than he might have expected, he saw that the stream matched the one that ran through the woods behind his cabin in Colorado, the one he'd shown to Lucky weeks ago. He stood on its bank now, not on the cliff where he and Lucky had looked down on it. Again, without surprise, he noticed the cliff take shape as he thought about it.

He knelt and drank from the stream. The water was cool and tasted fresh. He sat back on his heels and contemplated his next move.

His surroundings—even the clothes on his body— seemed real, but they responded to his thoughts. The only other times he'd experienced anything similar were in dreams. He remembered how Malachi had talked about the Tree as the place he found those caught between life and death.

Kev didn't feel like he was hovering at death's door though. Lucky had told him about her experience when she'd nearly died from the poison of that angelic sword. How between periods of blank unconsciousness, she'd seen nightmarish visions of herself and Josh. How she'd struggled against a darkness that tried to pull her under. How she'd somehow managed to make it to a tree on a hill, lit with a sunset glow, a tree filled with crows. And how Malachi had found her there.

Kev's only moments of unconsciousness had been those between the pain of Adrigon's lightning bolt and his aware-ness of the flickering light. So far at least, no nightmare visions. He wondered what that said about the state of his body. Too wounded to heal? Then why did he feel so okay? Healed? Then why was he trapped here? How could he find his way out? If he made it to the crow-filled tree, could Malachi find him there and bring him back? Did Malachi even know Kev needed to be found?

Enough.

If this place responded to his thoughts and wishes, then he knew what to wish for. He took another drink of water from the stream and then wished himself at Malachi's tree.

Even with Lucky's Naphil strength, it took both her and Mo to pull Malachi free from the Gates. As if, Lucky thought, his legs were being recreated inch by inch as they tugged him out of the Gates' flickering light. When he was completely free, the wings folded, hiding the light, and the humming stopped.

Lucky crouched and pressed her fingers to the side of Malachi's throat. "Do you have any idea where Katrin is?"

"Sure," Mo said. "She's at the safe house, checking on her patients. She sent me back here for more supplies."

"The safe house. Of course."

Lucky pulled her phone from her pocket and called Katrin. The healer promised to return to the brownstone as soon as she finished tending to her current patient.

"I'll get Malachi upstairs," Lucky said. "You can gather those supplies you needed."

"Are you sure you can carry him? That man weighs a ton."

Lucky chuckled. "Now that he's out of the Gates, I can handle him. I'm a lot stronger than I look."

Lucky took Malachi to the room she thought of as hers. Now that Bryn was living here, they had filled up all of Zeke's bedrooms. Hers was the closest they had to a spare.

By the time she'd gotten Malachi settled on the bed, Katrin had transported from the safe house. Lucky recognized her uneven gait, punctuated by the taps of a cane, before Katrin entered the room.

"You said you found him partially through the Gates?" Katrin asked, moving to Malachi's side.

"Yeah."

It took Katrin only minutes to perform an initial examination. "All his vital signs are good. On the phone you mentioned that you tried to use your Gift on my son. Did you attempt that with Malachi as well?"

Lucky shook her head.

"Try it now, please."

Lucky did as requested, and as with Kev, she found only threads of consciousness leading somewhere she couldn't follow.

"He's the same," she said. "Just like Kev, it's like he's—somewhere else."

Katrin's examination of Kev confirmed that he too seemed fine physically. "I haven't seen anything like this before. I'll have to do some research. I will also consult Sambethe—and Raphael if need be. In the meantime, I would like you and Mo to stay with them, in case there's a change."

"Sure."

The healer turned to go, but Lucky stopped her. "Katrin, at the safe house, how are the Still Ones? They're a collective. They must be grieving the loss of the rest of their kind."

Katrin looked puzzled. "No, they seemed fine when I left them. What do you mean the loss of their kind?"

"The Halls exploded. The explosion was supposed to destroy all the Dark realms." Lucky frowned. "But the Still Ones would know. If their world had been destroyed, the Still Ones would definitely not seem fine."

A hope she didn't quite dare acknowledge began to bud in Lucky's chest.

CHAPTER 16

Kev's first attempt was unsuccessful. As was his second. And third. But with each successive try, he added more details from Lucky's description to the picture of the tree in his head. And, finally, he felt it.

The massive tree sat atop a gentle hill, its branches bare of leaves, but laden with crows. The sunset streaked red, gold, peach, and purple behind it. The crows were cawing.

The image in Kev's mind possessed a depth that went beyond imagination. He knew that when he opened his eyes the real thing would be standing before him. Or he would be standing before it.

And he was. It was. He'd made it.

And what do you know, Malachi was waiting for him.

"Kev?" Malachi asked, surprise evident in his voice. "What are you doing here?"

Okay, maybe Malachi wasn't waiting for him. "I've been wondering that myself. I kind of hoped you were here to guide me back to my body."

A wry smile shadowed Malachi's mouth. "I would be happy to oblige, if I could figure out how to get back to my own."

"You didn't come here on purpose?"

Malachi's braids slid over his shoulders as he shook his head. "I had been with Margash and his team, helping them to prepare to track Adrigon and Helel's movements if they managed to escape when you invaded the Halls. Then Zeke alerted us about them setting the Halls to self-destruct. I had stepped through the Gates to return to Zeke's, where I could transport to the training center. But something went wrong in the Gates. It hurt. I blacked out. I do not know what happened to my body, though it apparently lives. My spirit ended up here."

"I don't know what happened to the Halls. Adrigon was on his way to start the self-destruct. We tried to stop him, but Helel set some kind of protective shield around them that Lucifer and I couldn't penetrate. Aidan and Lucky used their Gifts to get through the shield, but they didn't stop Adrigon either. The last thing I remember was taking one of Adrigon's lightning blasts to protect Lucky. Then I woke up here."

"So, we both had moments between life and death, but neither of us long enough that we should have even been aware of being here, let alone here still."

"What—?" Kev didn't even know how to phrase the question.

"I have walked the path between life and death many times. If either of us were close to physical death, we would not be this aware and present here. Nor would we be here if we had died—we would have crossed over. We should be back in our bodies, not caught in the in-between."

"Any ideas about why we might be trapped here?"

"No." Malachi lowered himself to the ground and folded his legs in a meditative posture. "But let me search the Tree. Maybe I can come up with something."

Malachi closed his eyes. Kev sat down beside him to wait.

While Lucky waited for Mo to return from taking the load of supplies to the safe house, she divided her time between Kev's room and Malachi's. Neither of the men showed any changes. Both appeared to be sleeping peacefully. Pulses and heartbeats remained steady.

Before leaving the room where Malachi slept, she pulled some leggings and socks and a sweater from the drawers. Back in Kev's room, she changed out of her fighting leathers into the more comfortable clothes and curled into a chair near the bed.

She thought of the days she'd spent waiting for Kev to regain consciousness after she had used her Gift to integrate him and his dragon. She had been so worried he would never wake up. That same worry filled her now.

She closed her fingers around the Light-Bringer's medallion, speaking as much to it—or to the connection with Kev that it provided—as she did to Kev's sleeping form. "Kev, wherever you are, you come back to me. Don't even think about leaving me here without you. You transported through wards you shouldn't have been able to pass to rescue me. You got out of the Heavens and into the training center, which shouldn't have been possible."

Lucky worried the amulet between her fingers and thumb, the shapes of sun and dragon rough against her skin. This time, she spoke directly to the amulet. "You took me into Kev's cell in the Halls, past wards that should have kept me out. Show me how to get to him now, how to bring him back."

She received no response. The medallion did not heat beneath her fingers. Kev did not miraculously awaken. Still, she felt a little better for having spoken the words.

She uncurled from the chair and pressed a kiss to Kev's still lips. She was crossing the hall to look in on Malachi when she heard Mo let herself in.

"Hey, honey, I'm home," Mo called.

"I'm upstairs with the guys," Lucky replied.

Mo met her at the top of the stairs. "Any change?"

Lucky shook her head.

"Well, on the bright side, that means no change for the worse either, right?" said Mo, ever the optimist.

"Right." Lucky gave her a half-hearted smile. "How were things at the safe house? The Still Ones still doing okay?"

"Yeah. Katrin was right. They seem fine. They're behaving just as they always have. Comforting the Nadachis and each other. No additional mourning that I can see."

The bud of hope in Lucky's chest began to open, and she allowed herself to give it voice. "Maybe Adrigon and Helel were wrong. Maybe the explosion destroyed only the Halls. Maybe the Dark realms weren't destroyed after all."

"I hope you're right." Mo squeezed Lucky's shoulder. "I'll go sit with Malachi, so you can stay with Kev."

"Thanks, Mo. I'm glad you're here."

Mo grinned. "Me too. I guess life was easier when classes and homework were all I had to worry about. But it certainly wasn't as interesting."

After she had settled the last of the Dark soldiers into the barracks, Bryn made her way back to the supply room. She unfolded one of the remaining cot mattresses on the floor, grabbed a pillow and blanket from the shelves, and allowed herself to succumb to the exhaustion weighting her limbs.

She didn't even bother taking off her boots.

She couldn't remember when she'd felt so tired. Quite a contrast to the excess energy that had buzzed through her the past few days. The only bit of zing left was that tingle in her palms. She curled her fingers into the slight irritation and dropped away.

Into she knew not what.

She fell through a mass of interwoven streaks of flickering multicolored light. Some streaks were so bright she had to half close her eyes to look at them. Others dim enough she almost missed their pale pulsing, catching sight of them only through the corners of her eyes.

She reached for the pale ones, wanted to touch them, but she fell too quickly. The farther she fell, the faster she dropped, streaking past the lights. And then there were no more lights, and she no longer fell so much as floated in a soft, welcoming darkness.

Then the darkness before her parted, and she saw the lights, bright and dim, tangled and intertwined like roots, around something that shone so white-hot, that even the glimpses she caught in the spaces between the tangled light-roots threatened to blind her.

That white heat would destroy everything, burn the worlds away.

She had to do something. She needed to help.

The colored root-lights seemed to dim a little, even as she watched. She couldn't let that happen.

She reached toward the dimming lights with both hands. And screamed as her hands caught fire.

Bryn jerked awake to the smell of singed cloth and a burning sensation in her palms.

She threw off the blanket and kicked at the smoking bits until they were extinguished. Only then did she look at her hands. An intricate pattern glowed like a red-hot coal in each of her palms.

She stared at her hands, so mesmerized she barely registered the sound of the door opening.

"There you are," said Aidan. "I've been looking all over for you."

Bryn looked at him mutely, then turned her palms to face him.

Aidan gasped. "You have sigils."

Something about the comment broke through Bryn's amazement. She chuckled. "You really do have a knack for stating the obvious sometimes, don't you?"

"Some people find it charming." Aidan beckoned her toward the door. "Come on. Zeke's back. He says he has news."

Time passed quietly.

Occasionally, Lucky would leave her post to visit with Mo or to go downstairs for snacks. Otherwise, she sat with Kev, while Mo sat with Malachi, while the conditions of both men remained unchanged.

Lucky had nearly fallen asleep over her book when a commotion from downstairs jarred her to wakefulness. The noise resolved itself to booted footsteps and Bryn's and Aidan's voices calling her name.

She was out the door and into the hallway, where she found Mo also headed for the stairs.

Aidan and a tired-looking Bryn met them at the bottom.

"How's Kev?" Aidan asked.

Lucky shrugged. "The same."

"And Malachi too," Mo added.

"Malachi?" Aidan and Bryn asked together.

Mo explained how they'd found him, and how his state seemed similar to Kev's.

"Well, hopefully we'll get some answers soon." Aidan gestured toward the basement stairs. "Zeke's back. He may know what's going on with Kev and Malachi."

Maybe he should have warned them, Aidan thought when he heard Lucky's and Mo's expressions of concern.

"Zeke, are you okay?" Lucky asked.

Instead of sitting behind his desk, Zeke had collapsed in one of the comfortable leather chairs. His face looked haggard, well beyond the forty-something years he usually appeared. Aidan knew Zeke, like all full-blooded angels, didn't require sleep, but he hoped the Cherub had some method of recharging, because he seemed in urgent need of a long nap.

"I will be fine, Lucky," Zeke said. "Please make yourselves comfortable. I will explain everything as best I can."

When everyone was seated, the girls in the remaining leather chairs and Aidan on Zeke's desk chair, which he had pulled close, Zeke told them why he had disappeared and what he had learned.

Aidan had heard part of the story already. When Zeke had shown up at the training center, looking like he was the one who'd been through Hell and back, he had shared the most important part with Aidan, Lucifer, Bryn, and all the members of the Fallen and Dark Forces. That was where Zeke started now.

"First, you need to know that the Dark realms were not destroyed when the Halls exploded."

"Yes!" Lucky exclaimed. "I had hoped so. The Still Ones at the safe house aren't in mourning, and I knew they would be if their world had been lost."

A smile lightened Zeke's weary face. "Good deduction, my dear. Their world and all the Dark realms are still intact. For now."

"For now?" Mo asked.

"The Tree came to the rescue. The Tree is a living thing, you know, made of all the raw creative energy that makes all our worlds possible. When the Halls exploded, the Tree did what it could."

Zeke had been holding something in his hand, rotating it, rubbing it between fingers and thumb like a worry stone. He placed the small item on the table the chairs were grouped around, pressing a button to activate the device. A three-dimensional image projected above the tabletop—an explosion halted in progress.

"The Tree could not prevent the explosion of the Halls, but it trapped it in a space-time bubble, so it would not expand outward, taking the nexus and the Dark realms with it."

Aidan leaned forward to examine the image. He could almost feel the force pushing at the bubble's edges.

"The problem," Zeke continued, "is that holding back the explosion is sapping the Tree's energy."

"That's why we've had problems rematerializing," Aidan said.

"Yes, the energy we can tap into to transport is limited, because the Tree's priority is containing the explosion. It is applying most of its considerable energy to that task. Even so, it cannot hold back the blast indefinitely."

"So, at some point, it is going to blow," Bryn said. "We just got a reprieve."

Aidan studied her, his brow knitting in concern. She looked and sounded almost as tired as Zeke.

"Yes." Zeke sighed and leaned back in his chair. "Unless we can figure out some way to contain or neutralize the blast. And, if we don't do it soon enough, the Tree may be so weakened that the blast will destroy more than the Dark realms."

"Seven hells," Aidan breathed.

"The Guardians are working on a solution. Their primary mission is to protect the Tree. I will be rejoining them as soon as I can. Even those of us Cherubs who are not Guardians are still energetically bound to the Tree and can give it what support we can while we determine next steps."

"Are you saying the Tree is drawing on your energy?" Aidan asked. "Is that why you look...?" His voice trailed off. He wasn't sure how to finish the question without sounding insulting.

Zeke chuckled. "Yes. That is exactly why I look somewhat closer to my real age than usual."

"Is that why *I* feel so tired?" Bryn asked quietly.

Zeke's gaze sharpened as he shifted his attention to Bryn. "It could very well be. You seem to have a natural connection to the Tree."

"I also have these now." Bryn held up her hands, palms out, and activated her sigils.

Lucky and Mo gasped.

Zeke's eyes narrowed. "When did those appear?"

"A little while ago. About the time you returned to the training center. But I don't understand why."

"Lilith's Banishment spell affected not only her but her descendants. You may not have been Bound to Nadach the way she was, but the spell blocked the Cherub traits you inherited from me. Now that the spell has been removed, those qualities are free to develop."

"Oh," Bryn said. From the shine of her eyes and her rapid blinking, Aidan suspected she was close to tears.

He rested his hand on her knee and squeezed.

When she placed her hand over his, he turned his hand up and threaded his fingers through hers. Her fingers tightened around his as if gripping a lifeline.

"So, what can we do to help?" Lucky asked.

"And what about Kev and Malachi?" Mo added.

"Malachi?" Zeke's eyes sharpened. "Aidan told me what happened to Kevin, but Malachi...?"

Again, Mo explained about Malachi and the Gates.

Zeke sighed once more then turned his gaze to Lucky. "What you can do is get them back." He looked at Aidan and Bryn. "And you two can help her."

Lucky sat forward. "But I tried to use my Gift on both of them. It's like there's a wall blocking me. I can't get to them."

"This is not about your Gift. It is about your connection to them. They are both your Makers. Something of each of their spirits lives in you. And that means you can help bring them back. Malachi will not need much help. Once the pathway is sufficiently repaired, his Gift will enable him to find his way back. You will simply speed up that process. Kevin does not have Malachi's Gift though, and he will need you to guide him back. That should not be a problem given the strength of your feelings for one another, and the way that"—he gestured to the medallion that hung round Lucky's neck—"seems to amplify your connection."

"I'm not sure how I can help," Aidan said. "Physically, Kev is fine. There's nothing for me to heal. And from what Mo said, the same is true for Malachi."

"*They* do not need to be healed. Their spirits are trapped in the Tree, in the in-between space between this world and the next. The pathway back must have been nearly destroyed when the Tree diverted its energy to contain the explosion. You and Bryn need to heal what damage you can."

"Heal the entire pathway?" Aidan's stomach knotted. "How are we supposed to do that? A little rip is one thing, but an entire path..."

"The Tree will guide you. I will escort you to Uriel on my way back to the Guardians. Lucky, you stay with Kevin and Malachi. Once Bryn and Aidan have repaired the pathway as much as they can, help guide Kevin and Malachi home."

CHAPTER 17

Lucky took a deep breath, opened her senses, and focused on Kev and Malachi. She and Mo had settled both unconscious men in Kev's bed. Lucky stood at the bed's foot.

Her first instinct was to use her Gift, to probe for threads and ribbons of thought and emotion that might lead her to them. But Zeke had said her Gift couldn't help now, so she resisted her instinct, relying instead on the heightened senses she had gained on her eighteenth birthday, when she'd learned what it meant to be a Sensitive, and which had stayed with her after the Making.

She could see Kev and Malachi lying still on the bed, but her normal vision was now overlaid with patterns of energy, lines dark and gold, auras unique to each. She could hear their hearts beating, the blood pumping through their veins. She could feel the warmth of their bodies, the sense of their aliveness all around her. Kev's warm, woodsy scent, so familiar to her now, wrapped her in tendrils of green. The spicy scent she recognized as Malachi's from the times she'd grappled with him during training sessions danced around her in flashes of dark amber.

Zeke had told her to focus on her connection to each of them as her Maker. She didn't know if she could hold both connections at once, but she did what she could.

She recalled the Making, how Malachi's Gift had swirled through her like dark wings and the caws of the crows who were his familiars. That memory brought a rush of others. The way he'd written fiery words in the air that had sunk into her skin like tiny coals when he'd helped her to call her Makers. How he'd carried her when she was too weak to walk on her own. How he'd found her in the darkness, on a hill topped with a huge crow-filled tree, bathed in the glow of sunset.

She took everything she remembered, knew, sensed of Malachi and spun it into a bridge reaching from his body here in this room to the tree on the hill with its sunset glow.

And Kev. Dear Kev. Beloved Kev. His first act as Maker had been to touch her so gently. Just his hand, his human hand, on her back, skin to skin, a touch as sweet as the brush of his fingers on her hair after his Gift had seared her, licking through her veins like hungry tongues of flame. "I've never been a Maker before," he'd told her after, his finger touching the medallion where it rested on her chest. The medallion she had seen in the vision when she had called him, when his dragon had shrunk, climbed up her arm, and disappeared into the medallion. The medallion he'd touched, his fingers wrapped around hers, his voice low and intense, when he'd asked her what she'd seen when she'd called him. The medallion that brought him to her in Nadach when her Gift had manifested, and brought her to him in the Colorado snow when the pony-tailed angel had attacked him. The kisses they'd shared after when he'd awakened her from her nightmare. The sculpture he'd made of her in the thralls of her Gift's Manifestation. The joy that filled her when he'd finally awakened after she'd integrated him and his dragon. More kisses, more touches. Her Kev.

She breathed it all in and breathed out a bridge for him as well, all the way to that same crow-filled tree.

Lucky held the connections as steady as she could, hoping they would serve as beacons once Aidan and Bryn had done what they could to repair the Tree's broken pathway.

Then she waited.

Bryn stood with Aidan before Uriel and Gabriel on the windswept plain she'd visited before when she and Zeke and Aidan had returned from the Tree. Then she had watched the Tree disappear, apparently into Gabriel's scroll, and the scroll disappear into the Book. This time, everything happened in reverse. The scroll arose from the Book, and when the scroll unfurled, the Tree appeared.

Uriel gestured toward the Tree. *Do what you came to do. We will wait.*

Aidan took her hand as they pushed toward the Tree through the buffeting wind. When they drew close, a sword appeared and blocked their way, just as Zeke had told her it would. "It will accept your blood," Zeke had said. "Blood of my blood."

Bryn held out her hands as Zeke had instructed, and the sword sliced across both her palms. The blade must have found her blood acceptable. It then faded away, leaving their path clear.

Bryn turned to Aidan and marked his forehead and palms with her blood. Aidan must have noticed the slight tremble in her hands. He threaded his fingers through hers, locking their palms together for an instant.

When they stood next to the Tree, Bryn pressed her bleeding palms against its bark. Aidan had told her that was how Zeke had opened the Tree when they'd come to find her. The Tree had absorbed Zeke's blood, and a door had appeared.

Not this time.

Bryn gasped as her palms vacuumed to the Tree. As if unsatisfied with a smear of blood, the Tree seemed to be drawing the life force from her veins through the wounds in her hands.

But for what it took, the Tree gave back in equal measure.

Bryn sank against the Tree as a wave of vertigo washed through her. She felt a fleeting sensation of the Tree's rough bark against her cheek, and then she was falling, falling, spinning into the light-streaked darkness of her recent dream.

Just as in the dream, she fell and fell through the light, until finally she floated in a sea of darkness. And, just as in the dream, the darkness parted to show a pulsing white-hot ball wrapped in tangled roots of colored light.

This time, though, her attention was caught by a single light-root, so dim it looked dark against the white heat of the pulsing sphere it helped to enclose. Bryn searched the tangle to follow the path of the dark and dying light until she found where it trailed away from the intertwined ball into the darkness.

She reached for it, pressing both palms against it, and like in the dream, she screamed as her hands caught fire.

"Bryn!" Aidan yelled.

It had happened so fast. One second Bryn had pressed her palms to the Tree's bark, just as Zeke had done when he had taken Aidan into the Tree. The next, she had collapsed against the Tree, screaming, fingers of flame flickering between her hands and the bark against which they seemed to be glued.

Aidan moved to stand behind her, his fingers brushing over her shoulders and down her arms. "Bryn," he said again.

"The Tree will tell you what to do," Zeke had said in his cryptic way. If that was the case, Aidan hadn't gotten the message yet. He had no idea what to do or how to help Bryn.

When his hands reached Bryn's, the Tree began to give up its message. Whether it was Bryn's blood on his hands or something else, Aidan didn't know, but his own palms sealed against the Tree beside Bryn's, so that his arms framed hers.

Something made him rest his ear against the Tree's bark. His nose was only an inch or so from Bryn's soft hair. The front of his body pressed into the back of hers.

Then his awareness of Bryn was eclipsed by his awareness of the Tree. He could hear something calling to him from inside it. He closed his eyes and expanded his hearing, listening deep into the Tree.

At first the rush of sounds overwhelmed him, the voices of worlds, so many worlds, but then he began to listen not just with his ears, but with his Gift. He had never thought of listening as a part of his Gift of Song before. He had always assumed the Gift was about making sounds, using his voice to create, to heal. But the Tree whispered to him, in Bryn's voice, in words that weren't really words, urging him to listen as only one with his Gift could do.

And, gradually, the sounds he heard with his ears fell away. And, with his Gift, he heard the music of the Tree, the songs of countless pathways and connections, weakened or broken, the continuous controlled rhythm that held the explosion of the Halls in stasis. He listened more deeply, learning the distinctive melodies of different pathways, and hearing Bryn's voice guiding him to the one he needed to heal.

And, slowly, slowly, all the songs stilled but one, its melody so faint and broken, Aidan wondered he could hear it at all, even with Bryn for a guide. And, as he listened, he began to sing, his voice picking up the broken thread and stitching together the notes he couldn't hear but somehow knew belonged. The longer he sang, the stronger his voice grew, bringing the song he threaded with it, both soaring higher and higher.

As his voice joined with that of the Tree, Aidan no longer knew if he sang or was sung. All sense of his physical body fell away. He became the pathway he sang, knew how it fit in the infinite network of endlessly branching connections that together made up the aliveness that was the Tree. He felt each note stitch itself into place, as if he were each individual note, the melody that joined them, and the glowing, pulsing energetic connection knit from the combination of notes and melody and singer and song.

Time and space disappeared. There was only the song.

Until with one last extended note, Aidan fell back into himself, his voice fell silent, and the song broke free and sang on its own.

The Tree released his hands, and Aidan dropped to his knees. His arms closed around Bryn as she fell against him.

They rested, spent, at the foot of the Tree.

It could have been minutes, hours, or days since he'd first found Malachi and the crow-filled tree. Kev had lost all sense of the passing of time, as if here on this hill, such a thing had no meaning or existence. In some sense, time must have passed. Malachi had returned from searching the Tree and confirmed that the pathway back to their physical realm existed only in tatters. Kev circled the tree, listening to the crows call and watching groups of them, in twos and threes, take flight and then return to alight in the branches. But he didn't know if he'd traced his path around the tree once or multiple times.

He walked back to where Malachi sat cross-legged, as he had since his initial foray into the Tree. Kev dropped to the ground beside him. Holding his right hand palm up, he activated his sigil and then willed a ball of flame to hover just above where the sigil burned. He created a second ball of flame with his left hand, then tossed the two fireballs back and forth. Again, he couldn't have said how much time passed while he did so. Then he merged the two balls into one larger one and passed it back and forth between his hands for another indeterminate period.

"Something is happening," Malachi said.

Kev snuffed the ball of flame between his hands. "I thought maybe you'd fallen asleep."

Malachi ignored Kev's comment. "I can feel the pathway. It is regenerating."

"That's good, right?" Kev got to his feet. "Is there enough of it there for you to guide us home?"

"Sort of."

Kev waited for Malachi to elaborate. When he remained silent, eyes still closed, Kev prompted, "Sort of?"

"I may be able to take myself, but I cannot take you."

"What? But what about your Gift?" Kev conjured another fireball as he paced in front of the seated Naphil. "Aren't you supposed to be able to move freely between the realms of life and death and take others with you?"

"Usually, yes. But this is different."

"How so?"

"When I find spirits here, guide them to this tree in order to return them to their bodies, I rely on my connection to both my own body and that of the spirit I escort. The pathway does not provide a map back to our bodies. Think of it more as a kind of extended door between our world and this place. Now that the door is open again, I am beginning to sense my connection to my own body. But I cannot sense yours."

Kev stopped pacing. "So, you return to your own body, and I stay here until you find mine and come back for me?"

"Perhaps." Malachi frowned. "Wait, there's something..."

Even as Malachi spoke, Kev felt it too, a kind of tug on his consciousness. It felt like... "Lucky," he said.

Then a vision as real as any he'd ever seen displaced all thought. A bridge stretching from where he stood under the crow-filled tree into the far distance—or maybe it was no distance at all—and Lucky waiting on the other end. Lucky receiving his power during the Making and giving something of herself in return. Lucky in Nadach when her Gift manifested, powerful, dangerous, and beautiful. Lucky kissing him in his bedroom at the cabin, and after, in his arms, her tears wet on his chest. Lucky laughing up at him, snow in her hair as she told him she loved him. Lucky in his room at Zeke's, standing at the foot of his bed, on which his body lay. His Lucky. His beloved Lucky. Calling him back to her.

"Go," Malachi said. "I will see you there."

Kev stepped onto the bridge and let it carry him home.

Kev and Malachi opened their eyes at almost the same time.

"They're back!" Mo exclaimed.

Lucky glanced from one to the other. "How do you feel?" she asked. It was all she could do not to launch herself into Kev's arms.

Malachi swung his legs off the bed, sat up, and stretched. "A little stiff, but otherwise okay."

Kev sat up, ran a hand over the place on his chest where Adrigon's lightning had struck him. "Same here. No lasting damage."

Lucky released the breath she hadn't been aware she was holding. She shot around the bed as Kev got to his feet and pulled him into her arms. The release of the fear she hadn't fully allowed herself to feel tightened her grip.

As if from a distance, she heard Malachi chuckle. "Shall we give these two some privacy? Maybe you can fill me in on what has happened in my absence, like who found my body and where?"

Lucky didn't hear Mo's reply. She was too focused on Kev's kiss.

CHAPTER 18

The fact that Aidan's arm around her shoulders offered him as much support as it offered her kept Bryn from feeling guilty about the arm she'd twined around his waist. Healing the pathway from the in-between had sapped them both.

They held on to each other as Gabriel and Uriel closed the link to the Tree and sealed its scroll back inside the Book. They held on to each other as they stepped into the Gates and out the other side into Zeke's basement. And they held on to each other as they climbed the stairs to the main level.

"I need a bed," Aidan said.

Bryn agreed. "Yes."

They reached Aidan's room first.

He sat on the edge of the bed, drawing Bryn down with him. He released her, pulled off his leather jacket and tossed it aside, then bent to remove his boots.

Bryn watched him. She didn't have the energy to move.

Boots gone, Aidan stretched out on the bed. He slid to the far side. "You can stay if you want," he said.

Before Bryn could even think of an answer, he had dropped into sleep.

Bryn watched him for a few seconds more, her eyes drooping. Then she tossed her own jacket aside, pulled off her boots, and lay down beside him.

Someone other than Harley was sharing his bed. Aidan could feel the warmth of another body at his back and hear the soft sounds of someone's breath. Carefully, he turned to face whoever had climbed in beside him.

In the not-quite-dark, the white streak in Bryn's hair almost glowed. A smile curled Aidan's lips. He remembered telling her she could stay. He hadn't allowed himself to imagine she might take him up on the offer.

With gentle fingers, he brushed the hair off her forehead.

Bryn's eyelids fluttered. "You're awake," she murmured.

"And so are you." Aidan's words were little louder than a whisper. "I didn't think you'd stay."

She didn't answer, and Aidan could feel her beginning to pull away.

His fingers brushed her hair again. "I'm glad you did."

"I was too tired to go any further," Bryn said.

She sounded more awake now. And she seemed so different from the Bryn who'd kissed him in the kitchen that Aidan half-expected her to shy away from him at any moment.

"Is that the only reason you stayed?" he asked.

He glided his fingers from the silky strands of hair to her cheek and jaw and down to her throat with its dark, tattoo-like Mark. He could feel her pulse beating against his fingertips. When she swallowed, he could feel that too.

She shook her head. "No. It's not the only reason."

"Good." Aidan's fingers lingered against her fluttering pulse.

"How—how are you?" Bryn asked.

Aidan's smile deepened. "Fine. Good. Right at this moment, maybe better than good." He moved a little closer to her. He could feel her breath on his lips. "How are you?"

Bryn shifted away from him and sat up, her arms around her knees.

"So, what happened to you?" she asked. "Back at the Tree?"

Aidan grinned. "Do you really want to know, or are you just trying to keep me at a distance?"

Bryn considered for a moment. "Both, I guess. But I do want to know. Don't you want to know what it was like for me?"

Aidan sighed and sat up as well, leaning back against his pillow. "I do. I don't know if I can explain what happened to me though."

He gave it a shot, pausing between words as he struggled to convey how the Tree, or she, had somehow guided him first to listen and then to sing, and how, finally, he had felt as if the Tree or his Gift or some combination of the two had turned him into song.

"That's beautiful," Bryn said when he had finished.

Aidan thought she was beautiful. "What about you?" he asked.

"I don't know if I can explain it either. I saw the energy from all the different pathways, wrapped like a tangle of roots around the explosion, and I found the one we needed. Somehow, I just knew which one it was. The Tree guided me, just like when I was inside it. I just knew.

"And then when I touched it, it was like I was the Tree, or the Tree was me. I felt your song. I didn't just hear it—I *felt* it. I knew it was you, making the pathway whole again, helping me to heal." She almost whispered the last words.

Aidan couldn't help but reach for her again. His fingers rested against the side of her neck. "Bryn," he whispered.

She unfolded her arms and legs and moved toward the edge of the bed. "I should go to my own room now," she said.

Aidan's hand snaked around her upper arm. "Please. Don't go. I want you to stay."

She didn't say anything, but she'd stopped moving, and she didn't pull her arm away from his grasp. He could see her chest rising and falling with her quickened breathing. His fingers caressed her arm.

"You don't really want to go, do you?"

After a long moment, Bryn shook her head.

After another long moment, she relaxed and let him draw her to him. He pressed his hand to her chest just below her collar bone.

"I can feel how fast your heart is beating," he whispered. His free hand drew hers to his chest. "Mine is pounding too. Can you feel it?"

Bryn nodded.

"I want to kiss you," Aidan said. "I've been thinking about it ever since that night in the kitchen. Will you let me?"

Bryn nodded again.

That was all he needed to know.

Tears rushed to Bryn's eyes when Aidan's lips touched hers. She felt them streak her cheeks even as she wrapped her free arm around him, pressing her hand against his back to pull him closer.

He must have tasted the salt of her tears. He stopped kissing her and raised his hand from her chest to brush across her damp cheek. "What's all this?" he asked. "If you don't want..."

Bryn pressed her fingers to his lips, stopping his words. "It's not that."

"Then what?"

Bryn shook her head.

She had no answer. Her tears were a mystery to her as well. She didn't want him any less than she had that night in the kitchen. If anything, she might want him more. But this was different. Then she had simply let her attraction for him have free rein and done what it demanded. Now, she felt as if what had happened at the Tree had somehow joined them on some deeper level, and she didn't know if she could ever untangle herself from him again. This—this would make that untangling even more difficult.

She felt as vulnerable as she had that first day they'd met, when she'd been so weak she could barely make it across the hall on her own.

The memory of their initial antagonistic exchange caused her to smile.

Aidan's fingers slid to her mouth. "And what's this?"

"I was remembering when we first met. I don't think you liked me at all then."

Aidan chuckled. "*I* didn't like *you?* I was ready to be your friend, and then you got all testy with me. Even your name was a dangerous topic."

Bryn laughed at the memory. Then she sobered. She raised her hand to his cheek, feeling the prick of his stubble against her palm. "I like you now," she whispered.

Aidan's hand covered hers where it rested on his cheek. "I like you too," he whispered back. "I like you a lot."

Bryn gathered her courage. "Then kiss me again," she said.

And he did.

Lucky wiggled out from under Kev's arm as carefully as she could.

Though he'd insisted he felt fine, he'd fallen asleep soon after she'd filled him in on everything that had happened while he and Malachi were trapped in the in-between. She had lain awake for a while, soaking in the feeling of him, warm and alive, in her arms, before finally letting sleep take her. Her stomach grumbling about its emptiness had awakened her.

She paused at the door when Kev shifted and sighed, but he didn't wake. She slipped into the hallway, nudged the door quietly closed, and descended the stairs.

The light from the streetlights gave the interior of the brownstone a twilight glow. Rather like that of Nadach on a normal day, Lucky thought. Quick upon the heels of that thought came another: the remembrance that Nadach was no more. Lucky sighed and closed her eyes. She still hadn't fully mourned the loss. She could only imagine how the Nadachis felt. Yes, the world had originally been created to serve as a prison of sorts for Lilith, but it had become a home to her and many others.

As Lucky crept through the living room, a soft sound drew her attention to the usually unoccupied couch. She smiled to see Mo's blonde hair peeping from under the edge of a blanket. Mo's help these last weeks had been invaluable. Lucky could hardly believe she had once thought she'd have to keep this world a secret from her best friend.

In the kitchen, Lucky rummaged through the fridge and cupboards for sandwich ingredients. She was placing the top slice of bread on her sandwich when Aidan entered the kitchen.

"Can I have one of those?" he asked.

"Help yourself." Lucky smiled. "There are other options in the fridge, if you want something else."

"These are good."

Lucky took a seat at the counter and watched as Aidan assembled his sandwich. He wore sweatpants and nothing else. She remembered a time not so long ago when the sight of his shirtless form would have sent her pulse racing. Now, she could appreciate the beauty of the slide of his muscles under his bare skin without wanting anything more.

"Do you intentionally run around without a shirt in order to show off?" she asked with a grin.

Aidan looked at her over his shoulder, one eyebrow raised. "One, it's not like I expected anybody else to be down here. Two, show off?"

"Yeah, show off." Lucky gestured at his bare torso. "I mean, look at all that."

Aidan turned to face her, arms out to the sides. "You like?" he asked.

Lucky chuckled. "Of course, I like. I'd have to be blind not to like."

"This could all have been yours."

Aidan's grin took the sting out of the words. Still, Lucky sighed as he turned back toward his sandwich making. "I know," she said. "I'm sorry I hurt you."

Aidan brought his sandwich to the counter and took a seat on the barstool beside hers. "I know you are. And I'm okay now."

"Yeah?"

"Yeah."

"Good." Lucky took a bite of her sandwich.

They chewed companionably for a while before Aidan spoke again. "You really love him, don't you? My brother."

Lucky nodded. "I do."

"Good." Aidan's eyes held hers as he spoke. "Because he's never loved anyone the way he loves you."

Lucky nodded again, and her lips formed a shaky smile. She couldn't speak around the knot in her throat.

They finished their sandwiches, and Aidan put the dirty plates in the dishwasher, while Lucky returned the sandwich fixings to their original locations.

"I maybe shouldn't ask. It doesn't really matter anymore, but I'd still like to know." Aidan propped himself against the counter. "Did you ever love me?"

Lucky closed the fridge and leaned back on the door for support. "Yes, I did. You swept me off my feet. I was this ordinary girl, barely out of high school, and you—you were the lead singer for Icarus, with that hair and those eyes and that voice. And those wings. You showed me how to fly. You were every fantasy come true."

"But?" Aidan prompted.

She gave him a rueful smile. "I don't know. Everything changed on the day of the Striking. After the ceremony, I felt so different, so emptied out of all I'd been before. And then came the Making. And Kev was one of my Makers. It's like a part of him lives inside me." She pressed a hand to her heart. "Here. And in the blood in my veins. And the power that runs through me." She looked at Aidan with tear-filled eyes. "He's not a schoolgirl fantasy for me. He's—necessary, like air or water. I don't know how I would live without him."

Aidan nodded, then smiled, then opened his arms. "Come here," he said softly.

Lucky hesitated only a second before accepting his embrace and pulling him into a fierce hug. "I've hated how awkward things have been between us," she said. "I've missed you."

"I've missed you too."

Aidan dropped a kiss on the top of her head and then pressed his cheek against her curls.

Lucky held him, her heart full to bursting.

Bryn awakened to find herself alone in Aidan's bed. Her hand slid to the space where he'd been sleeping. Still a little warm. He hadn't been gone long.

She sighed and rolled onto her back. If she had stayed asleep, he might have gone and returned without her knowledge, and she might have awakened later in his arms. As it was, she didn't think she could stay and await his return.

She felt far too vulnerable. Too much had happened. She felt both emptied out and full to the point of overwhelm. The Tree still reached tendrils into her consciousness, and her thoughts and emotions were filled with Aidan. She needed to put some space between them.

Moving quickly, she got up and gathered her discarded clothes and boots. After a quick check to make sure the hallway was empty, she slipped out of Aidan's room, closed the door, and ducked into her own room a little farther down the hall.

Safe inside, she climbed into her bed and pulled the covers snug around her.

Try as she might, she couldn't fall back to sleep.

Some traitorous part of her wished Aidan still slept at her side.

CHAPTER 19

The next morning, Aidan resisted the impulse to knock on Bryn's door. The pause before he turned toward the stairs was so brief, he could almost convince himself he hadn't involuntarily turned toward her room. Almost.

When he'd returned to his bedroom from his wee hours' foray into the kitchen, the lack of her had punched him in the gut. But he'd respected her need for space. And he respected it now.

This was Bryn, after all. His lips curled upward. She'd never made things easy for him.

He toasted a bagel, smeared it with cream cheese, sandwiched it, wrapped it in a napkin, and stuffed it in his pocket. Then he zapped himself to the training center.

He pulled the bagel from his pocket as soon as he rematerialized and took a bite as he pressed his palm to the security panel. He crossed the gym, waving to the soldiers who were training—some of them Fallen, some of them members of the Dark Forces he'd met the day before.

He'd polished off the bagel and was wiping his hands on the napkin by the time he reached the war room. Inside, he found Malachi and Lucifer, along with two members of the

Dark Forces Aidan had met the night the Halls exploded: the captain, a Dark Angel named Rimmon, and his commander, Danel, who, in appearance at least, seemed to be about the same age as Aidan.

Malachi inclined his head toward Aidan but wasted no words on greeting. He glanced from Aidan to Danel. "Rimmon and I have agreed that you two should start working together today. We need our Forces to function as one unit. You will share strategies and training methods and learn everything you can about each other's teams—our shared team now. What are our strengths, and where are our weaknesses? Magnify the former and eliminate the latter."

"Yes, sir," said Aidan.

"As you command," said Danel.

"You two are in charge here," said Malachi. "Rimmon will accompany Lucifer and me to meet with Margash and the Forces of Light."

"As will your brother, if he manages to get here in time." Even as Lucifer spoke, Kev burst through the door.

Aidan grinned. "Well, look who decided to join us."

Kev's hand stayed at his side, but Aidan saw the raised middle finger. He chuckled.

Lucifer raised an eyebrow.

Malachi's lips quirked. "Shall we go?" His words were less question than order.

"Nice job with the Tree yesterday, Aidan," Kev said as he followed the others out the door. "You and Bryn make a good team."

"Yeah," said Aidan. "We do."

Dominique's class had hardly begun when Zeke strode into the room. Bryn tried to focus on her new sparring partner, a Dark recruit of indeterminate gender named Alex, but she couldn't help stealing glances toward Zeke and Dominique. Fortunately, Alex seemed just as distracted.

When, after a brief conversation with Dominique, Zeke made his way toward her and Alex, Bryn gave up all pretense of sparring.

Zeke nodded to Alex. "I am afraid you are going to have to find a new partner." Turning to Bryn, he said, "Leave your training gear. You are coming with me today."

He waited at the door while Bryn stowed her gear. Lucky caught Bryn's eye as she was leaving, raising her eyebrows in question. Bryn shrugged and shook her head. She had no idea what her grandfather wanted with her.

And he didn't enlighten her soon either. He said nothing at all until they were outside the training center. Then, he only commented, "First, back home," before he took her hands and transported them both back to the hallway outside his study in the brownstone's basement.

He led her into the room that housed the Gates of Heaven, the massive carved wood wings that opened portals between worlds. He stopped directly in front of the Gates.

"I am taking you to meet the Guardians," Zeke said. "I intended to take you to them at some point soon, given your natural connection with the Tree. But after what you and Aidan did yesterday, they requested an immediate meeting— and I agree. None of them could have done what you did so quickly—and most of them have been serving the Tree for centuries."

"I didn't do it alone," Bryn protested. "Shouldn't Aidan come with us?"

Zeke shook his head. "Aidan has other duties. And he cannot be a Guardian as he is not of Cherub blood."

"*Be* a Guardian?" Bryn's heart felt like it might beat right through her ribs. "But I..."

Her objection died on her lips as she suddenly understood that *this* was where that path she'd taken when she'd been lost in the Tree had led. *This* was the unspoken agreement she'd made. The one that would change her life forever.

She raised her eyes to Zeke's. He must have read the recognition in her expression, for he held her eyes and slowly inclined his head, as if in acknowledgement.

"Ready?" he asked softly, offering her his hand.

Bryn nodded and placed her hand in his.

Zeke activated his palm sigil and pressed his hand against the Gates. The great wings spread, the brilliance behind them beckoning.

Bryn stepped with Zeke into the light.

The Archangel Michael and most of the Forces of Light had joined Margash's band of rebels. Not all of them had made it to the outpost, however, as several troops were needed to keep order throughout the Heavens now that Adrigon had been identified as Jahoel's killer. Enough of the Heavens' inhabitants still supported the Metatron's now deposed First that they'd taken to the streets in protest.

Kev had known support for Adrigon was strong, but he hadn't anticipated how many of Adrigon's supporters would remain loyal in the face of the evidence of his guilt. But, according to Margash, many denied the reports, while others suddenly accused Jahoel, who had always been well-respected, of crimes against the Heavens and its people, alleging Adrigon had only done what he had to do to protect them.

Whether through the help of some of those supporters or by other means, Adrigon and Helel had remained undetected since their departure from the Halls. None of the efforts of Margash's spies or those of any of the Forces—Light, Dark, or Fallen—had turned up any leads as to the pair's location. All attempts to track them had failed.

"Could Helel be using his Gift to hide them?" Kev asked. He knew they had to strategize, but all talk and no action was making him antsy.

"He does seem to have powerful protective abilities," Lucifer said. "How much do we know about his powers? If he can cloak the two of them with his Gift, how long can he do so? Surely, he couldn't sustain such a shield indefinitely."

Malachi's gaze sharpened. "Maybe we change tactics. Instead of attempting to locate Adrigon's or Helel's energetic signature, maybe we look for a consistent energy pattern that might indicate the kind of sustained magical output required to keep up a shield like that."

"I say we do both," said Rimmon. "Keep doing sweeps for their signatures, but also search for that pattern."

"Do not underestimate the power of our contacts in the realms," added Margash. "Our allies in the Heavens are keeping a close eye on the movements of Adrigon's support-ers to see if one of them might lead us to Adrigon. And theirs are not our only eyes. With our combined forces, we have informants on earth and throughout the Dark Realms."

Lucifer cleared his throat. "About that," he said. "The number of our informants in the Dark Realms seems to be shrinking. I have recently learned that many of the Dark are fleeing their realms and taking shelter in Elsewhere. Word of the Halls' destruction and the current state of the Tree has spread fast. Many have chosen to remain in their home worlds, but others do not want to take the risk of being incinerated."

Kev cringed. Leave it to Lucifer not to mince words.

"That means we will have to keep Elsewhere a safe neu-tral zone," said Malachi. He turned to Kev. "Go pull together a team from the Fallen and Dark Forces and get them to Elsewhere. Now."

"You got it," Kev said. Here was something he could do. Malachi must have read his mind.

How could so much have changed in so little time?

Lucky stood on the hill outside the Alliance Council Hall, staring down at an almost unrecognizable Elsewhere City. In the mere days since the destruction of the Halls, the city's borders had expanded until she couldn't see their edges. New construction and tent cities formed satellite communities stretching in every direction and dwarfing the original city.

"I guess when you have magical powers, it doesn't take long to put up a building," she said.

On Malachi's orders, Kev had assigned members of the Fallen and Dark Forces to patrol different areas of the growing city, to look out for any conflicts between the diverse peoples of the Dark Realms seeking shelter here, as well as between them and any denizens of the Heavens who might choose to visit the neutral zone. With the divide between Light and Dark growing ever wider, keeping the neutral zone neutral was of prime importance.

Rather than take a specific zone himself, Kev had decided to move from area to area to get as much of a feel for the whole as he could. When he'd told Lucky of his plans, she'd asked to come along. She was on the duty roster for later in the week, and she welcomed the opportunity to get in a little experience before her first real shift.

"Fly over first," Kev said. "Then we can wander around, take the temperature at ground level. So far, no one's reported anything more than minor disagreements. But it's early days yet."

Lucky summoned her wings, and then they were gliding down from the hill and winging their way over the city. They flew as low as possible, and Lucky caught the warmth and smell of smoke from open fires, the aromas of cooking meals, the sounds of laughter, snippets of conversation, and snatches of music. They flew over groups of children at play, families gathered for meals, and more raucous gatherings of adults in various forms, drinking, laughing, and dancing.

Each people seeking refuge from the vulnerability of their home world had created their own small community here, and so far, they all seemed to be keeping their distance from one another. Only in the original Elsewhere City did the peoples intermingle, and it was there that Kev signaled Lucky to drop back to ground.

They settled in an unoccupied area in a park near the main route into the original city. Lucky dismissed her wings as soon as her feet touched down.

"Did you get the sense that for some, this might seem sort of like a holiday?" Lucky asked.

Kev nodded. "Far from home, not knowing how long home will actually be there... Pretending it's a holiday probably helps them hope for the best."

He started toward the busy street, but Lucky caught his arm, her question for his ears alone. "Do you think the best is possible? Will all these people be able to go home soon?"

Kev let out a long breath. "I don't know. But sometimes you have to believe in the impossible—and sometimes what you think is impossible isn't after all." He caught her hand and brushed a kiss across her knuckles. "Like you being with me, for example. I thought that was impossible once."

Lucky chuckled. "Yeah, if someone like you could end up with someone like me, then neutralizing a world-destroying explosion is a piece of cake."

"Easy-peasy." Kev grinned. "Nothing to it."

Lucky followed him toward the street, thinking that, like Alice in Wonderland, she needed more practice believing impossible things.

The entire space was a whirl of blue wings and the continuous morphing of forms from human to bull to lion to eagle and back to human to start the whole sequence again. As part Cherub, Bryn could track the shifts fairly well. Still, after only a few minutes had passed, the refusal of any of the Guardians to settle on a definite shape caused her head to spin.

Only Zeke had consistently remained in his human form, and he looked at her now, his gray eyes narrowed in concern. Then he closed his eyes, and a stillness rippled through the crowd. The whirring wings disappeared, and one by one the Guardians took on their human guises.

"Better?" Zeke whispered.

Bryn nodded. "Thank you."

"They will not be able to hold these forms long. Since they do not dwell in the human realm, they have had no need to learn to stabilize their forms as I have."

"Can I learn to see them better as they are?" Bryn certainly hoped she could. If she was going to become a Guardian, she needed to be around the rest of them without getting dizzy.

It was Zeke's turn to nod. "Yes, with practice."

Bryn scanned the group of Guardians. Now that their forms had settled and their wings were hidden, she could see they numbered only a few dozen, instead of the hundred or so she had imagined. Zeke had told her they communicated telepathically, which was apparently how he had asked them all to take human form. They seemed to be doing it again now. Some quiet words were spoken in a language Bryn did not comprehend, but, for the most part, glances and nods were exchanged in response to messages she didn't even hear.

After a while, a single Guardian made her way from the back of the group toward Bryn and Zeke. She was shorter than Bryn, with a curvy figure. Her shoulder-length curls were a shade darker than her mocha skin, and her eyes a deep brown. She appeared to be about the same age as Zeke—that is, she looked to be somewhere in her mid-forties. Bryn knew Zeke was centuries older than he looked, so she guessed this woman's appearance to be equally deceptive.

The woman smiled warmly at Zeke and held out both hands to him. He took them in his and bowed over them.

"Hello, Eleni," he said, his voice rich and warm. "It is good to see you again."

"As it is to see you." Eleni's husky voice resonated like Zeke's, as if the sound could almost take physical form. She lowered the volume to a whisper, "You were always one of my favorites, you know." She winked at Bryn as she spoke.

Zeke chuckled. "I find that hard to believe. You have had so many pupils over the years." The smile drained away as he continued, "And no other so betrayed your trust."

"Nor did any other pay so dear a price." Eleni raised their clasped hands and pressed them to her forehead. When she released Zeke's hands and looked up, Bryn caught the glitter of tears before Eleni lowered her eyelids.

Bryn, shocked by the realization that this woman must be even older than Zeke, did not at first notice that Eleni had turned toward her. Belatedly, she took the woman's out-stretched hands, feeling an almost electrical charge in her fingers as Eleni's closed over them.

"I am to be your mentor," Eleni said. "I am pleased to take on the training of the granddaughter of one of the most honorable beings I have ever known."

Bryn found herself blinking away the sudden moisture that clouded her vision. "Thank you," she said. "I am honored by your gift."

Eleni's laughter was as husky as her voice. "You may not think it such a gift once your training begins."

"Bryn is no stranger to hard work," Zeke said.

"Indeed." Eleni's eyes dropped to Bryn's Raven Mark. "So, Bryn, shall we get started?"

CHAPTER 20

He may have decided to give Bryn her space, but Aidan hadn't expected days to go by without so much as a glimpse of her.

Not that he'd had much time to spend with her anyway. Between training with the combined Dark and Fallen Forces and pulling his shifts on Elsewhere, he'd been well occupied. Still, he would have expected to have at least seen her in passing as he had Kev, Lucky, Josh, and Ben. He'd even run into Mo on one of his brief stops at Zeke's. But of Bryn, he'd seen no sign—not since he'd left her in his bed in the middle of the night and come back to find her gone.

Well, maybe he'd see her on Elsewhere. He assumed she had been assigned patrol duty like all the others. His shifts had been quiet so far, and from what he'd heard, so had everyone else's. But he knew that could change at any time.

He exited the training center, so he was clear of the wards. Then he zapped himself to Elsewhere and made his way to the room in the Council Hall where the Forces had set up their base of operations. He found Lucky inside, her palm pressed to the identification screen.

"Signing in or out?" he asked.

The screen accepted Lucky's sigil, and she dropped her hand. "In. What about you?"

"In for me too. Looks like we're on duty together." Aidan pressed his palm against the screen and activated his sigil.

"Oh, good. I've hardly seen you lately. But we've all been so busy I haven't seen much of anybody—even Kev."

"What about Bryn?" Aidan asked. "Have you run into her at all?" Sign in complete, he followed Lucky to the door.

Lucky shook her head. "Not since Zeke pulled her out of Dominique's class a few days ago. I don't know where he was planning on taking her—and from the look of things, Bryn didn't either. I haven't seen either of them since."

"Zeke's been around. I haven't seen him, but I know Malachi has talked to him. Bryn hasn't been in any of her classes then?"

"Not the ones we have together anyway."

They exited the building and turned down the path toward the ever-growing city.

"I'm sure she's fine," Lucky added. "Zeke would let us know if anything was wrong."

"Yeah." Aidan knew she was right, but he couldn't completely quash the twinge of worry.

The sight of flames shooting up from one of the tent villages near the city's edge pushed that worry to the back of his mind.

"Seven hells." Aidan summoned his wings. Looked like they weren't going to have a quiet shift after all.

The fire turned out to be an accident.

Even so, by the time the flames were extinguished, the items damaged beyond repair cleaned up, and replacement tents located and erected, much of Lucky and Aidan's shift had passed.

Lucky handed a partially cleaned doll to its small owner. "Almost as good as new." She smoothed her hand over the child's hair, careful to avoid the sharp points of the horns that poked through the purple-black locks.

The little one smiled in thanks, lips parting to reveal teeth as sharp as the horns.

"I think they can take care of the rest of it," Aidan said. "Let's walk through the city before our shift ends."

As Lucky and Aidan said goodbye to the affected families and the neighbors who had come to their aid, Lucky marveled at the variety of beings inhabiting Elsewhere and the willingness of so many of them to help one another, even if they came from very different worlds.

The city's restaurants and bars teemed with patrons, and new street vendors appeared every day. Many of the items for sale—clearly food and drink—looked like nothing Lucky would have imagined to be edible if she'd seen them outside this setting.

A familiar logo caught her eye. "A Mixed Brew," she said, pointing to the sign. "That's the place Jaime took us after the memorial service."

She walked a little faster. "The shrine for Jahoel, where Bryn met the woman who saw his murder, is down an alley not far from here."

Lucky didn't recall exactly which alley housed the shrine, and it turned out to be farther away from the bar than she'd thought. By the time she saw the flickering candlelight that signaled the shrine's presence, her eagerness to share the site with Aidan was spiked with a sense of foreboding.

The buildings rising on either side blocked the natural light, casting the alley into shadow. When she had seen it before, all the candles on the shrine had blazed, filling the end of the alley with light. Now, only a few flickered, their light fading as the wax burned away.

"This doesn't feel right," she said under her breath. She pulled the dagger from its sheath on her thigh and slipped into the alley, hugging the wall.

"Agreed." Aidan moved silently to the opposite wall, drawing his own blade.

Lucky opened her senses just enough to heighten her natural perceptions. Within a few steps, she caught the slightly metallic scent of blood. She turned up the sensory volume a bit more, her eyes searching the pools of shadow. The scent of blood grew stronger, and now she could see the faint aroma trail and follow it as it strengthened and darkened nearer its source.

"There," she said, tilting her head toward a darker bundle in the massed shadows between them and the shrine.

Lucky knew at least part of what they would find even before they reached the body. Her heightened senses had shown her only the aroma trail from the woman's blood, no aura to indicate she yet lived.

Still, the sight revealed by the beam of Aidan's small flashlight caused her to gasp. The woman's throat had been cut through, her head severed from her body. Someone—presumably, her killer—had used her blood to mark the wall above her with characters Lucky couldn't read.

"Do you know what it says?" she asked.

Aidan nodded, his lips tightening. "It says 'Traitor.'"

Only when she stepped out of the Gates into the brownstone's familiar basement did Bryn allow herself to relax. She'd done it. She'd successfully completed her first round of Guardian training. She didn't even try to stop the grin that crept across her face.

She stepped into the hallway just as Lucky was exiting the gym.

"There you are!" Lucky said. "Where have you been? We've been worried about you. And what has you looking so happy?"

"How long have I been gone?" Bryn's head spun with information and experiences from her training. She remembered taking breaks for meals and short naps, but she had no real concept of how much time had passed.

Lucky's eyes widened. "You don't know? It's been almost a week since Zeke took you out of Dominique's class."

Bryn felt that grin curling her lips again. "Time really does pass differently in the Tree."

"That's where you've been? Where did Zeke take you?"

"I'll tell you everything, but first I'd really love a shower, and I need food."

"Come on then." Lucky pulled Bryn toward the stairs. "I'll fix us something to eat while you shower."

When they reached the main floor, Lucky headed toward the kitchen.

"Make it quick," she called over her shoulder. "I'm dying of curiosity."

Upstairs, Bryn made short work of showering and changing, despite lingering for a few moments under the hot spray. True to her word, Lucky had soup and sandwiches waiting in the kitchen.

She had set only two places at the bar. Bryn couldn't decide if she was relieved or disappointed that Aidan wouldn't be joining them.

"So, what's the scoop?" Lucky asked. "You've been in the Tree all this time?"

Bryn swallowed a spoonful of soup. "Not all of it. And it didn't seem so long for me. But, yes, a lot of the time I was in the Tree."

She told Lucky about Eleni, who, she had learned, held an almost mythic status among the Guardians. "She was Zeke's mentor. As in, she *taught Zeke*. She knows more than anyone about the Tree and how it works, how it lives and grows, how it can be wounded and how it heals, how it interacts with the Guardians." Bryn paused to eat a bite of her sandwich, then continued, "And she wanted to teach me. She could have assigned anyone to be my mentor, but she chose to do it herself."

"Does this mean you're going to be a Guardian?"

Bryn nodded. "Unless I really mess something up. I seem to have some kind of natural connection to the Tree. When I was lost in it, it tested me—chose me, somehow. Eleni says I catch on faster than anyone she's ever worked with—except maybe Zeke."

"Well, you are his granddaughter." Lucky pushed her soup bowl away and rested her arms on the table. "So, what kind of things did you learn?"

Bryn did her best to explain what she could. Some of what she'd learned were secrets, known only to those who were or would be Guardians—like how to access the Tree without Uriel and Gabriel, without going through the Place of the Book. She could never share that knowledge with Lucky or the others. Even Zeke had had the secret taken from him when he'd been stripped of his Guardianship.

For much of what Bryn could share, she struggled to find words. Her training had been mostly experiential, intuitive, and intimate. It was less like learning a skill than like developing a relationship. The Tree had chosen her, and now Eleni taught her and the Tree to know one another.

"You love it, don't you?" Lucky handed Bryn their rinsed bowls and plates to place in the dishwasher. "The Tree? This work?"

Bryn hadn't thought of it in those terms. She had only done what seemed right, inevitable. But Lucky's words fit. "Yes," she said. "For the first time, I feel like I really belong."

Unable to sit still, Kev prowled around his mother's lab, checking out the containers that filled the shelves. Katrin had asked him there so they could finally go over the results of the tests she'd done. But she had been detained at the safe house, leaving Kev alone with his thoughts about the woman Lucky and Aidan had found. She had helped them solve Jahoel's murder—and had then been killed for her efforts— presumably by one of Adrigon's misguided supporters.

It was Kev's job to keep Elsewhere safe.

And he had failed.

Of course, he hadn't known the woman would slip away from the soldiers who guarded her and return to the alley they had warned her to stay away from. Still, she had died on his watch.

After Lucky and Aidan had discovered the body, he had posted guards at the entrance of the alley. Too little too late.

Katrin materialized inside the lab's doorway without warning. "Sorry to keep you waiting. Put that down. It has nothing to do with you." She pointed her cane toward the chair he'd been avoiding.

Kev set the container of silvery liquid back on the shelf and took his seat as requested.

Katrin lowered into the chair behind her desk, supporting herself with her cane. She looked tired. Between the Nadachis and Still Ones at the safe house and the injured members of the Fallen and Dark Forces, she must have had little time to rest, even with Sambethe's help.

"Are you all right?" he asked.

Katrin spoke at the same time. "You seem anxious."

Kev smiled. "You first."

The curl of Katrin's lips only emphasized her weariness. "I am fine. Just tired. After we finish here, I plan to get some sleep."

"Good."

"Your turn."

"I wish I could have prevented that woman's death." Kev sighed. "And I'm also wondering what you've discovered about what's going on with me."

"I cannot offer you much. I can tell you that the drug Adrigon's people gave you is still affecting you. That is my fault, I'm afraid. As a Naphil, you are unable to fight it off as quickly as your fully angelic father. It may take several more days for the drug to work its way out of your system."

Kev had expected as much, but it was a relief to have it confirmed. "Okay. Anything else?"

"Something is still shifting in you. Some of your genes seem to be in flux. It appears your integration with your dragon is not yet complete."

"Can you tell what 'complete' might mean?"

Katrin shook her head.

"Any advice?"

Katrin chuckled. "Not any that you'll like. Be patient."

Kev's lips curled. Seems his mother knew at least a little about him. "I guess I don't have much choice."

"You can fight it or accept it."

Kev nodded. He just hoped he wouldn't have to accept what he feared he might—that he'd never be able to shift to the dragon again.

Aidan came awake to the sound of an indignant voice. "Are you stalking me now?"

He dropped his feet from their prop against the jamb of Bryn's bedroom door. The front legs of his chair hit the floor, and Harley jumped from his lap, chittering in protest.

Aidan stood up and stretched, then moved the chair from in front of the door. "Stalking? No. But there's something you need to know, and I wanted you to hear it from me."

He'd made Lucky promise to say nothing about what they'd discovered on Elsewhere if she saw Bryn before he did. Lucky had not only kept her promise, but had also let him know when Bryn was tucked safely in her room. He'd headed to Zeke's as soon as he could and camped out in Bryn's doorway.

He wanted to reach out and smooth away the tiny frown that wrinkled Bryn's brow.

"What is it?" she asked. "What's happened?"

Aidan shoved a hand back through his hair and blew out a breath. Now that the moment had arrived, he hardly knew what to say. There was no way to break it to her gently.

"You know the woman in Elsewhere, the one who saw Adrigon kill Jahoel?"

Bryn nodded, her frown deepening.

"She's dead. Murdered."

Bryn paled. "When?" The word was barely more than a breath.

"A couple of days ago. Lucky and I found the body. Whoever killed her painted the angelic word for 'Traitor' on the wall with her blood."

Bryn sucked in a breath and sank into Aidan's vacated chair. Elbows on her knees, she rested her face in her hands. "It's my fault. I did this. I told Zeke about her."

Aidan had known she would blame herself. He dropped to a crouch in front of her, pulled her hands from her face, and clasped them in his.

"It is not your fault. Zeke tried to protect her, told her to stay away from the alley. She escaped her guards."

"She wouldn't have wanted to leave the shrine untended." Bryn's eyes filled with tears.

Aidan slid one arm around her shoulders and another under her knees. He scooped her up and sat down on the chair with her in his lap.

Bryn stiffened for just a moment, then she relaxed against him, her head on his shoulder, and wept.

It took some time, but Bryn finally managed to convince the guards to let her enter the alley. One of them insisted on accompanying her.

Their footsteps offered a sad tattoo as they walked toward the now unlit shrine. Bryn took the lighter she'd brought from her bag and lit what candles she could. Then she replaced those that had completely burned away with votives she also pulled from the bag and lit them as well. When she had lit every candle, she stepped back and gazed at the blaze of light.

She glanced up at the guard. "May I have a few minutes alone?" She spread her arms to indicate the space around them. "There's no one here but us. I'll be fine."

The guard scanned the shadows pushed back by the candlelight, and seemingly satisfied, inclined his head. "Only a few minutes. Do not be long."

"I won't," Bryn promised.

The alley had been cleaned of the woman's blood. It no longer pooled in the shadows or marked the wall above where the body had lain. Although Bryn had not seen the woman's body or the bloody word, Aidan's description had painted the scene in her mind. Her mental image now filled in the details that had been scrubbed away.

She swallowed and pulled her attention away from the alley wall and back to the shrine. The now dead woman had tended the shrine ever since Jahoel's murder, had lost her life in part because she refused to leave the shrine unlit, returning to it even after word of her part in determining Adrigon's guilt had leaked and spread. Lighting the shrine had been the one thing Bryn had thought she could do for the woman.

She had lit it not only in honor of Jahoel, but also in honor of the woman who had given her life to tend it. Bryn sank to her knees, remembering how the woman had called her "bird girl" and said she shone brightly too.

If she hadn't found the shrine that night, if the woman hadn't decided to talk to her, if she, in turn, hadn't told Zeke....

Then they would still be looking for proof of Jahoel's killer.

But the woman would be alive.

Bryn sighed. Worrying over the past wouldn't change anything. The woman had helped them. Now she was dead.

At least candles burned on the shrine again.
Bryn heard a slight rustle behind her.
Then pain exploded through the back of her skull.
And everything went black.

CHAPTER 21

A flurry of curses tumbled from Aidan's lips.

"How could she have disappeared?" asked Kev.

"She asked for a few minutes alone." The guard shrugged. "There was no one else in the alley. I could not sense another being."

"You just did what she asked and left her alone?" Aidan bit out the words.

The guard nodded. "I gave her some time, yes. When she did not return to the entrance, I went back to fetch her. She was gone." He held up a cloth bag. "This was still there. She had brought it with her."

Kev took the bag from the guard and emptied out its contents. A few votive candles and a lighter.

Aidan closed his eyes. He should have known. He should have offered to take her to the shrine. He would never have left her alone where that woman had been killed.

"And you heard nothing? Saw nothing? Sensed nothing?" Kev asked the guard.

"No, nothing. Nothing at all." The guard looked stricken. "And that is my Gift."

"I know. That's why I assigned you as guard," Kev said.

"Helel," said Aidan. "If he didn't take Bryn himself, he must have used his protective powers to cloak whoever did."

"Why would they take her?" Kev asked.

Aidan shrugged. "To punish her for the part she played in Lucifer's escape? To show us they have the upper hand?"

Kev shook his head. "That's not enough reason."

"Maybe they found out she was the one who led Zeke to that woman?"

"Maybe." Kev thought for a moment. "But that doesn't explain why they kidnapped her. Why *take* her? Why Bryn?"

Aidan swore again when the realization hit him. "It's the Tree. She has a connection to the Tree. Somehow Adrigon and Helel must have found out about that."

"And they want to use her...," Kev began.

Aidan finished the thought. "To make the Tree release the explosion and finish what they started."

This time they both swore.

If only the room would stop spinning.

With her eyes still closed, Bryn pushed herself up to sitting. Her hand went to the ache at the base of her skull. She winced as her fingers touched the wound. Her short hair felt thick with dried blood.

She took a deep breath and tried opening her eyes again. After a few swirls, her surroundings settled into place.

She sat on a plush bed in a room more luxurious than any she'd ever seen. Rich brocade covered the walls, and thick rugs decorated the marble floors. The ceiling, high above, was painted with images of angels and edged with gold moldings.

Numerous mirrors reflected the room back on itself, making it seem even larger than it was.

It took Bryn a moment to realize the other purpose the mirrors served. They distracted from the fact that the room had no windows.

Where was she? And how had she gotten here? She had a vague memory of doing something in Elsewhere, and then nothing until she'd awakened here. Wherever here was.

A door, cleverly concealed by brocade draping, opened in one of the walls, admitting a white-robed girl carrying a tray. A white scarf covered her hair and wrapped around her throat, the ends trailing down her back.

"You are awake at last," said the girl. Her voice was soft and melodious but curiously absent of emotion.

She placed the tray, which held two golden bowls of steaming, scented water, two folded white cloths, and a few small, brightly colored jars, on a gilded table near the bed.

"Will you allow me to tend to your wound?" she asked.

When Bryn nodded, the girl unfolded a cloth and dipped it into one of the bowls. "Turn your back to me please."

Bryn did as requested. Though it hurt a bit at first, the feel of the warm water and soft cloth gradually soothed her, as if they washed away her pain along with the dried blood.

After patting Bryn's hair and wound dry, the girl smoothed cooling salves from the jars onto the cut. "It should heal quickly now."

Bryn watched as the girl washed her fingers in the second bowl, the first now tinted with Bryn's blood. Then the girl reached for the pillow on which Bryn's head had rested, and which Bryn now saw, her blood had marked. The girl slid the pillow into a sack she removed from the pocket of her robes, then slipped the straps of the sack over her shoulder.

Lifting the tray from the table, she said, "I will return with a clean pillow to replace the soiled one."

"Wait." Bryn rose from the bed as the girl moved toward the door. "Where am I? And why am I here?"

"I will return shortly," the girl said.

The door closed behind her, disappearing into the brocade wall.

As soon as class was over, Lucky transported back to Zeke's, changed clothes, and then zapped herself to the alley across from her grandmother's assisted living facility. She thought a visit with G-Ma might take her mind off her worry for Bryn. Besides, her last visit had been forestalled by the disruption of the Still One's world. Not that she had really gotten to visit with G-Ma then anyway. Lucky hoped that this time she'd find her grandmother awake.

Not only was G-Ma awake, but she was working at her art table. She greeted Lucky with a real smile and spread arms. "Lucky, my dear, come give your G-Ma a hug."

Lucky gladly complied, squeezing her grandmother tightly. "Hi, G-Ma. It's so good to see you."

When she stepped back from the embrace, Lucky looked at the photographs that covered the surface of the drawing table. "What are you working on today?"

"Family pictures. I thought I'd make a collage."

G-Ma picked up one of the photographs, smiling fondly. "Do you remember this?" She handed the photo to Lucky.

"I do!" The photo was of Lucky and Josh as children, playing in the sand at the beach along the shore of Lake Michigan. "We had so much fun that day, building sandcastles and burying each other in the sand."

"What about this one?" G-Ma handed her another photo.

Lucky laughed, as she looked at younger versions of herself, Josh, Uncle Matthew, and Aunt Beth, each holding a jack-o-lantern, while mimicking the carved faces. "Isn't there one of you? You always carved the best pumpkins."

"Probably somewhere in this pile." G-Ma chuckled. "You can help me look for it."

They looked at the family photos, talking and reliving the memories, for well over an hour. Then G-Ma reached out to touch the medallion that swung free when Lucky bent over the art table. "I need some pictures of you and your dragon," G-Ma said.

"My dragon?" Lucky asked.

"Your young man." G-Ma gave her a knowing smile. "Your dragon."

G-Ma had referred to Kev as Lucky's dragon before, though Lucky didn't know how her grandmother could possibly know who, or what, Kev was.

"How do you know?" Lucky asked.

"The same way I know your dragon and I—along with some others—live in you now." G-Ma touched a finger to Lucky's chest, just over her heart.

As Lucky stared into her grandmother's eyes, those eyes shifted. She had seen the change before and had written it off as a trick of the eye or her imagination. This time there was no mistaking it. For a long moment, G-Ma's hazel eyes were replaced by the uncanny cloud-dotted-blue-sky eyes of the Archangel Gabriel.

Of course, the door was locked.

As soon as the girl left, Bryn located the handle hidden in the brocade folds and turned it—to no avail. She hadn't really expected the door to open, but she'd had to try.

Fragments of memories flickered in her mind like candle-light. She grasped at the fleeting images, but they remained just out of reach.

She was sure of one thing though. However she'd come to be in this room, wherever it was, she hadn't come willingly. She figured whoever had brought her here had been the one who gave her the wound the girl had tended.

The dull throb had resumed its beat at the base of her skull, and the pain drew her back to the bed. She lay down on her side, facing the hidden door, and tugged one of the remaining pillows beneath her head.

Why would someone kidnap her and then lock her in such a luxurious prison with a servant to attend her?

It didn't make any sense.

Memory flickered again. Candles. The shrine. She had been at the shrine in the alley. The alley where the woman who had helped them had been killed. And where Jahoel had been killed before her.

Adrigon. He may not have dealt the blow, but she would bet he was behind this.

The door opened again, and Bryn sat up, wincing as the movement heightened the throbbing in her head.

It was only the girl, returning as promised with the replacement pillow. This time the tray she carried held a pitcher of liquid and a goblet.

She set the tray on the table, filled the goblet with the liquid from the pitcher, and handed the goblet to Bryn. "We thought you might be thirsty."

Again, her voice carried no emotion.

Bryn held the goblet but did not drink.

The girl removed the replacement pillow from the sack she carried and placed the pillow on the bed.

"Drink," she said. "I cannot leave the glass and pitcher with you."

Bryn sniffed the liquid in the goblet.

"Water," said the girl.

The girl was right. Bryn was thirsty. She drank.

The girl refilled the goblet. Bryn drank that too.

She thought better of it when her eyelids began to droop.

"And a little something to make you sleep," the girl said.

She took the goblet from Bryn's hand and helped her lay back on the pillows.

Bryn was too sleepy to protest.

Danel's voice rang out over the field, dismissing the group of Fallen and Dark soldiers he and Aidan had been training. Aidan's mind reverted to his concern for Bryn even before the troops had left the field.

The focus required to lead the soldiers through their paces was the only thing that kept his thoughts from continually retreading that well-worn path—was she okay? where could Adrigon have taken her? why couldn't anyone find her no matter what they did? wasn't there something *he* could do? The thought trail always led to the same place: a sense of frustrated helplessness that jacked Aidan's usual nervous energy to stratospheric levels. The inability to sate his desperate need to do something, anything, to find her and bring her back to safety made him feel like he might well vibrate right out of his mind.

"Are you sure you're okay?" Danel asked, not for the first time.

Each time he'd asked the question before, Aidan had put the Dark Forces' young captain off with empty reassurances—*I'm fine. Oh, yeah, no problem.* But this time, for whatever reason, he decided to tell the truth. Maybe because something in the young man's expression said he wouldn't stop asking the question until Aidan gave him an honest answer.

"Not really," Aidan said, rubbing the back of his neck. "I'm worried about my friend Bryn. Adrigon has her—at least, we assume he does—and no one can seem to get a trace on him or her. And all I can do is keep training the troops and wait—and wait and wait."

Danel's lips curved in a sympathetic smile. "You hate feeling helpless."

"Damn straight," Aidan muttered.

Danel nodded. "I understand. Your feelings for your friend are like those I feel about the possibly imminent destruction of my world. When I first came here, I thought my world was already gone. Now, I know there is still hope that it—and the other Dark Realms—may be saved. But I can do nothing to hasten that outcome. All I can do is focus on preparing myself and my troops to face Adrigon and his men when the time comes."

"We think that's why he took her." The words escaped even as Aidan wondered if he should burden Danel with the knowledge. "Bryn, I mean. She's a new Guardian—or training to be one—and she has sort of a special relationship with the Tree."

Danel frowned. "You think Adrigon took her because of this special relationship?"

"Yeah." Aidan sighed. "We think he wants to use her to make the Tree release the explosion."

Danel's expression darkened as understanding dawned. "And complete the destruction of the Dark Realms."

Aidan nodded. "She would never do it willingly. But I understand Adrigon's Gift makes it hard to resist his will. If he forces her to do this—even if he lets her live—I don't know how she'll recover from it. She's from Nadach. She knows what it's like to have your world destroyed."

"Nadach?" Danel frowned. "Your friend Bryn, is she tall, with a white streak in her hair?"

"Yeah." Aidan smiled, remembering how she'd gotten that white streak. "That would be Bryn."

"I met her," Danel said. "She took me to my room and helped me get settled that first day here. But she gave me a different name."

Aidan chuckled. "Branwen?"

"Yes, that's it."

"Bryn's a nickname. She says it's for friends only."

"She was kind to me," said Danel. "May she be returned to us unharmed very soon. I would like, someday, to be counted among those allowed to call her friend."

Bryn jerked awake, feeling something probing at the edges of her mind. Her gaze fell on the two angels seated in elegant armchairs across from the bed, and she was on her feet in an instant.

"I thought that might wake you." Adrigon waved a languid hand toward an empty chair drawn close to his and Helel's. "Sit, please. We have matters to discuss."

Bryn wanted to call her Raven and show them exactly how little interest she had in discussing anything with them. But she needed information too—about where they were holding her and what they wanted from her.

Saying nothing, she took the seat Adrigon indicated.

"I assume you are wondering why we have brought you here," said Adrigon.

That went without saying, thought Bryn. Though what she really wanted to know was how to escape. She made no response.

"You have something we want, you see," Adrigon continued, undeterred by her silence. "And whether you wish to or not"—his lips curved in a cold, confident smile—"you will give us what we want."

Still Bryn said nothing.

Adrigon turned to Helel. "Her silence grows tiresome, don't you think?"

Helel inclined his head. "Yes, Most High, quite tiresome."

Adrigon directed his attention back to Bryn. "Tell us what you are thinking right now."

Again, Bryn felt that probing at the edges of her mind. This time the intrusion delved further. Before she could gather her thoughts, she had begun to speak. "I'm thinking I want to wipe that self-satisfied smirk off your face, and I want you out of my head." Bryn tried to stop the words, but they kept coming. "And I didn't intend to say any of that."

The intrusion left her mind, and she stopped speaking, eyes wide and heart pounding.

"So much better than silence." Adrigon studied her for a moment. "Let's try that again, shall we? And understand that you want to tell me whatever I ask. I have heard you have a rather unique connection to the Tree. Tell me, do you know how to access it? Can you take us there?"

Bryn shook her head as Adrigon intruded into her mind once again. She felt the pull of his suggestion that she wanted to tell him, but the pull wasn't strong enough to sway her. She knew she didn't want to, even as the suggestion wormed into her mind. She pushed against it as hard as she could, and Adrigon's influence withdrew.

"Interesting," Adrigon drawled. "Your powers of resistance are substantial. No matter. You will still tell me what

I ask. The process will just be more painful for you. Now, tell me, can you take us to the Tree?"

This time when Bryn pushed against Adrigon's power inside her head, pain shot through her. But Bryn knew pain; she confronted it every time she shifted to her Raven form. She kept pushing, her heart pounding, her body shaking. Until the pain grew so great, she could no longer focus on anything. She screamed, her resistance crumbling. "Yes," she heard herself whisper. "I know how to access the Tree."

"Good. Very good," Adrigon said. "You see, there is no point in resisting. The more you resist, the more it hurts. And then you do as I want anyway."

Adrigon and Helel stood.

Bryn pushed through the pain that still crowded her being to call her Raven. But even as she started to shift, Adrigon was in her mind. "You do not want to do that, little Raven. There will be no shifting while you are in my custody. Nor will there be any self-harm."

Bryn called her Raven with all her strength. Like before, pain filled her, increasing in intensity until it completely wore away her resistance. Her still-human form crumpled to the floor.

"We have some preparations to make." Adrigon moved toward the door, Helel at his side. "Then you are going to take Helel and me to the Tree and make the Tree do my bidding."

Adrigon stopped at the door and turned to look at Bryn. Pain kept her on the floor, but she found the strength to glare at him.

"With a little Order"—Adrigon tapped the side of his head—"you will make the Tree release the explosion, destroying the Dark Realms just as we intended."

CHAPTER 22

Kev hadn't expected ever to return to the Metatron's council chamber, and certainly not so soon after being stripped of his role as *Ha-Satan*. He had to say he was a lot more comfortable this time around. Not only did he feel less vulnerable—not to mention warmer—in his extra-fire-proof fighting gear than in the ceremonial garb he had worn as *Ha-Satan,* but the guards stationed at the Gates had ushered him through the anteroom and into the council chamber without so much as suggesting a pat-down.

Things were a little different with Margash in charge.

The Archangel Michael, along with those members of the Forces of Light who maintained their loyalty to the Heavens rather than to Adrigon, had managed to quell the initial resistance. And, as word of Adrigon's guilt in Jahoel's murder had spread, more and more of the Heavens' inhabitants had withdrawn their support for him. Kev didn't know if this was due to a lessening of Adrigon's persuasive influence now that he seemed to have disappeared or to the deep-seated loyalty Jahoel had inspired. Either way, the outcome suited Kev fine.

A few holdouts espousing disbelief in Adrigon's guilt remained, but they had mostly fallen silent. Those staunch supporters, who included Tatriel, the former Second of the Metatron, had left the Heavens and, most likely, retreated to Adrigon and Helel's secret location. Like those of their leaders, the supporters' signals could not be tracked. It was as if they had simply disappeared.

Margash had agreed to assume the role of First of the Metatron, and Galiel, whose extreme views seemed to have lessened in Adrigon's absence, had agreed to assume the role of Second, until such time as two or more new members could be named. To distance the new partial Metatron from Adrigon's positions on the Dark and Fallen, Margash had invited Zeke, Malachi, Lucifer, and Kev to the instatement.

"Welcome, Kevin, son of Lucifer." Margash greeted Kev with a smile and a slight inclination of his head.

"Indeed, welcome," said Galiel, in warmer tones than Kev had ever heard from him. He also saluted Kev with the abbreviated ceremonial bow.

Kev returned their greetings and then joined Lucifer and Malachi where they waited by the doors that opened to the wide balcony overlooking the plaza. Soon after, Zeke swept into the room, wearing his ambassadorial ivory robes and bronze breastplate. After exchanging greetings and a few words with Margash and Galiel, he moved to join Kev and the others.

The guards ushered Kev and Malachi to one side of the doors and Zeke and Lucifer to the other. Then they opened the doors, standing aside for Margash and Galiel to step through, Zeke and Lucifer fell in behind them, with Kev and Malachi bringing up the rear. The four Dark and Fallen took their places on either side of the balcony as Margash and Galiel moved to front and center. The crowd in the plaza below cheered.

A brilliant flash lit the plaza, and Uriel appeared on the raised dais in the plaza's center. The Archangel filled the dais, his head rising higher than the balcony on which Kev and the others stood.

Kev noticed the searing touch of the Archangel's words in his mind when Uriel spoke. Otherwise, he paid little heed to the ceremony. His thoughts kept drifting to Bryn and the fate of the Dark Realms. He knew the Guardians, as well as a team made of members from the Forces of Light, Dark, and Fallen were doing all they could to find her and Adrigon and his followers. Still, some part of him couldn't help but feel that his time, as well as Zeke's, Lucifer's, Malachi's, and even Margash's, might have been put to better use. He knew the ceremony was important. The Heavens needed evidence of stable leadership. But if Adrigon managed to use Bryn to destroy the Dark Realms, Margash and Galiel's show of support for the Dark would surely mean little.

They had to find her. For Adrigon to succeed was unthinkable.

Bryn paced the circuit of her luxurious prison, racking her brain for a means of escape. Adrigon seemed to have eliminated all her options. She was stuck in this room, unable to shift to her Raven form. She'd tried, and the pain that resulted had put her back on the floor. She had thought she knew pain. After all, every shift to and from her Raven form hurt. But this pain was unlike anything she'd ever felt.

When she shifted to and from her Raven form, the pain was physical. When she resisted Adrigon's influence, physical pain was the least of what she endured. It was as if her whole being was annihilated, every bit of her crushed and compressed smaller and smaller until nothing remained but the pain of loss and the overwhelming force of Adrigon's will. How could she resist if she no longer existed?

Ceasing to exist, in fact, might have been her best option. In lieu of any other escape, she could have taken her own life to prevent Adrigon from using her as his instrument of destruction.

But he'd taken that option away from her too.

She turned her palms up and activated her sigils, greeting the slight burn with a sense of relief. She wasn't foolish enough to believe the sigils offered her any protection against Adrigon, but knowing he hadn't taken those too gave her some satisfaction.

At the sound of the door opening, she dropped her hands and let the sigils fade away.

It was only the white-robed girl. This time the tray she carried contained something wrapped in cloth as well as a pitcher of water and a glass.

The girl set the tray on the table and folded back the cloth to reveal what looked like a small loaf of bread. She filled the glass with water from the pitcher and then stepped away from the table.

"Eat, drink," she said in her expressionless voice.

Bryn made no move toward the table. "Forgive me if I seem lacking in gratitude, but the last time you offered me water, it was drugged."

"There is nothing in the water or bread," the girl replied. "The drug was to make you sleep so your body could heal itself. It has done so." She gestured toward the table. "Eat."

Bryn wasn't convinced she could trust the girl's word, but she was hungry. She didn't know how long she had been here, had no idea how long the potion had made her sleep, but she needed food. And she doubted that Adrigon would poison her if he intended to use her to complete the destruction of the Dark Realms.

She moved to the table and picked up the bread. The loaf was still warm. She broke a piece off the end, and the appetizing aroma made her mouth water. She put the piece of bread in her mouth and chewed slowly. It tasted as good as it smelled.

Bryn finished the bread and drank the glass of water. When the girl refilled the glass, Bryn drank that water too.

"Good." The girl picked up the tray and moved toward the hidden door. "Rest now if you can. You need to be strong to do the Most High's bidding."

The myriad weapons gleamed in their glass cases.

Lucky wandered among them, trying to reach out with her senses, to see if one would speak to her, call to her, reveal to her its name. She didn't really expect it to happen, but she needed to try all the same. She had convinced Aidan to let her into the weapons room. He'd opened the door for her and then gone to meet Danel to prepare for their next training session.

Alone, Lucky could take all the time she liked, without anyone watching.

She stopped in front of the case of basket-hilted swords that she found so beautiful and turned her senses up to full volume. Nothing. Yes, she could see energy arcing around the weapons, and she could detect the song of each one. But the energy around all of them remained stable, and none of them sang to her.

She moved to the next case and repeated the experiment. With the same result.

She feared she was wasting her time, but she had to try. She needed to do something other than worry about Bryn to occupy the time between classes. Finding her own special weapon would at least give her something to fight with if they ever managed to locate Adrigon.

She sucked in a breath and clenched her fists at her side. She had to believe Bryn was all right. If Adrigon intended to use her special Guardian powers, then he had to keep her safe, didn't he? Otherwise, she wouldn't be of any use to him, right?

Lucky clung to that hope as she moved to the next case of weapons. As well as to the hope that Bryn could withstand Adrigon's attempts to bend her to his will. Bryn was strong and, as Aidan had pointed out not so long ago, no stranger to pain. Surely, she could hold out against Adrigon until they were able to find her.

Of course, those searching for any trace of Bryn—or Adrigon or Helel or any of Adrigon's followers—were having no better results than Lucky was in her search for her weapon.

Maybe that was why she had come here.

If she could get the weapons room to reveal her special weapon, maybe she could also believe the trackers and energy tracers would finally yield some sign of Bryn.

The time had come.

Panic gripped Bryn's heart as Adrigon led her through the brocade-draped door, Helel hard on their heels. Fear of what she was about to be forced to do overshadowed her curiosity about what was on the door's other side. Not that she could see anything anyway. Helel had blindfolded her with a thick, though mercifully soft, cloth before Adrigon opened the door.

He'd also bound her hands.

Bryn decided to view the blindfold as a positive sign. If they meant to kill her after she'd done their bidding, surely, they wouldn't be concerned about what she saw. Then again, if they really did force her to make the Tree release the explosion and destroy the Dark Realms, she would welcome her own death.

She held out hope that she would be able to resist Adrigon's compulsion, but her failure to do so thus far fed the dread that pooled in her veins.

She stumbled when the path Adrigon pulled her along began to incline. His grip on her arm tightened painfully as he held her upright.

"Uphill," he snapped.

You could have mentioned that earlier, Bryn thought, though she refrained from comment.

She quickly developed a sense of the angle of incline. But she stumbled twice more when Adrigon failed to warn her of changes in footing. Each time his hold on her tightened. Bryn could feel the bruises even if she couldn't see them.

She had barely noticed the change in temperature as they climbed, but when Adrigon drew her to a halt, she realized the air was several degrees warmer than it had been when they first exited her room. She heard a sliding, scraping sound which she assumed indicated the opening of another door. An inrush of fresh air confirmed her assumption.

Adrigon pulled her through that door, and she heard it slide closed behind them. Then Adrigon gripped both her arms, and she felt the everywhere-nowhere sensation of transporting. When they rematerialized, Adrigon finally released her.

"You will take us to the Tree now," he ordered.

Bryn fought against the command until the pain buckled her knees. The key to the Tree was the deepest secret, the most sacred teaching, Eleni had given her. Bryn had sworn to use it only to protect and guard the Tree. She would not violate that promise, she could not.

But just as before, the pain dissolved her ability to resist. She had to do what Adrigon asked, but she didn't have to reveal how she did it. She bit her lip hard enough to draw the blood required to activate the key and thought, instead of speaking, the sacred words.

She felt the slight electrical charge as the magic began to take hold, and then the rising of the wind. What Adrigon and Helel didn't know, couldn't know, was that instead of taking them to the Tree, she would bring the Tree to them.

She heard them both gasp at the very moment she felt the inner alignment signaling the Tree's presence.

"Untie my hands," she said, her words just as much an order as Adrigon's had been.

One of them did as she asked. As soon as her hands were free, she removed the blindfold.

And there it was. The huge tree she had first seen on the windswept rocky plain in the Place of the Book. The same wind whipped around them here.

She pushed through the wind toward the tree, Adrigon and Helel close behind. When the sword appeared, she held out her hands. The blade sliced across her palms and disappeared.

"Do it," said Adrigon. "Make the Tree release the explosion. Do it!"

Bryn moved toward the Tree, heart pounding, tears streaking her face. She leaned into it, pressing her entire length, except for her bloodied palms, against the bark. "Help me," she whispered. "Don't let me hurt the Dark Realms. Don't let me hurt you."

Only then did she press her palms to the Tree. Just as before, the Tree absorbed her blood, suctioning her hands to the bark. Her sigils activated, and she felt the Tree drawing her energy through her palms.

"Do it!" yelled Adrigon.

"Help me," she whispered again. "Please help me."

And then she was falling through blackness, into the Tree, into its depths, into the heart of it all. And she dissolved again, not into pain, but into the Tree, spreading out through its veins and arteries and branches.

And then she was there, at what had once been the nexus that had housed the Halls and was now an enormous knot of roots and branches surrounding the explosion that roiled like a sun in its center. Bryn felt the fire of that explosion pushing outward, felt the force of the Tree holding it in.

"Release the explosion," she said, because she had to, because Adrigon willed it.

"Help me," she said, because she couldn't let Adrigon win.

And the Tree whispered, "Help me."

And the words vibrated through whatever remained of Bryn and echoed in the veins and arteries and branches of the Tree. "Help me, help me, help me."

And the Tree reached out and Bryn reached out. For help, for strength, for the Guardians, and for the Singer of the Song.

CHAPTER 23

One minute Aidan was leading the troop through the last exercise of the session, and the next he couldn't say where he was—perhaps in a waking dream.

Instead of blue sky and the grassy training field, he saw flashes of light and shadow that gradually resolved into glowing roots and branches, spreading and intertwining, each humming its own unique melody.

So many songs singing together should have sounded cacophonous, but Aidan could hear the distinct beauty of each one. He loved each light, each branch, each song. No, more than that. He *was* each light, each branch, each song. They belonged to him, and he belonged to them. They were he, and he was they. But the fire was coming. And they had to save themselves.

"Help me." The words whispered beneath the melodies. "Help me, help me, help me." And the voice that spoke the words was Bryn's.

The songs took him by surprise, ripping from his throat without his conscious volition. So many songs. Too many to be possible. His vocal cords burned, tore, shredded. Pain spiked through his arms, legs, and torso. But he sang. He couldn't have stopped even if he had had the will to. The songs had chosen him. He had no choice but to sing.

The multitude of notes flowing from his mouth arced and twisted. And in the vastness of his stolen vision, the glowing branches flickered and reformed, twining and interweaving around a gigantic ball of fire. The fire expanded, outward and outward, but still he sang until he could no longer see the fireball, so intricately entwined were the roots and branches around it. And he kept singing, adding branch upon branch.

And he continued to sing as the fire filled the branches, filled the roots, filled him.

"Help me," Bryn whispered.

And Aidan sang on, though the notes were like flames in his throat. The songs sang through him until he was no more, and only the fire and the songs remained.

Lucky heard the singing as soon as she left the weapons room. The sound was the most complex, multilayered, and eerily beautiful that she'd ever heard. She knew its source immediately.

"Aidan!"

She raced down the hall, through the gym, and onto the training field, pushing her way through the crowd of soldiers and trainees that surrounded the source of the song.

Then she stopped, as stunned and speechless as the others, her gaze locked on Aidan's body, where it hovered a few feet above the ground.

Though "hovered" might not have been the right word. Aidan's body hovered only in the sense that it defied gravity.

It certainly did not convey any sense of effortless floating. The only time Lucky had seen anything look as effortful was when she had watched Kev's body arching and twisting, flashing between human and dragon, when she had helped his two halves integrate.

Aidan's back was arched, his hands clenched, his muscles rigid with effort. His head was thrown back, his mouth wide, his throat stretched, as if the sounds he emitted were pulled from inside him by an external force.

Desperate to know, Lucky flipped on her extra senses, turning them up just a little. She knew better than to go all out. She was almost overwhelmed using her normal human senses.

Even with her extra senses set to low, what she saw took her breath away. Aidan's body wasn't levitating. It was impaled on a tree, a great glowing, pulsing tree, whose branches pierced Aidan's legs and feet, arms and hands, torso and throat. The multicolored light pulsing through the tree pulsed through Aidan too. And all the notes streamed from his mouth in colors and symbols that poured back into the tree, changing the rhythm of its pulsing colors.

Then all the colors turned to flame, burning through the tree and Aidan's body. Only the notes pouring from his mouth and back into the tree didn't burn.

It was beautiful and brutal. And Lucky couldn't look away.

Then the flames died, Aidan stopped singing, and the tree disappeared, dropping Aidan's body to the ground.

Lucky rushed forward and fell to her knees at his side.

She whispered his name, brushed his hair back from his forehead, pressed her fingers into his wrist to check his pulse. His skin was hot beneath her hands, his pulse thready, his breathing so shallow she could barely detect the rise and fall of his chest.

"How is he?" Miguel sank to a crouch on Aidan's other side.

"He needs Katrin," Lucky said.

"Help me," Bryn murmured.

A cool hand touched her forehead, her cheek. "It's all right," a soft voice said. "You're safe now."

Bryn knew she should recognize that voice, but she couldn't quite place it. She forced her eyelids to open.

Eleni smiled down at her. "Welcome back."

"W-where am I?"

"At the Guardians' Headquarters, in the healing wing."

Bryn tried to push herself up and gasped at the pain in her hands. Eleni pressed her back against the pillows. "Rest. You're still weak. You will be for a while."

Bryn lifted her hands, saw that they were both bandaged.

"What happened?" she asked.

She remembered merging with the Tree, reaching for the Guardians, reaching for Aidan. She remembered Aidan's song, the growing roots and branches surrounding the explosion, and then fire, so much fire. Her hands had burned where they pressed against the Tree.

"You did what Guardians do," said Eleni. "You protected the Tree."

"How did you find me?"

"We had been looking for you, for any sign of you, since Adrigon took you from Elsewhere. While we could find no trace of you or Adrigon or Helel, we felt you call the Tree. We followed the Tree to you."

"And Adrigon?"

Eleni shook her head. "He and Helel got away. As soon as we materialized, they transported. We were unable to track them."

"But the Tree is all right? What about the Dark Realms?"

"The Tree is safe, if wounded, and the Dark Realms are fine. Thanks to you—and your friend. You helped the Tree absorb the explosion. That's why your hands are burned."

"And Aidan?" Again, Bryn tried to sit up, but her weakened body refused to cooperate. If she, one with Cherub blood, a Guardian in training, who was meant to exchange energy with the Tree, had been so affected, what might Aidan have suffered? "How is he? Where is he? I want to see him."

"You will see him soon enough. Give yourself a bit more time to recover. Then Zeke will take you home."

Eleni had not answered her question about Aidan's condition, but before Bryn could press her mentor further, Eleni rose from her perch on the side of Bryn's bed. She held on to the bed for a moment, as if she might lose her balance.

"Are you all right?" Bryn asked.

Eleni nodded. "Just weakened. I, like all the Guardians, lent my energy to the Tree too."

"Oh," said Bryn. Eleni's comment only increased her concern for Aidan.

"I will leave you now," said Eleni. "Someone else is waiting to see you."

She exited the room, and Zeke stepped inside. He too appeared weakened. But a smile lit his face when he looked at Bryn. He crossed the room and bent to press a kiss to her forehead.

"How are you feeling, my dear?" His voice rumbled warmth all around her.

"I've been better." She smiled. "Also, worse."

Zeke chuckled. "You were very brave, and I am very proud of you, my granddaughter."

Bryn's eyes filled with tears. "How is Aidan?"

"He struggles. He is neither Cherub nor Guardian."

Bryn choked back a sob. "I didn't intend to hurt him. But when the Tree—we—reached out to him, it seemed the right thing to do. We—the Tree—and I—needed him."

"I know." Zeke stroked her hair. "You did what you had to do."

Bryn took little comfort in the words. She may have done what she had to do, but the fact remained that she was responsible for what had happened to Aidan. She couldn't rest easy until she knew she had caused him no lasting harm.

Despite his worry for his brother, a smile curved Kev's lips at the sight of a sleeping Lucky curled up in the chair next to Aidan's bed.

He leaned down and dropped a kiss beside her ear. "Hey, sleeping beauty."

Lucky's eyelids fluttered. Then she smiled. "Hey."

Kev trailed his knuckles over the softness of her cheek. "Go get some real sleep. I'll stay with him for a while."

"Are you sure? You just got home. You must be tired too."

"I'm fine. I don't need as much sleep as most Nephilim."

"What with being three-quarters Seraph and all." Lucky grinned. "Show off."

"It has its perks." Kev took her hands and drew her to her feet. "Seriously, you've hardly left his side for days. Go lie down for a while." He followed her gaze to where Aidan lay, still and pale as death. "I'll wake you if there's any change."

Lucky's fingers tightened around Kev's, but she kept her eyes on Aidan. "I keep seeing him, impaled on the Tree and singing colored flames. It reminded me of you flashing back and forth between human and dragon, in so much pain."

"He'll come out of it. Just like I did." Kev offered the reassurance as much for his own sake as Lucky's. Aidan appeared hardly to breathe. Looking at his unnaturally still form, it was far too easy to imagine the worst.

Katrin had assured them Aidan's body was healing—just much more slowly than usual for a Naphil. That slowness, Zeke had explained, was due to how much of Aidan's energy the Tree had taken. It was unheard of for an angel or Naphil without Cherub blood to unite with the Tree in such a way. Aidan had done something remarkable, but that act was not without cost.

Three days. Zeke and Eleni refused to let Bryn return to the earthly realm for three whole days. At first, the weakness of her body reinforced their proscription. By the third day, however, Bryn felt well enough to leave her bed in the healing wing. If she could walk about the Guardian's Headquarters, she reasoned, she should be perfectly capable of transmitting back to Zeke's. Eleni disagreed. And Zeke sided with Eleni.

Though Bryn chafed against their orders, she respected them both enough to comply. Even so, she arose so early on the morning of the fourth day that she was already impatient by the time Zeke knocked at her door.

She had reluctantly given in when he insisted on transporting her rather than allowing her to transport herself. The unsteadiness of her legs upon rematerializing in the Chicago brownstone made her grateful for his insistence. She leaned on him for support as they made their way to Aidan's room.

Lucky and Kev were both sitting with Aidan, and both greeted her with warm embraces. She wondered if they knew she was responsible for Aidan's condition. In any case, they offered no resistance when she asked for some time alone with him.

She sat down on the bed beside him and took his hand in hers. His skin felt cool to the touch, and the pulse at his wrist beat a slow rhythm.

"I'm sorry, Aidan." She traced the lines on his palm with her fingertip. "I didn't know what else to do. When the Tree reached out to you, it seemed like the right thing, the only way. I didn't know it would—do this to you."

She nearly sobbed at his lack of response. Some part of her had hoped—even believed—he'd wake up for her.

She pulled off her boots and lay down beside him. Finding his hand again, she threaded their fingers together. Tears leaked onto her pillow until she fell asleep.

Only when he awoke to the streamers of light and the sensation of song did he realize he had been drifting without awareness for a time he could not name. Nor could he name himself, who or what he was. He sensed there had been something before the timeless drifting unawareness, but the memory of that something lingered just out of reach.

Now, he knew only the sea of light in which he floated and the ribbons of song that surrounded him, enveloped him, held him afloat.

And something else. Warmth, giving shape to his space.

The streaks of light dimmed, and the songs faded as the warmth increased, solidifying his sense of the shape of himself, of his body. And, finally, concentrating in a single spot on that body. In his—what was the word? Palm. Yes, in the palm of his hand.

Aidan sucked in a lungful of air as he came fully awake, and the rawness of his throat warred with the small fire in his left palm for attention.

"Aidan?"

Bryn. He turned his head toward the sound of her voice. She lay on the bed beside him. It was her hand in his that burned. He lifted their linked hands, loosening his fingers enough to slightly part their palms. Both their sigils had activated. But Bryn's burned brighter. He could feel her energy licking at his palm, slipping up his arm to his heart, strengthening him.

Bryn gasped when she saw the small flames. "I'm sorry."

She tried to pull her hand away, but Aidan tightened his fingers on hers, flattening their palms together.

"I don't want to hurt you again," Bryn said.

"Not hurting." The words came out on a croak, each syllable sawing his throat like a dull blade. "Helping."

"Helping?"

He nodded. "Don't let me," he rasped, "take too much."

"Too much what?" Bryn whispered.

But Aidan's eyes had fluttered shut, even though his hand remained locked against hers.

Only then did she feel it. The tug at her palm. Similar to how the Tree took her energy, but much gentler.

She settled back against the pillow, focusing on her sigil, opening the flow of energy through her palm. "You can't take too much, Aidan. What I have I give freely." She had been the cause of his injury. The very least she could do was be an instrument of his healing.

CHAPTER 24

"It seems oddly quiet," Kev said.

Lucky agreed. As far as celebrations went, the party in Elsewhere was subdued. Though the strains of music and the delicious smells of various foods permeated the air, the gathering lacked the raucousness usual for such an event.

She stopped at one of the food tables, arrested by the intriguing-looking fruits on display. "I guess it's hard to go all out rejoicing in the salvation of your worlds when you still can't get home because the pathways used to transport there aren't working."

Lucky plucked a bright purple fruit from a small basket. The slight pebbling of the skin reminded her of an orange, but the flesh gave to the touch like a ripe stone fruit. "Do you know what this is? Is it safe for me to eat?"

"It's safe." Kev selected a spiny dark green specimen. "It's a midnight plum, and that one looks perfectly ripe. This is called a horned melon. It's not at all like what we think of as melons though."

With his dagger he cut off the end of the longest protrusion and then sliced through its base, removing it from the fruit. He slurped the pulp from inside the spine and then inserted the narrow end into the soft fruit his knife had exposed, making a kind of straw. He held the straw up to Lucky's mouth. "Try this first. The plum is sweeter."

The pulpy liquid tasted tart, like some combination of lemon, lime, berry, and cucumber. "That's good," she said, and Kev offered her another sip.

"Now try the plum," he said.

She bit into the fruit, and her mouth exploded with sweetness. "Oh, it's like blackberry pie! Delicious!"

Kev bent his head and licked the dribbling juice from her chin, before planting a kiss on her lips. "You're delicious," he said and kissed her again.

Lucky leaned into the kiss, her free hand sliding around to his back to pull him close.

"You do remember you're here to ensure peace is kept, right?"

Lucky drew away from Kev and looked up into Josh's laughing brown eyes. She raised her eyebrows and shifted her gaze deliberately from the pastry her cousin held in one hand to his other hand which clasped one of Ben's.

Josh, just as deliberately, bit into his pastry.

Ben laughed. "All quiet in the fourth quadrant. Looks like the same is true in the third."

"Yes," said Kev. His arm, still around Lucky's waist, tightened briefly before he released her. "Though we should keep moving. We'll head back to the first quadrant."

"And we'll take the second," Ben said. "Alert us if you run into any trouble—or anything too fabulous to miss."

Kev chuckled. "You do the same."

"See you later." Lucky waved as Josh and Ben moved off into the crowd.

She finished her plum and wiggled her sticky purple fingers. "I should wash this before my fingers become permanently glued together."

"There's a fountain in a small plaza down this way." Kev's hand moved to the small of her back to guide her between the tables and stalls. "You can rinse your hand there."

Lucky wondered why she didn't remember any fountain. Her question was answered when they reached the plaza. The fountain wasn't large or ornate, just a burble of water spilling from the mouth of a bull's head mounted onto the wall of a building on the far side of the plaza. The water splashed onto the paving stones and drained through a recessed grate.

She left Kev watching the festivalgoers and walked across the mostly empty plaza to the fountain. She wet her hands in the cool water and scrubbed away the purple stickiness.

Finished, she turned from the fountain, shaking water droplets from her hands, and stopped dead. Helel and Adrigon stood a few feet from her. Just beyond them, the air shimmered. She could see Kev talking to someone at the plaza's edge, but it was as if she were looking through water.

She called Kev's name, but he didn't turn. Her voice seemed to bounce back at her, echoing inside the shimmering chamber that surrounded her, Adrigon, and Helel. The smile that curved Helel's lips chilled her blood.

"What do you want?" She reached out for Adrigon's mind even as she spoke.

Her Gift hit a wall just as surely as had her voice.

Adrigon shook his head and tutted, as if disappointed in her. "You did not think I would come to you unprepared? I know your power. I felt it in the Halls, remember? As to what I want, that would be the amulet you wear around your neck. And you, I believe, want to give it to me."

He held out his hand like he expected her to place the amulet into it, and she felt his power probing at the edges of her mind. She pushed against it with everything she had, and the mental intrusion dropped, along with his hand.

"Interesting." His face hardened. "In that case..."

He moved so quickly. Before Lucky had an inkling of his intentions, he'd grabbed her, one iron-hard arm trapping her own arms against her sides, as his other hand ripped the chain from her neck. In an instant, he again stood beside Helel, dropping her locket and the Light-Bringer's Medallion from the broken chain into his palm.

He gave the locket a cursory glance and tossed it aside, then closed his hand around the amulet. "Thanks for this." He and Helel disappeared, leaving his mocking words hanging in the air.

Lucky looked to where he had tossed her locket in time to see it roll into the recess beneath the fountain and drop through the grate.

He floated in a sea of healing warmth. Heat and energy pulsed into his palm, filling him and surrounding him. He breathed it in, let it seep through his skin and bones into his core. He drank deeply, drawing it into him, taking what his damaged body needed to be whole again. The warmth flowed through him, and through him, and through him.

Aidan opened his eyes, something in him aware that something had changed, though he couldn't say exactly what. Then he felt it, or rather, the lack of it. Bryn's energy no longer burned into his palm.

"Bryn!"

His voice did not rasp his throat as it had before. Nor did it rouse Bryn. She lay, pale and unmoving, at his side.

Aidan swore. "I told you not to let me take too much." He ran his hand over her arm, her throat, her face. She felt cool to the touch. "Gods, Bryn, what have you done? What have *I* done?"

He gathered her into his arms and began to sing.

At least, that's what he meant to do. But his breath carried no sound. The notes he needed wouldn't come. Like words on the tip of the tongue, they were there but not there. He felt them, waiting to be sung, but he couldn't quite grasp them. They remained stubbornly out of reach.

Seven hells.

Aidan slipped his arms from around Bryn's limp body, releasing her to the pillow's embrace. He didn't want to leave her, but if he couldn't help her, he had to find someone who could.

"They have to be somewhere in Elsewhere." Kev's grip on Lucky's hand tightened as he drew her closer to him. "They took Bryn from here, and now they've attacked Lucky here. They can't be that far away."

"Not necessarily. They could have tracked Bryn and Lucky here," Ben said. "Bryn first, once they found out about her abilities with the Tree. They might have decided to take the medallion from Lucky only after Bryn and Aidan foiled their original plan."

"True." Ben had a point, even if Kev did find it more than a little disturbing. He really didn't like the idea of Adrigon, Helel, and their minions keeping tabs on Lucky—or Bryn, for that matter. He released Lucky's hand and wrapped his arm around her instead, tucking her against his side.

"Why would Adrigon want the medallion anyway?" Lucky pulled away from him enough to look up at him. "It connects me with you, but..."

Kev cursed. Gods, how had it taken Lucky's words to remind him that it was the medallion that kept each of them aware of when the other needed help? Until they got it back, he wasn't letting her leave his sight.

Josh raised his hand. "Didn't you tell me that the medallion enhances the power of the person who wears it? Zeke said that was why the Archangels made the medallion for Lucifer in the first place, right, when he went off to rule the Dark realms as the Light-Bringer?"

"I'd forgotten about that. It's become so much a part of me since then..." Lucky's voice trailed off, and a frown wrinkled her brow.

"What?" Kev asked.

She shook her head. "Nothing. Just thinking."

"Well, you can keep thinking while we check in with Margash's team. I want the trackers who are looking for

Adrigon and Helel to double down on their efforts in Elsewhere. Ben could be right. Adrigon and Helel could have tracked you and Bryn from anywhere. But my gut tells me they're close, and I'm not going to ignore that." Kev looked at Ben and Josh. "We shouldn't be too long. You two keep the party safe until we get back."

"You got it," said Ben.

Kev wrapped his arms even more tightly around Lucky and transported them both to Elsewhere's Gates. Lucky was about to get her first glimpse of the Heavens.

"Stop fussing over me." Aidan resisted the impulse to push Katrin's hands away from his throat. "Bryn's the one who needs help."

"I have done everything I can do for her. She is too far gone for my skills to pull her back. But she will remain stable until Malachi can get here."

Katrin lifted a scalpel from a tray of instruments and drew the blade across the tip of her finger. "Heal me," she ordered.

Aidan stared at Katrin's outstretched hand, watched the blood well on her finger. He closed his hand around hers, opened his mouth, but only a whisper of sound escaped. "I can't." He released her hand, letting his own fall to his lap. "I can't sing."

Katrin wiped the blood from her finger with a clean cloth. "Bryn's life energy restored yours. But she couldn't restore your Gift. The Tree took it all, drained you. You will recover, but it may be some time before you can sing again."

She sounded so matter of fact. Katrin wasn't one to waste energy on useless worry. Aidan, on the other hand, felt like he could jump out of his skin. Bryn's life was in jeopardy, and his Gift had deserted him. "Where is Malachi anyway? Can't he get away?"

"He is in the Heavens with Margash and his team. They may have a lead on Adrigon's location. Since Malachi and his crows have some skill in tracking, he is needed there. I told him he need not rush."

"What?!" Aidan almost knocked his chair over in his haste to get out of it. "Of course, he needs to rush. She's trapped between life and death. Death, Katrin! I am not going to let her die just because we have a lead on Adrigon's whereabouts."

Katrin raised an eyebrow and gave him a look that reminded him she had been a General in the Forces before she became a healer. "As I believe I have already said, I have stabilized her condition. She will not worsen before Malachi arrives."

Aidan blew out a breath and raked a hand through his hair. "You're right. I know he'll get here as soon as he can." He sighed again. "I just—I can't lose her too."

Katrin squeezed his shoulder. "You're not going to lose her, Aidan. *We're* not going to lose her. Malachi will be here soon, and he'll bring her back."

Lucky sat in the hall outside Bryn's room, watching Aidan pace in front of the closed door. Malachi was in there with

Bryn, walking between the worlds to retrieve her from death, just as he'd done for Lucky all those months ago.

"Is this what you did when Malachi had to come after me?" she asked.

Aidan stopped pacing, leaned his back against the wall, and then slid down until he sat on the floor across from her. "Yeah. Until Kev dragged me downstairs for tea with threats of Zeke's wrath if I wore a hole in his rug. And I spent some time in the gym."

Lucky chuckled. "Want to go down for tea now? Or to the gym?"

Aidan shook his head. "I want to be here when Malachi brings her back."

"Yeah. I get that." Lucky had no doubt about Aidan's feelings for her cousin. Her golden-haired friend wore his heart on his sleeve.

"So, Adrigon has the Light-Bringer's Medallion now?" Aidan asked.

Lucky sighed and leaned her head back against the wall. "He does. And now Kev is afraid to leave me alone. He only let me come back from Margash's war room without him because I came with Malachi. It's like he thinks I'm helpless without the medallion. I've gotten pretty used to it myself, but still..."

"He doesn't think you're helpless," Aidan said. "But the medallion warned him if you needed him. Now he won't have that warning."

Lucky's eyes filled with tears. "And neither will I. It warned me about him too." She wiped the tears from her eyes with the heels of her hands. "Damn Adrigon anyway. As if it wasn't enough for him to steal the medallion, he had to go and throw my locket down a drain. The locket didn't mean anything to him, but it meant something to me. Wearing it kept G-Ma and my mother close to me, and he took that away from me too."

"He didn't take your mother and grandmother away from you, Lucky. They're with you no matter what. You don't need the locket to hold on to them."

Lucky squeezed her eyes shut as more tears burned. She remembered what G-Ma had told her after the Making: *My life is in you now.* Lucky had never really known her mother, but she knew she was somehow with her too—even if the locket with her picture was gone. "I know, but I still want it back."

"Has the lead on Adrigon's location panned out at all?"

"Not yet. But the trackers are adjusting their methods, and Malachi sent some crows to Elsewhere to see if they can find something angels and Nephilim can't."

"They just might. Those birds of his are something else."

Lucky nodded. She hoped the crows turned up something. Just as she hoped Malachi would find Bryn.

In the meantime, all she—and Aidan—could do was wait.

She could also worry about the fact that the medallion was now in Adrigon's hands. If the amulet increased the wearer's power, that not only meant her powers would be weaker than they had been while she'd worn it—and she had worn it ever since she'd been Made Naphil—but also that Adrigon's powers would be stronger.

"We couldn't defeat Adrigon when he didn't have the medallion. How can we hope to do it now?"

Aidan's blue eyes blazed into hers. "You can't think like that, Lucky. If we give up, he's already won. We have to defeat him. And we will—no matter who has the medallion. We'll find Adrigon, Helel, and the others, or they will eventually come out of hiding. And we'll end this."

Lucky wanted to share Aidan's conviction. And she did, really, if she could get past how defeated Adrigon's theft of the medallion made her feel. She had come to think of the amulet as almost a part of her, and yet he'd taken it with such ease, as if she had no claim on it at all. For some reason, Adrigon's possession of the medallion made her doubt nearly everything she'd held to be true about herself.

But that was what Adrigon wanted her to feel, wasn't it? He wanted her doubt to undermine her power.

She wasn't about to give him that satisfaction.

She latched on to the anger that flared, feeling her palm sigils heat in response. "You're right," she said. "We'll end this. And soon. Adrigon won't know what hit him."

She was, and she wasn't.

She was flashes of light, snatches of song, aches of emotion, and awareness that stretched into branches and roots. Worlds beyond worlds. Beyond words.

She wasn't, and she was.

And when she was, she dreamed she weighed no more than one of the black feathers from her Raven wings. And yet she was immense, free of her physical body and its shifting forms. Held aloft by a sea that surrounded her, filled her, bathed her in the deepest, truest love she'd ever known.

And she was the sea.

And the sea was the Tree.

And all its branches were her fingers and its roots her toes.

The voice came as a surprise.

Though maybe it wasn't a voice. She didn't exactly hear it. It was more like something spoke directly into her awareness. A sense of sound, of feeling, of words. Repeating. Until she finally grasped their meaning.

You must go back.

Back where?

Memories flooded through her. Lilith and Nadach. Jaime and Alicia. Lucky. Aidan. Zeke. The Fallen. The Tree and the Guardians. Adrigon. The Tree again. And Aidan. And the Tree. And Aidan. And Aidan. And Aidan.

Had she saved him?

You must go back and see, said the ocean that surrounded her and was her.

Yes, she replied. Yes.

And suddenly she found herself on a hilltop, beneath a tree filled with crows and awash in all the colors of sunset. Malachi stood before her, the sunset glow reflected in his amber eyes, his hand outstretched.

"Are you ready to return?" he asked.

"Yes," she said again and took his offered hand.

CHAPTER 25

The door closed, shutting out Lucky's, Jaime's, and Alicia's voices. The silence fell like balm on Aidan's ears. Jaime and Alicia had joined his and Lucky's vigil shortly before Malachi had reported Bryn's safe return. Consequently, Bryn's room had been a little too crowded for Aidan's taste—until now.

He moved from where he'd been standing at the foot of the bed to perch on the mattress beside Bryn.

"Don't think I don't appreciate what you did for me." He took Bryn's hand and threaded his fingers between hers. "But don't ever do that again."

"It was my fault you were hurt. I did what I could to help." Bryn's voice still sounded weak, but Aidan knew she was on the way to healing.

He raised their joined hands to brush his lips across her fingers. "You let me take too much of your life force. I almost *killed* you. Promise me you'll never sacrifice yourself like that again."

Bryn shook her head. "I can't promise that. Not if you're in danger again and I can do something about it."

"Gods, Bryn! Your life for mine is not a trade I'm okay with. When I woke up and you—" Aidan's voice broke. "I tried to sing you back, and I couldn't. I couldn't sing. The notes wouldn't come. I thought I'd lost you." He didn't try to hide the tears in his eyes. "I don't want to lose you, Bryn. I can't lose you."

And he wasn't the only one getting emotional. He could see tears glistening in Bryn's eyes too. "I can't lose you either," she whispered.

He released her hand to pull her into his embrace, breathed in the scent of her hair. "Then I guess we'll just have to keep each other safe, won't we?"

"How was class?" Bryn asked. "Did you tell Dominique I can't wait to get back?"

Lucky flopped into an armchair across from the sofa on which Bryn half-reclined, Lilith at her blanket-covered feet. "I did. She said she knew you must be impatient to return. She also said to tell you not to expect her to give you any special treatment, even if you are something of a hero and all."

Bryn shook her head, looking embarrassed, and Lucky grinned. "You are, you know. You saved the Tree, despite Adrigon's hold on you. And then you saved Aidan. That seems pretty heroic to me."

"I just did what needed to be done."

"Which is what it means to be a hero, don't you think?" Lilith patted Bryn's feet. "To do what must be done, no matter the consequences to yourself. I always knew you had it in you, even if you didn't know it."

Pink tinted Bryn's cheeks, and she waved her hand in a way that reminded Lucky of Lilith. "Enough about me." Bryn turned to Lucky. "Tell me about your encounter with Adrigon. Aidan said Adrigon had to take the medallion from you, that he couldn't persuade you to give it to him. Is that true?"

Lucky's hand rose instinctively to where the medallion and locket used to rest on her chest. She could feel their absence as a kind of phantom limb. "Yes. I could feel him trying to get into my head, and I pushed back as hard as I could. I think that pissed him off. The next thing I knew he'd grabbed me and ripped the chain with the medallion and my locket off my neck." She frowned. "He was able to block me too. He said something about being prepared to face my Gift."

Lilith tilted her head. "Your Gifts *are* related. The Gift of Madness allows you to influence thoughts and emotions, especially emotions and their intensity. It also gives you the ability to see how those thoughts and emotions are both separate and intertwined, and to alter the connections between them."

"Exactly!" Lucky leaned forward in her chair. "That's how I was able to help Kev with his dragon." She lost some of her excitement, remembering what else she'd done with her Gift. "And to hurt William and his father the night they attacked us."

Lilith nodded. "The Gift of Order is similar. It allows Adrigon to influence thoughts and emotions, but more by implanting a thought and linking that thought with a desire. In other words, he can make people want what he wants them to want."

"And if you resist, it hurts," said Bryn. "A lot."

"Like how it might feel if you didn't answer when Zeke summoned you?" Lucky asked.

"No." Bryn shook her head. "I mean, I've never resisted Zeke's summons, and I know the need to be where he wants you to be gets stronger if you don't go. But that feels—I don't know—maybe something like an itch. What Adrigon does"—her gaze dropped as she again shook her head—"I've never felt anything like it. It hurts so much it's like you don't even exist anymore. You stop resisting because there's no you left to resist."

Lilith looked from Bryn to Lucky, lips pursed. "I get the feeling most people don't even try to resist. That you both did—with remarkable degrees of success, I might add—must tell us something."

"Besides the fact that they both inherited their grandmother's stubbornness?" Zeke followed his comment into the room and dropped into the remaining armchair.

"Eavesdropping, Ezekiel?" Lilith asked.

Lucky envied her grandmother's ability to speak volumes with the lift of one elegantly arched eyebrow.

Zeke chuckled. "Not intentionally, Lilith. I could not help but overhear."

"You do have a point though." Lilith pursed her lips. "I am the common thread here. Could their mixed blood provide them with some protection against Adrigon's Gift?"

Zeke drummed his fingers on the chair arm. "It very well might. I have studied all the records on Adrigon's Gift Margash has been able to obtain. Nothing hints at resistance from any of those he is believed to have influenced. But they are all full-blooded angels."

"Which makes sense, given Adrigon's hatred for those of us with mixed blood. And I guess Bryn and I are about as mixed as you can get." The irony curled Lucky's lips. "It seems only fitting, really, that what Adrigon thinks of as our impurity would weaken his power over us."

"Indeed." Zeke's gray eyes caught and held Lucky's. "I am beginning to see why Sambethe was so insistent you be Made Naphil."

They followed the cawing of the crows.

Malachi led the way. Kev, Aidan, Miguel, and Danel fell in behind him. They had materialized in the hills and cliffs of a remote part of Elsewhere, far from Elsewhere City and the burgeoning tent cities. Now, Malachi's familiars, the crows that could navigate even between the worlds of the living and the dead as he did, guided them the last steps of the way.

The birds perched on the gnarled branches of a few small trees clinging to the side of what looked to Kev like a solid wall of rock.

"Clever," said Malachi.

He gave a command to the birds, and they began pecking at the rock face. Within seconds, the glamour crumbled and fell away, revealing a door built into the cliff wall.

"They have found an entrance," Miguel said into his holocom. He relayed their coordinates to the members of the backup team, who, Kev knew, would monitor the entire area for signs of movement, of anyone coming or going.

"Can your crows see through any glamour?" Danel asked.

Malachi slid his fingers around one side of the door's edge. "If the glamour is between them and the energy signature they are tracking, they can. But they must be close to the energy signature to detect it."

Kev moved to the other side of the door, his fingers searching the seam for an opening mechanism.

"How did they detect it?" Aidan asked. "Helel's protection has blocked every other form of tracking we've tried."

Malachi crouched to examine the door's base. "Once the crows are within range of the signature they seek, nothing can hide that signature from them. They are psychopomps, after all. They guide souls between life and death. Locking on to energy signatures is essential for what they do."

"Which made them the ideal trackers for us," added Kev. He too crouched to reach the bottom of the door. "I got nothing, Malachi."

"Let me try." Danel stepped close to the door and laid both hands against it. "I have some affinity for locks."

Kev and Malachi moved out of Danel's way.

Eyes closed, Danel moved his hands over the door inch by inch. Kev had almost decided the Dark soldier's efforts would yield as little as his and Malachi's when Danel stilled.

"Ah," he breathed. He followed the syllable with a quiet incantation, then stepped back as the door released, and the panel slid into the rock face.

"Way to go, Danel." Aidan moved into battle stance.

The others took similar positions. After a few seconds of no movement other than the crows stretching their wings or preening their glossy feathers, the men edged toward the opening.

Miguel notched an arrow into his bow. "I would have thought that would have triggered an alert."

"Agreed." Malachi again led the way. "But perhaps Adrigon and Helel have become a little too confident."

"Especially since Adrigon stole the Light-Bringer's Medallion," Aidan said.

Kev growled. The image of the angel grabbing Lucky and yanking the chain from her neck—while he stood, unknowing, only a few yards away—haunted him.

"We'll get it back." Aidan cast Kev a sidelong glance. "That amulet was never meant to belong to the likes of Adrigon."

The anger in Aidan's voice equaled Kev's own, reminding him that the Light-Bringer's Medallion had been Aidan's long before it had belonged to Lucky. Lucifer had given it to his youngest son when he'd renounced his wings. Kev wondered if Aidan now felt as if he'd lost the amulet for a second time.

Kev scanned the interior of the narrow, high-ceilinged cavern they'd entered. Nothing but empty rock walls and floor, lit with a dim glow that emanated from a passageway that sloped down into the hillside.

Malachi gestured toward the passage. "The crows will keep watch outside."

Danel coaxed the door closed. The group donned their glamour and began their descent.

The underground hideout was larger than Aidan had expected. But he supposed Adrigon had to provide all his misguided followers a place to stay. Odd, then, that the place seemed so empty.

They searched through countless rooms and found no one. Only the kitchen seemed inhabited. There, a small group of servants lifted vacant eyes from their work when Aidan and the others approached. Aidan wondered if one of them was the girl Bryn had told him about.

At first, each of the servants offered some small resistance to being taken away from their work. But the glamour the Fallen had cast, as well as Malachi's free use of Adrigon's name and title seemed more than enough to convince the servants to do as he asked.

"The Most High has requested we bring you to the surface," Malachi said. He gestured to Miguel and Danel. "They will accompany you, while we look for the others whose presence the Most High desires."

"Of course," said the woman who appeared to be the senior member of the group. "Whatever the Most High wishes shall be done."

How Adrigon could have removed his servants' wills so completely Aidan didn't know. Maybe Zeke, Katrin, and Sambethe could learn more about the extent of the angel's Gift while they worked on releasing the hold he had on these poor people.

Provided they could get those people out of here.

Aidan waved to Miguel and Danel as they escorted their charges toward the passage to the cliff-face door. Then he followed Malachi and Kev into one of the remaining tunnels that branched off the central hub.

Like the others, it was uninhabited. As was the next.

"They have to be here somewhere, right?" he asked Malachi. "I mean, the crows did track them here."

"There must be another exit," said Malachi.

"Maybe they were alerted to our presence after all." Kev closed the door on another unoccupied room.

They had covered only a few more yards when Malachi exclaimed, "The crows!" and turned to run back through the tunnel to the central hub.

Aidan and Kev raced after him. Within seconds, Aidan's holocom buzzed an SOS from Miguel.

Cursing under his breath, Aidan followed Malachi and Kev up the ascending passageway, weapons at the ready.

Aidan felt the air from the open doorway before they reached the top. He could hear the disturbed caws and squawks of Malachi's crows. And he smelled brimstone.

"What fresh hell?" he muttered.

He didn't have long to wait for the answer. No sooner had he, Kev, and Malachi ascended out of the passageway and into the narrow cavern than one of Adrigon's lightning blasts hit the stone floor in front of them, sending shards flying.

Kev dove toward the open doorway where Adrigon and Helel stood, backed by roughly a dozen armed angels.

Miguel and Danel crouched at either side of the opening, weapons drawn. The servants they had escorted huddled at the far end of the cavern.

Aidan summoned and flamed his wings, flying after Kev as Adrigon sent another blast into the cavern.

Aidan's flaming wings were enough to make the group back away from the door. He cleared the opening and hovered long enough to provide cover for Malachi, Miguel, and Danel to make it outside before he winged upward.

Two of Adrigon's troops shot up after him, their own wings igniting.

Seraphs. Seven hells.

Fending off the two angels called on every skill Aidan had honed since rejoining the Forces of the Fallen. In the milliseconds he had to spare a thought for anything but his next move, he hoped the rest of his team was faring better. But the sounds of battle and the ever-renewing scent of brimstone gave him little hope.

He heard the roar before he felt the heat.

And both caused his heart to leap with renewed hope, even as they seemed to surprise his angelic antagonists.

Taking advantage of their momentary distraction, he sent his spear flying into the throat of one, while his sword slipped past the other's guard to slice into his neck. Before he'd drawn back to deliver a second blow, both seraphs had dematerialized, and his spear had returned to his waiting hand.

Winging about, Aidan found that Adrigon, Helel, and all the rest of their troops had likewise disappeared. Their numbers had been replaced by the Fallen and Dark soldiers who had come in response to Miguel's distress call.

And blocking the cavern door, wings outspread and neck arched, stood Kev's huge dragon. Aidan laughed when his brother roared again, shooting his fiery breath skyward.

Looked like one of them had his Gift back.

CHAPTER 26

A shadow fell across the metal sculpture in front of Lucky seconds before Kev stepped around the bench on which she sat and dropped to the ground to sit cross-legged at her feet.

"Dominique said I would find you here." He wrapped a hand around her calf and rested his chin on her knee.

His smile and the warmth of his hand dissipated the foggy tendrils of worry that had brought Lucky to her favorite spot at the training center.

"It helps me clear my head." Lucky threaded her fingers through his hair. "And I feel close to you here."

Kev's smile grew wider. "Oh, yeah?"

Lucky leaned forward and rested her forehead against his. "Yeah."

When he kissed her, she slid off the bench and onto her knees so she could wrap her arms around him and hold him close. Her love for him made her heart ache in her chest. She could feel the corresponding ache in him in the sweet-hot slide of his lips on hers and in the caress of his hand on her cheek when he finally released her mouth.

"I was so worried about you," she whispered. "What happened with Adrigon?"

Kev rose to his feet, drawing her up beside him. "Walk with me."

He waited until they had exited the meditation center before he answered Lucky's question. As he explained how Malachi's crows had led them to Adrigon's hideout, how the team had found only a few servants inside, and how they had then been ambushed by Adrigon, Helel, and their troops at the entrance, Lucky silently cursed Adrigon for the thousandth time. How did he always manage to stay a step ahead of them?

"Adrigon was blasting his lightning bolts into the cave entrance, and I dived past the debris to get through the door. I could feel the heat building in me, and I didn't want to go supernova inside with the rest of the team. Aidan flew out after me and used his flaming wings as cover so Malachi and the others could get out. I put myself as far away from them as I could while staying within flaming distance of Adrigon and his minions."

"What happened when you supernovaed?" Lucky asked.

"That's just it." Kev grinned. "I didn't. I shifted, Lucky. It took a little while, but I shifted. The drug has worn off. I think my dragon, combined with the arrival of our backup Forces, scared them off." His grin faded. "So, yeah, they got away. But we were able to save the brainwashed servants. Maybe Katrin, Zeke, or Sambethe can at least learn something that will help us while they figure out how to free those people from Adrigon's influence."

"Hopefully." Lucky curled her hand around his arm and leaned against him. "I'm glad you have your dragon back."

"Me too. I'd much rather shift than turn into a deadly fireball that destroys everything near me."

After a couple of steps, Kev stopped and turned to face Lucky, brow furrowed.

"What is it?" she asked.

"There was something else. I don't know if I can even explain it. But when I shifted, I felt like something was—missing. I had the dragon, I had the Fire, but there was something—more—just out of reach. And that something seemed somehow connected to you."

"Connected to me?" Lucky felt her own brow knit. "How so?"

"I've been wondering about that. You know how the medallion is supposed to enhance the powers of whoever wears it?"

Lucky nodded.

"We know it connected us, right? Well, I think, maybe, because of that connection, it enhanced my powers too."

Lucky's eyes widened. "When Malachi took me to find my weapon and nothing called to me, he said something about a weapon not always looking like a weapon. And that night out in the snow on Zeke's patio, you asked me if I called the medallion when I called my Makers. I've been wondering since if, somehow, the medallion is my weapon. But, if it was, I would know, right? And Adrigon couldn't have taken it, could he?"

Kev shrugged. "I guess there's no reason you'd have to know. And, even if it's your weapon, he could take it. But you could call it back—with the name revealed at the Bonding."

Lucky sighed, her spirit sagging. "But there was no Bonding. I don't have a name to call."

"That doesn't necessarily mean the amulet's not your weapon." Kev looked thoughtful. "Have you tried to call it in other ways?"

Lucky blinked. "What do you mean?"

"Maybe visualizing it. Feeling for it with your extra senses."

Nothing like that had occurred to her. Lucky shook her head. "I didn't know it could work that way."

Kev shrugged. "It might not, but it's worth a shot. When I summon Pacifer and Aegis, I don't just think their names. I feel them in my hands. In a way, it's like they're always with me."

"Like the wings." When her wings first appeared, Aidan had explained to Lucky that they always existed as energy. Summoning them simply converted that energy into matter. Maybe weapons—at least Bonded ones—worked the same way. "Okay. Here goes."

She closed her eyes, took a deep breath, and visualized the amulet on its chain around her neck. She could see the rays of the sun and the raised shape of the dragon. She felt the texture of it against her fingers, the weight of it on her chest, the heat it emitted when it carried messages between her and Kev.

She held the image, the texture, the weight, the heat. Held them, then let the sensations melt into her like the fiery letters of Malachi's words when he'd helped her call her Makers.

And something brushed the edges of her mind, a whisper, a breath, not quite heard, not quite felt. Then it was gone.

She opened her eyes. Kev looked at her, eyebrows raised.

She shook her head. "Nothing. Well, maybe something. Maybe not. I'm not sure."

"Keep trying," Kev said. "That maybe something could turn into a definitely something."

"I will. Later. Right now, I need to get to my next class. Dominique's making sure I learn how to use those weapons I'm not Bonded to."

Standing on her toes, Lucky brushed a kiss across Kev's lips. He wrapped his arms around her, and she let herself lean into his warmth and strength.

"It will come back to you, Lucky," Kev said. "Somehow."

Lucky wished she felt as confident as he sounded.

Aidan's arrival provided all the excuse Bryn needed to switch off the treadmill and sink onto a weight bench to catch her breath.

"How's the recovery coming along?" Aidan asked.

"I barely broke a jog, and look at me. What do you think?"

Aidan's lips quirked. "Is that impatience? From you? What a surprise."

Bryn narrowed her eyes, and his quirked lips stretched into a grin. "Come on, Bryn. It's going to take longer than a couple of days to get all your strength back." Grin fading, he dropped down beside her. "You nearly died. For me. I'd consider it a favor if you'd go a little easier on yourself."

Bryn sighed. "It's just so frustrating. All those days recovering from what happened with the Tree and now this. I'm sick of being an invalid."

"You're not an invalid. You're just not at 100% yet. Neither am I, for that matter."

"You still can't sing?"

Aidan shook his head. "No. Katrin tested me again today. No song, no healing. I don't know when—even if—it will come back."

"The Tree took it all." Bryn looked at the floor, avoiding Aidan's eyes. "*I* took it all." After a brief pause, she turned to meet his gaze, chin lifted. "But I couldn't have done otherwise, Aidan. If I had it to do over again, I'd do the same thing. Even though it nearly killed you."

Aidan's hand moved to cup her chin, his fingers lightly caressing her cheek. "I know you would. And that's exactly what I'd expect of you. You did what you had to do, Bryn. And I don't blame you. Sure, I want my Gift back, but if the loss of my power is the cost of saving the Tree? Well, I consider it worth the price. I'm glad—and proud—to have been a part of it."

Bryn's eyes filled with tears. "I hope you don't have to pay that high a price."

"Me too."

Aidan's fingers feathered across her throat as he released her, and Bryn wanted to catch his hand and hold it there over her pulse. She looked away, hoping he hadn't seen the longing in her eyes.

He took a deep breath, exhaled. "Katrin said she and Sambethe are close to figuring out how to break Adrigon's hold on the people we brought back from his place in Elsewhere."

"Good." Bryn remembered how vacant the girl who had visited her had seemed. Had she and the other humans willingly succumbed to Adrigon's control, or had he taken over their minds against their will? "I wonder how they'll react, what they'll remember."

"Hopefully, something that'll help us find Adrigon and Helel and stop them once and for all." Aidan rose to his feet and turned to face her. "In the meantime, are you ready to take me to meet Eleni?"

Bryn stood too, the movement bringing her body within millimeters of Aidan's. Her breath caught in her throat. She hadn't realized he was that close. "As soon as I shower and change. I'll be quick."

"We need to leave in fifteen minutes. Don't make me be late." His breath warmed her cheek when he spoke.

She looked at him, eyebrows raised.

"I'm just saying." He grinned. "I want to make a good first impression."

Bryn chuckled and stepped around him to head toward the shower. "Meet you upstairs in ten."

"I was just getting ready to call you," said Josh.

Lucky hadn't even closed the apartment door behind her, but the "Well, hello to you too" that rose to her lips died unspoken with one look at her cousin's face.

"What is it?" she asked. "What's happened?"

"It's G-Ma. She fell and hit her head—hard. I think on the corner of her art table or something. Dad said it's all cut and bruised. The assisted living place called him to say they'd sent her to the emergency room in an ambulance. He's still at the hospital. They're admitting her since she keeps going in and out of consciousness. I was getting ready to head that way and figured you'd want to come too."

CHAPTER 27

"I'm too pumped to go home, Bryn." Aidan's body felt electric with energy. "Want to check out one of the bars in Elsewhere City?"

He hadn't really known what to expect from the meeting with Eleni. Given her role among the Guardians and the fact that she was not only Bryn's mentor but had also been Zeke's—a concept that still blew his mind—he'd been excited to meet her. He'd also hoped she could shed some light on what exactly had happened with him and the Tree. But he had had no idea that just being around her and talking to her would energize him so. He hadn't felt this good in—he couldn't remember how long, certainly not since the Tree had used his Gift to heal itself.

"That sounds great. I'm not ready to go home either." Bryn sashayed across the lawn of the Alliance Council Hall. She seemed to have plenty of energy too, as if she were completely healed.

"Does Eleni always have this effect on people?" Aidan asked.

"What effect?" Bryn turned in circles beside him.

Aidan laughed. "Are you kidding me? You're practically dancing. I can almost feel you vibrating. And I have more energy than I know what to do with."

He grabbed her hands, and they spun each other in circles all the way to the top of the hill leading down to Elsewhere City, where they collapsed in laughter on the grass.

"I haven't ever noticed it before," Bryn said, once she could speak. "But, now that I think about it, I felt it as soon as she joined us in the room. And by the time she left, I was almost giddy."

"Almost?" Aidan chuckled.

Bryn grinned. "Well, you had something to do with the spinning and falling."

Aidan jumped up and offered her a hand. She took it without protest, and he pulled her to her feet. "You were dancing before that though. You can't deny it."

"True." Bryn left her hand in his as they started down the hill. "It just feels so good to have this much energy. I feel like my old self."

Aidan squeezed her hand. "That's great. Do you think this will last?"

Bryn shrugged. "I haven't noticed any lessening since Eleni left us. And I think she felt it too—even though she didn't say anything. She seemed even more alive than when I've seen her before."

Gasping, she stopped in her tracks, drawing Aidan to a halt as well. "Aidan, do you think this means the Tree is getting stronger? It drained the Guardian's energy when it was weak and needed help. And it almost took everything from you to heal itself. Maybe it's stronger now, so it's giving that energy back to us, giving us back what it no longer needs."

"Maybe so." Aidan swung her hand as they continued down the hill. If that was the case, he wondered, if the Tree was returning their borrowed energy, would he be getting his healing Gift back soon?

Lucky drifted in a white stillness, her skin dotted with the slight stings of tiny cinders. She was waiting. Something or someone had called her here, but she didn't know who or what or why.

A sense of anticipation built even as the stillness deepened around her. She felt a flutter in her chest as something began to take shape in the distant whiteness. Lucky's heartbeat increased as that something drew closer. After some time, she saw that it was a robed and hooded figure. When only a few feet separated them, Lucky recognized the face inside the hood as G-Ma's.

G-Ma stopped directly in front of Lucky, so close that Lucky could have touched her, though Lucky did not. This robed and hooded G-Ma, with lowered eyes and folded hands, seemed somehow removed from the humanness of a touch or an embrace. When G-Ma raised her eyes, Lucky saw, without surprise, that they were the pupilless, cloud-dotted-sky eyes of the Archangel Gabriel.

G-Ma/Gabriel held out their folded hands, and Lucky put her own hands, palms up, beneath them. They placed whatever they held in her hands and then folded her hands around it, holding her hands together with theirs. Lucky felt something slide up her arms to her chest, a recognition, a welcoming, a homing, a connection she could not name.

G-Ma/Gabriel nodded, and then they were gone.

Lucky opened her eyes, blinking away the residue of the dream. She stretched to relieve the crick in her neck. She had fallen asleep in the chair beside G-Ma's hospital bed. Josh, on the couch against the wall on the opposite side of the bed, had also fallen asleep. Lucky could hear his gentle snoring. G-Ma lay unmoving in her bed. A nurse would come and check on her soon. Someone had stopped in to do so every hour or so since Lucky and Josh had talked Uncle Matthew into letting them take the night shift.

Lucky started to reach into her pocket for her phone to check the time, and something fell from her hand into her lap. She picked it up, and time stilled. Her breath caught in her throat as she stared at the object in her hand.

It was her locket, which she had last seen when it dropped into a drain in Elsewhere.

Bryn was grateful to be back in class, if disappointed that Dominique had paired her with Lucky. Usually, Dominique had each student spar with someone of equal or slightly better skill level. Lucky had greatly improved since her days in Elsewhere, but she was still nowhere near as skilled as Bryn— when Bryn was at normal capacity. Since Bryn was still recovering, Dominique had not only insisted she take it easy, but had forced her to do so by pairing her with a less experienced partner. Even though Bryn had protested that she felt fine, almost back to normal, Dominique had refused to budge.

Bryn found no consolation in learning that Dominique had been right. As expected, Bryn won every bout, but not as easily as she should have. She even felt a little winded by the time the class ended, which didn't improve her mood. She hadn't noticed a drop in energy since returning from Elsewhere the day before, but she clearly hadn't fully recovered. Maybe she had been wrong about feeling back to normal.

"I can't believe it's taking me so long to recover." She took a pull from her water bottle. "I should have beat you in a third of the time and with half the effort."

Lucky laughed. "I'll try not to be insulted by that." Then, she sobered. "I know you're frustrated, Bryn, but considering what happened, you're doing great. You and Aidan both almost died. Even a Cherub-demon-human blend like you isn't going to recoup in a few days the amount of life energy you spent saving him. And you were already drained from merging with the Tree. You'll be back to beating me in five moves in no time."

"Three." Bryn grinned.

Lucky rolled her eyes. "Okay, fine. Three."

Lucky lowered the zip on her sparring jacket, and something gold caught Bryn's eye. "That looks like—"

Lucky followed her gaze. "My locket. Yeah, it was the weirdest thing. I was in the hospital with my G-Ma. I fell asleep and had this dream where she—well, it was sort of her and sort of the Archangel Gabriel—handed me something I couldn't see. When I woke up the locket was in my hand."

"It's the same?"

"As the one Adrigon tossed down the drain in Elsewhere? Yes, complete with all the little dings and scratches it's accumulated over the years. I just put it on a new chain."

Bryn frowned. "That is weird."

"I know. And you know what's even weirder? I feel stronger, more centered, more focused since I put it on."

Bryn raised an eyebrow. "Are you saying that's why I didn't beat you sooner?"

Lucky punched Bryn's arm. "I'm serious. I've been wearing it all day, and I've really felt stronger. It doesn't make any sense. I've worn this locket almost every day since I turned sixteen, and I never felt different before."

"Did you feel weaker or less centered when you weren't wearing it?"

"Maybe." Lucky's brow knotted. "I was so upset that Adrigon had taken it and tossed it aside. I'm not sure I noticed anything different except how upset I was. And if I had, I would have assumed it was because of the Medallion."

"That makes sense."

Lucky opened her mouth as if to respond, closed it, and then looked at Bryn for a few seconds without speaking. "I had thought," she finally said, "that maybe the Medallion was my weapon. Now, I'm starting to wonder if it isn't the locket."

"That's the last of them." Aidan returned the final weapon to its slot and activated the control to retract the drawer and close the panel. "And I've gotta go."

"Your turn for Elsewhere City patrol, correct?" Danel asked.

"Yeah." Aidan sighed. "I'm kind of bummed about it. I really want to see what new tech Miguel has come up with."

Danel closed the weapons room door behind them. "I know. I have been looking forward to his training session all day." His lavender eyes danced with humor. "Fortunately for me, I do not have a prior commitment."

Aidan nearly flipped the young man the bird, but he wasn't sure Danel would recognize the gesture. "Fine. I see I'll have to look for sympathy from someone else."

Danel chuckled. "Maybe you can find some in Elsewhere."

This time Aidan did flip him the bird. He was rewarded with a burst of laughter that faded as he dematerialized.

He rematerialized in Elsewhere and signed in for his patrol, a smile curving his lips.

The murmur of Aunt Beth and Uncle Matthew's conversation did nothing to keep Lucky awake. She, Josh, and his parents had been sitting with G-Ma for a couple of hours now, and though it was only mid-afternoon, Lucky kept drifting off despite her best efforts. Josh had left only moments ago to get sustenance from a nearby coffee shop, after the entire family had agreed that the free hospital coffee was undrinkable. Lucky decided to give into the temptation to nap while he was gone. It wasn't as if G-Ma was awake anyway.

No, wait. G-Ma was awake after all, and she looked more herself than she had in months. She was wearing her favorite faded jeans and the soft sweater Lucky had always liked to snuggle against. When she opened her arms, Lucky hugged her fiercely.

"I've missed you so much," Lucky whispered.

"I know, my darling girl. I've missed you too." G-Ma pulled away enough to look into Lucky's eyes. "I don't have much time, and there are things I need to tell you." Her eyes filled with tears. "Oh, you are so dear to me."

G-Ma pulled her close again, and Lucky felt tears flood her own eyes.

Then G-Ma drew back again, her hands wrapping around Lucky's upper arms. "I'm not going to wake up again, and that was my choice." She tapped the locket on Lucky's chest. "This is my gift to you. It ties you to me and to my Marie. And to Lilith. To all your mothers. And to all we have each given you. There is great power here." She moved her finger to tap not the locket but Lucky's chest. "And here. You will need that power very soon."

Lucky's fingers fluttered to the locket. "But how...?" She sniffed, unable to finish the sentence.

"Ask Gabriel. Together, we helped to make you Naphil. And that has forever bound us. Gabriel will tell you more." Her hands moved to Lucky's cheeks. "I must go, but do not grieve for me, child. This is my path, my choice. I will always live in your heart, as you will in mine."

She kissed Lucky's cheek and wrapped her close once more. "Tell them all I love them so. And be brave, my girl—as I know you are. So strong and so brave. And so very loved."

Lucky nearly sobbed when she felt G-Ma's lips press against her forehead. "I love you too, G-Ma. So much."

"I know, dear one." G-Ma's hands moved to Lucky's cheeks again, and she gazed into her eyes without speaking, her lips curved in a soft smile. "You have everything you need. And I must go now."

Even as G-Ma faded away, Lucky felt herself enveloped in the warmth of her grandmother's love.

"G-Ma," Lucky gasped, dragging herself out of the dream and out of her chair to stand at her grandmother's bedside. Uncle Matthew and Aunt Beth were on either side of the bed, holding G-Ma's hands. G-Ma's breath sounded labored.

Lucky ran a hand over her grandmother's hair, tears flowing down her cheeks.

"What's going on?" Josh came through the door, a tray of coffees in his hand.

"This is it," Lucky whispered. "She's leaving."

"What?" Josh, Uncle Matthew, and Aunt Beth all spoke at once.

Lucky wiped the tears from her cheeks with her free hand. "She came to me in a dream. She said to tell you all how much she loves you, and that she has to go now."

"No." Josh thrust the tray of coffee onto a table and rushed to the bedside to place a hand on G-Ma's knee. "She can't..."

But G-Ma's breathing grew even more labored.

"Mom." Uncle Matthew's voice broke on the word.

Then G-Ma drew a last rattling breath, and no more.

Lucky wrapped her arms around G-Ma's shoulders and sobbed on her chest.

Kev felt a faint buzzing like electricity in his veins. He'd first noticed it the evening before, but he hadn't really paid it much attention in the last several hours. Assisting with the heightened efforts to locate Adrigon, Helel, and their followers had demanded his full attention. Now, as he scanned the huge screen in Margash's command center, the buzzing penetrated his awareness again. It wasn't the same as the fire in his veins before he'd supernovaed, and yet it reminded him of that feeling.

He pushed the sensation to the back of his mind and focused on what Ithrael, the angel leading the tracking team, was saying.

"This is what we wanted to show you." Ithrael gestured toward a blank area in the middle right of the screen. The rest of the screen showed myriad dots of light, like brightly colored stars in a night sky, in changing patterns and configurations. "Finally, thanks to several angels with enhanced abilities to sense disparate energetic patterns and technology upgraded to their specifications, we discovered this anomaly in the energy signatures in Elsewhere. This absence indicates where neither the angels nor our upgraded sensors can trace any energetic patterns."

She zoomed in so the blank space filled more of the screen. "Note how this area changes shape. Let me show you a recording from the last couple of your hours."

Ithrael flicked a finger and the image on the screen shifted, its irregular boundary narrowing in places and expanding in others. After a few seconds, a small section separated from the larger mass, as if it were spawning, and then the smaller area disappeared and reappeared across the screen. A few seconds later, it returned to its original location and remerged with the larger mass.

"That has to be them," Kev said.

"Yes," Malachi agreed. "Adrigon and Helel, or possibly Helel with someone else, leaving the protected base and then returning. The other changes could be the natural expansion of the base's protective field as people move near the perimeter."

"Agreed." Ithrael moved her fingers again, and a gridded map of Elsewhere overlay the screen.

Kev leaned in for a better look. "The new base is much closer to the old than I would have guessed."

Malachi studied the map for a few seconds. "We start planning the attack immediately. This time I want Michael's help."

Malachi had taken two long strides toward the door when movement on the screen caught Kev's eye. "Malachi, wait! Ithrael, zoom out!"

The screen shifted and reconfigured.

"Holy hell," Kev breathed. Blank spaces appeared throughout Elsewhere City and the greater tent city surrounding it. Then the blanks began to fill with brightly colored stars. "I think Adrigon's beaten us to the punch. Looks like they're attacking Elsewhere City."

CHAPTER 28

The renegade Angel of Light appeared out of nowhere, and Aidan winged sharply right to avoid impact, only to pull up short as more angels appeared in the air around him. He could see even more on land in the tent city below.

Without conscious thought, he summoned his sword and spear. Good thing too. Just as he felt them materialize in his hands, the angel nearest him noticed his presence and moved to attack.

The last thought Aidan spared for anything other than the battle at hand was to hope Gareth, his patrol partner, was able to call for help. Because no matter how skilled he and Gareth were, they were only two. And they couldn't defeat this army without reinforcements.

"Zeke," Josh said.

Lucky too felt the itchy tug in her mind. She released her hold on G-Ma and moved around the bed toward her cousin.

Aunt Beth put her hand on Josh's arm. "What did you say, honey?"

"We have to go," Josh said. "I'm sorry, Mom, Dad, but Lucky and I have to leave."

"Where would you possibly have to be that's more important than this?" Uncle Matthew's question held equal parts anger and bewilderment.

"We can't explain right now." Lucky wiped tears from her eyes. "But we really, really have to go." Zeke's summons was already burrowing into her brain. Her eyes flashed to Josh's. "It's urgent."

He nodded. "We gotta get out of here."

Lucky held back a sob. "I'm so sorry, G-Ma, but I know you understand."

"How could she understand?" Aunt Beth turned confused, tear-filled eyes to Lucky. "I know I certainly don't."

Uncle Matthew rounded on Josh. "Son, what is going on?"

"You know we wouldn't do this if it wasn't important, right?" Josh grabbed Lucky's hand and pulled her toward the door. "Just trust us. Please."

"We'll explain later," Lucky added, "if we can."

Her aunt and uncle's expressions of confusion and disbelief followed them out the door.

The extra one-on-one training session with Dominique had helped, Bryn had to admit. Dominique had taken her through some new moves as well as shown her some different techniques for executing moves she already knew. But the best thing she'd done was help Bryn relax. She hadn't babied Bryn or treated her as if she needed remedial work. Instead, Dominique had provided tips for executing powerful moves with less effort, for fighting smarter instead of harder. Those tips had helped Bryn realize she could still perform well even if her energy wasn't quite back to peak.

"If I'd known all this earlier, I could have beat Lucky more easily," she said when Dominique ended the session.

"That's why I wanted to do this after our regular class." Dominique stowed her weapon and then stepped aside so Bryn could stow hers. "You needed to see the difference between how you fought with Lucky earlier and how you fought with me after learning these techniques."

"Thank you. This was really helpful..." Bryn's voice trailed off as she realized Dominique wasn't listening to her.

Then Dominique snapped back to attention. "Seven hells," she breathed. "Zeke has summoned me to the War Room. It must be something to do with Adrigon." She pulled combat gear from the closet and began donning it over her training clothes.

Bryn did the same. "I'm coming with you."

"If you weren't summoned, you may not get any farther than the War Room."

"I'll take my chances."

Bryn followed Dominique through the training center to the large meeting room.

Members of the Forces already filled the room, and more came in behind Bryn and Dominique.

Across the room, Bryn saw Lucky and Josh, their colorful street clothes standing out in stark contrast against the black of the Forces' battle gear. Her friends had come here in a hurry. Apparently, Zeke had summoned them too.

Why hadn't he summoned her?

Bryn forced the painful thought to the back of her mind, as Zeke called for attention.

Then, as she listened, her self-concern faded away. Adrigon and his army had attacked Elsewhere City. Aidan was there when the attack began.

Part of her heard Zeke's voice explaining that the combined Forces of Dark and Fallen, under Danel's direction, had already been deployed to the battle, and that Malachi had enlisted the help of the Archangel Michael, so he and the loyal Angels of Light would soon be coming to assist, if they weren't there already. But mostly she worried about Aidan.

Only he and one other soldier had been in Elsewhere City at the time of the attack. Only two of them to fight an entire army.

She dragged herself back to attention when people started to leave the room. Zeke was giving orders about who was to report where and do what. When she heard him direct Lucky and Josh to get geared up and report back to him, she pushed her way through the crowd toward them. Dominique called her name, urged her to wait, but Bryn ignored her.

She didn't care if she wasn't fully recovered. There was no way she was going to stand idly by while everyone she loved risked their lives.

Zeke may not have summoned her, but she was going to help—whether he wanted her to or not.

Kev reformed high in the sky over Elsewhere City. He had transported to a location above the colored stars he'd seen on Ithrael's screen, so he could get a bird's eye view.

He hadn't waited for the first troop of Fallen to deploy or for word from Malachi on when Michael's Angels of Light would reach Elsewhere. As soon as he'd learned Aidan and Gareth had been patrolling when Adrigon's army arrived, he'd summoned his wings and transported.

The largest number of Adrigon's renegade angels seemed to be on the ground, attacking the Dark inhabitants of the tent cities. Multiple fires had been set, and Kev could hear screams of terror. Even so, it looked like the refugees from the Dark worlds were holding their own. Some of Adrigon's soldiers were already down.

Scanning the figures fighting above the tent cities, Kev spotted Aidan's golden head. His brother was fending off two of Adrigon's men, and Kev saw another Dominion winging in their direction. He shot a fireball into the third angel's wing.

That got his attention.

With a snarl, the angel altered course and headed straight for Kev.

Kev summoned Pacifer and dived to meet him.

The fireball was Aidan's first indication that help had arrived. He saw the flaming missile out of the corner of his eye and knew it heralded the arrival of either his father or his brother. He didn't know which until several dodges and parries and a few well-placed spear thrusts finally put him into a position to behead one of his two opponents. As the angel disappeared in a dust of gold and Aidan spun out of reach of his other attacker's sword, he caught a glimpse of Kev in combat nearby.

A quick scan as he circled back to face his attacker revealed additional support. At least one troop of Fallen and Dark had now engaged with Adrigon's renegades. Small groups of fighters in combat peppered the sky all around him.

He didn't have time to check the status of the ground war. The other angel was on him. Aidan raised his sword to block his opponent's blow, and the impact reverberated through his arm. He flamed his wings and the angel backed off, giving Aidan the advantage he needed. With the other angel in defense mode, Aidan moved in for the attack.

Lucky reformed at the coordinates Zeke had provided with his final words still echoing in her head and her hands still linked with those of Josh and Bryn. They stood on the hill near the Council Hall, with Elsewhere City and its burgeoning tent cities stretching below them.

Winged battles peppered the sky above the tent cities, and the cities themselves were in chaos. Sounds of combat and screams of terror accompanied the smell of smoke rising from the fires that consumed many of the tents.

"Holy hell," Lucky breathed.

"Just hell. Nothing holy about it." Josh's words came out on a growl. His eyes glowed Wraith-red, and his fists clenched, causing the heavy muscles in his arms to bunch.

Lucky's eyes widened. No matter how many times she saw it, she didn't think she would ever witness her scholarly cousin's transformation without surprise.

"If Zeke wanted us down there," Bryn nodded toward the sprawl of tent cities, "why did he send us up here?"

"Because he wanted you to meet up with us."

Lucky took some comfort in the fact that both Josh and Bryn seemed as startled as she was at the sound of Lilith's voice. The number of people accompanying her grandmother surprised her even more. Lucky recognized Mather and Alicia's mother among them.

"How...?" she managed.

"Amazing what a little silencing spell can do." Lilith bowed with a flourish. "I've brought along the strongest of my sorcerers. We intend to do everything in our considerable power to protect our Dark sisters and brothers—and defeat Adrigon. We will break up into smaller groups and enter different parts of the tent cities."

Luil moved forward from the back of the group. "I will accompany my daughter and her friends." He cocked an eyebrow at Lucky. "If I may?"

Lucky nodded.

The remaining sorcerers divided into groups. To Lucky's relief, Mather was not one of the few who chose to accompany Luil. To Lucky's surprise, Lilith appointed Mather the leader of his group. Did that mean she had forgiven him for attacking her granddaughters?

Lilith made quick work of assigning each group a point of entry into the tent cities. Then she wished them all luck. "And may Adrigon rue the day he decided to attack us."

Even as Lucky cheered along with the others, she wondered if Adrigon would actually show up.

And if he did, could she do what Zeke had told her to do?

She was no closer to answering the question when Luil indicated it was time to move.

She, Josh, Bryn, and Luil transported to an empty area on the outskirts of the tent cities. Soon after they reformed, a bright portal opened nearby, and the sorcerers who had joined their party stepped through.

Luil took charge of the group, and Lucky found herself grateful for his leadership as they headed into battle.

Kev hadn't realized how very many angels Adrigon had recruited. When he'd rushed to help Aidan, he'd assumed Danel's arrival with the combined Forces of Dark and Fallen would even the numbers on their side.

He'd been wrong.

For every member of the Forces that joined him and Aidan, it seemed two more of Adrigon's angels appeared. If many of the inhabitants of the tent cities had not had fighting skills, magic, or other powers to bring to their own defense, the Dark and Fallen would have been greatly outnumbered.

Even so, Kev had changed his mind about the Dark refugees holding their own. The fires in the tent cities had spread, and from what he could gather in the split-seconds he had to check on the progress of the larger battle, it appeared as if the refugees accounted for more of the wounded and fallen than did Adrigon's troops.

Kev wished he could call his Dragon, but he knew it wouldn't help their cause. Adrigon's full-blooded angels could be killed only by beheading, but his dragon fire would be fatal for the mixed-blood Fallen and Dark who battled alongside him. So, he fought with his sword and the occasional carefully aimed fireball, looking for any opportunity to penetrate the defenses of the angels he fought against.

His latest opponent, a huge Dominion who reminded him of the guards who had insisted on patting him down every time he'd entered or left the Metatron's Council Chamber back when he was *Ha-Satan*, flew at Kev, sword raised and ready to strike. Kev dived toward the Dominion, dismissing his wings and jack-knifing under the angel's sword to plow into his midsection. While the Dominion struggled to regain his balance, Kev grabbed on to the angel with his legs, leaned back, and sliced Pacifer toward the angel's throat. The Dominion managed to block the blow.

Then something rippled through the air like a wave through water, rocking them both. Kev saw a momentary flash of fear in the Dominion's eyes, even as he felt an answering exultation. They both knew what that ripple heralded.

The Archangel Michael with the Forces of Light.

Kev took advantage of the Dominion's distraction to strike again. The angel's sword glanced off Pacifer, slowing the blade but failing to stop the blow. The sword sliced through the Dominion's neck.

As the angel dusted to gold, Kev summoned his wings.

All around him, members of the Forces of Light were engaging in the battle. No sooner had he felt the first impact of a new opponent's blade against his own, than he became aware of more angels of Light fighting beside him. The numbers were now in their favor.

The tide had turned.

It wasn't long before Adrigon's renegades began to fall. The air filled with the gold dust of beheadings and the groans of those too wounded to continue to fight. From the cries of victory coming from the tent cities, it sounded as if the ground forces had fared equally well.

Kev drew a breath of relief, then winced, when he felt a touch in his mind, an intrusion, an attempt at invasion. A voice began to whisper, a persuasive voice, an awful whisper.

Adrigon!

Kev pushed at the intrusion, and pain shot through his head. The persuasive whisper offered relief if he would only do what it said. No way in seven hells that was happening. Kev pushed harder, resisted with everything he had. After some agonizing moments, the pain subsided, and the whisper was gone.

But all around him, Kev saw many who hadn't been able to resist. The Forces of Light who had come to the aid of the Dark and the Fallen now turned against them and joined with Adrigon's remaining renegades. Kev knew what they heard in their minds: "Kill the Dark. Kill the Fallen. The polluted do not deserve to live."

The tide had turned again.

CHAPTER 29

Michael's Angels of Light had arrived just in time.

Bryn had watched the number of fighters among the Dark refugees dwindle as more and more had fallen to the swords of Adrigon's renegades. She had felt her own hopes of victory dying along with the hopes of those around her. The rage that had fueled her when she had first witnessed the destruction of the tent cities—and the dead and wounded among their inhabitants—had begun to turn to despair.

Now, she fought with renewed energy, her weapons her Raven beak and talons rather than the sword strapped to her back. The Angels of Light had shifted the balance in their favor. Adrigon's men were outnumbered.

And soon, Adrigon's men had fallen.

Bryn shifted from half-Raven back to her human form and looked around, her gaze searching the smoke for Lucky and the others.

There. The sorcerers had magicked a protective shield for a group of refugee mothers and children. Lucky, Josh, and Luil were among the fighters who guarded the sorcerers.

Bryn had taken only a few steps toward them when she felt Adrigon's push in her head. With recognition came resistance. And with resistance came pain. It was only a fraction of what he'd inflicted on her before though, and it faded quickly when she continued to resist.

Even as her own pain subsided, she felt the energy around her begin to shift. She saw Angels of Light wrestling with their pain, and she saw them begin to give in.

"Oh, no," she breathed.

She ran for Lucky as fast as she could run.

"What the—?"

Aidan knew Adrigon had turned the Angels of Light against them. He'd felt Adrigon's intrusion in his own mind and somehow—he wasn't sure how—had managed to resist it despite the pain. Then he and the other Dark and Fallen had had to go on the defensive against the Angels of Light who, moments before, had been fighting by their sides. Now, they were outnumbered again, and—*seven hells!*—he really hadn't expected his father to be one of his attackers.

"Abomination!" Lucifer loosed a fireball directly at Aidan's head.

Aidan dodged enough to prevent a direct hit, but the fireball singed his hair and ear in passing. Still, that didn't hurt half as much as the hatred on Lucifer's face.

Thankfully, the other Angels of Light seemed to have found other targets. Aidan needed all his wits about him to defend himself from Lucifer without really wounding him.

"What? Are you afraid to fight your father, half-breed? Your human blood makes you weak." Lucifer sent another fireball Aidan's way and dived toward him, sword in hand.

Aidan dodged, felt the heat of the fireball as it zipped past him, and raised his sword, bracing for impact.

Then someone flew between him and his father, intercepting Lucifer's blow.

Kev!

Together they had a chance against Lucifer.

He couldn't say the same about his fellow members of the Forces. They couldn't withstand the Angels of Light if Adrigon's hold on them wasn't broken soon.

Lucky couldn't believe how easily she resisted Adrigon's intrusion into her mind. As soon as she felt the nudge of persuasion, she pushed against it. After a few seconds of pain, it was gone. Easy as that.

"Did you feel that?" she asked.

Both Luil and Josh raised their eyebrows in question.

"Feel what?" Josh asked.

Luil gestured toward the pockets of Angels of Light all around them. "Perhaps whatever they are feeling."

"Yes, exactly what they are feeling." Lucky recognized the signs. The angels' faces reflected confusion, resistance, pain, and then acquiescence.

The realization of what that acquiescence meant hit her just as Bryn grabbed her arm. "Lucky, it's Adrigon. He's getting to them. The full-blooded angels. They're the only ones he can control."

"Or the only ones he's trying to control," said Luil. "His Gift is stretched thin. If he can control those least able to resist him, he trusts they will take care of the rest of us."

Bryn's hold on Lucky's arm tightened. "This is it, Lucky. You must stop him. Like Zeke said, your Gift is the best—maybe the only—weapon we have to combat his power."

"I know what Zeke said, Bryn, but I'm not so sure. Adrigon can resist me, just like I can resist him. And besides, how am I supposed to get past Helel's protection—assuming I can even find them?"

"No problem finding them." Josh pointed skyward.

High above the tent cities and the remaining battles that dotted the sky, Adrigon and Helel hovered. They weren't even trying to hide.

With her senses turned up, Lucky could see a dark cloud emanating from Adrigon, could feel the menace in its expansion, as more and more of the Angels of Light fell under his control.

The weight of responsibility settled in Lucky, and her entire body felt charged with electricity. Bryn was right. If she could get into Adrigon's head, maybe she could stop him.

"Do what you can, Lucky." Josh said. "Otherwise, we don't stand a chance." He took his place alongside the Dark refugees whose children they protected and moved into battle stance. "Not that we won't go down fighting."

Beside him, Bryn shifted back to her half-Raven form.

Luil stepped closer to Lucky. "I will take care of Helel, daughter," he said. "You take care of Adrigon."

The tingling in Lucky's body intensified. She squared her shoulders, nodded.

"Let's end this," she said.

Here goes nothing. Kev called his dragon and transformed in an instant. The dragon might not be the best opponent against Adrigon's renegades, but he might be just the thing for keeping at least some of the brainwashed Angels of Light—and his father—busy, buying some time for someone to get to Adrigon.

No, not *someone.* He was buying time for *Lucky* to get to Adrigon. Her Gift was their best shot now.

Before Lucifer could strike Aidan with his sword, Kev flamed his father's sword arm just enough to knock him out of commission for a few minutes. Then he showered the closest group of Adrigon-controlled Angels of Light with enough dragon flame to piss them off and make them turn in his direction.

Move quickly, Lucky, he thought, and flamed them again.

Luil must have used some heavy-duty cloaking spell. Less than a hundred yards separated Lucky and her father from Adrigon and Helel, and the angels seemed none the wiser.

"Now, to take care of Helel," Luil said in Lucky's ear. "Look there." He pointed to a spot behind the two angels.

As Lucky watched, shapes began to appear. Shadow creatures, like the ones who had disrupted Mo's mother's country club dance in what seemed to Lucky another lifetime. Like smoke, the creatures moved toward Helel. By the time he became aware of them, it was too late. They had already wrapped him in arms that Lucky knew from experience wielded much more strength than their shadowy appearance would indicate.

"He will lose consciousness in seconds," Luil said. "Be ready."

The vibration in Lucky's body grew stronger. This was it. This was what everything in her life had been pushing toward since Josh had taken her to see Icarus and she had first met Aidan. This was why she had been Made Naphil.

Could she do what they expected of her? Was her Gift strong enough to defeat Adrigon?

Helel's head dropped, and Lucky knew he would have fallen had Luil's shadow creatures not held him in midair. Adrigon, apparently sensing the loss of Helel's protective shield, turned toward his companion.

The vibration Lucky felt moved inward and settled in the center of her chest, at the spot where her locket rested. Or where it usually rested. Now, it hovered a few inches away from her body, as if pulled by a magnet.

A glint of gold on Adrigon's chest drew her eyes. She had that sense of recognition, of homing and connection, she had felt in the dream when G-Ma/Gabriel had dropped their unseen gift into her hands. She had felt it again when she'd fastened the new chain around her neck and the locket had nestled against her skin.

The locket had called her, had come to her, and she could feel the pull of it now reaching for the medallion and of the medallion reaching for it—and for her.

She had been told the names of weapons revealed themselves in the Bonding, but she had no sense of a name here. What she felt, what she knew, was beyond naming, deeper than language, a oneness as primal as being itself. The locket and the medallion didn't belong to her, and she didn't belong to them. They were the same. They were one. She was the locket and the medallion, and they were her. She didn't have to call the medallion to her. It, like the locket, was already part of her.

Even as the truth of this sank into her skin and bones and heart like the tiny cinders in her dream, she felt a familiar burn in the center of her chest. She knew the medallion now rested alongside the locket even before her world exploded into light, time stilled, and she hung suspended, her heartbeat loud in her ears as images, feelings, and sensations rushed through her.

She saw the Dark refugees battling against the brainwashed Angels of Light. They fought, and bled, and many of them died. She saw the Forces of the Fallen and Dark falling to those who had been their allies. She saw it all: the fights in the tent cities and all the battles in the skies above. She saw Dark mothers and fathers die protecting their children. She heard their cries. She smelt the smoke from the burning tent cities, the metallic scent of blood, and the acrid odor of fear. She saw Josh and Bryn wounded and bleeding but still struggling with the others to hold their line of protection. She saw Aidan and Kev battling their own father. And—holy hell!—she saw Malachi defending himself against Zeke. Even Zeke had fallen prey to Adrigon's persuasion.

The pain of all this suffering combined with her own to drive multiple blades into her heart.

All the suffering, all the heartbreak of the Dark and Fallen, all the losses they had already endured, now compounded by the necessity of battling their allies and friends, poured through her.

And she saw the Still Ones, those in the Chicago safe house and those remaining in their own, wounded world. She saw all the beings in all the Dark worlds, all the Light worlds, all the Fallen worlds.

So many sights and sounds and smells. So much laughter, so much happiness, so much joy, so much love. And so much pain, so much heartbreak, so many wounds and lacerations. Colors, chords, scents, textures, feelings, and emotions. All of them woven together, beating together, vibrating through her, and she couldn't comprehend them, couldn't contain them, couldn't hold them.

Lucky felt as if her mind and body were ripping to pieces.

Then, somewhere in the back of her mind, she heard Malachi's voice. Malachi, helping her call her Makers, speaking fiery words that circled around her, and telling her to stop struggling and let the words in.

She listened. She stopped trying to comprehend all the sights and sounds, the feelings and sensations. She just let them wash through her. She saw them, heard them, felt them, and then let them go.

And, gradually, they fell away.

And she saw and heard and felt what lay underneath it all. Threads, or ribbons, of light connected everything and everyone, each humming with its own song. And, where Adrigon extended his Gift, a dark, pulsing cord twisted and tangled the ribbons, distorting the songs, or drowning them altogether, with an incessant, discordant drone.

She reached out with her own Gift, following the cord to its source, and then riding the ribbons of light that naturally connected them. And this time Adrigon's mind offered no resistance. Whether he was too stunned or too weakened by the loss of the medallion to put up any resistance, or whether her spontaneous Bonding with the medallion had strengthened her beyond his resisting, she didn't know. And she didn't care. She simply took advantage of the opportunity.

Adrigon's mind was a knotted jumble. The dark pulsing cord had entangled the ribbons of his own thoughts and emotions as thoroughly as it had entangled those on whom he'd used his Gift. It was as if his power had rebounded on him, imprisoning and controlling him even as he tried to control others.

Lucky traced the twisted path of the cord to the deepest, largest, most stubborn snarl. The threads and ribbons of Adrigon's thoughts and emotions glowed faintly through the cord's knots and tangles, reminding Lucky of a tree struggling against the strangle-hold of a parasitic vine.

There! Deep in the center of the snarl, she could see the bulbous tangle where the cord began. Light leaked through a few tiny gaps in the mass where the core of Adrigon's thoughts and emotions curled.

Lucky imagined hacking the knot into pieces. She could wield her Gift like an axe, cutting at the knot until it fell away. With no root, the tangles growing from it would wither and die.

And Adrigon would wither and die too. His thoughts and emotions were too entangled with the knotty cord to survive.

A rush of power filled Lucky. She could end him, this hate-filled angel who was willing to destroy worlds to get what he wanted. She could break his hold on the Angels of Light and make sure he'd never have such power over anyone again. All she had to do was apply her Gift just so.

She reached for the knot with her Gift, the image of a sharp-edged axe firm in her mind. This was what he deserved. She could make him pay for everything he'd done. The sense of her own power was coldly intoxicating. She had never wanted anything as much as she wanted to destroy Adrigon and his followers and everything he stood for.

The realization hit her like a fist to the stomach.

She was no different than Adrigon. This desire to destroy, this part of herself that she had first seen when her Gift manifested, and her righteous justification of it, made her just like him. They were both driven by the same desire to protect their own and destroy those they saw as enemies. And the thought of that destruction gave them both a hard, cold pleasure.

Kev had told her she had to accept that part of herself. And, for the first time, Lucky understood what he had meant. Seeing, feeling, and accepting her own destructive desires made her recognize her kinship with Adrigon. She could use her Gift to destroy him, just as he had used his Gift to control and destroy so many others. If she did, her Gift would rebound on her just as his had on him. If she acted on her desire to destroy him, that part of her would grow stronger—while the part of her that had recognized her kinship with him, that kept her from using her Gift to destroy, would weaken.

Was there another way? Could she stop Adrigon without destroying him? Lucky didn't know, and a part of her didn't even want to try. The pulse of her power urged her to do what she knew she could.

But the warmth radiating from the center of her chest advised otherwise. It spread through her entire torso and down the length of her arms. Lucky let the feeling guide her.

Instead of chopping at the knotted tangle at Adrigon's core with an axe, she saw herself surrounding it with the same warmth that now filled her whole body.

The vibration in her body changed, and she felt a similar change in the knotty coil.

Then the knot began to soften, and gradually, so gradually, to unwind. The colored ribbons of Adrigon's emotions flashed and swirled. He was afraid. Lucky could sense his fear. Her own heartbeat quickened in response, but she continued radiating warmth.

She remembered how Aidan described healing with his Gift of Song. The right notes just came to him, he said, and when the healing was complete, the song stopped, without conscious effort on his part. What she did now likewise seemed to stem both from her and from something apart from her, something bigger than her. She didn't control her Gift, so much as provide a medium through which it could move and work. She let go of her ideas of what could or should happen and let the warmth flow through her, trusting her Gift to do its work.

It was like being released from a prison he hadn't known he'd been in. Kev had sensed that something was missing ever since he'd regained his ability to call the dragon, but he couldn't have said what that missing something was. He still couldn't have named it, but he knew it wasn't missing anymore. Midway through showering a group of Adrigon-controlled angels with flame, he felt the shift. All the fire that had burned in him when he hadn't been able to shift at all, all the power of the supernovas he'd experienced in his human form, knitted itself into his dragon. He was no longer a dragon who breathed fire. He was dragon-shaped flame, living fire that could expand and retract at will, unbound from the size and shape of his formerly flesh-and-blood dragon.

The flame he breathed must have changed too. The angel he dowsed last, after he'd become the Fire Dragon, wasn't burned. Instead, she shook her head as if waking from a fog. Her brows drew together as she looked around her. Then she brandished her sword and shot toward a be-spelled Angel of Light whose sword was on course for the back of Danel's neck. She blocked the blade and shifted the angel's attention to her, leaving Danel none the wiser.

Kev rained flames on the nearest group under Adrigon's control, and the result was the same. The angels shook off Adrigon's hold like the vestiges of a dream and rejoined the Dark and Fallen they had originally come to aid.

Kev's heart leapt. Maybe he could do something besides buy Lucky time after all. Or more likely, he and the others had already bought her enough time. He could feel the bond between them again, even stronger than before. He'd bet his flame proof fighting gear that she had something to do with what had just happened to him. In fact, he'd bet his flaming life on it. Because the new form of his Gift and the sense of wholeness that filled him had to be the culmination of the integration she'd performed for him. He'd never felt so fully alive or so fully himself.

With an exultant roar, he spun to dowse the next group with flames.

Help me. The mental command hit Bryn with such force that she stumbled. She would have fallen right into the path of her opponent's blade had Josh not knocked her out of the way.

The words whispered to her in her own voice, but she knew where they came from. The download of images that followed had her abandoning her half-Raven form and scrambling inside the protective circle the sorcerers had erected against Adrigon's followers and the hijacked Angels of Light. She couldn't fight anyone with the Tree filling her head, and she didn't want to be a liability to Josh and the others.

She huddled with the Dark children and the adults unable to fight until the flow of images stopped and their message settled into her mind and heart. When she was certain her thoughts were her own again, she left the circle, gestured her thanks to the sorcerer who had aided her entrance and exit, and looked for the fastest path out of the wreckage of the tent cities. Then she drew the swords from the sheaths on her back, summoned her Raven wings, and took to the sky to find Aidan.

"Don't flame me! I'm on your side!" Aidan shouted, as the dragon-shaped fireball that had replaced his brother's scaly alter ego blew a fiery geyser in his direction. Sure, he was kind of in the middle of a wad of too many Angels of Light turned Adrigon-minions. Still… "Watch where you aim that thing!"

When the flame hit him, though, it didn't hurt at all. It felt warm, even pleasant. Weird…

At least the thought of getting flamed had pumped some adrenaline into his system. He needed that to keep fending off his former allies—not to mention his father.

Wait. The hostile angels around him seemed to be re-grouping, moving away from him, and Lucifer winged Aidan's way with a concerned look on his face, not a weapon in sight. Aidan raised his guard just in case his brainwashed father had decided to try a new tactic.

"Are you all right, son?" Lucifer came to a hover a few feet away. "I had never grasped the extent of Adrigon's power. That he could have turned me against my own children…" His voice trailed off as he gazed at Aidan.

"All right?" Aidan raised an eyebrow. "Let's just say I'm unsettled. Are you sure you're back to normal? No lingering desire to wipe out the mixed-blood mongrels?"

Lucifer winced. "While I see no visible wounds, it sounds like you have some invisible ones. You must know I don't believe any of things I said—or condone the things I did—

while under Adrigon's control. I would unsay and undo them if I could."

"I get it. It's just…" Any further response Aidan might have made was wiped from his mind by a flurry of black wings as Bryn nearly barreled into him.

She stopped before she hit him. Even so, the tips of her dual swords ended up a little too close for comfort. "Whoa! Be careful with those things."

She slid the swords into the sheaths on her back with a combination of strength and grace that took his breath away.

Her intense gray eyes locked onto his. "I need your help, Aidan. I know how to fix the pathways, but I can't do it without you. The Tree needs us—now."

Aidan shook his head. "I can't leave before we end this."

"Go," Lucifer said. "Your brother seems to be making short work of this."

He was right. Kev's new dragon crop-dusted the skies, and, for whatever reason, the touch of the dragon's flames seemed to break Adrigon's hold on the Angels of Light.

Still Aidan hesitated. "But I can't… Bryn, the Tree took my Gift the last time. I've got nothing to give it."

"Just trust me." Bryn clasped her fingers around his hand. "Please."

He took a deep breath, paused, nodded. "Okay."

Even as the word left his lips, he felt himself fading into everywhere and nowhere.

CHAPTER 30

Lucky felt the warmth leaving her almost as if she were waking from a dream. She had no sense of how long the warmth of her Gift had flowed through her. She sensed it had done what it needed to do, though she couldn't say exactly what that was.

As her connection to Adrigon's mind fell away, she became aware that Luil was gripping her upper arms and that she gripped his arms in return.

"Did it work?" she asked.

"Yes." Luil grinned. "It worked beautifully, my daughter. See for yourself."

He moved to the side, so she could see beyond him to where an oversized, chain mailed being with iridescent blue-black hair that seemed to float on a breeze held a sobbing Adrigon by the base of the wings with one huge hand. One of the Angels of Light bound Adrigon's hands behind his back and slipped a hood made of some glowing silver substance over his head.

"The Archangel Michael?"

Lucky hardly needed Luil's nod.

He answered her next question before she asked. "The hood is to block Adrigon's Gift—in case he tries to use it."

"What about Helel? Did they get him too?"

"Yes. Some of Michael's soldiers have already taken him away. My shadow beings held him until the Angels of Light were able to come for him."

"Then it's over?" Lucky asked. "We won?"

A warm smile curved Luil's lips. "Yes. We won." He pushed back some strands of hair that had fallen into her face. "Thanks to you."

Lucky went weak with relief, and her eyes filled with tears. When Luil pulled her close, she didn't resist. She laid her cheek against his chest and wept.

They had won, but far too many had lost their lives in the process. Kev made another pass over the devastation of the tent cities. With his heat vision, he scanned the bodies of those who had fallen for signs of life. And, just like the last two passes he'd made, he turned up nothing. Everyone down seemed to be down for good.

He sighed and winged back toward the park where the survivors had gathered.

They had come together not so much in celebration as solidarity. While Adrigon's defeat had brought relief, too much damage remained in his wake for rejoicing. Not only had many lost their lives, but many others now had to live with the knowledge that they themselves had taken the lives of allies and friends. Under Adrigon's control though they may have been, their hands, their weapons, had been the instruments of death. That awareness added layers to their grief.

Even for those whose friends—or family members—had successfully fought back and survived, reunion was also a reckoning. Kev had had to overcome some residual distrust of his father, and he knew Aidan had done the same. Lucifer, for his part, had made no secret of how rocked he had been by the ease with which Adrigon had turned him against his own sons.

Kev gathered even Zeke hadn't been immune. He overheard the Cherub apologizing to Malachi, while he looked at his hands as if they belonged to a stranger. "Some part of me knew you were my friend and colleague—or, at least, had been so—but that seemed irrelevant, eclipsed by the overpowering thought that, as a Naphil, you were the enemy and had to be destroyed. It may be some time before I stop second-guessing my own thoughts."

"It may also be some time before I see you the way I once did," Malachi said.

"Understandably so."

If Malachi made any verbal response, Kev didn't hear it. But he did see Malachi, after only the slightest hesitation, take the hand Zeke extended.

Kev wondered how many of Adrigon's original followers—so many of whom they'd beheaded and turned to dust—would have been as stunned as his father and Zeke about what Adrigon had made them believe and do.

"Kev!"

He turned toward the sound of Lucky's voice, his eyes searching for the shape of her. He caught sight of her and Luil pushing through the crowd toward him. He rushed to meet them and caught her in his arms.

"You did it!" he said into her hair.

"We did it." She pulled back to take his face in her hands. "I heard about your Fire Dragon and his purifying flame."

Kev grinned then turned his face to kiss her palm. "That wouldn't have been possible without you. It took a while—probably longer because of Adrigon's blasted drug—but that integration thing seems to have finally done its work."

"This might have had something to do with it too." Lucky's hand moved to lift the chain around her neck.

"The Medallion!" Kev reached for the amulet where it dangled beside Lucky's locket. "How did you get it back?"

Lucky shrugged and shook her head. "It came to me—in what I guess was a kind of Bonding. It seems the Medallion and the locket together, somehow, are my weapon. I think they strengthened my Gift enough for it to defeat Adrigon, but I can't explain how or why or even what I did."

"Whatever it was, it worked. You did well, my daughter." Kev had almost forgotten about Luil until he spoke.

"Thank you for your help," Lucky said.

Luil inclined his head. "I think I will find the rest of our sorcerers and see if we can help restore some order to the tent cities."

Lucky said goodbye to Luil and then looked at Kev, her eyes glistening with tears. "These poor people. So much death, so much loss. Even their makeshift homes have been destroyed."

"I know." Kev tucked her against his chest. "Looks like others have the same idea as Luil. Let's see what we can do to help."

Aidan hadn't expected to rematerialize in a different part of Elsewhere. But he recognized the hills and cliffs from their search for Adrigon's base.

His fingers tightened around Bryn's before releasing them. "What are we doing here?"

"I'm going to call the Tree. Since it's already come to me once here, it will be even easier to summon it this time."

Aidan's gut clenched. So, this was where the fun had begun last time. "Oh, right," he said. "I'd forgotten you can summon it."

Bryn didn't answer. Her eyes were closed, and her lips shaped words he didn't understand.

He felt the sudden charge seconds before the Tree appeared, complete with heavy winds and guarding sword.

Bryn caught his hand and drew him toward the sword.

He didn't understand what she was doing until the sword sliced across his palm.

"Ow! You could have warned me."

Bryn let the sword cut her own palm, then grabbed Aidan's hand again, pressing her bloodied palm against his.

Hand in hand, they pushed through the wind to the Tree.

Side by side, they touched their palms with their commingled blood to the Tree's bark.

Aidan almost sighed with relief when the Tree simply absorbed the blood and opened a glowing door.

He followed Bryn inside.

And the door closed, leaving no trace it had ever been.

They were in a kind of clearing in a forest, from which opened countless paths. As Aidan looked around, path upon path appeared. Paths crisscrossing, intertwining, and intersecting one another. Though he couldn't see them, he sensed additional pathways all around him—to either side, above and below—radiating out from the clearing in all directions.

Bryn led him to the middle of the clearing, dropped to her knees, and drew him down beside her. As he knelt, Aidan saw that the floor of the clearing looked like wood. It was ringed and grained like a cross section of a gigantic tree.

Bryn sat back on her heels, raised their joined hands, and threaded her fingers through his so their palms pressed together. "Place your other hand on the Tree," she said, lowering her free hand to press against the wood.

Aidan did the same. As soon as his palm touched the wood, both of his palm sigils activated. Instinctively, he tried to pull his hand from Bryn's, but her fingers tightened, pressing her palm more tightly against his. He felt again the connection of their sigils, the exchange of energy, he had first felt when she had given him her life energy after his last encounter with the Tree. This time though, he could feel the energy flowing both ways. And he could feel their commingled energy flowing through his other hand into the Tree.

The hand that pressed against the Tree grew warm, and the ringed wood beneath them began to glow with a pale green light. The light expanded to fill the space around them, and in the green glow, Aidan could see the ghostly images of the pathways he'd only sensed before, so many he couldn't begin to count them. A nexus. No. The answer came to him as both his own deduction and as an awareness rising in him from his connection to the Tree: not *a* nexus, *the* nexus, the nexus where the Halls had been—visualized in a way he and Bryn could comprehend.

"Help me." The words, in Bryn's voice, whispered through his consciousness.

Unlike the last time, when the Tree had commandeered his Gift and taken what it needed, this was a request. The whispered words urged him to sing.

Aidan could feel the notes, the melodies, waiting to be sung. But when he opened his mouth, there was no sound.

Heat grew where his palm sigil pressed to Bryn's, and then Bryn began to sing. Aidan knew the notes before she sang them. He provided the song. She gave it voice.

The heat between their hands intensified, and now Aidan could see into the Tree as he had done before. Colored paths, like branches and roots, pulsing with light, growing brighter and brighter as Bryn sang, as he sang through Bryn.

His hand was burning now, and a kind of pressure built inside him, radiating up through his legs and arms, to his chest, his heart, his throat. It grew and grew, and then he was singing, his voice mingling with Bryn's.

Then Bryn's voice fell away, and Aidan sang alone. The song was as many-layered and impossible as the one he'd sung when the Tree had hijacked him to heal itself. But this time, he felt no pain. The Tree healed him as he healed the Tree.

And Bryn made both healings possible.

The Tree and Aidan filled Bryn's entire being. She could feel both the vastness and strangeness of the Tree and the immediacy and intimacy of Aidan. Or was it the other way around? Sometimes the Tree felt as close and intimate as her own heartbeat while Aidan seemed vast and mysterious. Their energies circulated through her, and she guided them, showing them how to help each other.

She sensed where the Tree needed strengthening, even where new growth beckoned, and she guided Aidan to those places. At the same time, she somehow knew how the Tree could complete Aidan's healing, could return to him his Gift of Song, and she guided the Tree to him as well.

Time and space lost all meaning. Bryn saw herself as a kind of pathway, a conduit for primal, healing energies. And when those energies had done their work, when the pathway was no longer needed, she opened her eyes. The last notes of Aidan's song hovered in the green light, accompanied by the hum of the pathways that surrounded them.

"It's done," she said, and Aidan nodded.

She lifted the hand she had pressed against the Tree and let it rest on her lap. Aidan raised his hand to his knee.

Slowly, Bryn uncurled the fingers that had welded his palm against hers, stretching them and then dropping that hand too to her lap.

They knelt in silence until the green glow faded.

Then Bryn led Aidan out of the clearing and through the door that opened into Elsewhere.

Only after the Tree had faded away did Aidan break the silence. "What exactly did we do in there?"

Bryn had almost forgotten he wasn't a Guardian, that he couldn't feel the Tree stretching its new pathways. She smiled.

"You'll see," she said.

CHAPTER 31

Two memorial services in one day.

Lucky took a deep breath and tightened her grip on Kev's hand as they joined the throng outside the temple in Elsewhere.

They had left G-Ma's memorial only a couple of hours ago. There, Lucky had laughed and wept as friends and family had shared stories about her grandmother. She had even managed to share one herself, although she'd finished it with tears running down her cheeks. When she'd taken her seat, Kev had wrapped his arm around her shoulders. Josh, seated between her and Ben, had taken her hand.

In the days between the battle in Elsewhere and the memorial, Lucky and Josh had managed to explain everything, as best they could, to Josh's parents. Uncle Matthew's and Aunt Beth's reactions had moved from disbelief to shock to a stunned acceptance. Even as they had struggled to understand what she and Josh had revealed to them, Lucky had felt the depth of their love. She had almost cried when they had insisted on inviting Kev and Ben to dinner.

"They love you—and we love you," Aunt Beth had said. "We want to meet them."

Lucky wished G-Ma could have met them too.

Now, she and Kev and Josh and Ben counted themselves among the thousands attending the ceremony for all those lost in the battle. Lucky felt the weight of their deaths. The connection she had felt with all of them, the sense of their suffering, still haunted her.

Lucky and the others moved into the line of mourners processing down the colonnade at the temple's entrance. It seemed to Lucky that the towering stone angels and the Still Ones atop their columns shared their grief.

Inside the temple, they located Aidan and Bryn—few beings had hair as perfectly golden as Aidan's—and made their slow way down the aisle to slide onto the stone bench beside them.

After murmured greetings, they sat in silence while the remaining mourners took their seats. The solemnity of the occasion called for silence, but even if it hadn't, Lucky would have had little to say. The grief she shared with everyone around her spoke for itself.

When everyone was finally seated, the silence deepened as those participating in the ceremony moved onto the dais. In addition to the Archangel Uriel, the group included a leader from each of the Dark realms whose members had sought refuge in Elsewhere. There were so many of them. So many different worlds, each with so many now dead.

For some reason, Lucky remembered looking around at all the weapons in the weapons room at the training center and thinking, "So many ways to die." Many hands may have wielded many weapons to create the deaths they mourned today, but those weapons and those hands were all guided by Adrigon. Adrigon was the real weapon. Adrigon and his blasted Gift.

No, Lucky thought, the problem wasn't his Gift. She knew plenty of people with Gifts powerful enough to cause massive destruction. *She* was one of them. The problem was Adrigon's hatred of the Dark and Fallen. That hatred was the real weapon, and his Gift had enabled him to spread the hatred even to those who didn't naturally share it.

Lucky found it difficult to pay attention to the ceremony. She kept thinking about the battle—and about the Bonding, when the Light-Bringer's Medallion had come to her and she'd experienced such an awareness of everything, of everyone, and how she'd felt such pain and such joy. She hadn't been able to hold it all then, and she certainly couldn't grasp it all now. But she couldn't let it go either.

An exquisite sound broke through her reverie, drawing her attention to the performer on the dais. A horned being with purple-black hair clothed in multicolored robes held an iridescent black orb that seemed to be an instrument played using subtle hand motions. Lucky's thoughts fell away. She opened her senses to experience more of the performance: sight, sound, touch, taste. The sweetness and bitterness, the softness and harshness, the beauty and sorrow, brought tears to her eyes.

Kev's hand tightened on hers, and Lucky turned to look at him. The smile that curved his lips and crinkled the corners of his eyes made her heart ache.

The music faded and the performer left the stage.

In the silence that followed, Lucky felt the cool dampness of the tears on her cheeks, the warmth of Kev's hand in hers, and the subtle pulse of the ache in the center of her chest.

Like the other memorial Lucky had attended in Elsewhere, this one ended with fire. This time Lucifer and the leaders from the Dark realms made the flames. As the pyre grew, Uriel spoke the ritual words of remembrance. The formal ceremony ended with the fire still blazing, and those in attendance moved out of the temple to circle the pyre.

Lucky, Kev, Bryn, Aidan, Josh, and Ben kept to the outer edge of the circle. When the flames had nearly disappeared, Zeke approached them, accompanied by a human-sized Archangel Gabriel.

"Gabriel would offer his condolences," Zeke said to Lucky.

Gabriel bowed his head, then looked at Lucky through the cloud-swept eyes she'd sometimes glimpsed in G-Ma's face.

And to Lucky, it was as if those eyes became movie screens. Scenes from her life with G-Ma flashed across them: momentary glimpses of incidents from Lucky's birth, through her childhood, and up to her visits with G-Ma at the assisted living facility. Lucky's heart felt full to bursting. Tears streamed from her eyes.

Gabriel opened his arms, and it seemed the most natural thing in the world for Lucky to move into his embrace. And it was G-Ma's arms she felt around her, G-Ma's familiar frame she felt in her arms, G-Ma surrounding her, enfolding her, with love.

When Lucky finally stepped out of the embrace and looked into Gabriel's eyes, they were again their normal cloud-swept blue.

"How?" Lucky whispered.

Your grandmother and I have been connected since your Making. Gabriel's voice flashed like lightning in her mind just like she remembered, but this time the lightning was tempered by something human, something of G-Ma. *Humans are rarely called to be Makers, but when such a thing happens, I serve as surrogate and conduit during the Making. I cannot serve as surrogate without passing something of myself to both the Made and the human Maker. Likewise, something of the human Maker remains with me.*

Gabriel's words solved several mysteries for Lucky, but she still had some questions. "How is it possible for humans to be called as Makers at all? How did I call G-Ma?"

It is only possible if the human is a Sensitive.

"But G-Ma wasn't a Sensitive. If she were, she would have warned me—and my mother. She would never have let either of us reach our eighteenth birthday without knowing."

Your grandmother's Sensitive powers were dormant. She was only a carrier until Alzheimer's opened a part of her mind that activated her abilities to some extent, making it possible for her to see beyond her time and space.

Tears again filled Lucky's eyes. "That awful disease gave her something good?"

Zeke put his hand on her shoulder. "Most things are neither all bad nor all good. They are mixed."

Lucky thought of her Gift, and Kev's, and Aidan's. She nodded. "I guess that's true."

Your grandmother wishes you to know that she would not change anything. She lived a full life, and she considers herself fortunate to have chosen how it would end.

"She sacrificed herself to help me." Lucky sniffled.

Not just you. She knew you would play a vital role in this battle, and she wanted to ensure you had everything you needed. I confess I provided her some additional assistance—if only to counterbalance the damage the Wraiths did when the bit of Archangel in her attracted them.

"That's why they were so interested in her!" Josh exclaimed.

Joshua Monroe. Gabriel turned from Lucky to her cousin. *Your grandmother wants you to know she loves you and is proud of who and what you have become.*

"She knows what I've become?" Josh looked as if he might be close to tears as well.

Gabriel inclined his head. *She knows. She also knows how well you have handled your transformation.*

"Thanks," Josh said on a sniffle. "Tell her I miss her."

She knows that too.

Josh smiled. "Yeah, I suppose she does."

"Thank you, Gabriel," Lucky said, "for sharing G-Ma's messages. For all you've done. For helping G-Ma get the locket back to me. We all owe you and her thanks for that."

Many others are to be thanked as well.

"Yes." Lucky thought of all those whose bodies had burned on the pyre. "Very many."

Including you. I am proud to have been a part of your Making, Lucky Monroe.

The Archangel Gabriel was proud to be a part of her Making. Lucky could barely find her voice. "Th-thank you. I'm—honored—and grateful."

Gabriel inclined his head. Then he disappeared in a flash, leaving behind a fading after-image.

"How about that?" Josh put his arm around Lucky and gave her a squeeze. "Our G-Ma is connected to an Archangel. Wait until Mom and Dad hear about this."

Bryn was changing out of the clothes she'd worn to the memorial when she felt the shift, the settling. She yanked on her workout gear, rushed to Aidan's room, and knocked on the door.

"I'm almost ready, Bryn," he called, "but come on in."

She pushed the door open.

"If I'm moving too slowly for you, I can just meet you in the gym." Aidan's voice was muffled by the faded blue t-shirt he was pulling over his head.

Bryn ignored the remark. "It's finished," she said. "Can you feel it?"

For a split-second, Aidan looked confused. Then his eyes widened, and his brow furrowed.

"I'm not sure." He closed his eyes and tilted his head. "Maybe. There's been a kind of dissonance in the back of my mind since we visited the Tree, and, yeah, it just resolved." He opened his eyes and looked at Bryn. "So, what exactly is it that's finished?"

Bryn frowned. "You really don't know?"

Aidan shook his head. "I really don't."

"I can see it as well as feel it. Well, what I see is more like a symbol, a kind of representation."

Aidan shrugged. "I got nothing like that."

Bryn thought for a moment, then his words from just before clicked into place. "But you've got sound, right? Dissonance and resolution. You hear music?"

"Yeah. The music has been in the back of my mind, almost outside my awareness, since we helped the Tree absorb the explosion of the Halls. After our last visit to the Tree, it changed—got louder, became more dissonant—and I really heard it. Then I realized it had been there for a while, even though I hadn't been conscious of it before. Now, it's changed again. No more dissonance."

"But it's still there?"

Aidan nodded.

"What is the music telling you? If you could see it instead of hearing it, what would it show you?"

Aidan closed his eyes again, a frown between his brows. He made small movements as he listened to the music inside his head. And then his movements became more pronounced, and the frown dissolved. When he opened his eyes, Bryn could see her own excitement reflected there.

"Seven hells," he breathed. "Does Eleni know? Do the other Guardians?"

"I assume so, but I don't know for sure."

"Bryn! Aidan!" Zeke's bellow flew up the stairs like an arrow from a bow.

"I think they know," said Aidan.

CHAPTER 32

Only a few days had passed since the memorial, but Elsewhere looked completely different. Those who could sense the repair of the Tree's pathways had wasted no time passing the news on to those who couldn't, and joy at the ability to return home had if not replaced, at least alleviated, the grief and sorrow of loss. Some of the Dark refugees had already returned to their home worlds, but many had wanted to end their time in Elsewhere with a celebration.

Lilith and some of the sorcerers she'd trained in Nadach had lent their magic to the cause, and the party had come together quickly. Lucky, Alicia, and Mo had arrived early to help with some last-minute arrangements that, as Alicia put it, "someone without a shred of magic could do."

"I'm so glad you agreed to help with this," Alicia said. She eyed the serving bowls Lucky had unceremoniously placed on the table and, within seconds, had rearranged them so that the shapes and colors of the bowls and their contents somehow looked artistic and purposeful.

Lucky chuckled. "I'm not sure you need my help. What you just did would never have even occurred to me."

"Me neither." Mo placed a vase of flowers in the opening Alicia had left on the table. "Centerpieces, though, even I can manage."

Alicia's quick fingers repositioned a couple of the blooms, and Mo laughed. "Or not. It looked fine to me before, but now—wow! And you say you can't do magic."

Alicia beamed, moving on to the next table. "It's easy for me. I see how things go together—shapes, colors, flowers, herbs, all kinds of things."

"That's part of what makes you good at healing," Lucky said.

Alicia's hands stopped their motion. "Huh. I'd never thought of it that way. I guess it is." She resumed her arranging. "I'm starting my training soon, you know, to be a healer."

"Alicia!" Lucky plunked the laden tray she'd been holding onto the table and threw her arms around her friend. "That's wonderful! What made your mother change her mind?"

Alicia grinned. "I did. I finally told her it was what I wanted to do and nothing she could say or do would stop me. She looked stunned and didn't say anything at first. Then, after a long pause, she said, 'Well, if that's how you feel, I suppose I must respect your choice.'"

"Good for her," said Lucky.

"And good for you!" Mo added.

"Thanks. It made me wonder if she's just wanted me to stand up for myself all along."

"That's possible," Lucky agreed. "Whatever the reason, I'm glad she's finally decided to let you do what you love."

"Me too."

Alicia and Mo moved down the table, and Lucky retrieved the abandoned tray and followed.

"I'm really excited." Alicia took some bowls and platters from the tray and arranged them on the table around the centerpiece Mo had put in place. "Not only has Katrin agreed to take me on as an apprentice, but Sambethe said she would also give me lessons when she's released from Raphael's supervision."

Lucky's fingers tightened on the tray. "Sambethe? They're releasing her, then? Allowing her to teach?"

Mo placed the last centerpiece and looked at Lucky, a furrow between her brows. "I know you don't trust her after what happened with Josh, but she's been great with all the Nadachis and Still Ones at the safe house. Katrin couldn't have managed everything without her."

Lucky hmphed. She hadn't been happy about her friends working so closely with Sambethe. Now, with both of them seemingly on Sambethe's side, she liked it even less.

Alicia contemplated the final bowl on Lucky's tray, shifted a few things around on the table, and moved the bowl from the tray to the space she'd prepared.

Then she turned and contemplated Lucky, her hands on her hips. "You have a right to be upset with her—I know that—but I think you should give her another chance. You might find she's not as bad as you think."

Lucky set her jaw, then sighed. "Josh told me pretty much the same thing. I guess if he can forgive her, I can at least talk to her."

"Atta girl," said Mo.

Alicia smiled her approval. Then, her gaze moved past Lucky, and her smile brightened. "Jaime!"

"How's my girl?" Jaime scooped Alicia up in his arms and spun her around before setting her back on her feet. "Are you almost finished? Everyone's gathering at the stage in the park. I hear we don't want to miss the opening remarks."

Jaime's words wiped all thought of Sambethe from Lucky's mind. "We definitely don't," she agreed. "Bryn has been dropping hints and smiling like the Cheshire Cat."

Alicia cast one last glance around. "I think this looks great." She took the tray from Lucky's hand and tucked it underneath one of the tables, where the tablecloth hid it from view. "Let's go. I can't wait to learn about Bryn's big secret."

Eleni moved to the front of the stage amid cheers and applause from the crowd. Aidan's fingers closed around Bryn's, and Bryn released the breath she hadn't realized she'd been holding.

When the cheers faded, Eleni expressed her joy that all those who had taken refuge in Elsewhere could now return to their home worlds and her gratitude for being included in their celebration. Then came the moment Bryn had been waiting for.

"As a long-time Guardian and trainer of Guardians, it is my honor and privilege to share some exciting news with you. The restoration of the pathways from Elsewhere to the Dark worlds and between the Dark worlds is not all we have to celebrate today. The recent healing of the Tree also created new pathways between Dark and Light. Travel to the Heavens is no longer restricted to those with access to the Gates. The Tree has united Light and Dark once more!"

Eleni beamed as the crowd cheered. When the roar subsided, she continued, "And for that we can thank the two newest members of the Guardians—Branwen, of the line of Lilith, and Aidan, son of Lucifer."

Cheers erupted again.

Bryn held onto Aidan's hand as they moved forward to stand with Eleni. When Aidan grinned and raised their joined hands, the cheering grew even louder.

Bryn's connection to the Tree was like a live wire. She could sense the vibrations of all the new pathways. The energy of creation buzzed through her veins and spilled out in both tears and laughter. Somehow, the destruction of Nadach and of the Halls had given rise to this newly connected world. The promise of it salved her grief—and seemed to do the same for the cheering crowd.

After the cheering had quieted, Eleni continued, "The Guardians would like to offer Bryn and Aidan each a token of appreciation for their service."

Turning to face Bryn and Aidan, she opened a small box she had cradled in her palm to reveal two small, stylized silver Trees. She pinned one on the shoulder of Bryn's vest and the other on the raised collar of Aidan's jacket.

"In a few days, we will welcome you more formally into the fellowship of the Guardians," she said. "But wear these knowing that the Tree has chosen each of you as one of us."

The Tree had chosen them. The thought was both exhilarating and humbling. Not long ago, Bryn hadn't even known the Tree existed. Now, she had become a Guardian, and the Tree was woven into her very being. And Aidan, who had come to mean so much to her, was a Guardian too.

After the pain of losing Nadach, she had finally found a home.

The Metatron's council chamber was almost unrecognizable. Not that the room itself had changed. It still held the same crystalline furniture, and the same silver-white light streamed through the high windows. But Kev had never seen the place occupied by so many people, dressed in so many assorted colors, all talking together. The formal part of the meeting was over, but informal conversation continued. That's what the chamber had been missing all along, Kev thought, a variety of voices from the Light and Dark realms.

As he scanned the room, Kev's gaze caught Lucifer's. A moment later, his father was at his side.

"You look as if you approve of this new order of things." Lucifer gestured toward the room at large.

Kev nodded. "I do."

"As do I."

"And why wouldn't you?" Kev grinned. "Now that you're a member of the new Metatron."

Lucifer's smile was unexpectedly humble. "I was gratified when Margash asked me to consider it. We both wanted a Metatron that could serve both Light and Dark. I think Ba'al and I strike a good balance with Margash and Galiel."

"I agree. I also trust the Advisory Council will keep the four of you in line. You'll have a lot of input from a lot of different perspectives." Kev gestured toward Zeke as he joined their group. "Including from this one."

Lucifer acknowledged Zeke with a tilt of his head. "Those perspectives are essential. Our worlds are all connected now. It is time we learn to cooperate and work together. It may be difficult, but all our worlds will be richer for it."

"Well put," said Zeke. "It seems Margash made a wise choice."

"Thank you, Zeke. I know I speak for the whole Metatron in saying we are grateful for your participation in the Advisory Council."

"I am glad to be of service." Zeke turned toward Kev. "Shall we go? I fear we have missed Eleni's announcement. The party is well under way by now."

Kev shrugged. "We knew the gist of it anyway. Still, I am sorry to have missed seeing her recognize Aidan and Bryn."

"I regret missing that too. But all of us being here together does celebrate them in a way. What they did made this possible," Zeke said.

"Your granddaughter and my son." Lucifer couldn't have looked prouder. "Together they made the prophecy come true. They united Light and Dark."

Lucky contemplated the various brightly colored beverages on the refreshment table. Without a clue about their ingredients, she could only base her decision on appearance. She finally chose a dark berry colored drink with a gold-green swirl.

"Good choice. Dragon plum and night melon. It's one of my favorites." The words came from behind her, but Lucky recognized the voice.

She had half a mind to put the glass back on the table and walk away, but she'd promised Alicia and Mo.

"Hello, Sambethe." Lucky turned to face the small, white-haired woman. "I don't know that I want to base my choice of beverage on your recommendation."

Sambethe's lips twisted, and she inclined her head. "Touché. I understand your reluctance, but in this case my words are true. The drink is delicious and refreshing. It would be a shame for you to miss the experience because you distrust me."

Lucky suppressed a sigh. She picked up the drink and took a sip. Sambethe hadn't lied. "It really is good. I've never tasted anything quite like it."

Sambethe also picked up a glass of the dragon plum drink. She gestured toward a small bench beneath a nearby tree. "Would you be willing to sit and talk with me while we enjoy these?"

This time Lucky did sigh. "Sure. Why not?"

Still, she couldn't bring herself to start a conversation after they had sat down on the bench. She didn't know how long they would have sat in silence if Sambethe hadn't spoken.

"I did not want to have to do what I did to your cousin, you know. But I saw no alternative. Every vision of the future that came to me showed division and destruction and death on a scale much larger than we have experienced. Every vision, except one in which you were Made Naphil. I could not see how your Making would alter things in our favor, only that it would. And I could not convince the Council."

"So, you decided to force our hands."

Sambethe inclined her head. "I saw my chance, and I took it. And while I regret the pain it caused you, I cannot regret the decision. I see now what I could not see before. Your Making was the catalyst that"—she made a sweeping gesture with one arm—"made all this possible."

Lucky's brow furrowed. "I did manage to stop Adrigon, if that's what you mean."

A smile curved Sambethe's lips, and she shook her head. "Stopping Adrigon was indeed important, yes, but I was referring to much more than that. What else made this celebration possible?"

"Everyone did, everyone helped." Lucky shook her head. "I don't know what…" Then she gasped. "Kev, his Fire Dragon's flame. And Bryn and Aidan, what they did with the Tree."

Sambethe's smile widened. "Yes, yes! Without your Making, Kev would not have become the Fire Dragon. And Bryn and Aidan would not have met, let alone become Guardians, because she would not have left Nadach. It took all of you— and you, Lucky, were the key."

The truth of Sambethe's words fluttered in Lucky's chest along with her quickened heartbeat. "But Josh," she said.

"I knew you would choose to save him, Lucky. I deemed what I did a necessary risk."

"And you didn't know my blood would change him."

Sambethe shook her head as if replying to a question. "No, I did not." Her eyes twinkling, she added, "I do not think he minds it though."

"No, he doesn't. He told me as much." Lucky took a sip of her drink, swallowed. "He forgave you long before I did."

Sambethe tilted her head. "You have forgiven me then?"

Lucky chuckled. "I hadn't. Until just now."

"Then I am glad we had this chance to talk." Sambethe raised her glass and tilted it toward Lucky. "To new beginnings."

Lucky clinked her glass against Sambethe's. "To new beginnings."

Aidan had hardly let go of Bryn's hand since they had walked out on the stage to accept Eleni's gift. His connections to the Tree and to Bryn sang in his blood. The two combined made a heady melody. He barely took in his surroundings, so aware was he of the humming in his veins and the girl beside him.

He shifted his hand to thread his fingers with hers.

Without conscious thought, he guided them away from the crowd to a more secluded part of the park. Away from the throng of people, the song thrumming through him quieted, but his heartbeat picked up speed. The long, sheltering branches of a weeping willow beckoned, and he turned his steps toward it. Bryn followed his lead without comment.

Aidan pushed aside some of the wispy branches, grateful to find that no one else had sought the privacy the willow afforded. He drew Bryn into the tree's shelter and down onto the soft grass. After they were seated, he released his hold on her hand only to glide his fingers back and forth over her fingers and palm.

"Do you feel it humming in you—your connection to the Tree?" he asked.

Bryn's fingertips slid over his, mirroring his touch. "I feel it, but not so much as humming though. It's less of a song for me than it is a vibration, a frequency—or a mix of frequencies."

"I get that." The touch of Bryn's fingers made it difficult to shape words.

"It's strange, isn't it? I mean, the Tree feels like such a part of me, and I feel such a part of it. But, at the same time, I almost can't believe it chose me—chose us."

Aidan cast Bryn a sidelong glance, his mouth quirked in a half-smile. "You find it hard to believe the Tree would choose a mixed-blood demon-human-Cherub and a half-Seraph Naphil?"

Bryn chuckled. "When you put it that way…"

"Your doubt makes perfect sense?"

"Exactly!" Bryn's eyes widened. "But maybe that's why it chose us. Our mixed blood is what made it possible for us to resist Adrigon. Maybe it also made it possible for us to help the Tree. We're Guardians of a different sort."

"I like the way you think." Aidan's heart pounded in his chest, and now words tumbled out of him. "In fact, I like everything about you. *Like* isn't even a strong enough word. I *love* everything about you." There, he'd said it. He took a deep breath, and said it again, more slowly. "I love you, Bryn. And

I love the idea of being a different kind of Guardian with you."

Bryn rested the hand Aidan wasn't gripping like a lifeline against his cheek with a tenderness that took his breath away. "Oh, Aidan, I love you too. So very much."

He kissed her. She kissed him back. It felt like coming home.

When they paused for breath, Bryn asked, "Will you miss being part of the Forces of the Fallen?"

"Yeah, I will. I haven't been back with the Forces for all that long, and I do enjoy it." He paused, considering. "But being a Guardian—that feels right—even if it also feels strange and new and a little scary." He squeezed her hand. "Plus, I get to do all that strange, new, slightly scary stuff with you. I'm all in for that."

"Me too." Bryn grinned and kissed him on the nose. "All in."

She looked so happy and so beautiful and so Bryn that Aidan had to kiss her again.

When the kiss ended, he sighed. "Now that I know you love me back, I guess we could be a little more social—go find our friends and check out the party?"

"Yes, we definitely should." Bryn stood up and held out both hands to him. He took them and let her pull him to his feet. "We have so much to celebrate."

Aidan couldn't have agreed more.

"Oh, there's Katrin." Sambethe pointed out the healer in the crush of people around the refreshment tables. "I have something I need to discuss with her regarding your friend Alicia's training. Do you mind?"

"Of course not." Lucky rose to her feet when Sambethe did. "I'm glad we talked. And I'm glad you're going to be one of Alicia's teachers."

Sambethe smiled. "I am glad too. On both counts."

Luil appeared at Lucky's side as Sambethe's small form disappeared in the crowd. "You and Sambethe have come to a resolution then?"

"Were you eavesdropping?"

Luil chuckled. "Only a bit."

Lucky gave him a mock indignant glare, then nodded. "We have. I can get why she did what she did. Deciding what's right can be messy sometimes, can't it?"

"Messy?" Luil frowned. "I had not considered that before, but, yes, I suppose it can be."

Lucky raised her eyebrows. "You hadn't considered it? Is that because of the whole 'I am Shedim, I want what I want' business?"

Luil's eyes narrowed. "Are you making fun of me?"

Lucky grinned. "Only a bit."

"I suppose I deserve it. For what it's worth, I think I may be moving beyond 'I want what I want'—at least a little."

Lucky remembered how he'd helped her with Adrigon and how he'd been there for Lilith when Nadach had been destroyed. "Yes," she said. "I think you are."

"Finding you, getting to know you, helped with that." Luil's hand cupped her cheek. "Knowing I have a daughter made me want to be better, to be the kind of father you deserve. I may not be able to reach that mark. I will always be Shedim. But I will do my best."

Lucky slid her arms around him and pulled him close. "I think you're doing just fine."

Luil's arms closed around her, and she sniffed and buried her face in his shirt. She refused to cry outright.

"Where will you and the other Nadachis go?" she asked as she stepped out of the embrace.

"Many of us will stay here in Elsewhere. My mother is building a castle outside Elsewhere City. Others have chosen to live in the Earthly realm. Still others may go to other worlds. We have many options."

"You said, 'Many of *us*.' Does that mean you are going to stay in Elsewhere?"

Luil nodded. "Yes. I will stay with Lilith and help to train those who come to us in the ways of magic."

"And that won't be too boring for you?"

"Are you kidding?" Luil grinned. "People learning magic can get into all kinds of trouble."

Lucky laughed. "It should just suit you then."

Scanning the crowd, she caught site of Bryn's distinctive, white-streaked black pixie cut next to Aidan's unmistakable golden curls. She waved and called their names.

When they approached, Lucky raised her eyebrows and looked pointedly at their clasped hands. Bryn's cheeks grew a little rosier, and Aidan grinned from ear to ear.

"Looks like congratulations are in order," Lucky said.

"And about time too," added Luil.

Aidan looked surprised. "You knew?"

It was Luil's turn to raise his eyebrows. "Didn't everyone? I knew the first time I saw the two of you together."

Bryn's cheeks pinked even more, and Aidan looked a little embarrassed. Neither seemed to know how to respond.

Lucky looked from one to the other and then threw her arms around first Bryn and then Aidan. "I'm so happy for you! And I'm so excited about the Guardian thing. You have to tell us more about what happened with the Tree—well, everything that isn't a closely guarded secret."

Bryn and Aidan took turns filling in all the details they could. By the time they'd finished their story, Mo, Alicia, and Jaime had joined their group.

"Not that the Tree talk isn't exciting and everything," said Mo, "because it really is—exciting, I mean, like, *really* exciting. But it sounds like the music is starting in earnest, and I think some serious dancing is in order. Am I right?"

"Absolutely!" Lucky laughed. Mo's enthusiasm was irresistible. Even Luil followed along as Mo led them toward the music.

Josh and Ben must have had the same thought. They were just stepping up to the platform that served as a dance floor when Lucky and the others arrived. Ben, having shed the glamour he assumed when he was around only humans, positively glowed, so much so that Lucky imagined his gold-dusted bronze wings could spring from his back at any moment.

"Impressive, angel boy," Lucky said as she scanned Ben from head to toe.

"I know, right?" Josh gestured at his own jean-clad form. "I feel so underdressed."

Ben laughed. "This has nothing to do with clothing, darling. It's all about my sparkling personality."

"'Sparkling' doesn't even begin…" Mo stared at Ben, unable to finish the sentence. "If you showed up like that to an Icarus show, you would be so fan-mobbed."

"Yeah," Ben grinned. "But then Aidan would get jealous because everyone would be like 'Aidan who?' I do what I must to keep the band together."

Aidan rolled his eyes. "I think that's our cue to dance."

Bryn laughed and waved to the group as he drew her onto the dance floor.

"Follow them!" Mo encouraged. "We came here to dance, so let's dance. The band may not be Icarus—or play anything recognizable—but they're good."

Lucky agreed. The band members appeared to come from multiple different worlds, and the music was unlike anything she had ever heard. But it was interesting, energizing, and very danceable.

The group piled onto the platform after Aidan and Bryn. As the others paired off into couples, Lucky and Mo danced around Luil. He had them both laughing with his intentionally awkward moves.

In the middle of the second song, the medallion and locket warmed on Lucky's chest just as she felt a familiar hand on her shoulder. She spun around and into Kev's arms.

"You found me," she said.

"Yep. Just followed the pull of the Medallion." Kev swung them around to the beat of the music.

"And the locket," Lucky said. "It's together that they create the big magic."

Kev's lips curled into a sensual smile. "Together, *we* create the big magic."

Lucky chuckled. "Yes, we do. Seriously, though, it's both the locket and the Medallion. The two of them, together, are my—weapon. Though 'weapon' doesn't really seem like the right word."

"What do you mean?"

"Well, weapons are about harming people, about separation." She held the locket and Medallion between her thumb and fingers. "These are more about connection. They connect the different parts of me, they make my Gift stronger, and they connect me to you—so much so that we can pass through wards for each other. Even more than that, they help me see how we're all connected—all of us and all the worlds."

"And that connection is our strength."

"Yes, exactly."

Kev looked thoughtful. "That seems to be how the new Metatron is operating too, with the help of an Advisory Council of beings from the various realms."

"With the new pathways between Dark and Light, it's more important than ever." Following Kev's lead, Lucky swung away from him and then spun back around to let him pull her close. "And speaking of those new pathways, it gives me shivers to think Bryn and Aidan were a part of that."

"I know." His gaze searched for Aidan and Bryn among the dancers. "They're going to be wonderful Guardians."

"And what about you?" Lucky smiled up at him. "What are you going to do?"

"In the long term?" Kev shrugged. "I'll continue working with the Forces—and try to use my new Fire Dragon powers for good."

"And in the short term?"

Kev pulled Lucky closer. "In the short term, I'd like to visit a certain cabin in Colorado with a certain person I love. I want you to see how beautiful it is in the spring."

Lucky's smile widened. "I can't think of anything I'd rather do."

"Good." Kev spun her away again. "Because I already told Zeke and Malachi we'd be gone for a few days."

Lucky spun back into his arms and poked him in the chest. "You told them without even asking me? You were so sure I'd say yes?"

"Mmm, I do know you pretty well."

"Yes, you do." Lucky thought of the sculpture he'd made of her, and his easy acceptance of the Dark side of her Gift. She rested her hand against his cheek. "You helped me know myself."

"You did the same for me."

The warmth in Kev's eyes triggered that sweet ache in the center of her chest again.

Scattered around the dance floor, Lucky could see her family and friends—Josh and Ben, Aidan and Bryn, Alicia and Jaime, and Mo and Luil, now dancing as a threesome with Lilith—and so many others—Light, Dark, and Fallen. Although she didn't see them, she knew Zeke, Malachi, Lucifer, Katrin—and, yes, Sambethe—were among the crowd.

She remembered those who could not be there—the Nadachis, Still Ones, and so many others—lost to the conflict with Adrigon. And G-Ma, beloved G-Ma.

So much sorrow and so much joy.

Lucky snuggled against Kev's chest, her heart holding it all.

ACKNOWLEDGEMENTS

First, apologies to my readers for how long it has taken me to finish this final book of the Light-Bringer Series. A lot of life has happened in the last few years, and months with great progress were often followed by months of no work on the book at all. Your comments about how much you have enjoyed reading *A Gift of Wings* and *A Gift of Shadows*, as well as your questions about when the final installment would be published, kept me going over all those years. Thanks for hanging in there!

As always, I want to acknowledge my beta readers for the insightful comments and suggestions that have made this a better book. Thank you, Kathy Boyer, Kel Carver, Terri Carver, Peter Jabin, Stephanie Lindemann, and Hannah Woodard.

Many thanks to Ravven for another gorgeous cover. You have brought Lucky—and this story—to beautiful visual life.

Thanks again to my readers—for reading and for your patience. I have so enjoyed spending the last several years with the characters in these books, getting to know them and telling their stories. The characters feel like family to me. I hope you love reading their stories as much as I loved writing them.

ABOUT THE AUTHOR

Stephanie Stamm is the author of the Light-Bringer Series of NA/YA urban fantasy novels. She lives with her spouse, a shy cat, and a part-time dog on a small urban farm near Atlanta, Georgia.

Website: www.stephanieastamm.com
Facebook: www.facebook.com/stephaniestammauthor

www.ingramcontent.com/pod-product-compliance
Lightning Source LLC
Chambersburg PA
CBHW030806260626
47169CB00001B/208